I0612437

NIKOLAI II

Her Russian Protector, Book 6

Roxie Rivera

Night Works Books
College Station, Texas

Copyright © 2014 by Roxie Rivera

Cover Art Photograph Copyright © 2011 Dani Dunca Photography

All rights reserved. No part of this publication may be reproduced, distributed or transmitted in any form or by any means, including photocopying, recording, or other electronic or mechanical methods, without the prior written permission of the publisher, except in the case of brief quotations embodied in critical reviews and certain other noncommercial uses permitted by copyright law. For permission requests, write to the publisher, addressed "Attention: Permissions Coordinator," at the address below.

Night Works Books
3515-B Longmire Drive #103
College Station, Texas 77845
www.roxierivera.com

Publisher's Note: This is a work of fiction. Names, characters, places, and incidents are a product of the author's imagination. Locales and public names are sometimes used for atmospheric purposes. Any resemblance to actual people, living or dead, or to businesses, companies, events, institutions, or locales is completely coincidental.

Book Layout ©2013 BookDesignTemplates.com

Ordering Information:
Quantity sales. Special discounts are available on quantity purchases by corporations, associations, and others. For details, contact the "Special Sales Department" at the address above.

NIKOLAI II (Her Russian Protector #6)/ Roxie Rivera. -- 1st ed.
ISBN 978-1-63042-025-3

Acknowledgements

Big, warm virtual hugs and so very many heartfelt thanks to all the readers who stuck with me during the setbacks that delayed this sequel. Your kind notes and messages were just so very amazing. I'm a lucky girl to have so many wonderful readers!

And, of course, huge thanks to Rimma for schooling me on Russian language and culture. Any mistakes in the book are mine and mine alone!

P PROLOGUE

April

"Where are we going?" My gaze darted from the windshield to the strong, proud profile of my husband's handsome face. The pale blue glow from the dashboard lights highlighted all the features I loved so much. Unable to help myself, I reached across the short distance between us and trailed my finger along the scar on Nikolai's jaw. My fingertip traced the curving line of his chin and dipped into the shallow cleft there.

"It's a surprise, *zolota*." He cast a sinfully sexy smile my way, and my core trembled wildly. The realization that this smile was mine and mine alone did crazy things to my heart. With everyone else, he maintained that impenetrable wall. Others were met with a coldness that chilled to the bone with a single, sharp glance.

But not me. Never me. With me, Nikolai was warm and loving because I was his *solnyshka* and his *zolota*—his sun and his gold.

"You said you don't like surprises." I tapped his lower lip, and he responded by playfully nipping at my finger and making me giggle.

"I don't, but it's different when it's a surprise for you."

"Why?"

"Because it simply is." He turned his head and kissed my palm before turning his attention to the wet highway that he deftly navigated. Rarely did Nikolai drive us anywhere. For security reasons, he usually preferred to let Kostya, Sergei or Danny handle that rather mundane duty. Tonight was special for some reason. He had even chosen to drive the Continental coupe that he babied so much.

"Did you enjoy the opera?" He grasped my hand and interlaced our fingers.

"I did." That morning he had surprised me with tickets to a performance and instructions that I was to be ready to leave the house by six. After a quick shopping trip with Erin and Bianca, I had popped in to see Holly Phillips at her salon so she could work her magic.

"I'm glad." He lifted my hand and kissed the back of it. "What did you think of dinner? If you didn't enjoy the private dining at the theater, we can visit one of the restaurants in the Theater District the next time. We won't have a problem getting a table."

No, we definitely wouldn't. That was one of the perks to Nikolai owning one of Houston's finest and most popular restaurants. He had contacts at all the hottest places in town. "I enjoyed the dinner and dessert at the theater, but I enjoy trying new places."

"Then I will make different arrangements for our next night out." He rubbed his thumb in a slow circle along the back of my hand.

The idea of having a regular date night with Nikolai filled me with such happiness. Before our rather rushed wedding, we hadn't had a chance to date like a normal couple. A crazed psychopath, an angry drug lord and my fugitive father had complicated things and pushed us into a hastily arranged wedding without a real courtship.

The city was quieter now and the underworld seemed to be in a calm period, but I knew better than to think it would last. Sooner or later, all hell would break loose—and Nikolai would be right in the center of it.

Not wanting to entertain those terrifying thoughts, I jokingly replied, "If I had known you were a patron of the opera and had a box, I might have studied German or Italian instead of Russian and Spanish."

He laughed. "Every year, I hope they'll announce one of Tchaikovsky's operas on the schedule, maybe

Iolanta or *Eugene Onegin*, but every year, it's Wagner or Puccini. Not that I don't enjoy their operas but..."

"I understand."

As he exited the loop and merged into one lane traffic with heavy construction, his hawk-like gaze skipped to the rear view mirror. Instinctively, I glanced at the passenger side mirror. Though the rain drops made it difficult to see, I spotted the black SUV following us and stiffened. The memories of the blitz attack that had nearly killed him were too fresh.

"Easy," he said and squeezed my hand. "It's Artyom and Danny."

Looking more carefully, I relaxed. It was one of the black Escalades from Nikolai's fleet. "Have they been trailing us all night?"

He glanced at me with amusement twitching his sinful mouth. "What do you think, *rybka*?"

The pet name brought a smile to my face. "I think you probably had some of your men in the audience."

He nodded. "Kostya enjoys the opera. He brought Boy with him and stuck him in an aisle seat near the rear. Artyom and Danny stayed in the SUV, just in case."

Just in case we needed to make a hasty exit amid a hail of gunfire or worse, I silently finished.

He must have known what I was thinking. "You're safe with me, Vee. No one will ever hurt you again."

I wanted to believe him. I wanted to believe that no one would ever harm us again, but I knew better. If my life had taught me anything, it was that there were no guarantees. "You can't promise me that."

"*Solnyshka*." He unlaced our fingers and slid his hand to the back of my neck, cupping me gently but firmly. "You are my wife. You belong to me. I protect what's mine."

It was an outrageously alpha statement, but I understood that was simply Nikolai's way. From him, that was the strongest declaration of love possible. "Do you belong to me?"

"Always," he answered without hesitation. "Forever."

"So how do I protect you?"

He shot me a strange look. "That's not your concern."

"It is," I insisted. "If you take care of me, I'm supposed to take care of you."

"You do take care of me, Vee." He caressed my neck. "In your own way," he added. "In the way that means the most to me."

"I worry about you." We didn't speak of his role as the Russian mob boss of Houston very often. It was a fact that was acknowledged and accepted between us, but it wasn't a topic that we discussed. Even now, I felt uncomfortable bringing it up. "I read the newspapers, and I see what's happening with the cartels in Mexico and I—"

"Vee," he murmured softly. "Don't."

"But—"

"Do you trust me?"

There was no question about that. "Yes."

"Then trust that I will tell you what you need to know," he said. "If I say nothing about my work, that's a good thing."

"I know."

His jaw visibly clenched at my whispered reply. It wasn't a sign of irritation with me. No, he was angry with himself. "I'm sorry."

"For what?"

"Dragging you into this life of mine," he said. "You deserve so much better. If I was less selfish, I would have made sure you ended up with a man like Misha or Viktor or Leonid."

I blinked at the mention of Yuri Novakovsky's fellow billionaire oligarchs who visited Samovar every time their business trips brought them to Houston. "You being selfish and wanting me all for yourself has nothing to do with it. I never would have been happy with those men."

"You don't know that. You never tried."

"I didn't need to try dating men like that. It was you, Kolya. It was always you." Narrowing my eyes at him, I reached over and pinched his leg through the crisp fabric of his trousers. "And why are you trying to convince me I should have run away with one of Yuri's friends? Do you regret marrying me?"

"Never." He hurriedly and firmly reassured me. "You are the best thing that ever happened to me. Marrying you was the proudest moment of my life and the smartest decision I have ever made." He caressed my neck and traced the shell of my ear with his thumb. "Because I love you, I want the best for you. It would have been better for you to marry an obscenely rich businessman who could give you everything you deserve."

I reached up and clasped his hand between both of mine. "You've given me everything I want and more. I don't need *things*, Nikolai. I only need you."

He eased on the brake as we approached an intersection. The yellow light switched to red and he made a full stop. With his foot on the brake, he surprised me by leaning over, cupping my face between both hands and capturing my mouth in a deeply sensual and possessive kiss. I gripped his arms as he flicked his tongue against the seam of my mouth and silently asked for entrance. A little whimper escaped my throat when the kiss took an erotic turn that left me trembling inside.

Always aware of his surroundings, Nikolai gently ended our kiss seconds before the light turned green. His hand returned to the back of my neck where he tenderly caressed my skin. We drove in silence for a few moments before he finally spoke again.

"I only need you," he echoed my words. "*Only* you. Everyone else—*no one else*—matters to me like you do." A happy smile curved his mouth, and his thumb glided along the curve of my neck. "You look so beautiful tonight."

I actually blushed. "Thank you."

Nikolai turned down a street that ran parallel to a rather rundown shopping center. All of the storefronts were closed except for one—a tattoo parlor I recognized as the one his preferred artist owned. He didn't pull into the parking lot but instead navigated down the side street and into the employee lot out back. It was a shadowy space that would have made me nervous had I been alone, but I feared nothing with my husband at my side.

As he parked, I twisted in my seat to face him. "What are we doing here?"

He switched off the engine and unlatched his seatbelt. Leaning across the center console, he flicked off my belt and pushed it away from my shoulder. His fingertips grazed my cheek and jaw before gliding over my lips. Holding my gaze, he asked, "Do you know what today is?"

"Friday." I noticed Danny hurrying from the SUV to take up a position at Nikolai's door. He quickly unfurled an umbrella and waited for his boss to exit the car.

Nikolai chuckled softly. "Yes, but more specifically."

"Um...it's Friday. It's April the..." My voice trailed off as the significance of the date struck me. "Oh."

"*Da.*" He nodded solemnly. "Eleven years tonight." His hand slid down my neck, over the curve of my breast to the flat expanse of my belly. He rubbed a slow, warm circle there, his palm moving over the gunshot scars hidden by the diaphanous amethyst chiffon of my evening gown. "Eleven years since the night I nearly killed you."

The awful, ugly truth hung in the air between us. Flashes of memories I had tried to suppress came roaring back to life right before my eyes. The shame of my involvement in the attempted hit on Nikolai's life made my stomach lurch. I had been an easily tricked child, a little girl so desperate for her father's love that she had agreed to burglarize a house, but that didn't make me any less guilty for what had almost happened that night. Nikolai had fought off my father and escaped with his life before very nearly taking mine.

"We were bound together forever that night. You and me," he said, his hand going still on my abdomen. "I never imagined it would lead us to this life we share, but it has. It was fate that you would become my queen."

My eyes widened at his description. "Your queen?"

"You would prefer *koroleva*?" he teased.

"Kolya! Be serious!"

"I am being serious." He played with the loose waves of my hair that cascaded around my shoulders. "That's what they're all calling you. The Night Queen," he clarified. "Because you rule the underworld with me."

"Hardly," I argued. "I'm just your wife. I'm just—"

"You aren't *just* anything, Vee. Not to me and not to them." He captured my mouth in a lingering kiss. Pulling back, he held my gaze. "Come. It's time for your coronation."

I blinked, and the pieces fell into place. "You've brought me here to see *Igla*."

He laughed at the nickname the men of his family had given to the Hungarian ex-pat tattoo artist who had spent most of his adult life in Moscow. *Igolochkoy* was a Russian embroidery style where the threads were punched through the fabric using a sharp needle. "You've been eavesdropping again."

"Your men should be more discreet."

He shot me a look before sliding out of the front seat. Danny handed over the umbrella that shielded Nikolai's tuxedo from the warm drizzle and stepped back to give him some space. My husband walked around the car to open my door. Reaching in, he grasped my hand and guided me out into the night. His palm settled against the small of my back and he gently pressed me toward the rear entrance of the tattoo shop that Arty now manned. The street captain with the shaved head and grass green eyes winked at me as I passed.

Inside the shop, we were greeted by the infamous tattoo artist. The older man sported a thick, long white beard and heavy ink from the top of his neck to the tips of his fingers. No doubt his torso, back and legs were equally as decorated. Nikolai called him by his real name—Tomi—but the artist only nodded before taking us to his private studio at the rear of the shop. It was so quiet in the space that I wondered if he had shut down the business to see us tonight.

With Arty and Danny guarding the door, Nikolai shut it behind us. Clearly at ease in these surroundings, he slipped out of his tuxedo jacket and bowtie, dropping them on Tomi's desk. He accepted the sketch the artist thrust his way and studied it with a smile. Handing it to me, he asked, "What do you think, Vee?"

I examined the surprisingly feminine and delicate crown Tomi had drawn. The design wasn't very big, but it was incredibly detailed. It was done in the style of a Russian tiara, the type one of the Feodorovna empresses might have worn. Tomi had incorporated Nikolai's pet name for me by using beautiful little sunbursts. There was a pretty crest in the center but it seemed unfinished.

As if reading my mind, the artist handed me a pencil. Addressing me in Russian, he said, "You're the only one I've ever allowed to alter my designs."

Understanding that this was something I should consider an honor, I reverently took the pencil and the drawing to the nearest flat surface. I didn't have to think twice about what would go in the center of the crest. I sketched in my husband's Cyrillic initials. Soon they would mark my skin, forever branding me as his.

When I handed it to Tomi, he actually cracked a small smile. "Good," he said before taking the pencil and cleaning up my addition with harder, cleaner lines.

Nikolai's hands settled on my shoulders. The heat of his chest seeped into my back. His lips brushed my ear. "You don't have to do this. I thought you might like to have one done. You've always been fascinated by them, by what they mean and how they're earned."

Glancing back at him, I asked, "Have I earned this one?"

He pressed a tender kiss to my throat. "You've earned so much more than this. It's the least I can give you. The very least," he whispered before turning my face and claiming my mouth.

"Where will it go?" I tried to ignore the nervous wobbling in the pit of my stomach and focused on the beautiful piece of art that would soon adorn my body.

"Where would you like it to go?"

"You choose. It's your gift to me."

His eyes sparked with a primal flare that made my insides tremble for a reason that had nothing to do with nervousness. I pressed my thighs together as Nikolai walked to Tomi's small desk and grabbed a rubber band from the container on the corner. When he came back to me, Nikolai gathered my hair in his hands and twisted the strands into a high bun that he secured with the rubber band. His lips skimmed the back of my neck. I sucked in a shocked breath when his tongue flicked against my skin.

"Here," he decided. "You'll wear my crown here."

I gulped and nodded. It would be easy to hide by wearing my hair down—and to show off whenever I wanted by choosing to wear my hair up. The idea of Nikolai seeing his mark on me when we were alone thrilled me. "Yes."

With a satisfied hum, Nikolai took my hand and tugged me toward the chair in the center of the room. The red leather was worn in spots but it seemed sturdy and comfortable. I was taken aback when he sat first and leaned back. When he patted his lap, my lips parted to protest, but he squelched the words with one heated look.

Ignoring Tomi's amused stare, I straddled Nikolai's lap as daintily as possible. The flowing skirts of my evening gown came in handy. They were loose enough and so full that I didn't have to worry about the fabric bunching along my thighs or hips.

"Look at me." Nikolai commanded my gaze. "This is going to hurt. Not as bad as the other pain I've caused you." He shot a pointed look at my stomach. "But it won't be pleasant."

I interlaced our fingers and gave his hand a squeeze. "I'm not afraid."

"No," he agreed and kissed me lovingly. "You never are."

Behind us, Tomi readied the necessary supplies. I leaned against my husband, accepting his strength and finding comfort in his soothing warmth, as Tomi prepared my skin and applied the stencil. Nikolai's powerful arms kept me from flinching when the first bite of the needles registered. I stared into his handsome face, enthralled by his pale eyes, and found myself wondering, not for the first time, how he managed to look at me with such love and kindness one moment and offered others that cold, icy glare the next.

The pain of the needles stabbing into my skin blossomed from one small spot to the entire back of my neck. After some time, the heated burn morphed into a strange numbness that I didn't mind so much. My fingers began to tremble, and Nikolai simply held my hands tighter. The all-black design didn't take as long as I had expected, and before I knew it, Tomi was wiping away the blood and ink and handing us a pair of mirrors.

With my skin throbbing and feeling a bit lightheaded, I used the mirror I had been given to catch sight of the reflection from the one Nikolai held behind my head. The delicate and darkly beautiful mark on my skin seemed as if it had always been meant to fit right there. Maybe it had. Maybe Nikolai was right. Fate had thrown us together eleven years earlier, and now here we were, married and in love, the king and queen of Houston's underworld.

"Do you like it?"

I caught the slightest hint of uncertainty in my husband's voice. Smiling at him, I nodded. "I love it."

He leaned forward and kissed me then, the scorching heat of his lips against mine promising a night I wouldn't soon forget. Tomi bandaged my neck, and Nikolai carefully shifted me off his lap. He steered me toward a chair in the corner and slipped his jacket around my shoulders.

"Drink this," he said, taking a can of my favorite soda from Tomi and pressing it into my hands. "The sugar rush will help."

"Thank you." I sipped at the ice cold drink and glanced up at him when he started to remove his cummerbund and shirt.

As if reading my mind, he nodded. "It's my turn."

Consciously ignoring the painful pulse along my nape, I watched as he took his place in the chair and bared the back of his neck for Tomi. He was tall enough that he rested his chin on the top of the headrest while the ink master tattooed a matching but more masculine crown on his skin. I wondered how many other pieces the artist had done for my husband. The more elaborate art, the iconography on his forearms, the onion domed churches topped with steeples and crosses that took up his entire back, those were definitely Tomi's work. There was also the pair of interlocking Orthodox wedding crowns and our names that Nikolai had hired the man to ink over his heart on Valentine's Day.

Some of the tattoos, the faded ones with blue and green tints, had been done during his stints in some of Russia's worst prisons, back when Nikolai was younger and restless and prone to risky decisions. They were simpler pieces—numbers and letters, shields and crosses, spiders and daggers—that held secret meanings. Each tattoo told part of Nikolai's history with Maksim Prokhorov's criminal family.

With his father's crime family, I silently added. That was a secret we hadn't told anyone. Only Yuri, our priest, the parish deacon and my father knew the truth about Nikolai's father's identity. We intended to keep it that way. There was nothing but danger that would come from letting that fact become more widely known. It was best for everyone to think that Nikolai was simply Maksim's chosen man in Houston.

My thoughts turned to the massive cross in the center of his chest and the stars just under his shoulder blades. He had two matching stars on his knees. They were tattoos that very few men in the life earned. I didn't know whether he had gotten them before or after he had earned his position as the *pakhan*, the boss, of Houston. It wasn't a question I dared ask or one he would likely answer. There were lines I didn't cross in our marriage and that was one of them.

I didn't like it, but that was the bargain I had made when I had agreed to marry him. We weren't like our friends. He wasn't going to tell me everything, and I had to find a way to be okay with that. I hadn't yet discovered how I was supposed to do that, but I prayed that someday I would figure it out. I hated not knowing what was happening. I hated the nights when I stared at the ceiling waiting for him to come home, all the while knowing that I couldn't ask him where he had been or what he had been doing.

I worried that someday all that secrecy was going to tear us apart. Marriages were supposed to be built on truth, but our foundation had some serious holes in it. One good gust of wind—and the walls of our house might crumble in on us.

"*Solnyshka*?" Nikolai's concerned voice interrupted my thoughts. He didn't even seem to feel the needles buzzing along his skin as Tomi worked the vibrating tattoo gun back and forth. Brow furrowed, he gazed at me with worry. "Do I need to call in Artyom?"

I shook my head and offered a sweet smile. "I'm fine. It's been a long day."

He didn't seem totally convinced but let it go. Feeling steadier, I gripped the can of soda and stood. I pulled his tuxedo jacket tighter around my shoulders and enjoyed the familiar, comforting scent of him that curled around me. While the crown tattoo took shape on Nikolai's skin, I perused the framed art decorating Tomi's walls. His tattoo style leaned more toward the traditional end of the spectrum, but the ink and pencil drawings with vivid swaths of color that he had proudly hung on his walls convinced me he had been classically trained in the fine arts.

Lost in my silent critique of his art, I didn't even realize he had finished Nikolai's tattoo until Tomi appeared next to me. He issued a little huff of laughter. "They aren't as good as yours, but I like them."

I glanced at him with surprise. "I think they're better than mine. Much better," I added softly and with a touch of envy in my voice. Gesturing to the street scene that had held my interest, I said, "Your style reminds me of Goncharova."

His light blue eyes widened noticeably. He glanced at his drawing and then back at my face. "You're serious."

"Of course." I tilted my head as I studied the scene again. "It's the way you've drawn the motorcycle that makes me think of her work."

"Would you like to take it?" Tomi gestured to the drawing.

As an artist, I understood what it meant for him to offer the framed canvas to me. "Yes, thank you. I'd love to hang it in my studio."

A smile brightened his face. He reached for the drawing and carefully took it down from the wall. With a surprisingly bashful tone of voice, the hard-looking man handed the framed piece to me and offered three words in Russian, "For the queen."

"Thank you." I hugged the drawing to my chest.

Shrugging into his shirt behind Tomi, Nikolai watched us with a pleased expression. When he joined us, he slipped his hand under the jacket draped around my shoulders and retrieved a thick envelope from the cleverly concealed pocket there. He exchanged the envelope and a handshake with Tomi and walked me out of the room.

I didn't miss Arty's curious glance as he tried to locate the new ink we both sported. My lips twitched with amusement when he gestured for Danny to take the lead. I glanced back at the captain as we walked down the hall and caught his surprised gape at the bandage covering the back of my neck. I had to bite back a laugh when he winked at me and made an approving thumbs-up gesture with the hand that still had all its fingers.

Outside, the rain had finally stopped. I slid into the passenger seat, and Nikolai reached down to gather up the hem of my skirt, clearing it from the door. He leaned in and captured my mouth with a playful kiss. I grasped his shirt, holding him hostage, and boldly flicked my tongue against his. He growled, the sound low and rumbling in his chest, and gently pried my hand from his shirt. His forehead touched mine. "Soon."

I practically vibrated in my seat as we made the drive back to our home. The dull ache along the back of my neck spurred thoughts of my friends and their reactions. Bianca would be aghast by the placement of the tattoo. She wouldn't come right out and call it tacky, but she would give me *that* look. Lena would probably frown and mutter something about gang tats. Erin would be her usual sweet-as-pie self and would probably gush over the romantic gesture. Benny would simply smile and call it beautiful.

The longer I thought about it, the less I wanted to share my new secret. Deciding to keep it discreetly covered by my wearing my hair down, I stared out the window and wondered what other surprises this night would bring.

We reached the house without any problems and parked in the converted carriage house in the rear of the property. Nikolai waved at Arty and Danny, sending the pair off for the evening, before escorting me across our backyard. He paused every now and then to inspect the newly blooming plants in the garden and flower beds he tended with such care.

Holding my hand, he led me through the side entrance and into the mudroom. He pressed a tender kiss to my temple. "I'll meet you upstairs."

Nodding, I rose on tiptoes and pecked his cheek. "Don't be long."

"I won't."

Trailing my fingers down his arm, I reluctantly parted from his side and made my way upstairs while my husband went through his usual nightly routine of making sure the house was secured. I paused at one of the upstairs windows overlooking the front yard and noticed two men talking on the sidewalk. One I immediately recognized as Kostya, but the other was unfamiliar. I assumed he was some new recruit, a young street soldier happy to stand guard on our home for the chance at gaining Nikolai's favor.

Some of the magic and excitement of our night faded as the reality of our life together hit me. Suddenly the tattoo no longer felt so romantic. It felt more like a public symbol of ownership and a sigil of protection. I could practically hear the thoughts of the underworld denizens who might see the mark still burning and throbbing on the back of my neck. *Don't touch that one. She belongs to Nikolai.*

"Vee?" He appeared behind me on the stairs. When I glanced back at him, his brow knitted and his mouth quirked to the side with worry. "Do you regret it?"

My stomach clenched. "What?"

"The tattoo," he said, coming to join me and taking the jacket from my shoulders. He dropped it onto one of the nearby slipper chairs before sliding his hands around my waist and embracing me from behind.

I relaxed when I understood what he meant. "No."

He nuzzled into the side of my neck and breathed in deeply. "I should have talked to you about it first. It was wrong of me to spring it on you like that. You're not one of my men champing at the bit to be branded as one of my soldiers. I should have given you time to consider it."

I laughed at that. "You do remember your proposal to me, right?"

He growled against my throat. "Not my best or most romantic moment," he conceded.

"No, but it definitely set the tone for us." I reached back and caressed his jaw. "We seem to make our best decisions relying on gut instinct."

His wide palm rested against my abdomen. He splayed his fingers against the front of my evening gown and playfully nipped at the fleshy spot where my neck curved into my shoulder. I let loose a mewling sigh and pressed back against his hard, powerful body. "Kolya..."

He tugged on the zipper running along my left side and pushed the empire-waist gown off my body. It pooled around my feet in a billow of purple chiffon. With one hand, he unsnapped my strapless bra. The other was busy drawing ticklish circles on my bare stomach. Standing in only a seamless nude-colored thong and high-heeled sandals, I felt acutely undressed. My nervous gaze flitted to the window. "Nikolai, they'll see us."

The possibility of one of his men getting a peek at me momentarily cooled his ardor. He hoisted me up in his arms, kicked aside the outrageously expensive dress and carried me to our master suite at the end of the hall. Placing me down on the bed with surprising reverence, he tapped the tip of my nose. "Stay."

Leaning back on my hands, I watched him slowly strip. My greedy gaze roamed his naked and heavily tattooed body. He had the natural physique of a swimmer. Where I had to run every morning to keep fit, he needed only a few mornings a week at Ivan's gym to look that damned good.

My gaze drifted along the myriad scars, some of them puckered and pink and others thin and white, marring his skin. The reminders of the pain and violence he had known in his life always saddened me. He had escaped the horrors of a sickeningly abusive orphanage and survived as a homeless child on the streets of Moscow with Ivan at his side. Later, the two men had brutally conquered those same streets before coming to Houston to make inroads for the Prokhorov family.

Sitting up all the way, I lingered on the fresh scars from the December attack that had nearly killed him. The stab wounds he had sustained hadn't healed correctly, not after he had slipped out of the hospital in the middle of the night with my cousin Eric, a Houston detective, as his accomplice. Instead of resting and recuperating, Nikolai had gone to great lengths to save me that night and in the weeks that followed.

He brushed his hand over the black eight-pointed star sitting just beneath his left collarbone. "Do you know what these mean? What I did to earn these?"

My gaze flicked to his somber eyes before settling on the frightening star he touched. They were the tattoos only a man who had reached the highest and most secretive echelon of the Russian mafia earned. Voice soft, I nodded and whispered, "Yes."

He stalked toward the bed with that predatory grace I found so thrilling. Standing so close I could feel the heat waves radiating from his skin, he asked, "What else do these stars on my chest and my knees mean?"

Focused on his pale eyes, I didn't miss the dangerous flash in his icy irises. "That you will kneel before no man."

"*Da.*" Then, deliberately and with glacial slowness, he slid to the floor and knelt in front of me. I held my breath as he peppered light yet stunningly erotic kisses along my thighs. He lifted his head and pinned me in place with a scorching look that made my heart swell and my stomach wobble violently. "Only you, Vivian. You are the only one in the entire world who can bring me to my knees."

His bold confession struck me as both an incredible compliment and a reverent warning. I wielded an immense power over him, the sort of power other men dreamed of having, and I had to be careful in the way that I used it.

With a silent but meaningful look, he dropped his head and resumed the sensual trail of kisses along my thighs. Overwhelmed by arousal and love for this beautifully complicated man, I fell back to the bed and closed my eyes. My hand traveled down my own belly and didn't stop until I felt his thick sandy-colored hair beneath my fingertips.

A pleasured sigh escaped my lips when he parted my legs and began to torment me with that wicked, wicked tongue of his. "Nikolai..."

1   Chapter One

June

"Vivi, turn your webcam. I can't see the full piece."
The staccato accent of Niels Mikkelsen's voice echoed
in the sunroom Nikolai had converted to a home studio
for me. "The easel with your new work is blocking my
view."

"Hang on." I wiped the palette knife I had been using on the nearest rag, cleaning away the ridge of ceru-
lean blue oil paint clinging to the metal, and dropped
it on my worktable. I moved a few steps to the left
and turned the stack of art books supporting my lap-

top and webcam so Niels could see the painting I had finished earlier that week. Sliding to the side, I asked, "Can you see it now?"

"Yes!" Excitement filled his deep, masculine voice. "My goodness, you've really grown since the last show." Rustling sounds filtered across the speakers as he moved aside the papers and files on his desk and leaned in for a better look. "But you're also returning to your roots, I see. Mixed media?"

"Layers," I said. "It's about the layers."

"Yes," he hummed his agreement. "You're maturing. I can see that you have found something very interesting to say."

The compliment from the Danish billionaire and world-renowned collector of modern art brought a smile to my face. Although he had enjoyed my show earlier in the year, Niels hadn't wasted the chance to deconstruct my paintings and encourage me with criticism that he delivered with an academic air. "I'm glad you like it."

"I do." He slid back into his seat, the leather creaking and the springs of the chair groaning. "I suppose I don't have to look very far for your muse."

"And who would that be?" I glanced at the screen to see him watching me rather intently. The handsome face filling my laptop screen could have easily been printed on the glossy front of a men's magazine or in a couture editorial. He had the strangest eyes, the hazel color an enthralling mix of whiskey brown with jade flecks, and sharp cheekbones. The intensity of his gaze made me glance away. If he had been an alpha wolf, I would have been a pack member who happily bared her neck in submission rather than risk being torn to pieces.

"That Russian of yours, of course." Leaning back in his chair, he interlaced his fingers behind his head. "Where is Nikolai? Usually when we have our chats, he's hovering in the background." He clicked his teeth. "Such jealousy."

I rolled my eyes at the way he tried get a rise out of me. Nikolai didn't hover, but there was no love lost between the man I loved and the Danish tycoon who was sponsoring my debut on the international art scene. "He's probably on his way home." I peeked at the clock in the lower right-hand corner of my screen. "We're headed to a barbecue with friends in a little while."

"How very domestic," Niels replied rather dryly.

"I rather enjoy domesticity."

"I'm sure that you do." There was no mistaking the slight tone of censure to his voice. "Playing house is all very well and good, but remember that you have other talents beyond flower arrangements, cooking dinner and keeping house."

I shot him an annoyed look. "You are so abrasive sometimes."

He shrugged. "What you call abrasive, I call truth. You have an amazing talent as an artist, Vivian. If you continue nurturing your gift and maturing in your art, you have a truly bright future ahead of you. Husbands and children have a bad reputation for ruining the promising careers of young women."

His words stung in a way he couldn't have imagined. I fought the urge to touch the gentle curve to my belly that I easily hid with my painter's smock and loose dresses. Just days before walking the stage to accept my bachelor's degree, I had discovered that I was pregnant. It had taken only the simplest calculation to realize that we had likely conceived our first child the night we had marked our bodies with matching tattoos, the night Nikolai claimed me as his queen.

The discovery had filled me with elation and terror. Elation because I couldn't imagine anything sweeter or more wondrous than creating a beautiful new life with Nikolai. Terror because I secretly feared that the madness that had driven my mother to suicide lurked within me. Pregnancy had been the trigger that sent her down that long spiraling road of mental deterioration that included an attempt at drowning me before finally hanging herself in a motel room.

My stomach lurched violently—and not with morning sickness—at the thought that even a single seed of her illness had begun to sprout within me. Nikolai had been so overjoyed by the discovery that we were expecting a child, and I couldn't bear to burden him with my admittedly overblown worries. My mother had shown symptoms of her mental illness earlier in life. So far, I had operated on an even keel.

Once again, I convinced and reminded myself that I was simply overreacting. It was just first-time pregnancy nerves and the unknown ways adding a child to the life I shared with Nikolai would change things. *You're fine. You're being a drama queen. Let it go.*

"Vivian?" Niels called to me. "Have we lost the connection?"

"No." I turned toward the screen and smiled at him. "I spaced out for a second thinking of some last minute things I need to take care of before we leave for London on Sunday."

"You're staying with Yuri?"

"We are."

"I'm going to leave Amsterdam in the morning. My first stop will be the gallery to make sure everything is exactly the way it needs to be." He tapped his fingertips on the gleaming burled wood of his desk. "Has Lena been prepping you for the press?"

"She has. I'm sure we'll discuss it during the flight."

"Did she mention Tatiana Melnikova?"

The name didn't ring a bell. "No. Why?"

He waved his hand. "One of the journalists I was speaking with earlier in the week at a gallery showing in Berlin mentioned that he was coming to London to see your new collection. He asked whether this Tatiana woman had sponsored your show, and I thought she might run in your circle of friends there in Houston."

I took a moment to think about the many acquaintances we had but came up empty-handed. "No. Sorry."

"She's probably some rich Russian who wants to shove her way onto the art scene. It's little matter." He leaned forward. "We need to discuss your plans for next year. We should consider another show in the spring in Houston and then perhaps something in New

York. You'll need to give some serious thought to the agents I've recommended and—"

"Niels," I gently interrupted, "let's get through this show first." I didn't want to tell him that early next year I would be waiting to go into labor. I had just started the eleventh week of my pregnancy and was due in mid-January. Though I had no plans to give up painting, I also had to be realistic about juggling studio time and travel with a breastfeeding infant.

"Fine," he agreed with a slight frown. "We'll table this discussion until I see you in London."

I had no intention of taking up this discussion that soon but didn't feel like pushing the issue. "Sure."

He nodded. "I'm very sorry that we didn't get to have our dinner last week, but my business over here couldn't be rescheduled. I'm very much looking forward to seeing you next week. And your husband," he added as if it were an afterthought.

"Niels."

Startled by Nikolai's greeting, I glanced over my shoulder and spotted my husband sauntering into our sunroom-slash-studio. He carried one of the ripe, juicy peaches from the trees in our backyard. I had been craving them so much lately, and he never failed to pick the perfect one each time he came home.

Crossing the studio, he set aside the peach when he reached me and placed a hand on my shoulder. His fingertips grazed my neck, and I leaned into his touch, seeking the comforting, familiar warmth of him.

"See?" Niels said with a laugh. "Always hovering in the background."

Ignoring the barb, Nikolai asked, "How's business, Niels? Everything floating along nicely?"

I didn't miss the slight narrowing of the Danish businessmen's eyes. The two men had just shared some secret communication. Judging by that brief and almost imperceptible micro-expression, Niels wasn't pleased. What did Nikolai know?

"Business is fine. Better than ever," Niels replied. "And you? How are the new partnerships working out? Because I always find that mergers can be a bit...messy."

That reference I did understand. Though Nikolai tried to shield me from all the dirty details of the underworld, not even he could keep the whispers about my father and his father going into business south of the border from me. Judging by the newspaper articles I read online every morning, the cartel my father had once served so faithfully seemed to be preparing to go to war with him and the men who had chosen to follow him.

"After some corporate restructuring, things will settle down."

In any other setting, the words would have been innocuous. In this instance, they were ominous and threatening. Corporate restructuring could only mean one thing—hits. They were probably going to happen from the top down. Did he mean my father? Or his? Or the cartel?

"Let's hope." Niels leaned forward and folded his arms on the desk. "Your wife is looking exceptionally beautiful today. One might even say she's positively blooming."

Did he know? How? I had gained less than five pounds and dressed so carefully. Was it that easy to see now? I schooled my features and refused to let him have the satisfaction of knowing he had rattled me.

Nikolai took it in stride. "Yes, I'm a very lucky man."

"You truly are." Niels held his gaze. "See that you remember that. Pamper her. Spoil her. Remind her that she's precious. There is no end to the long line of men who would happily take your place." He pushed up the cuff of his shirt and glanced at his watch. "I have to get to a meeting. I wish you both safe travels. I'm looking forward to seeing you next week."

"Same here," I assured him, though I doubted Nikolai shared my sentiment.

"Until then," Niels replied with a smile.

"Bye."

The second the video-call ended, Nikolai reached out and shut my laptop. He muttered under his breath, but I heard every word. "Insufferable fucking prick."

I swatted his arm. "Be nice."

"I am extremely nice. He is extremely annoying."

I stroked the silky fabric of the tie I had chosen for him that morning. "You shouldn't let him get to you. He enjoys pushing your buttons."

"Because he's perverse," Nikolai grumbled.

"Yes," I agreed, thinking of the stories Lena had told me about the man's rather dark sexual desires.

"He's incredibly helpful when it comes to my career, but there's no rule that says I have to rely on him as my shepherd through this new world." Not wanting Nikolai to have something else to stress about when he already had so many burdens to bear, I said, "After the show, I'll put some distance between us."

"No." Nikolai combed his fingers through my hair. "He's the best contact to have in your network. I can't stand the way he openly flirts with you, but I won't ask you to cut ties with him." He pressed a tender kiss to my forehead. "You're right. I shouldn't let him get to me. He only enjoys it more when he gets a reaction from me."

Not wanting to talk about Niels anymore, I gestured toward the peach. "You brought me a snack."

"Of course," he said in between light kisses that he dotted along my cheek. He nibbled my neck before sucking on a sensitive patch of skin. "But first I think I'll have mine."

"Kolya," I whispered, my toes curling against the floor. "Now?"

"I've been thinking about you all day. I couldn't get out of Samovar fast enough." He tugged on the strings tied at the small of my back and peeled my smock away from my dress. Tossing it aside, he spun me around and pressed me back against my worktable.

"Are we alone?" I nervously glanced at the closed door. Ever since Erin and Ivan's wedding, Nikolai had beefed up our home security. Danny, Boy, and Arty were all familiar faces around the house these days. Sergei had officially left my husband's employ a week earlier and had been freed from the family after the underground bare-knuckle tournament. I didn't know the full score there, but I sensed Nikolai, Sergei and Bianca were keeping a big, fat secret from me.

A week earlier, I had overheard Arty talking to Kostya about *nochniye volki*, the Night Wolves gang, but both men had clammed up the second they noticed me coming out of the library. I wanted to know everything—but I *didn't* want to know everything. I tried to remind myself what Nikolai had said to me in April. I had to trust that he would tell me what I needed to know.

"No one will bother us." He placed his hands on either side of me and lowered his head, capturing my mouth. His passionate kiss made me dizzy with desire.

I clutched at his arms and whimpered, "Kolya."

"God, Vee," he said, tearing his lips away from mine. "That sound does crazy fucking things to me."

I gulped and tried to catch my breath. He grasped my hand and dragged it down between our bodies. "Feel what you do to me."

My heart beat wildly in my chest, thumping against my ribcage like a hummingbird on a sugar high. Though I had come into our marriage a virgin, I had quickly gained confidence in my sexuality under Nikolai's loving, encouraging hands. Even so, I still blushed madly when my fingertips found the hard outline of his cock. He pressed my hand against it, and I grasped him through the fabric of his perfectly tailored trousers.

Groaning my name, he leaned into my hand and kissed me again. His fingers tangled in my hair and tightened into a fist as he tugged my head back, exposing my vulnerable throat to his lips and teeth. I shivered with arousal and whimpered even louder as he laved and nipped at my neck. Stroking him through his pants, I tried to slow down my racing breaths. A rush of wet heat pooled between my thighs, and my breasts ached with anticipation.

Not that I had to wait very long. He crouched slightly and slid his hands to the backs of my thighs. In one swift movement, he hoisted me right up onto my worktable. He shoved aside clean brushes and tubes of paint to make more room for me. His tongue stabbed against mine while his dexterous hands made quick work of whisking away my paisley print skater dress and panties. I hadn't worn a bra that morning because pregnancy had made me so sensitive and uncomfortable.

Taking a step back, Nikolai shrugged out of his jacket and loosened his tie. His hungry gaze roamed my naked body as he unbuttoned and rolled up the sleeves of his shirt. "I wish you could see yourself right now. You remind me of a wood nymph perched on the edge of that table. All you need are wings."

I smiled at the description. "There's a costume shop on the way to Bianca's house."

He laughed. "Don't tempt me."

"I'm your wife. I'm supposed to tempt you."

"Mission accomplished," he murmured and moved closer to me. His gaze slid to the art supplies lining the center of the table. He ran his fingers over the bristles of the many brushes standing upright in the mason jars I preferred for their storage. "These are clean?"

"Yes." I watched him carefully. What did he have in mind?

Nikolai plucked a big, fat *hake* brush from the jar where I kept miscellaneous tools. Though I had never been very good at the *sumi-e* style of painting, I liked the effect the brush made on canvas. After watching my fellow artsy friend Hadley Rivera teaching the ink wash technique to her students at the arts center she owned, I had gone right out to my favorite supply store to buy four of them.

But Nikolai had no intention of using that brush to paint...

"Oh!" I sucked in a surprised breath when he trailed the brush along my neck, down my chest and across my breast. He swirled the super soft bristles around my nipple. It felt incredible, and my body responded instantly. The puckered peaks tightened, and I broke out into goose bumps.

My gaze darted to Nikolai's face. His lust-darkened eyes were focused on my breasts as he teased them with the brush. Raw need flared in his irises. When he lowered his head and suckled me, I nearly slid off the table. My delighted moan echoed in the room. He gripped my waist, holding me in place, and continued to torment me with the brush and his mouth.

"Lean back," he ordered.

In a haze of lust, I did as instructed and leaned back on my palms. He pushed my thighs apart and bared me to his heated gaze. I held my breath as he dragged the fat brush down my belly, swirling it around my navel before guiding it even lower. The feathery bristles glided over my bare lips, and I shuddered. "*Oh.*"

He smiled wickedly and swept the brush up and down the seam of my sex. My fingers curled behind me, my nails scratching at the surface of the table, and I fought the urge to shut my legs and stop the sensual torture. He tossed aside the fat, soft calligraphy brush and selected a bright brush from the jar where I stored my oil brushes.

I bit my lower lip when he parted the most delicate part of me with his fingers. He slipped his fingers down to my opening and encountered the slick wetness seeping from me. Holding my gaze, he slowly penetrated me with one and then two fingers, burying them to the knuckle in my sheath. Stomach trembling, I felt those first curls of desire blossom in my core. I shuddered when the sable bristles of the paintbrush grazed my clitoris.

"You aren't the only artist in this house." Nikolai whispered against my lips before flicking his tongue against mine. "Let's see if I can paint a brilliant masterpiece."

I surrendered to his erotic kisses while his nimble fingers did crazy, dirty things to me. The firm strokes of the paintbrush drove me wild. My aching nub throbbed almost painfully as I moved closer and closer to the edge. The coil of bliss in my belly tightened. In and out, his fingers plunged into my soaking core.

Round and round and side to side, the paintbrush flicked at my pulsing clitoris.

My breaths were shuddery now, almost panicked. A flutter invaded my belly—and I exploded with sheer ecstasy. I rocked my hips and lifted my bottom right off of the table, riding Nikolai's hand while his mouth skimmed my throat and my breasts. He had learned all the secrets to my body and knew when I had had enough. His fingers went still and his kisses turned gentler and sweeter.

The paintbrush dropped to the table with a clatter. He cupped the back of my head and ravished my mouth. I clung to his chest, fisting his shirt in my trembling hands. When he broke our kiss, he pulled back just enough to gaze into my eyes. "Look at you. Lips swollen, pupils dilated..." He teased his tongue against mine. "You're practically begging for my cock."

I gripped his belt and jerked him toward me. "Do you want me to beg? I'll happily slide down to my knees right now."

He chuckled darkly and touched his lips to my forehead. "The tile floor in here is too hard. I won't have you bruising your knees for me."

Amused by his reply, I smiled at him. He picked up the peach he had brought me and held it up to my mouth. I could smell the citrus scent of the all-natural cleaner he used on the produce from his garden and small orchard. Though he preferred to garden organically, he was taking no chances with me or the baby.

I took a small bite of the peach. The yellow flesh yielded easily and spilled sweet juice on my tongue.

Nikolai stunned me by dragging the exposed fruit around my right nipple, spreading the sugary nectar all over my skin. I inhaled a sharp breath when his tongue followed the same path. "Nikolai!"

He just laughed mischievously and continued painting my breasts with the peach juice and lapping it up with his tongue. I marveled at the sight of him. He had been so tense lately. Seeing him grinning and hearing his laugh filled me with such happiness. I loved knowing that I was the one he came to for comfort and relaxation. I was the only one who could put a smile like that on his handsome face.

The peach left a wet trail down my belly to the vee between my thighs. I held my breath and waited to see if he would take it any farther, but he stopped just short of where I wanted his touch most. His tongue traveled the same wet line but kept on going until it hit the jackpot. I threw back my head and spread my thighs as he went down on me. He zeroed in on the rhythm I loved most, flicking and fluttering his tongue over that swollen kernel until my thighs were tensing.

But the moment I started to get close, he stopped. "No!" I thrust my hips toward him, but he was already standing.

Grinning devilishly, he swept me up into his arms and playfully swatted my bare bottom. "Patience, Vee."

"Please," I pleaded and wrapped my arms around his shoulders. Nuzzling into his neck, I nipped at him and sucked hard on his skin. "I want you."

He carried me to the wide, low chair in the corner and deposited me on the plush upholstered cushion. "I'm yours, Vee."

Reaching for his belt, I ordered, "Show me."

2 CHAPTER TWO

Nikolai's heart hammered in his chest. Vivian gazed up at him with that sultry smile and her brilliantly blue eyes, and he was fucking lost. Sometimes he was taken aback by how confident she had become as his lover. He held still as she unbuckled his belt and unbuttoned his trousers. She lowered his zipper and freed his cock from his boxers.

His eyes closed briefly at the feel of her soft, warm hand gliding along his throbbing shaft. It was the wet, hot glide of her tongue around the head that made them pop open again. Nostrils flaring, he breathed in deeply and stared down at the raven-haired nymphet bobbing up and down on his cock. He loved watching his erection disappearing between her lips. The swirl of her tongue was even better.

"*Solnyshka.*" He threaded his fingers through her hair and tried to maintain control over the raging urge to pump his hips. Deeper and deeper, she swallowed his length on every down stroke. His balls ached, and he wanted nothing more than to be buried in her tight, slick pussy. "Enough."

She dragged her mouth all the way back to the tip and held him there for a long moment before finally allowing him to slip free. He wiped her lower lip and smiled when she bit down on his thumb. Brushing his knuckles along her cheek, he said, "Turn around. On your knees."

She hastily complied with his instruction and gripped the arms of the chair. Her perfect little ass wiggled side to side as she presented herself to him. He caressed her back and bottom before gently, carefully, probing her with his fingers. She was so fucking wet he could hear his digits sliding in the slickness between her thighs. His cock pulsed, and his groin tightened. He had to get inside her. *Now.*

Cock in hand, he guided the blunt crown into her and thrust forward. He held onto her hips and withdrew from the wet heat enveloping him. She moaned with pleasure and pushed back to meet his next forward motion. He picked up the pace but tried to be mindful of the force he used. Since discovering her pregnancy, he had been eaten up with worry. He would do anything to keep her and the baby safe. *Anything.*

"Kolya." She breathed his name on a sigh and reached back to grab his hand. "So good." Her fingers gripped his wrist now. "Oh, God. More. *More.*"

Hearing her beg for his dick shattered his control. He had never been able to deny her anything and wasn't about to start now. He gave her exactly what she wanted and fucked her harder and faster. She gripped the top of the chair now and cried out again and again. The keening sounds echoed in the room.

When she lowered her head, her black hair fell away from her neck and revealed the tattoo. *My tattoo.* Unable to help himself, he ran his fingers over the dark mark. It was a primitive thing, but he couldn't stop the grip of possession and ownership that clutched at his heart. *Mine.*

Wanting to feel her come and to remind her who lived to give her pleasure, he leaned forward and slipped his hand between her thighs. His arm brushed her belly, and he felt the slight curve there. As petite as she was, she was already showing. Soon their secret would be difficult to keep. The fear that kept him awake at night stabbed his chest. He muscled it down and focused on beautiful Vivian who writhed with need beneath him.

With the practice that came from learning his sweet wife's body, he found her clit and expertly strummed it. His name poured of her mouth in an unending litany as she chased her orgasm. He felt that first flutter of her pussy and smiled triumphantly. "Let go, Vee. Give it to me. Come. *Come.*"

She did. With a white-knuckled grip on the chair, she trembled violently and climaxed. Bending down, he licked the tattoo on the back of her neck and then bit down before riding her hard and fast. She cried out his name, and her cunt clutched his cock, setting off his own explosion. Buried deep inside her, he jerked roughly and filled her with his seed.

He fell against her back and panted against her neck. "Vee." He whispered to her in Russian. "*Ya obozhayu tebya.*"

She clasped his forearm. "I love you."

Reluctantly, he pulled away from her and found some paper towels on her worktable to clean them up. When she tried to stand, he noticed her unsteadiness and instantly leapt to her side. He caught her before she fell. "Vee! Are you all right?"

"Sorry," she said a bit breathless. "I'm just dizzy."

He silently cursed himself for being so careless with her. She was pregnant and carrying his child. He needed to be more careful with her.

"Come here, baby." Not bothering to get her dressed, he sat in the chair and tugged her down on top of him. He hooked his foot along the side of the ottoman and dragged it closer. Stretched out together on the comfortable chair and stool, they enjoyed a quiet moment. He brushed his fingers through her hair and caressed her bare back.

The new painting she was working on caught his attention. She had been using palette knives for this one and only palette knives. The layers of oil paint created a depth and richness that made the colors seem so incredibly vibrant. There was something about this painting that unsettled him though. The longer he stared at it, the more convinced he was that she was trying to tell him something important. He could almost feel the waves of conflict and uncertainty flowing from the piece.

His hand traveled to her belly, and he placed a protective hand over the spot where his child was growing. Not for the first time, he wondered if he should have taken measures to delay their family. Vivian had been through so very much since Christmas. She had nearly been killed and trafficked. He had rushed her into marrying him so he could keep her safe. Now, she was pregnant with what he, selfishly, hoped was the first of many children.

But she was young and had her entire life ahead of her. Her career as an artist was just beginning to blossom. Soon she would have a child, and while he was prepared to do everything he could to support her dreams and aspirations, he feared motherhood might impede her journey. The guilt gnawed at him. He should have been more responsible and put her future first.

"You're terribly pensive today." She stroked his jaw. "Is everything all right?"

He kissed her palm and turned the question around on her. "Is everything all right with you?"

Vivian glanced at him. "Yes. Why?"

"The last six months of your life have been filled with changes."

"They were good changes." She cuddled in closer to him and pressed her cheek to his chest.

He bit his tongue rather than reminding her that she had married a mob boss. Good wasn't the adjective he would have used to describe that change. Embracing her and kissing the top of her head, he murmured, "I'll do anything to make you happy, Vee. Whatever you want. Whatever you need. It's yours if you ask me."

"I am happy." She kissed his jaw. "With you." Trailing her fingers down his chest, she asked, "How was work?"

He understood that she was asking about the restaurant and not his other work. Grunting at the memory of the spat between waitresses, he said, "Lidia and Jessica got into it again. I could hear them squawking at one another from my office."

"What was it this time?"

"I have no idea. I didn't ask. I sent them both home and took them off the schedule for two days." Wrapping her hair around his finger, he admitted, "You were right about Lidia. I probably should have let her go after the night she purposely dumped that glass of wine on Bianca."

"Bianca told me that Lidia apologized to her. She accepted the apology and wiped the slate clean."

He made an irritated noise at that. "Bianca is too sweet for her own good. Sergei will have his hands full with her."

Vivian snorted indelicately. "In more ways than one."

He laughed. "Listen to you! I should be ashamed at how badly I've corrupted you." Her soft giggle inspired a smile. "Do you need to do any last minute shopping before we leave for London next week?"

"I don't think so. I'm going to see Holly on Friday for a quick trim and to have Maria do a manicure. I'd like for us to have everything packed by Thursday."

"That won't be a problem." He mentally arranged his schedule for the upcoming week. It was going to be a busy one for him. One of his most loyal soldiers was being released from prison, and he needed to finalize the arrangements for his crew while he was out of town with Vee. Kostya would be in charge, and Arty would be his second. He had no doubts when it came to his two most trusted men, but he worried about his fugitive father-in-law Romero and Julio Jimenez, the cartel's main man in Houston, coming to blows.

There were already rumblings on the street that Romero was going to challenge the cartel and do it using backup from Maksim. The two old bastards were already running guns south of the border and causing serious headaches for him. Nikolai feared Vee's father would try to make his move against his old cartel while he was away in London and the city was vulnerable. He had to shore up his alliances before leaving so that Kostya was in the strongest position possible.

But he didn't want to think of any of that right now. Lush and naked, Vivian was curled against him. He didn't want any of the ugliness of the underworld to touch her.

"We have our first doctor's appointment on Tuesday. Don't forget that you're supposed to meet me there at two."

"I won't." The prospect of the first glimpse of their baby on ultrasound excited him. It still seemed a bit unreal, but he was certain that seeing their baby would make it all more final. "I wouldn't miss it for anything."

"How much longer are we going to keep this quiet?"

"I don't know. As long as possible." Hating the position they were in, he interlaced their fingers and smiled at the paint smudges staining her skin. Because she deserved to know the truth, he confessed, "Our fathers are stirring up trouble with Lorenzo Guzman. Until I can get that mess sorted, I don't feel comfortable announcing your pregnancy. You read the Mexican newspapers, Vee. You know what the cartel is capable of doing."

He swallowed hard and placed his hand against her stomach. Fingers splayed, he silently vowed that nothing would stop him from keeping them both safe. *Nothing.* "We have to be careful until things go quiet down there."

She sighed loudly. "Our dads really suck."

He chortled at her remark. He would have used a stronger word to describe the situation. "They do seem to enjoy making things difficult and dangerous for everyone."

"Is it worth it? All this trouble they're causing?" she clarified. "I mean, what are they going to get out of going to war with the cartel?"

He planned to use all the favors he could call in to avoid a war. He had a reputation for negotiating his way out of stalemates like these and hoped he could prevail upon Maksim and Romero to see the light. A war would be bad for everyone in the underworld.

"Money," he said finally. "It's always about money, *solnyshka*."

"Greedy bastards," she grumbled.

He laughed softly and kissed the top of her head again. "Do you think you can stand up now? We need to shower and change soon or else we'll be late for dinner with Bianca and Sergei."

"I just need to remember to move more slowly when I'm changing positions." She let him help her stand and humored him with a smile when he tugged her dress down over her head. He slipped her panties into his pocket and earned a frown. "Remember to put those in the hamper. I'm pretty sure Boy will die of embarrassment if my undies tumble out of your suits when he takes them to the cleaners on Monday morning."

He tried to imagine the look on the kid's face if he got a peek at the sexy little panties Vivian preferred. Of course, he hadn't missed the way the kid stared at her when he thought no one was paying attention. He couldn't blame Boychenko for wanting to look, but he trusted the kid knew better than to even think about crossing that line.

Upstairs, he joined Vivian in the shower. She had piled her hair high on top of her head to keep it from getting wet. She still hadn't shown off the tattoo in public yet, and the one on the back of his neck wasn't visible because of his shirt collars. He rather liked that it was something just for them and didn't mind that others hadn't seen them.

"Will you be all right in here alone?" He eyed her carefully. "Are you still dizzy?"

She poked his stomach. "You worry too much. I'm fine."

"I'm your husband." He kissed her temple and smoothed his hand along her belly. "It's my job to worry about you and the baby. When I married you, I swore vows to protect you and care for you. That means making sure you don't pass out in the shower."

Her expression softened. "I really am fine."

Taking her at her word, he exited the shower and grabbed towel. He rubbed his skin dry and wrapped the towel around his waist before heading for their large walk-in closet. He paused as he passed Vivian's racks of clothing and ran his fingers along the soft fabrics. It was a simple thing—a silly thing, really—but the sight of her things mixed in with his filled him with the most incredible sense of contentment.

She was here with him—in his house and in his bed—and shared his name. She was exactly where she was always meant to be. By bravely choosing to love him, with all his flaws and his sordid past, Vivian had given him something so precious. She filled his home with love and happiness and gave him a reason to be a better man.

He wasn't stupid enough to believe that he would ever be good. No, that fucking ship had sailed and sunk a long time ago. He wasn't like Sergei. He couldn't be redeemed in that way, but he could be better. He would do anything to make Vee proud of him. Even now, he was using leverage and leaning on Romero to avoid bloodshed. A few cleanly executed hits would be quicker than negotiating, but he couldn't bear the thought of Vivian looking at him with mistrust and disappointment.

"Kolya?" The shower had shut off and he could hear Vivian opening vanity drawers.

"Yes?" He called out to her as he selected a pair of jeans and a lightweight shirt. Around the house, he was comfortable wearing a polo, but he didn't want to bare his arms at Bianca's home because he wasn't sure about the guest list.

"I got distracted earlier when you came home, and I forgot to ask you something."

He picked out a pair of Italian leather wingtip boots. "Oh?"

"Niels said that a journalist he met a few days ago asked him about a Russian woman who was coming to the show in London. He didn't recognize her name, and he wondered if she was someone from our social circle. Her name wasn't familiar to me."

"What was it?"

"Tatiana Melnikova."

The boots dropped from his hands and hit the hardwood floor with a thump.

"Are you okay?"

"Yes." He quickly recovered and snatched up his shoes. "I dropped my boots."

"Oh. So Tatiana? Do you know her?"

"No." Guilt squeezed his chest in a vise-like grip. Fuck. *Fuck*. Even though it would be easier, he couldn't lie to her. Swallowing roughly, he confessed more loudly, "Yes."

Boots in hand, he left the closet and found her standing in the doorway of the bathroom. Wrapped in her robe, she clutched at the labels and peered at him with confusion. "Why did you change your answer?"

Tossing his boots onto the closest chair, he expelled a noisy breath and rubbed the back of his neck. There was no easy way to say it. "Tatiana Melnikova isn't her real name. It's a fake. It's a name and an identity I bought for her. Her real name was Tatiana Filipova—and she was my fiancée."

Vivian's face slackened, and her delicate hand moved to her throat. "You... But..."

"It was before you, Vee." The look of betrayal etched into her beautiful face slashed at his heart. "Years before you ever came to Samovar," he hurriedly explained. "You were still in high school, and your grandparents were alive."

"Why didn't you tell me?"

I didn't think you would ever find out. But he couldn't say that. He couldn't admit that he had been hoping to never have this conversation with her. "She had to disappear. There was no reason to tell anyone about it. Besides it was a long time ago, Vee. She doesn't matter."

"You don't get to decide something like that unilaterally." Her sharp tone surprised him. "How would you feel if you found out I had been engaged to another man before you? That I had been planning to become his wife and have his children and build a life with him?"

Jealousy burned through him. Slashing his hand through the air, he insisted, "It's not the same, Vee."

Incredulous, she threw out both hands. "How?"

"Because I didn't love her! She was handpicked by Maksim to form an alliance with a rival family. It was a way for Maksim and her father to align their interests. That's it. It was a practical decision."

"People might think you're describing our marriage."

"How?"

"My father and your father found a way to align their interests." She looked like she might start crying at any second, and it fucking killed him. "The night you proposed to me, you had been in meetings with the cartel and taking phone calls from Moscow. Did Maksim tell you to propose to me?"

"No! It wasn't like that for us."

"Are you sure?" She arched one dark eyebrow. "You asked me to marry you because you were catching heat from all sides. You gave me your name to protect me."

"I asked you to marry me because I fucking love you, Vivian." Irritated that she would even compare their marriage to the sham that he would have had with Tatiana, he snarled, "You are the only one—the only fucking one—I have ever loved. *Ever.*" He gritted his teeth and tried to maintain his cool. "Don't ever question my love for you. It's the one thing I won't abide."

"Then why did you lie to me just now? I asked you if you knew Tatiana and you said no."

"I panicked." He wasn't proud to admit it. "I haven't heard her name in years. That's a complicated and very messy chapter of my life that was supposed to be closed forever. Everyone thinks Tatiana Filipova is dead or that I had her killed. No one would dare to say her name in front of me. That's the way it needs to stay. Her new identity—Tatiana Melnikova—has no connection to mine."

"Why?" Her eyes narrowed with suspicion. "For a man who says he didn't love her, you've gone to extremes to save her life and to avoid talking about her."

Just tell her. Tell her the whole ugly, sordid truth about Tatiana and be done with it.

But he couldn't. He had given his promise, and he never broke his word. Surrounded by a minefield, he had to tread carefully. "Tatiana was caught with another man," he added. "She humiliated me in front of my crew and in front of *krestnii otets*. In front of Maksim," he clarified, in case she had any question as to the godfather he meant. "Her father and mine would have killed her if I hadn't told Kostya to get her out of the country. Even if someone suspected she was still alive, she would be fucking dead to me and to everyone in this family and her own."

The anger faded from her face. Vivian held his gaze "I don't ask you questions about your other business, but when I ask you a question about something that impacts our marriage and our relationship, I expect you to tell me the truth."

His gut clenched. Though the urge to tell her everything about Tatiana and the reason she had run and how she had escaped her father's control was strong, he refused to pull Vivian into it. There were too many innocent people who could be badly hurt by the truth, including one person that Vivian loved dearly. He wouldn't put her in the position of knowing too much and having to choose whether to keep that painful secret.

"In the future, if you ask me about a woman from my past, I will tell you the truth." He couched his answer in carefully chosen words and silently prayed she would leave the topic of Tatiana alone. There was no good that would come from dredging up that ancient history and putting so many lives at risk.

She seemed mollified by his answer. "I'll tell Niels that she's an old friend of yours."

He shook his head. "Don't tell him anything about her. She won't be coming to the show."

"But the journalist—"

"She won't be coming to the show. I'll make sure of that." He intended to put Kostya on the task of tracking her down and giving her a warning. After he had helped her escape, Tatiana had sworn that she would never contact him again. He intended to hold to her to that promise.

Vivian didn't seem happy about his instruction. "Fine. If that's the way you want to handle this."

"It is." Crossing the distance between them, he clasped her sweet face between his hands and grazed his thumbs along her cheeks. "Vee, in my entire life, you are the only woman who has ever managed to melt the ice around my heart." He touched his forehead to hers. "Whatever I had in the past doesn't matter. It's us, our marriage and our family that matters to me. I love you."

"I love you," she murmured, "but don't lie to me. I can't—I *won't* stand for it."

"Nor should you," he agreed. Knowing that he asked so much of her, he pulled back and gazed down into her eyes. "You've given me your trust, and you've accepted all the bullshit that comes with the bad choices I made before I met you. I don't take that for granted. I know what you've sacrificed to be with me."

There was so much more he wanted to say, but he couldn't find the words. Vivian caressed his jaw, and he saw understanding reflected in her sapphire eyes. He whispered his love for her before tenderly capturing her mouth. She surrendered to his seeking mouth and wordlessly forgave him. He didn't deserve her forgiveness, but he selfishly accepted it all the same.

Eventually they separated and dressed. He finished before her and went downstairs to choose a bottle of wine to take as a gift to their hosts. He had chosen his favorite Australian Shiraz from the collection in the butler's pantry when he heard heavy footsteps approaching from the adjacent dining room.

Glancing toward the doorway, he caught sight of Boychenko. By the looks of it, the blond kid had final-

ly gotten the message from Arty about the expecta-
tions for the street soldiers. Instead of the T-shirt and
jeans the kid had been wearing the last time Nikolai
had seen him, Boychenko had paired a dark polo with
khaki chinos and nice shoes. It was an improvement
and a step in the right direction.

"Boss?"

"Yes?"

"One of your neighbors was at the back gate. The
judge," Boychenko explained. "He says he needs to see
you. I wasn't sure if you wanted me to let him inside
so I left him in the garden with his dog."

Boy had only been on the house security detail for
a short time, but he had quickly learned that Nikolai
didn't like anyone who wasn't part of the family in his
home. "I'll go speak with him." Gesturing toward the
back of the house, he said, "Grab the keys to my Land
Rover and pull it out of the garage for us."

"Yes, sir."

"And Boy?" The kid paused and looked back at
him. "Artyom tells me that you're doing well on the
street. You've done a good job here at the house and
with Vivian." He leveled a stare at the younger man.
"It's important to me that she's surrounded by people
I can trust."

"I understand, boss."

He was sure the kid did. If Boy wanted to climb
higher in the organization, he would earn his place
much more quickly by proving himself trustworthy and
willing to do whatever Nikolai asked of him. "Good."

Boy left to finish the errand he had been given, and Nikolai carried the bottle of wine across the house with him as he trailed in Boychenko's footsteps. He opened the back door and found Judge Fitz Walker crouched down under a tree and scratching between his Mastiff's ears. The dog slobbered happily while the judge, dressed in workout clothes, smiled at him. A widower who had lost his wife to a heart attack the prior winter, the man had had a rough run of luck lately including a small house fire and that dog seemed to be the only thing that made him happy.

"Judge, my apologies for the wait." He approached the man but didn't hold out his hand. Though he was cordial with the man, they weren't friendly. More importantly, he didn't want dog hair and saliva all over his hands.

"It's fine." The older man stood, his knees creaking with the movement. "Roscoe and I were walking by, and I thought I would see if you were available to chat."

"I have a few minutes." He glanced back at the house. "My wife and I are heading out for the evening." Always mindful of the balance of favors owed to him, Nikolai was only too happy to help a federal judge in any way he could. "What can I do for you?"

The judge glanced toward the grass and fidgeted with the leash attached to his patiently waiting dog. "It's my daughter. She's in trouble."

Nikolai's lips settled into a thin line. If a man with so many connections was coming to him, trouble was probably an understatement. "What sort of trouble *exactly?*"

"Drugs," the judge said somberly. "She's been an addict for years. We tried everything to get her clean, but nothing worked. Helen, my wife..." His voice broke and he cleared his throat. "It killed her. All the stress and the worry," he said. "It killed her."

The raw emotion in the other man's voice made him uncomfortable, but he didn't try to interrupt the judge.

"Julie's attached herself to a drug dealer. She won't come home. I think...I'm worried that they're *using* her."

Nikolai's jaw clenched. It wasn't unheard of for dealers to surround themselves with young women that they pimped out to their friends and business associates.

"She won't let us—me—talk to her. I've tried, but the last time I went to see her, those goons put a gun in my face."

"You should go to the police."

"I can't." The judge looked stricken. "I don't want them to see her like that. I have to work with these people."

Nikolai ran his tongue around his inner lip. "Which crew is she with?"

"I don't know."

"What's the boyfriend's name?" He expected to hear the name of one of Lalo Contreras' men but that wasn't what came out of the judge's mouth.

"Bobby Pham. He runs with a Vietnamese gang."

"Pham?" Nikolai repeated. "You're sure?"

"Yes."

The name wasn't familiar to him, and he made sure to know every dealer on the streets, from the high level kingpin wannabes like Lalo to the lowest slinger who bought dope on credit and tried to carve out a piece of action.

"What's he selling?"

"Cocaine."

Nikolai tried to make sense of that. Only the cartel and their associates were allowed to move weight around the city. The Vietnamese weren't in that circle so how the hell were they getting their hands on product?

"I'll look into it." He was going to do more than that. "Give me a few days."

The judge's face relaxed with relief. "Thank you." He hesitated. "Whatever you need—"

"I won't hesitate to ask," Nikolai assured him.

The judge nodded. His gaze skipped behind Nikolai and he smiled. "Vivian!"

"Your Honor," she replied with a smile as she joined them.

"You're looking lovely this evening," Judge Walker complimented.

"Yes, you do," Nikolai agreed as he wound his arm around her waist. She wore a striking rust-colored dress with flowing sleeves that ended right above her elbows and a hem that flirted with her knees. The silhouette was deliberately loose and hid the early stage of her pregnancy flawlessly. But that line of buttons down the front of her bodice had his fingers itching to pluck at them.

The gold bracelets adorning her wrist jingled as she reached down to ruffle Roscoe's ears. Seeing her with the dog set his mind into motion. Maybe it was time to add a dog or two to their growing family. He thought of Yuri's great beast of a guard dog but tossed aside the idea. No, Vivian would want something gentler for their children. Gentle but fierce enough to protect his family, he amended.

"Well, I won't keep you two," the judge said and gave Roscoe's leash a tug. "Thank you for the advice on my honeysuckle. I'll let you know if it works."

"Please do." Nikolai watched the judge leave the backyard before guiding Vivian toward the idling Land Rover. Boychenko waited nearby while he got his wife situated in her seat. After closing the door, he flicked his fingers and gestured for the kid to walk around the back of the SUV with him. He stopped near the rear cargo door. "Bobby Pham?"

"Sure," Boychenko said with a nod. "He's one of Mr. Lu's nephews. He runs counterfeits for the old man. DVDs, purses, shoes. It's all good shit though. Top notch."

"Just counterfeits?"

"The last I heard," Boy confirmed.

"When you get off tonight, I want you to find out where he operates. Do it quietly."

"Sure thing, boss."

"And be careful, huh? Everyone is tense right now. Lots of trigger happy fingers, yes?"

"Right." Boychenko nodded dutifully. "I'll be careful and quiet."

Satisfied the kid could handle the task, he slid into the front seat of the SUV and handed the bottle of wine to Vivian. She studied him as he buckled up. "Everything okay?"

He glanced at her and smiled. "It will be."

But a nagging voice warned him that it was going to get a hell of a lot worse before that happened.

3 CHAPTER THREE

Three mornings later, a soft buzzing sound roused me from a dead sleep. Bleary eyed, I turned onto my side and slapped at my bedside table to grab my iPhone. I squinted at the screen and groaned. It wasn't even four a.m. yet.

I didn't recognize the number and considered letting it go to voicemail. But what if it was important? The thought that one of our friends might be in trouble spurred me to answer. "Hello?"

"Vivian."

I stiffened at the sound of my father's raspy voice. "Dad?"

"I know it's early, but I need to speak with Nikolai."

I glanced at my husband. Face down on the bed, he had one arm draped across my waist and his leg hooked across both of mine. I could feel his warm, deep breaths skittering across my skin. The sheet had fallen down around his taut backside. Last night he had come home in a rather amorous mood. By the time we were finished writhing together in bed, we had been too tired to even contemplate slipping into pajamas. We had passed out in a tangle of limbs.

"It's four in the morning, Dad."

"I know what fucking time it is," he snapped. "Put him on the goddamn phone."

Irritated, I hissed, "I don't know who you think you're talking to, but I'm not one of your grubby MC brothers. You do not call my house at four in the morning and speak to me like that. *Me entiendes?*"

A tense silence stretched between us. The rough, gravelly tones of his laughter filtered across the speaker. "Yeah, kiddo, I understand you. Sounds like you've finally found that backbone. They're right. You are becoming the queen."

I ignored the remark. "What do you want?"

"I need to speak with Nikolai. Now. It's important." He paused. "Please."

"Hang on." I lowered my phone and reached out to stroke the back of Nikolai's neck. "Kolya? Wake up."

He bolted upright and instantly covered my body with his own. Pressing me down onto the mattress, he protectively shielded me and the baby. "What is it? Did you hear something?"

"No." I gently caressed his face. Even in his sleep, he never truly relaxed. I worried so much about the stress he endured day after day. "Relax."

He expelled a slow breath but didn't move away from me. Dropping his head down, he nuzzled his nose against mine. "What time is it?"

"A little before four," I answered quietly. Holding up the phone, I gave it a shake. The screen lit up his face with a bluish glow. "You have a call. It's my dad."

Nikolai grunted with annoyance but took the phone from me. He rolled onto his back and tugged the sheet up around my shoulders. "Yes?"

I heard my father's voice but couldn't make out the words. The conversation was short and mostly one-sided.

"I'll call you back in a few minutes." Nikolai ended the call and placed my phone on the bedside table. He leaned over and kissed my cheek. "I have to go downstairs. Go back to sleep."

Downstairs. To his office that Kostya swept for bugs. To the burner phones that couldn't be traced. I grasped his hand and stopped him from leaving. "What's going on?"

He squeezed my fingers in a reassuring grip. "Nothing that you need to worry about, Vee." He planted his mouth against mine and lingered. "Get some rest. I kept you awake too late last night."

"I'm not complaining."

"Good." His hand followed the outline of my growing curves. "I intend to keep you awake again tonight."

I giggled as he tickled my sides. "Kolya! Stop!"

He placed a noisy kiss on my cheek. "Go to sleep. I'll wake you for breakfast."

I didn't have the energy to argue with him. First trimester exhaustion was still kicking my butt. I had been lucky to avoid the worst morning sickness, but I couldn't seem to get enough sleep.

From my spot in bed, I watched him disappear into the bathroom and emerge in only his pajama bottoms. He left the room quietly and closed the door behind him. Hugging my husband's pillow, I closed my eyes and tried to sleep. My mind reeled with troubling thoughts. My father hadn't contacted me since January. For him to call this early in the morning? It was very serious.

Though it would be so easy to sneak downstairs and eavesdrop, I stayed in bed. My heavy eyelids drifted together, and I surrendered to the siren call of sleep. Sometime later, I woke to the sound of a knock at the bedroom door. Sitting up, I clutched the sheet to my bare chest and glanced at the clock on Nikolai's side of the bed. It was after nine!

"Vivian Ivanovna?" Artyom's rough voice penetrated the door.

I smiled at the way he called my name in that ultra-respectful way. He used my grandfather's name instead of my father's for obvious reasons. Clearing my throat, I asked, "Yes?"

"I have your breakfast."

"Oh. Um...just a second." I carefully slipped out of bed, making sure to take my time to avoid dizziness, and found my nightgown and robe neatly draped across the foot of the bed. *Nikolai.*

I dressed and pulled my hair into a low ponytail. When I opened the door, I found Arty waiting patiently in the hallway. He smiled down at me. "*Dobroye utro.*"

"Good morning."

"May I?"

"Yes." I stepped aside and let him into our bedroom. He carried the tray to the sitting area by the window that overlooked the backyard and placed it on the leather ottoman there. I sat in my favorite chair and gestured to the empty seat. "Would you like to stay?"

He glanced around the bedroom and shook his head. "I don't think the boss would like that."

"It's only breakfast."

"It's your bedroom." He grabbed the neatly folded napkin, unsnapped it and draped it across my lap. Artyom wasn't about to put either of us in a situation where wagging tongues might start rumors. With a playful smile, he took one of the pears from the tray and walked to the open doorway. Leaning against the frame, he took a bite. "There. Now we can talk."

Amused by his compromise, I perused the offerings on the tray and decided to have the yogurt sweetened with a drizzle of honey and raspberries first. "Thank you for breakfast."

"I only made the tea. The boss put this together before he left. He told me to let you sleep in and wake you at nine."

Not at all surprised that Nikolai had arranged all of this, I ran my fingertips across the soft, lush petals of the three Madame Berkeley roses he had clipped and placed in a small vase for me. The apricot petals had a tinge of pink on the tips. "Where is Nikolai?"

"He had to leave unexpectedly."

I picked up the mug of tea and took a sip. The ginger and orange blossom flavor soothed my nausea. "Business?"

"*Da.*"

"My father?" I noticed the slight tic in his cheek and sighed. "What's he done now?"

"It wasn't your father. It was one of his men." The tight-lipped captain warily admitted that much but I sensed he wasn't going to tell me much more.

"It's bad?"

Arty crunched another bite of the sweet pear and nodded. My gaze was drawn to the tattoos on his hand. He lacked the five dots that Nikolai, Ivan and a handful of others had. It meant that he had never been to prison. The grinning devil on the back of his hand always freaked me out. He had the year of his birth inked onto his fingers, on the spaces between the joints and the nails. There was a typical thief's talisman on his thumb, and a scarab on his pointer finger. The asterisk on his middle finger wasn't a symbol I recognized.

Glancing away from his hand, I asked, "So I guess you're going to be my shadow today?"

"Yep." He turned the pear in his big hand and sank his teeth into the soft flesh. "You're getting a new one tomorrow. A full-timer to replace Sergei," he explained.

"Oh? Is Danny going to take over?"

"No. Danny is moving up the ladder." He made a walking motion. "The boss has decided that Ten will be responsible for you."

I blinked with shock. "Wait. Ten? As in Anton Vasiliev?"

"Yes."

"But he's in prison," I sputtered.

Arty shook his head. "He got out this morning."

Why in the world wasn't I told this? Irritated that Nikolai had kept this decision from me, I stabbed my spoon into my yogurt. A thousand arguments against being placed in the care of man with Ten's reputation raced through my mind but I clamped my mouth closed. That was a conversation I would have with Nikolai. Speaking of my husband... "Do you think Nikolai will be back by this afternoon?"

He shrugged. "Maybe. Why?"

"I have an appointment." We were supposed to have our first look at the baby today, and I really, *really* didn't want to drag a mob captain to my first prenatal visit.

"If the boss isn't back in time, I'll make sure you get there." He finished off his pear. "Is it at the salon?"

"Not exactly," I murmured and tucked into my breakfast.

"You let me know when you're ready to leave. I'll take you." He pushed off the door frame. "Do you want to paint here at the house or do you want to go to the studio?"

"I'll stay here today."

"Okay." He gestured over his shoulder. "I'll be downstairs. Boy and Ilya, one of my other guys, is here. If you need anything, you call for us. Yes?"

"Sure." He started to leave but I stopped him. "Artyom?"

"Yes?"

"I'm going to be totally nosy for a second. You can tell me to mind my own business if you'd like."

He actually laughed and held up the hand that was missing two fingers. "You want to know the story behind this?"

"No!"

"It's all right. Everyone wants to know."

"No, really. I—"

"Luka Beciraj."

I didn't know that name. "Who?"

"You know Besian?"

"A little." I dipped my spoon into the yogurt and stirred it around. "I used to see him around Samovar. He was at our wedding."

"Luka is his cousin, and he's the big boss over in Tirana. He runs that family with an iron fist."

I didn't know a lot about the Albanian crews, but I did know they were all about their family ties, loyalty and honor.

"I made the mistake of taking something from Luka." Artyom held up his hand. "So he took something from me—with a chisel and a hammer."

My eyes widened at the brutality of it. "Jesus."

His shoulders rolled nonchalantly. "I got off lucky. Two fingers? It's a small price to pay."

"A small price?" I shook my head. "You guys are crazy sometimes. You know that?"

He laughed sadly. "Yes."

I scooped up a spoonful of the yogurt and raspberries. "I was going to ask about the tattoo here." I tapped my finger to indicate which one I meant. "I've never seen a ring tattoo like that one."

He glanced at the asterisk on his hand. "It means I have no father."

I frowned. "That's not what Nikolai or Ivan's orphan tattoos look like."

"They were abandoned. I disowned my father. It's different."

"I see." I suddenly had a sneaking suspicion that the green-eyed captain had a life story similar to mine. More than once, I had dreamed of disowning my own father.

Artyom tapped his knuckles against the door frame. "We'll be downstairs."

Certain the men all had money on the World Cup matches, I waved my hand. "I don't mind if you watch the games."

He grinned. "I was going to ask, but I thought I'd wait until after your breakfast."

Feeling lucky, I asked, "Are the books still open?"

He seemed surprised by the question. I couldn't blame him. The fact that I sometimes indulged in gambling was one I kept very quiet. He glanced at his watch. "Yes. Why? You want to drop a buck on the chalk? It's Portugal."

I tried to remember all the sports talk from Bianca and Sergei's barbecue. "Make it two."

"You got it."

After Artyom left, I pushed aside thoughts of chisels, hammers and Albanian blood feuds and enjoyed my breakfast. I stopped halfway through to grab my phone. I went straight to the Mexican newspapers I scanned every morning and looked for clues as to why my father would have called and why Nikolai would have left without a word. There were the usual reports of cartel violence, but I didn't see anything that tied back to Houston.

Uneasy and prickling with dread, I finished my breakfast, showered and dressed for the day. I dropped off my tray in the kitchen and handled a bit of house-work. We had a housekeeper who came by twice a week, but I rather enjoyed the mundane, quiet tasks. They gave me time to think or unwind.

But today I couldn't shake the feeling that something bad was happening.

Alone in my home studio, I perched on a stool and stared at the two finished canvases and the blank one that sat on my center easel. I wasn't sure where the hell I was going with this new collection. *Find something to say.*

God, there was so much I wanted to say. I just didn't know how to do it. Layers, mixed media, vibrant colors—there were so many choices. I needed a

cohesive vision. My other collections had all come together so easily, but this one? No, this one evaded me.

Rather than attempting a new painting, I opened
one of my favorite art books and studied the pages of
oil paintings completed only with palette knives. The
technique had long fascinated me, and I had been in-
corporating it in my work for some time now. I selected a trio of colors and squeezed small dollops on a
palette so I could practice different strokes and layers.

I kept glancing at my phone, checking the time and
expecting a message or phone call from Nikolai. Biting
my lip, I decided to send him a text instead of calling.
My finger hovered over the screen for a few seconds
before typing in a message.

V: Doctor's office in one hour. Call me!

When I didn't hear from him after fifteen minutes,
I debated whether to cancel the appointment or go on
my own. We needed to keep our pregnancy quiet, but
I also needed to start my prenatal care. My hand drifted to my stomach, and I bit my lip. I had to make a
decision—and I was choosing the health of the baby.
We were leaving for London in a few days, and I needed to know everything was all right.

I cleaned up my mess and looked for Arty. He sat
forward on the edge of a couch in the media room and
watched a soccer match. Boychenko leaned against the
opposite wall and split his attention between the front
yard and the television. He seemed tense, and it occurred to me that Arty had years of practice playing
cool and dealing with the blowback of this life. What-

ever problem had dragged Nikolai out of bed so early clearly had Boy rattled.

"Artyom?"

He instantly muted the television and rose to his feet. "What can I do for you?"

"That appointment? I need to leave soon."

"Sure." He glanced at Boy. "Get Ilya. You'll follow us."

Boy nodded and left to find the guard who was probably hanging around the backyard. Arty switched off the TV. "Which vehicle would like to take?"

"Parking is going to be a nightmare unless we valet."

"Valet? Where are we going? A hotel?"

I swallowed anxiously. "No, you're taking me to the hospital. The new women's hospital downtown," I clarified.

"Hospital?" Concern darkened his face. "Are you all right?"

I touched his arm. "I'm fine." I lowered my voice. "I'm pregnant."

"Pregnant? But that's fantastic! Congratulations!" He looked as if wanted to hug me but held back. His expression quickly turned more serious. "Oh, but this is a very bad time for—" He stopped suddenly. "I mean—*shit*. What I mean is—"

"I know what you meant," I interjected. "We've had the same thought."

He rubbed the back of his neck. "Boy and Ilya? I trust them, but two mouths means two more chances for the news to get out. I assume that you and the boss want this quiet until things settle down."

"That's the idea."

"I'll tell them to stay here. You and I will leave in the Land Rover, but we'll switch to one of the fleet cars we keep in the parking lots around town. No one will be able to follow us that way. I'll make sure that your trip today is as secret as possible."

I clasped his hand and smiled warmly. "Thank you."

"It's my job." He touched my shoulder. "Let's go."

Half an hour and a vehicle switch later, we were riding an elevator up to my obstetrician's office. I gripped the handle of my purse and wondered where Nikolai was. I had texted him four more times during the drive and still there was no response. My emotions were all over the place. Anger, annoyance, frustration.

"He'll be here," Arty assured me as we reached the office door. "He's probably running a few minutes late. As soon as I see him, I'll send him inside to find you."

"You don't have to wait out here." He seemed hesitant to follow me inside the office. I didn't blame him. It was a strange situation. "It might be a while."

"I'll wait. It's no problem."

"All right."

Inside the office, I checked in and took the stack of paperwork to an open chair. Balancing the clipboard on my lap, I filled out the pages of medical history and insurance information. I couldn't fill in all of Nikolai's medical history so I had to leave spots blank. They still hadn't called me back by the time I had finished the paperwork so I fished my phone from my purse and texted him again.

V: Doctor's appointment in five minutes. Please call!

But he didn't answer.

A nurse popped her head out of the door that led back to the exam area and called my name. I glanced back at the entrance, expecting to see Nikolai rushing through the door like some scene from a movie, but he wasn't there. With a sad sigh, I followed the nurse to the triage station to be weighed and have my blood pressure and temperature taken. When that was done, I was led to a room and given a gown and a sheet.

Alone in the room, I sat on the edge of the exam table and nervously fidgeted. I tugged the gown tightly closed and used the sheet to cover my legs. My gaze flitted around the room. There were posters about breastfeeding, birth control and the anatomy of pregnancy on the walls. The poster about post-partum depression caught my attention. All those worries and fears bubbled to the surface.

The door opened, and hope flared within me. It was him. It just had to be him, rushing into the room, breathless and apologetic.

But it wasn't Nikolai. It was my doctor.

Plastering a smile on my face, I shook her hand and shoved down the feelings of disappointment and bitterness that threatened to overwhelm me. *Where are you?*

CHAPTER FOUR

Rubbing a hand down his tired face, Nikolai blew out a noisy, frustrated breath before sliding out of the backseat of the SUV. He buttoned his jacket and adjusted his aviator sunglasses, all the while scanning his surroundings like a hawk in search of prey. Flanked by Danny and two others, he grimaced at the muggy heat that greeted him. Even at nine in the morning, the humidity and warmth were oppressive.

Kostya waited for him at the entrance to the climate controlled storage locker. The hard line to the other man's mouth didn't bode well. "They're all inside. I've swept the area and the men for bugs. I've confiscated all the cell phones." He held out his hand and wiggled his fingers. "I need yours."

Nikolai retrieved his phone and handed it over. Kostya switched off the power, peeled a red sticker off his shirt and pressed it onto the phone before dropping it into a bag he carried. "The new guy is here. He came light. No heavies."

New guy? *Shit.* The lack of sleep over the last few weeks was getting to him. He had completely forgotten that there was a new player in town. His decision to wipe out the Night Wolves after they been caught gathering intel on Vee and had attempted to kill Bianca in her own store had left a power vacuum in the hierarchy of the white supremacist groups.

He didn't like working with them, but it was a necessary evil. Their hatred for others sickened him. Though he was no saint, he had his lines and codes. He didn't touch innocent people—children, wives, girlfriends, parents. That had always been his rule. He didn't cross that line. Ever. But these men who were so twisted up by skin color and religion? They didn't follow those rules. It made them reckless and dangerous and difficult to predict.

But he needed to fill that power slot. It was better to invite in someone with a power structure behind him than to let the smaller gangs around town fight it out on the streets. In some ways, he felt like a bit like the CIA installing and propping up a dictator who would follow the party line.

So overtures had been made and a new man from the main Aryan group out of Dallas had been sent down to Houston. Nikolai couldn't remember his name. *I need more coffee.*

As if reading his mind, Kostya said, "His name is James Mueller. They call him the Red Baron." He actually flashed a smile that revealed how stupid he found that nickname. "He's not your typical skinhead loser. I think you might actually like him. You know, except for all that white power bullshit."

"We'll see. Where did you put him?"

Kostya laughed mischievously. "Between Nickel Jackson and Mr. Lu. It's our own little version of the U.N. Security Council in there."

Nikolai chortled at the mental image of a racist sandwiched between a Vietnamese importer and the burly black gangster who ran all the action in the area of the city known as the Bloody Nickel.

"By the way, boss, Julio wants a private meet after the council finishes."

Nikolai groaned. "He's not going to like what he hears."

Kostya shrugged. "I'm just the messenger."

"Where did you seat him?"

"Between Besian and Mr. Lu and across the table from Spider."

Nikolai knew and respected the Calaveras MC vice president. He suspected Spider didn't like this mess any more than he did. That fucking phone call this morning threatened to push the cartel and the MC into a war.

Back in April, the big story around town had been the hit-and-run death of a high school kid leaving a concert up in the The Woodlands. The poor kid had been clipped and dragged by a motorcycle. The rider had jerked the kid free and sped off, leaving him in the middle of the road where he was hit again by a truck.

The cruelty and coldness of that death had bothered Nikolai. Within a day of the story hitting the news, Kostya had quietly informed him that the kid was actually the godson of Julio Jimenez, the Guzman cartel's top guy in the city. Kostya had believed the kid was really his biological son so Nikolai had put out feelers to find the asshole who had killed the boy. It would have been a nice gift to the cartel and a good deed that would buy him some goodwill down the line.

Because of the motorcycle connection, he had specifically asked Romero to get the Calaveras on it. The bastard had sworn up and down that none of the MCs in town had anything to do with it. The rider that night hadn't been wearing a kutte or colors. He was just some random guy on a Harley.

Except that he wasn't.

Romero had been lying through his fucking teeth and had been forced to admit to that this morning. It had been his closest friend, Mando Fernandez, the damned sergeant-at-arms for the Calaveras MC, who had killed the kid. He had been doing a bit of freelance work that night so he hadn't been wearing his vest or riding his usual bike. Mando had called Romero the next morning, after the kid's identity was revealed, and Romero had given him orders to keep his trap shut. They had planned to take that secret to the grave.

But someone had found out and told Julio. Now Julio wanted blood. Nikolai didn't blame him. The thought of someone hurting his child was like a spear to the chest. The person who made the mistake of even trying to touch his son or daughter would know a gris-ly and violent end. He would make sure of it with his bare hands.

As Nikolai entered the storage container for the quarterly council get-together, he still didn't know what the hell he was going to do about this situation. The fact that Romero had known the whole time ran-kled him. This was something he had needed to know but his father-in-law had kept him in the dark.

Romero had let this fucking wound fester and rot— and now Nikolai had to decide how far up the limb to amputate.

He glanced at the guards lining one wall. Each boss brought one man inside to watch his back. The rest of them remained outside. Even before he opened the door that sealed off the secret chamber portion of the container, he could hear the raised voices from inside. This council had been started to keep the peace and negotiate easements when it came to territories dis-putes. Usually the meetings were peaceful and short but the summer heat had a way of inflaming tempers. There was a lot of business on the table today, and Nikolai had a bad feeling it was going to be like trying to wrangle cranky toddlers in a daycare center.

He stepped inside the room and swept his gaze around the sparse interior. A round table, some chairs, no windows. He glanced at the familiar faces seated at the table and mentally catalogued their allegiances, strengths and weaknesses. If he didn't get what he wanted through negotiation, he would apply pressure to those weaknesses.

When he dropped down into his chair, Nikolai spotted the cup of coffee waiting for him. Kostya, of course. He took a sip while the room quieted down. The new guy, blond and green-eyed and dressed impeccably in a grey single-breasted suit, looked uncomfortable as Nicky and Mr. Lu leaned across him and hissed at each other. He let his gaze linger on Julio Jimenez who looked unnaturally calm. Spider drummed his fingers on the table and assiduously avoided looking in Julio's direction. Beside him, Besian unwrapped a jawbreaker and popped it into his mouth. They exchanged a look before the Albanian mob boss dropped back into his chair and rolled the hard candy around his mouth.

"All right. Let's get this shit over with," Nikolai stated. He gestured toward the Red Baron. "This is James Mueller. He's with the Brotherhood out of Dallas." There were murmurs of introductions around the table. Just in case Mueller had any funny ideas about his position on the totem pole, Nikolai made sure to end them. "He won't have much to say today. He's here to listen."

Mueller simply nodded.

Nikolai tapped his fingers on the plastic lid of his coffee cup. "Who is up first?"

"Me." Julio waved his hand, and Nikolai's stomach clenched as he expected shit to get real and loud fast. "We have an issue that needs to be addressed. It's between me and him."

The knot in his stomach eased when Julio pointed toward Mr. Lu. The elderly man held up both hands and immediately started to protest. Julio began to talk over him, and Nikolai stepped in like a father separating arguing children. "Come on. One at a time. Julio?"

"Our market share is dropping around the city, and it's not because the red ribbon campaigns are working. Our dealers—Lalo and his men—are reporting that someone is undercutting their prices and flooding the market with product. It's coming from his territory."

"No, no, no." Lu waved both hands. "We don't deal in drugs." He stated his position firmly, and Nikolai didn't detect a hint of untruth. Apparently the old man was in the dark about his nephew's activities. Boychenko had reported back with an address and half a night's worth of observation that confirmed Bobby Pham was dealing.

"Bullshit," Julio spat back. "I had two guys do buys from a dishwasher at a pho shop and a massage parlor."

"I can't control every single lowlife in my territory." Mr. Lu turned his attention to Nikolai. "If there are side deals going on in my backyard, I'll take care of it." He glanced at Julio. "You should have come to me first. This didn't have to be escalated as a council matter."

"I wanted it out in the open, in front of everyone," Julio said and cast a look at Spider. "But if Lu says that he'll take care of it, I take him at his word."

Nikolai sipped his coffee. This was far from settled, but he wasn't going to get involved. Not publicly, at least. "Next item?"

"That's me." Nicky raised a dark hand glittering with gold jewelry. "And Lu."

The old man made an irritated noise. "I told you that all purchases are final."

"No, no, no, no, no." Nicky pounded his finger against the tabletop like a nail going into wood. "You guarantee the shipments."

"Yes, I guarantee the shipments. I guarantee that they arrive and are transferred to you. That's my guarantee. I don't guarantee what's in the boxes!"

Nicky leaned across the table, forcing Mueller back into his seat. "How in the hell are my boys supposed to push lean when the syrup is bad? Huh?"

Ah, now Nikolai understood the issue. Nicky bought huge quantities of promethazine and codeine from Chinese suppliers to sell to users who mixed it with lemon-lime soda to get high. They called it lean because the kids who drank that shit started to tilt and lean after a cup or two. It used to be easy enough for Nicky's guys to doctor shop to get their ingredients. With the DEA cracking down, Nicky had turned to Mr. Lu who imported and delivered the cough syrup without incident.

"What the fuck do you want us to do about it?" Besian rolled the jaw breaker around his mouth. The sound of it knocking against his teeth irritated Nikolai but he tried to ignore it. "Lu is right. We pay him for shipping and customs. That's it."

"He gave me the supplier contact. That's on him," Nicky insisted. "He's on both sides of this deal. He's taken a cut from the supplier for making the contract, and he's getting my shipping and handling fees. Now he's telling me that he can get me the good stuff from a different factory—at twice the price and only if I clear the debt on that last shipment that I can't even give away." Nicky shook his head. "This shit ain't right, y'all."

Mr. Lu started to argue about his policies, but Nikolai had had enough of it. Besian caught his eye, and they shared a look of understanding. It was time for the gangster version of good cop, bad cop.

"You know, Lu, it sounds like you're losing your touch, old man." Besian crunched what was left of the jaw breaker between his back teeth. "You've got kids selling some of that sweet Colombian *llelo* right in your backyard, and now you're making the whole Fifth Ward sick with your bad syrup."

Mr. Lu sputtered. "That is not—"

"Nicky, maybe I should put you in contact with my man. He can get you anything you want from anywhere in the world." Besian made the offer with a smile, but it was a threat as dangerous as a knife to the throat for Lu. Without the confidence of the men at this table, he couldn't do business. If they started using Zec for their shipments, they would cut the old man off at the knees.

"Look," Lu interjected hastily, "we don't have to be so drastic." With a resigned sigh, he turned toward

Nicky. "I'll take back the shipment, and I'll get you a clean shipment on my dime to replace it."

"I want the same price for the new shipments," Nicky countered.

"I can't get it for that price," Lu insisted.

"Bullshit. You and your—"

"Enough," Nikolai interrupted. "Nicky, the market is the market. When prices rise, we all have to adjust." He looked to Mr. Lu. "At the same time, it's better to ease these types of price changes onto our customers. So let's talk about a six month discount." Knowing that Nicky wanted a good deal and Lu had to think about thin margins, he started off at a number that left room for negotiations. "Thirty percent?"

"Impossible!" Mr. Lu vehemently refused. He waited two heartbeats before countering, "Ten."

Cheap old bastard. "Twenty-five."

"Fifteen."

"Twenty," Nikolai said, his voice lower and sharper.

Lu sighed. "Yeah. Okay."

Nikolai glanced at the man who ran the Fifth Ward. "Do we have a deal?"

Nicky gave a slight nod. "Yes."

"Good." Nikolai placed both hands around his coffee cup. Fully expecting Julio to bring up his issues with Mando, he asked, "Anything else?"

"Pussy," Besian said, fishing a new jaw breaker from his pocket.

Nikolai's mouth settled into a grim line. His family didn't touch the skin trade, but several of the men at the table had lucrative business lines dedicated to it. "What about it?"

"In the last two months, I've had to send my guys out to chase away the corner girls who have been hanging around the strip clubs." He popped a green candy into his mouth. "They come in vans from Nicky's district and hang around the parking lots. Instead of spending money to get into a VIP room in my clubs, the customers are taking their dollars outside to visit these cut-rate streetwalkers. It's cutting into my bottom line and draws police attention. Lights and sirens are bad for business."

"Look, man," Nicky sat forward, "Sugar's sits on the edge of the buffer zone. Do you expect me to hook GPS tags on my girls? They walk the streets. I can't help it if they cross an invisible line."

"Invisible line my ass," Besian growled. "I'm pretty fucking sure they can see the huge hot pink lips blinking on top of Sugar's. This is you making plays and edging into my territory." He swept his hand along the table. "We've talked about this. We agreed—"

"We agreed that you get the high-end action," Nicky cut in with a wag of his finger. "You get the security business for the high-end escorts Alina runs out of her brothel and the strip clubs. I have all the street action. *That* was the deal. But you've been pinching my girls and running your escorts around my territory."

"That's not the way it happened," Besian argued. "I can't help it if your girls are tired of giving fat fucks handjobs in back alleys and getting their knees dirty over at the Flying J parking lot. Employee retention isn't my problem. You should take that up with Alina." He crunched another jaw breaker. "We're just her hired muscle."

Nickel Jackson rapped one of his golden rings on the table. "Don't give me that line. You and Alina have been running your games for years."

Wading into the fray, Nikolai said, "Maybe we need a bigger buffer between your two territories."

Julio agreed with a slow nod. "I'm with the Russian on this one. Every time we meet, you two squabble about territory issues. Your business interests intersect too much. We could partition off a strip between the two of you and give it the Hermanos."

Now that didn't surprise Nikolai one bit. The Hermanos street gang was closely allied with the cartel and helped maintain their presence here in the city.

"We have businesses in that area around Sugar's," Mr. Lu mentioned. "We could take it."

Nikolai noticed that Spider didn't make an offer to take the piece they were discussing. He was smart and practical and likely anticipated it would be more trouble than it was worth to his MC. Nikolai considered the new man at the table. "Mueller."

"Yes?" By the look on his face, he already knew what was about to be asked of him.

"How would you like to be the new owner of ten Houston blocks?"

Mueller rubbed his thumb over his watch face. "Real estate is my legit business. I'll buy anything if I can get a good price."

"Then today is your lucky day because I'm giving it away free," Nikolai remarked.

After the expected grumbling from Besian and Nicky over the new arrangement, they settled some of the smaller issues and ended their meeting. Nikolai tensed when he noticed Julio passing Spider, but the two men didn't exchange a word.

"Trouble in paradise?" Besian asked in that maddening way of his. The man could ferret out a secret faster than Kostya. "What's that saying around here?" He dug around in his pocket and produced another jaw breaker. "Oh. Right. Too many chiefs and not enough Indians."

Nikolai snatched the candy away from Besian, the plastic wrapper crinkling loudly as he closed his fingers around it. "I can't listen to you crunching another one of these." He stuffed it into his own pocket. "You're going to ruin your teeth."

Besian issued an amused chuff. "Yes, Papa."

Nikolai shot him a warning look. "What is with the candy?"

"I'm trying to cut back on the smokes," Besian explained. "Apparently they kill people. The candy helps me fight the urge to light up."

"You're going to need a dentist and a gym if you keep this up," Nikolai warned. "All that sugar? You'll be trading lung cancer for diabetes."

Besian shot him the finger. "What about you? How did you stop?"

A memory flashed before his eyes. Suddenly he was rifling through his desk drawers and coat pockets at

Samovar in search of a pack of cigarettes. He couldn't understand why they kept disappearing. Certain one of the employees with cash flow problems was pinching them, he had gone into the locker room to check the cubicles.

Desperate to feed his habit, he had opened the first locker—and froze at the sight that greeted him. Two stacks of cigarette packs, some brand new and sealed and others half empty, sat on a shelf in the locker. It wasn't the discovery of his stolen cigarettes that had stunned him. No, it was the realization that he was staring into Vivian's locker. His gaze had settled on the photos taped to the door and interior walls. All but one were Vivian with Lena, Erin and Bianca at various social gatherings—college football games, concerts, night clubs and the beach.

But that one photo taped to the left wall, down low where it was almost easy to overlook, had ensnared him. It had been snapped a few months earlier when the staff at Samovar had blindsided him with a birthday cake before the doors opened for lunch. More than anything, he had been startled someone had discovered his birthday. Until, of course, he had spotted Vivian standing near the rear of the small crowd, her fingers interlaced and her expression a mixture of excitement and fear. Somehow she had wheedled that bit of information out of one of his friends. Vanya, he was sure. The former street fighter had a soft spot for Vivian.

But soft spot didn't even begin to describe what he felt toward the blue-eyed beauty who had completely upended his carefully arranged world. So when she had bitten her lip and silently pleaded with him to just sit the hell down and pretend that he enjoyed the off-key notes of his staff singing *Happy Birthday* that's exactly what he did.

For her. Because, if he was being truly honest with himself, everything he did had been for her and only her since the moment he had discovered her bleeding, broken body in the front yard of that house.

When it was time to cut the cake and partition out small squares to the staff, Vivian had been the one who came forward with a knife to handle the task. Someone had snapped a photograph of her by his side, a sweet smile on her face and the hint of one ghosting across his. It was a totally innocent photograph and rather unremarkable to anyone who didn't know what to look for—but he knew and he saw it.

He had taken that photo and tucked it into his wallet. Later, with a couple of drinks in him, he had discovered the decency to be embarrassed and a little bit ashamed for stealing from Vivian. The photo had meant something to her, but he suspected it meant more to him. Looking at that photo, he could almost imagine that it had been just the two of them. Together. Happy.

Even now, more than two years later, he still tugged that photo out of his wallet on occasion and ran his finger along her face. Their home was decorated with dozens of photos of the two of them, but that one meant the most to him. It was the first. It had been so important to him that he had secretly scanned and saved it, just in case he ever needed another copy.

Realizing he had drifted into his thoughts, Nikolai stood up and glanced at Besian who wore a slightly bemused expression. "Vee asked me to quit so I did."

Besian seemed surprised by his honesty. "Just like that?"

"No. I tripped up quite a few times but I kept trying." *For her.*

"Well," Besian said on a low breath and rose from his chair, "then I'm fucked. I'll never meet a woman like your little artist. God knows I've looked."

"Because there are no other women like Vee," he answered matter-of-factly. Thinking of the women Besian paraded around town, he made a simple suggestion. "Stop looking in the wrong places."

"Oh, there's a list then? Of right and wrong places?"

It was one thing to discuss women with his closest friends, but giving relationship advice to a rival boss? Not really his thing. Deciding to cut this discussion short, he pointed out the obvious. "Stop dating your employees."

"You married your employee."

Affronted that Besian would even think to compare Vivian to the naked, glitter-dusted girls dancing on his stages, he glared at the man. "That's my wife you're talking about, Besian. We are friends, but don't think for one fucking second that distinction means anything when it comes to her."

The Albanian boss held up his hands. "Hey, come on. I didn't mean it like that."

Irritated with Besian, he asked, "Are we done?"

"We will be as soon as you tell me what the hell is going on between the cartel and the Calaveras. I have side deals with the MC for bikes and bike parts. Do I need to cut back on those shipments and add more security?"

"It's business as usual. The issue is personal. It has nothing to do with the cartel or the club."

"You sure?" Besian glanced at the closed door and stepped closer. "I'm hearing shit, Nikolai. Worrisome shit," he added seriously.

He had been hearing the same worrisome shit, but he shrugged it off. "There are always rumors. That's the nature of our world."

"It's not only rumors. I saw something the other day. Something very strange."

Nikolai narrowed his eyes. "And what was that?"

"I took 59 to Laredo last week to check up on our operation there. Do you know what I saw?"

"Drug mules. Drug dealers. Corrupt deputies." He listed the usual things one might find on that stretch of highway. US 59 was notorious for drug traffic and heavily favored by the cartel.

"Hector Salas, Lalo Contreras and two of Mr. Lu's nephews all left the same hotel. I was sitting in the lobby reading the paper when I spotted Lalo first. I didn't think much of it because, hell, he's the cartel's street man. When I spotted the two Pham boys and

Hector?" Besian shook his head. "That's not a coincidence."

Hector Salas had a reputation as the cartel's fixer and top enforcer. His father had been drug lord Lorenzo Guzman's best friend, but it was his mother that was really interesting. She had been the sister of Eddie Rivera, one of the richest men in the country. A cartel squabble twenty years earlier had killed her. She had been violently and brutally murdered.

According to the stories around town, Hector's father had sent him to Houston to live with Eddie and his family. By all accounts, Marco Salas had promised his wife their son wouldn't follow in his footsteps. Clearly he had failed. From what Nikolai knew of the story, Hector had served ten years in the military before being dishonorably discharged and tossed to the wolves. The cartel had come calling, and the rest was history.

The puzzle pieces started to fit together now. Lorenzo Guzman was feeling the squeeze south of the border. Rival cartels were gaining strength and market share. He had Romero, once a friend and now his enemy, making plays in his backyard with the support of Maksim. Were Lorenzo's captains and street soldiers thinking of staging a coup? How did these Vietnamese kids fit into this? There were so many Latino street gangs in Houston. Lalo and Hector could have picked any or all of them to start running product and setting up new supply lines so why the Pham boys?

"I'll look into it." Nikolai headed for the door. "I hate these shady, backroom deals."

"Whatever happens? My crew stands with you."

Nikolai glanced at Besian and nodded. The Albanians had some lucrative businesses and sidelines in the city but they didn't have strength. They limited their growth by only allowing those who were connected by blood or marriage to join the ranks. It cut down on the sort of backstabbing bullshit that was probably happening right now inside the cartel—but it meant they needed the protection of a bigger organization.

"We're with you," Nikolai confirmed.

"And the others?" Besian gestured toward the closed door with a lift of his chin. "If the cartel implodes, we're going to have the barbarians at the gate. We'll need every man we can get."

"Yes, we will." Already doing the math and thinking of the dozens of ways this could end, Nikolai left the storage locker with Besian at his side.

"Oh. I forgot." Besian snapped his fingers. "Everything is ready for Ten's party. You get him to the warehouse, and I'll handle the rest."

Nikolai wasn't thrilled by the welcome home party that had been arranged by the captains, but he wasn't about to stop them. Ten had given six years of his life to protect the family so he was willing to turn a blind eye to whatever was going to happen tonight at Besian's warehouse.

"No alcohol, Besian." He fixed the slightly shorter man with a pointed look. "They'll force him to piss at his first meeting with his parole officer tomorrow morning. They're going to be watching him closely. He has to do everything by the book or else he'll have to go back inside and finish up his ten years."

"Hey, I'll take care of him. He's in good hands."

"He better be." Nikolai thought of Artyom and his mangled hand. "Because Luka isn't the only one with chisels and hammers in his garage."

Besian issued a dark laugh at that one. "I almost believe you."

Standing alone, Nikolai noticed Mueller and Julio lingering nearby, both wanting to speak with him. The others were long gone. He had wanted to speak with Spider but that would have to wait until he could track him down and corner him. Because he was certain the discussion with Julio was going to be a long one, he flicked his fingers at Mueller.

"Take a walk with me, Red Baron."

5 CHAPTER FIVE

Nikolai didn't even try to hide his smirk at the irritation that flashed across James Mueller's face upon hearing his nickname. Side by side, they slowly walked away from the container. Mueller spoke first. "I fucking hate that name."

"Should I even ask why it was given to you?"

"No."

He decided not to poke. "This new territory you've been given? I wouldn't try to set up shop there. You and your kind won't last a week in that neighborhood. Put some men there to keep the peace and leave it at that. Don't try to grow or put down roots. Nickel's men will try to push back and agitate so keep that in mind when you choose your men. "

"Not quite the welcome wagon I had expected," he replied, hands buried in his pockets.

Nikolai stopped and pivoted to face him. "Do I need to remind you what happened to the last lightning bolts and swastika crew that tried to gain a foothold here? Because I'm sure Kostya would love to take you for a ride so he can give you all the details."

"Look," Mueller whipped of his sunglasses, "I get it. Those Night Wolf assholes didn't play nicely in the sandbox. They were young and reckless. We aren't. When it comes right down to it, the only color I care about is green. So if we can find a way to work together and make some money doing it? Great. If we can't, we'll close up shop and move on to more hospitable territory."

"Sounds like a reasonable plan," Nikolai agreed, glad to see the man understood the score here.

"That strip of territory you've given me is a shit sandwich, Kalasnikov, but I'm going to grab it right off that silver platter, take a big ole bite and smile. You run the show here, and we are not looking to upset that balance."

While Nikolai didn't appreciate the imagery of that rather colorful metaphor, he studied Mueller's face and saw no signs of lying. "What is it that your crew wants?"

"We want the ice trade in town. That's it."

"I'm not the man to ask for that. That action is city-wide, but Nickel holds the biggest share of the market. I doubt he'll be very accommodating if you get anywhere near his territory." And that was putting it nicely. Knowing what he did of the way Nicky Jackson had gained control of the Fifth Ward, he believed Mueller was in for a long, painful ride.

"You'll find I can be very persuasive." Mueller slipped his sunglasses back into place.

Nikolai didn't comment on that.

"This is a bit awkward, but my wife wanted to know if yours would be interested in exchanging contact info. Mindy is trying to get settled here. She's looking for a hair stylist, a spa, a personal shopper. Shit like that," Mueller said with a wave of his hand.

He had to bite back a guffaw at the idea of Vivian interacting with Mueller's wife. In case the man wasn't aware, he enlightened him. "My wife's father is Romero Valero."

"I'm aware of that."

"Then you're aware of the fact that Vivian is half-Mexican, yes?"

Mueller shrugged. "Like I said, when it comes to color, I'm only interested in the green printed on hundred dollar bills."

"Vivian's inner circle is full." Because it wouldn't kill him to extend a little kindness and earn some favor, he said, "She enjoys the salon and spa Holly Phillips owns. It's called Allure. I'm sure your wife can find the details online."

"Thanks." Mueller seemed to get the hint. "I'm sure I'll see you around town. Mindy likes to run with the philanthropist set. She's begging me to get a box at the opera. I hear you have one."

Nikolai nodded. The idea of running into Mueller at the one place he enjoyed when he needed a well-earned dose of relaxation and culture pissed him off. From now on, he would have to remind Vee to vet the guest lists for the society and charity invites that landed on their doorstep every month.

Mueller patted his chest and retrieved his cell phone. His mouth slanted with a smile. "It's my wife. We're closing on our new house this afternoon. River Oaks," he said. "The country club area. You're near there, right?"

Nikolai saw right through the innocent façade. The man was one of the most successful real estate agents in Dallas. Mueller would have no trouble finding out exactly where Nikolai lived, when he had bought his house, how much he had paid for it or the recent tax bill. "Yes. In one of the historic homes."

"Home? Estate more like," Mueller said with a laugh. "I have to take this." He extended his hand. "I hope this is the beginning of a prosperous relationship."

Nikolai shook his hand and fought the urge to wipe his palm on his jacket. Leaving Mueller, he moved toward Julio who gestured to his SUV. Nikolai hated getting into other people's cars. Kostya stood next to the vehicle and made the smallest gesture with his fingers to let Nikolai know he had checked the SUV during the meeting. It was safe and free of tracking and listening devices.

Inside the middle seat with Julio, he waited for the other man to speak. He didn't dare reveal his hand until he was certain of what the other man knew. Julio sat stiffly, his hands clenched into fists. Nikolai eyed him warily. This guy was hanging on by a thread.

"I'd like to think that you and I have a good working relationship," Julio said. "We've done business for years. There has been friction, yes, but we've always managed to find a way to negotiate our way around it. The two of us—you and me—we've always kept the big bosses happy and away from each other's throats."

"We have." Nikolai wondered where he was going with this speech.

"I don't expect loyalty from you. We don't play for the same team. But some common fucking courtesy would have been nice," he growled. "How could you stand there at my boy's funeral and watch me put my son in the ground all while protecting that scum piece of shit who killed him?"

The pretense of the boy being the godson was gone. Nikolai didn't have to think too hard to understand why a man would deny a child his name and raise him outside his home. Life as Julio's son would have been exceedingly dangerous. By all accounts, the boy had enjoyed a normal, happy life before that awful night.

"I didn't know." Nikolai turned in his seat so Julio could clearly see his face. "I didn't know until this morning. Had I known that one of those MC bastards had killed that boy—*your* boy—I would have trussed him up myself and delivered him to you wrapped in a fucking bow."

Julio studied him for an intense and unnerving moment. His eye twitched, but his hands relaxed. "I want him. Now."

"I'm working on it, Julio, but Romero didn't call me until after he sent Mando on the run. The guy is in the wind."

"So put your spy on it!"

"He is. Kostya will find him, but it won't be easy. It might take some time." He hesitated. "Have you talked with Romero?"

"This morning."

"Good." Nikolai had all but ordered his father-in-law to open a channel of communication with Julio. He wanted them to work this out but had feared he would be the one forced to step in and make it right.

"Not good," Julio retorted. The man's fists tightened again. "He offered me money. Can you believe that shit? He asked me what my son's life was worth."

Nikolai's stomach revolted at the sheer audacity of it. He shouldn't have been surprised. Romero had abandoned Vivian in a home with an armed man to save himself. If he wouldn't go back to save his own flesh and blood, he sure as hell wasn't going to be motivated by fatherly love to do the right thing for Julio.

"Do you know what I asked him?"

"No."

"How much is Vivian's life worth to him?"

The words registered slowly, and Nikolai turned his head to stare at Julio. An icy cold spilled through his veins and settled in the pit of his stomach. In that moment, his ability to think and reason like a human being vanished. He was reduced to his most primal state. He felt like a lion preparing to defend his mate and their cubs. *Protect. Kill. Protect.*

Very calmly and with a voice that sounded unnaturally relaxed, Nikolai stated the facts. "You're under a great deal of stress, and you're still grieving for your son. I'm going to let this go today."

In a flash of movement that startled Julio, Nikolai clamped his hand around the man's throat and shoved his temple against the window. Julio's head whacked the glass with a loud thump and his skin squeaked as he tried to fight free. Nikolai grasped the man's hand, drawing back his thumb into a stress position, and held him there, weak and trapped.

Hissing like a viper, he warned, "But if you ever make the slightest hint of a threat against my Vivian, I'll kill you." He squeezed his fingers around Julio's throat. "I'll fucking kill you, and I'll take my time doing it. Kostya will be mopping up the scene for weeks after I'm finished."

His warning given, Nikolai held his hand on Julio's throat a moment longer, pressing his fingertips into the other man's flesh to be sure there would be bruises. He wanted Julio to look in the mirror every morning for the next week and remember what had happened here. This wasn't an empty threat. Nikolai would end any man who tried to hurt his wife and his baby.

Letting go, he reached for the door handle and exited the SUV. Julio coughed and cleared his throat.

Before he shut the door, Julio said, "One hundred thousand, Nikolai. That's all she's worth to him."

Gritting his teeth, Nikolai slammed the door and strode to his vehicle. Kostya hurried to catch up, and Danny's brow furrowed with concern as he quickly opened the rear door so Nikolai could get into his vehicle. Kostya dropped into the driver's seat and eyed him in the rearview mirror. Smartly, he said nothing while Nikolai tried to regain control of his raging temper.

He didn't know who he wanted to hit first—Julio or Romero. Julio had crossed the line by threatening Vivian. It wasn't her father who had killed his boy. It was Mando Fernandez. Julio had no business whatsoever dragging her into this mess. She was innocent in this.

And mine. She's mine, and he's fucking crazy if he thinks he can even joke about putting a hit on her. The disrespect was outrageous. Fucking outrageous.

"One hundred thousand dollars," he grumbled while reaching for his seat belt.

"Boss?" Kostya twisted in his seat. "Do we need to hit up the bank?"

Kostya didn't mean a normal bank branch. He meant one of the locations where they stowed hard currency.

"No." He sat back and wiped his face with his hands. "Julio threatened Romero over this bullshit by asking him how much Vivian's life was worth to him."

Kostya sucked in a shocked breath. "And?"

"And what do you think happened?"

"Well I heard him talking so at least you left him alive," Kostya dryly replied. "I didn't bring my black bag of tricks."

The dark humor did little to ease Nikolai's anger. "Romero put a price of one hundred thousand on Vivian. On his daughter. On *my wife*."

Kostya wisely didn't speak.

"She took the fall for him. She believed in him. She *loved* him like all little girls love their fathers—and he abandoned her. He left her there to die. He left her there for me to kill. He left her behind to fend for herself while he went inside and did his ten year stretch. And what's she worth to him? A handful of stacks." His jaw clenched so tightly it started to hurt. He thought of sweet Vivian, always optimistic and kind, always believing the best in everyone, and wondered how the hell she had been saddled with such a shit for a father.

"But she's precious to you, boss." Kostya spoke the words in a tone that was meant to calm him. "She's precious to you, and she knows that. She knows that you value her above all things. She knows that you would do anything for her."

The reminder eased the fury inside him. "We need to get out in front of this. Julio is a ticking time bomb. He's going to blow. Romero will yank and yank on that chain, and Julio is going to lose it. He can't touch Mando because the man has no wife or family so he'll go after Romero."

"He's got a stripper."

"What?"

"A stripper from Sugar's," Kostya explained. "Her name is Tawny. She didn't come in to work the last few nights. She's gone on the run with Mando, but she has family in the area. I'll shake them down and see if she's made contact with them."

"Do it—but keep it quiet, yes? And put out some feelers on hit men. Julio won't use one of the squads on the cartel payroll. He'll hire this out. He'll go free-lance with a *sicario* or maybe even one of the Professionals."

Kostya inhaled a long breath as he considered the possibilities. "There's the Ghost or the Liquidator. Either way, it's not good."

"We can contact the Liquidator. He's got standards and a code. You know his rules."

"Yes." Kostya had a professional relationship with the man everyone knew as the Liquidator. He had three younger brothers who also worked in that rather peculiar line of business—the Collector, the Fence and the Cleaner. They were ungodly expensive but they did quality work. "If someone tries to buy a contract on Vivian, they'll know about it. They'll turn it down, but they'll know."

"No, I want them to buy it. I want them to buy it and come to me. I'll triple the fee and pay them for the identity. Fuck it. Offer them whatever they want. Let them name the price. Triple, quadruple, quintuple—it makes no difference to me. I'll pay it."

"All right, boss. I'll get on it." Kostya put the car in drive and eased on the gas. "So much for a quiet year, huh?"

Nikolai exhaled roughly. "It was too good to last."

"Yes." They drove in silence for a few minutes. "Where to next, boss?"

"The meetup with Romero," he said, glancing at his watch. They were running late. Although Nikolai valued punctuality, he didn't even blink an eye at the thought of making Romero wait. For a moment, he considered filling the three hour drive with a phone call to Vivian, but he didn't want to wake her if she was still sleeping.

And what would he tell her? Your father's best friend killed a cartel kid and now he's on the run so the cartel and the MC are probably going to slaughter each other in the streets?

Jesus. Nikolai scrubbed his face again and wished he hadn't left his coffee on the table. Gazing out the darkly tinted window, he tried to play the various angles. He couldn't find a single way to end this without bloodshed.

For a moment, he actually toyed with the idea of calling Detective Eric Santos. He and Vivian's cousin had never seen eye to eye but the detective was a stand-up guy who would do the right thing. His contacts were almost as good as Kostya's. He could find Mando, snatch him up on an outstanding warrant and sweat him in a gen pop holding cell to force him to talk.

Once he was on the inside, Mando would have to fold to protect his club. The district attorneys and Feds would be tripping over themselves to cut a deal and get any information they could. Mando was too loyal to the MC—a real ride or die man—to flip on his boys, but he might spill the secrets he knew about the cartel. If that happened, the cartel would find a way to shut him up on the inside. Either way, he would be off the streets and no longer one of Nikolai's problems.

It was the cleanest way to fix the situation—but Nikolai's men would see it as the ultimate betrayal. There was still some grumbling over the way a Fed informant Besian basically owned had been used to clear out the Night Wolves once and for all. If Nikolai went to Eric, it would cast a long fucking shadow. Every step he made would be questioned. Suspicion would dog him. He needed his men to believe in and trust him implicitly and without question. He couldn't have dissension in the ranks.

So what to do? For once, he honestly didn't know. He couldn't see the answer. *I'm losing my edge.*

Still plagued by questions, he barely registered the minutes and miles ticking by. Too soon, their vehicle was pulling into the agreed meeting spot. The SUV sat still for less than a minute before the passenger side door opened and Romero slid inside. Kostya exited slowly and quietly to take up a guard position outside.

Romero had come incognito—jeans, Mexican football jersey, sneakers and a baseball cap pulled low. He had started to grow out a beard. Somehow it made him look even harder and rougher. There were streaks of silver in the dark, coarse hair. His age was finally catching up to him.

Whipping off the hat, Romero scrubbed his fingers through his hair. "Fuck, what a mess."

Nikolai twisted in his seat to face his father-in-law. "You offered him money?"

Romero arched an eyebrow. "Yes. And?"

Taken aback by the familiar facial movement, Nikolai accepted that no matter how much he wished he could pretend that Vivian had nothing in common with her old man she was still his daughter. "And? Are you seriously going to fucking sit there and act as if you didn't just insult Julio? A man who lost his only son?"

"It was an accident."

"Bullshit." Nikolai slashed his hand through the air. "I read the police report. His light was red. He ran it and clipped that kid. Instead of staying behind to help the kid, Mando left him in the street to die. A little boy!"

"He was sixteen."

"And Vee was eleven when you left her behind," Nikolai angrily retorted.

"Yes, she was eleven when you shot and nearly killed her." Romero dared him to find a comeback. "How is my baby girl? I hear she's settling in quite nicely as your queen. Apparently she made quite an impression at the fight."

A vision of Vivian in black and gold at the warehouse where he hosted the bare-knuckle tournaments taunted him. God, she had been breathtakingly beautiful. He had been torn between wanting to scold her for doing something so risky and wanting to sweep her into his arms and kiss her until she was breathless with arousal and blushing in submission.

"She's strong, brilliant and nurturing. She's found her place." *Right next to me.*

Romero made a throaty noise. "You're still going to London this weekend?"

"Yes. We leave on Sunday."

Romero glanced out the window, but not before Nikolai caught an expression that resembled regret. "That's good. I'm glad she's getting this chance."

Nikolai wasn't about to invite him to tag along or tell him that Vivian wanted him there. She didn't. "What are we going to do about Julio and Mando? We can't let this keep spinning out of control. Julio just threatened Vivian to my face. I can't allow this to play out in my city."

Romero stared at the windshield. He seemed to be carefully weighing his options. "I'll talk to Julio again." He held up his hand before Nikolai could interrupt him about the money. "I'll find a way to make it right."

"He wants Mando. Unless you tell him where to find your friend, he's going to start crossing names off lists—and he'll try to start with Vivian."

Romero's dark eyes flashed with a warning. "He won't touch my daughter."

"Your daughter *and* your grandchild." Nikolai hadn't been planning to reveal her pregnancy to her father yet, but it might be the only way to make Romero do the right thing. "We're pregnant. Eleven weeks."

Romero didn't say a word. He seemed completely stunned. "Vivian," he said finally. "A baby?"

"Yes."

Romero's throat moved up and down. He swallowed audibly. He seemed to be searching for the right words. Finally, he found them. "I don't particularly like you, Nikolai. I've learned to tolerate you."

High fucking praise indeed.

"When I heard you were going to marry Vivian, I didn't like it, but I honestly couldn't think of a better man for her."

The statement rocked Nikolai to the core.

"I don't mean that in the traditional way." Romero kept his gaze fixed forward on the windshield. "I mean that in the sense that by simply being my daughter Vivian is in a great deal of danger every day. My list of enemies is a mile long and growing every day. There aren't very many men in this world who could keep her safe *and* love her." He paused. "But you do."

"I do," Nikolai agreed. "I will."

"You have to watch her carefully," Romero instructed. "After the baby comes," he clarified. "Katya was always wild and unpredictable. Those were things I loved about her—until I didn't. Until I realized that she wasn't *right*. That she was broken up here." He tapped his temple. "It was having Vivian that flipped some switch. She was never the same again."

"Vivian isn't her mother." Nikolai growled the words.

"No, she isn't, but she's a woman and things happen to women after they have babies. You have to watch her. Keep her safe. Keep the baby safe."

Was Romero thinking about the day Katya had tried to drown Vivian as a child? The day a neighbor had broken down the door to save her? Was he thinking about all the times that Katya had abused Vivian while he was off running errands for the cartel or riding with the club?

"You don't have to worry. I'll keep them safe."

Romero finally looked at him and nodded. With a rough sigh, he reached for the door. "I'll get this thing with Julio taken care of while you're in London. It'll be safer for Vivian that way." He opened the door and climbed out of the SUV but didn't immediately close the door. "When you get back, we need to have a long discussion."

"About?"

"Our next moves," Romero said, as if strategizing together was the most natural thing in the world.

"*Our* moves?"

"It's time the two of us stop barking for our masters. It's time to cut the leashes."

Nikolai stared at the door that Romero quickly closed. Was his father-in-law proposing what he thought he was?

"How did it go?" Kostya asked as he fastened his seatbelt.

Nikolai replayed his father-in-law's parting shot. "I honestly don't know."

Kostya swiveled in seat, bracing his hand on the console. "What the hell does that mean?"

"It means things are going to change. Whether we're ready for it or not," he added ominously.

Kostya let that sink in for a moment. No doubt, he was already running the various scenarios and making lists of all the dirty deeds that would need to be done to protect the family. With a disturbingly cool shrug, Kostya said, "Fuck it. We'll make it work. We always do."

That was just like Kostya to put it all in perspective. "True."

Turning back toward the windshield, the cleaner announced, "I'm starving. Let's have a steak and a beer and forget this shit morning ever happened. Then we'll head back to Houston and track down Ivan and Ten."

Happy to let someone else make a decision, even if it was something as simple as lunch, Nikolai dropped his head back against the seat, closed his eyes and nodded. "*Da.*"

6 CHAPTER SIX

Nikolai grinned warmly as Ten strode into the coziest private dining room at Samovar with Ivan and Kostya right on his heels. Only a few inches shorter than Sergei, Ten sported similarly broad shoulders and the physique of a fighter. He had obviously burned a lot of prison time exercising in the yard. No longer did he wear his hair long. It was clipped short, but he had a scruffy beard now. There were a couple of new tattoos on Ten's neck and arms, all of them marks Nikolai had sanctioned from the outside.

"Boss." Ten extended his hand, but Nikolai surprised him by embracing the other man tightly. Ten stiffened, but Nikolai didn't hold it against him. He had spent enough time on the inside to understand how difficult it was to allow other people to invade his personal space.

Stepping back, Nikolai let his arms drop to his sides. "You look good."

"I feel good." Ten glanced around the dining room, his eyes darting toward the corners almost as if he expected to find men lurking in the shadows.

"It takes time, Ten." Nikolai cast a look at Ivan who studied his friend with a mixture of sadness and understanding. "You'll adjust." He gestured toward the table where the best the restaurant had to offer awaited them. "Come. Eat."

Though Nikolai preferred the seat with the best view of the room, namely the entrance and exit points, he let Ten have it tonight. Ivan dropped down into the other chair and reached for his silverware. Always so easy in social settings, Ivan took control of the conversation and kept it light and fun. The stories he told were intended to draw Ten back into the life he had left behind and familiarize him with the changes that had occurred during his time inside.

Sitting back and pushing away his dessert plate, Ten shook his head. "I still can't believe you're married. I never thought I'd see the day that you let yourself be chained to one girl."

Ivan toyed with his wedding band. A faint smile played upon his mouth. "When you meet Erin, you'll understand. Most days I can't believe she agreed to marry me."

Nikolai chuckled at that. He understood what that was like. There were mornings he woke up and simply gazed upon Vee's sleeping face because he couldn't quite believe that she was his wife.

Ten stared at Nikolai's wedding band. Unlike Ivan who had chosen to wear his according to the American custom, Nikolai wore his on the right hand because it was the Orthodox way and Vivian's preference. "You wouldn't believe the kites that were flying between cells when the news hit that you were going to marry the machete's daughter."

"I can imagine." Nikolai folded the edge of his napkin as he pictured the small folded notes attached to long strings of floss soaring through the air between cells. Deciding this was as good a time as any to bring it up, he said, "I wanted to speak with you about Vivian."

"Should I leave?" Ivan asked, already rising from his chair.

Nikolai swept his hand through the air. "Stay."

Ivan sat down and reached for his fork again. It was a move that didn't surprise Nikolai in the least. Far from it, actually. The sight of Ivan cleaning his plate, refusing to leave even one tiny scrap of food behind, took Nikolai back to their shared childhood. Cold, hungry nights hadn't bothered Nikolai that much. He had turned that hunger into anger and used it to fuel his survival and his rise through the ranks.

But Ivan? Ivan hated being hungry. Whenever he ate, he made sure to finish every morsel available to him because as a child meals had been meager and few and far between. Despite finding success and wealth with his investments and business, Ivan was still that scared, hungry kid deep down inside. Erin's love for him had gone a long way toward easing some of those deep-seated fears but some habits would never change.

Turning his attention toward Ten, Nikolai began a conversation he expected the other man was not going to like. "I realize that you had hoped to be slotted into a job at Alexei's dealership or with the gym," he motioned toward Ivan, "until your probation was finished but I need your skills somewhere else."

Looking slightly uneasy, Ten said, "The conditions of my parole—"

"Will not be impacted by what I'm about to ask of you," Nikolai assured him. "You will follow them to the letter. Your new duties will never take you anywhere near those types of activities or people."

Ten's eyes narrowed. "What sort of job is this?"

"I need you to guard my wife."

Ten's lips parted with shock. He clamped them shut and worked his jaw back and forth. His prized enforcer had the worst fucking temper so Nikolai steeled himself for a blowup.

But it never came.

Nostrils flaring slightly, Ten inhaled a steadying breath. The muscles in his neck were flexed, and his hands were curled into fists atop the table, but he maintained control. Finally, he said, "If this is what the family needs me to do, I'm happy to take the job."

"Ten." Nikolai sat forward and tapped the table. "This isn't a punishment or a demotion. Even if you were legally free and clear, I would still ask you to do this for me. I need the very best men I know watching

Vivian. Sergei is gone, and if I thought Ivan would come out of retirement for me, I'd ask him."

Ten's shoulders dropped and the insulted look on his face faded. He asked the most obvious question. "Are we going to war?"

Now it was Ivan who tensed. Apprehension darkened his face.

"Not yet," Nikolai answered. "Not if I can help it."

"Then why me?" Ten seemed honestly confused by the request. "I was your best enforcer. I was the man you called to do the jobs no one else could. I trained Sergei for you and made sure there was someone to keep this city in line while I was away. To ask me to babysit your wife?" He touched his chest. "I'm sorry, boss, but it seems like a waste of my skills."

"Vivian is absolutely precious to me. She's my one weakness—and my enemies know it." Nikolai didn't like admitting that aloud but Ten deserved to know the truth. "She was already a target because of her father, but now that she's my wife, she's the biggest target in the city. Something is coming." He rubbed his thumb along the spot where his pulse beat on the underside of his wrist. "I can feel it."

"The cartel?" Ivan asked the question everyone plugged into the underworld wondered.

"Lorenzo Guzman is losing control. Romero will make a play, but he's not the only one. It could get messy." He held Ten's gaze. "I need to know Vivian is safe, especially now."

"Especially now?" Ten repeated.

"Now that she's pregnant." Nikolai dropped that bombshell without warning. "It won't be easy to hide much longer." He was talking to Ten man to man now and not as his boss. "Will you watch over them for me? I need to know they're safe."

"Yes." He answered without hesitation. "Of course."

Nikolai glanced at Ivan who drew a finger across his lips. He wouldn't breathe a word about the pregnancy, not even to Erin.

Leaning back in his chair, Nikolai said, "Sergei has agreed to talk to you about guarding her. He was with her the longest so he knows her the best. They bonded like brother and sister." He hesitated as he considered the hard, violent man in front of him. "I don't expect that sort of friendship between the two of you, but I need to know that you'll treat her...gently."

Ten shot him a look of consternation. "Boss, I'm not going to sit here and defend my reputation. I'll treat your wife with the same respect I give you—but I don't need a friend or a sister."

Nikolai lifted both hands. "Fine. That's fine."

"When do I start?"

"Tomorrow." Nikolai gestured toward Ten's messy beard. "You can keep that but clean it up." He eyed the other man's jeans and polo shirt. "We need to get you some new clothes."

Ivan took the lead on that one. "I'll take care of it. We can go see my guy in the morning after we visit his P.O. and the DPS office for his license. Then I'll drop him off at your house?"

Nikolai nodded. "We have a new kid at the house who can do all the driving until you have everything arranged. He's young and has a clean record."

"Boychenko?" Ivan grabbed his glass of water and finished it. "He's a scrappy little bastard. Sergei might actually be able to turn him into a fighter. He'll always be a featherweight but he's got potential."

"Wait." Ten seemed confused. "Roman?" He held up his hand to measure five feet or so from the floor. "The kid who bags groceries at his grandmother's little market?"

"The market is gone," Nikolai said, "and Roman is nineteen. He's working for Artyom now." Recognizing that lost look in Ten's eyes, he shrugged. "A lot happens in six years."

Ten nodded slowly. "Yeah."

Fully aware that the shock of being released from prison made it easy for a man to slide into depression, Nikolai decided it was time to send Ten on his way. A celebration would be good for him. It would remind him of all the friends who cared about and had missed him. He needed to feel surrounded and supported. He needed to be made whole again.

He walked them out the side entrance while they waited for one of the valets to bring Ivan's Escalade. He shared a look with Ivan as the other man slid behind the wheel of his vehicle. Like brothers, they could communicate without saying a word. *Keep him out of trouble.*

"They'll be fine."

Nikolai searched the nearby shadows for Kostya. He hated the way the former covert operative skulked in the darkness. There weren't many men who could get the drop on him, but Kostya was one of them. Thankfully they were on the same side.

"Ivan will take care of him. He won't let Ten fuck up his parole." Kostya finally emerged from the shadows. "You want me to drive you home?"

Nikolai shook his head. "No. Are you heading to the party?"

Kostya shot him a look that said *of course.* "I'm catching a ride with some of your line cooks. If you need me—"

"I know how to find you," Nikolai replied.

Kostya took exactly four steps down the street before turning suddenly. "Shit." He reached into the back pocket of his jeans and retrieved a cell phone. "I forgot I had this."

Nikolai accepted it from him and tucked it into his own pocket without a glance. Vivian wasn't in the habit of texting or calling him unless it was important. If it had been something that needed his immediate attention, Artyom would have found a way to get a message to him through Kostya or Danny.

He spent more than an hour in his office going over paperwork. Samovar and the legitimate and very successful businesses he owned wholly or partly around the city were the major sources of his personal income. Early on, he had recognized that building a legitimate portfolio was the only way to stay out of prison. So he had kept his eyes open for business opportunities and had availed himself of Yuri's head for finance.

His first forays into legitimate earning hadn't been smooth or above-board exactly. Truthfully, the first few car washes and bars that he had acquired had been on defaulted loans he had extended. The construction company that he intended Sergei to run in the near future had been purchased when the previous owner needed fast cash. Any time a man left the family—men like Ivan or Alexei—he made sure to fund their startups. Twenty or twenty-five percent ownership here or there added up quickly.

While his crew earned tidy sums off of their illegal activities, he made sure they were receiving the bulk of their income through the side businesses. That way they weren't tempted to get stupid and surrender to the promise of easy but dangerous money. Their hands were dirty, but they weren't *that* dirty. He stayed on their asses about paying taxes and keeping out of trouble.

Thoughts of avoiding the trouble brewing around the city plagued him as he drove home. There were so many pieces to this puzzle, and he could no longer tell where each one fit. He finally had the one thing he had wanted most—a family with Vivian. His stomach in knots, Nikolai accepted that one wrong move could cost him everything.

As he drove by Judge Walker's house, he thought of his promise to help the man extricate his daughter from a bad situation. The morning after giving the order, Boychenko had given him the address and a quick rundown of the situation after a few hours of watching the house where the woman was living. It wasn't going to be easy to get her out of there, not if her habit was as bad as Boychenko's investigation had uncovered. She was hooked on that sweet Colombian candy *and* her dealer.

After he parked in the garage, Nikolai ambled toward the side gate that granted him access to the alley. He walked the shadows like a man used to living in them, completely at ease and not the least bit afraid of what might lurk in them. Frankly, the types of people who hid in the shadows were more likely to be afraid of him. Well—all of them who weren't Kostya.

The judge left his back gate unlocked. Nikolai frowned at that. Anyone could get in here. Bad people even. *Like me.* He entered the backyard and used the flagstone walkway. He had traveled twenty feet before he heard the unmistakable *click* of a revolver cylinder slamming into place. With a quirk of his mouth, Nikolai stood perfectly still and lifted his hands. The porch light suddenly illuminated the backyard and blinded him from seeing anything on the screened-in porch.

Playing along with the judge's game, he slowly lifted his jacket and turned in a circle. Seemingly satisfied that he was unarmed and had no ill intentions, the judge flipped the light off. The *thunk* of the gun landing on a table echoed in the night.

"Awfully late for a social call, Nikolai."

"I work odd hours." Hands on his hips, he waited for the judge to invite him onto the porch or send him away. Realizing he hadn't heard a peep from the judge's dog, he glanced around the backyard. "Your gate is unlocked. Did Roscoe escape?"

"He's at the vet. Someone poisoned him. With cocaine," the judge growled. "Those bastards took my daughter, and now they're trying to kill my dog."

"So the gate is unlocked and you're sitting in the dark with a revolver—"

"And a shotgun."

"And a shotgun," Nikolai repeated, "because you think they'll come back and you're hoping to unleash some of that Texas justice?"

"My castle. My guns."

Nikolai didn't doubt the judge would blow a hole in the first unfriendly face that peeked over the hedge. "When did the poisoning happen?"

"This morning," the judge answered. "I let him loose to do his morning business, but he didn't come back to the house. I found him out near the garden shed. He had eaten half a pound of bologna laced with drugs."

Nikolai scratched his fingers through his hair. He wasn't sure what pissed him off more. Was it the fact that some lowlife thug had gotten *this* close to his own home, to his wife? Or was it the fact that some dumbass drug dealer thought it would be a good idea to threaten a federal fucking judge in a boss's backyard?

This was bad. There would be cops crawling all over this poisoning and digging into it. Though he didn't want to get dragged any deeper into this argument between the judge and Bobby Pham, he nevertheless extended his help to the man. "I've located your daughter, but it won't be easy to get her out of there."

The judge finally emerged from the darkness of his screened-in porch to the door he had propped open with a heavy planter holding a wildly overgrown aloe plant. "Is this where you shake me down for money?"

"No. This is where I tell you that these types of things tend to be noisy if they're rushed. It's easier on everyone if we do this quietly."

"What does quietly mean?"

"It means we do it my way. It means that it takes some time."

"Time?" The judge raised his voice, clearly exasperated. "I don't have time. She's been there too long. If I don't get her out soon—"

"You asked for my help, and I'm telling you this is the best way. If you don't want my help, by all means, do it yourself. But I warn you it won't go well for either of you."

"Is that a threat?"

"It's free advice. I suggest you take it." Biting back his frustration, he sighed. "I want to help you, Judge, but you have to work with me. You rattled their cages. Poisoning your dog was a warning. I suggest you heed that warning. Leave this ugly business to men like me."

Not wanting to argue with an armed man who was probably teetering on the edge of a breakdown, Nikolai pivoted on his heel and left the judge's backyard without another word. He stepped onto his property and instantly spotted the silhouette of a man leaning against a corner of the pergola. The flare of a lighter illuminated Ilya's face—and the flowers smashed between his arm and the wood.

"Get off the roses," Nikolai scolded. Vivian loved sitting under the pergola in the morning. She often sketched the beautiful blooms. He had one of the delicately shaded drawings in his office at Samovar.

"Sorry, boss." Ilya spoke around the cigarette clamped between his lips and straightened. "It won't happen again."

"See that it doesn't." He glanced around the yard. "Where is Boychenko?"

"The kitchen."

"Arty?"

"Inside." Ilya took a long drag and held the smoke in his lungs before slowly, almost decadently, exhaling it in a curling plume. "There was some trouble four houses down, boss."

"I heard."

"When I saw the cops in the alley, I called a guy I've got in my pocket, up at the police station. He told me his girlfriend who works in a vet's office had seen the judge's dog. He was poisoned."

Not for the first time, Nikolai was impressed by Ilya's network of gossips and informants. "Do we know who did it?"

"You're not going to like this answer." Ilya blew out another lungful of smoke.

Subtly shifting away from the breeze that carried the smoke, Nikolai tried not to inhale the familiar scent of it. With the stress piling up on his shoulders, he had a raging craving for a Marlboro red. "Just tell me."

"It was the judge's daughter."

Nikolai narrowed his eyes. "You're sure."

"I took one of the baskets you keep on the porch, picked some peaches and tomatoes and visited your neighbors. I told them you were going out of town and your wife wanted to share the extra produce out of the garden before you left. Your peaches will open any door on this street." Ilya chuckled darkly at his off-color remark. "The old lady who lives next to the judge? In the brick house?"

"Mrs. Laramie."

"Right. That one." The bright tip of his cigarette bounced as he gestured with it. "I asked her about the judge's dog. I said that Vivian was really worried because she wanted to get a puppy and if there's some psycho running around poisoning dogs... It was a complete bullshit tale, but I figured it would soften her up, get her talking." Ilya waved his hand. "So the old lady tells me not to worry because it's just family trouble."

"Family trouble," he repeated dubiously.

"She says that the daughter and the parents argued like crazy before she moved out. Apparently the fireworks were like the Fourth of July over there. She told me that she saw the daughter drop something over the fence this morning. The old lady gets up early to fish in the summer so she knows everything that goes on in this neighborhood." Ilya took a final drag on the cigarette before stubbing it out between his shoe and a brick paver. "Did you know the people across the street, the ones with the white front porch, have swinger parties? She says that she can see everything with her binoculars."

Actually, Nikolai did know that the Jamesons were rather peculiar when it came to their bedroom games. Kostya routinely ran surveillance on the neighborhood and had uncovered some truly bizarre goings-on down at that house.

Not wanting to discuss his neighbors' sex lives, he asked, "Did she mention it to the police?"

"The swinger parties?"

Nikolai clicked his teeth. "No. Julie poisoning her father's dog."

"Oh. No."

"Why not?" Nikolai's gaze drifted to the cigarette butt that had been crushed on his sidewalk, and Ilya bent down to pick it up without having to be asked.

Pocketing his trash, Ilya shook his head. "She says that she isn't going to get involved. She did once before, when the girl was in high school, and she caught some older guy sneaking into the girl's bedroom. It didn't end well. Apparently the daughter went crazy, smashed the old lady's windshield and slit her tires. She's dangerous, boss." He pointed to the back gate. "Do you want us to put more men out here until you leave for London?"

"Ten will be here tomorrow." That was all he needed to say. More men in the house would unnerve Vivian and make her feel unsafe. That was the very last thing he wanted.

Leaving Ilya outside, Nikolai took the sidewalk to the backdoor and entered through the mud room. He was surprised to find Boychenko sweeping the kitchen. Eyebrows raised, he watched the kid dump the dustpan into the trashcan tucked into a lower cabinet. By the looks of the counters and sinks, he had been busy.

If any of the men on his crew ever saw the kid doing chores like these, they would rag on him until the day he died, but Boychenko didn't seem the least bit fazed to be discovered this way by his boss. The kid offered a self-deprecating smile as he twisted the red plastic ties on the garbage bag. "Miss Vivian got sick after dinner. Arty has forbidden me to cook ever again."

The Miss Vivian thing always amused him. Born and raised in Houston, Boychenko was the strangest mix of Texan and Russian when it came to his manners. Nikolai offered the kid an encouraging look and lied right through his teeth. "I'm sure it wasn't your cooking. Vee has a nervous stomach. She's been very stressed about the upcoming show."

"Just in case, I've tossed everything and cleaned the kitchen for her."

"You didn't need to do that. We have a housekeeper who comes tomorrow morning."

"It was no big deal, boss." He hefted up the bag. "Do you need any other chores handled before I head home?"

"No, but there is something else I need you to do."

"Anything."

"Get the names of the men who run with Bobby Pham. I want to know where they live, what they drive, where they eat, who they fuck—everything. Understand?"

"Yes. I'll get it done."

"I know you will." Of that, Nikolai had no doubt. This kid was hungry and ready to prove himself. "Oh." He snapped his fingers, remembering something he had forgotten that morning. "Your uncle. The one who lives near Conroe?"

"Valery?"

Nikolai nodded. "Does he still breed dogs?"

"Sure. Mastiffs and Great Danes." Boychenko got a funny look on his face. "I heard Ilya making up that story about Miss Vivian wanting a puppy. Was that real?"

"It might be. Tell your uncle I'd like to speak with him when I get back from London."

"Okay. Night, boss."

He locked the side door behind Boychenko and started loosening his tie as he crossed the kitchen. When he stepped into the entryway, Nikolai noticed Arty sitting on the second floor in the seating area there. Normally Artyom kept downstairs after Vee turned in for the night. Thinking of the way she had been sick after dinner, he assumed the captain had simply wanted to be close to her in case she needed help.

Nikolai shrugged out of his jacket and tugged free his tie as Artyom came downstairs. The somber expression the other man wore unsettled him. "What's wrong?"

"Your phone is off?"

He touched the hard lump outlined in the jacket tossed over his arm. "Kostya had it because of the meeting. He didn't give it back. Why?"

"Boss, did you forget something?"

"Forget something?" He rolled through his mental datebook but couldn't think of anything that he'd forgotten to do. "No."

Standing in front of him, Artyom suddenly looked disappointed. "Vivian."

A quiver of panic struck his chest. "What about her?"

"She had an appointment today. An important one," he emphasized.

And then it hit him.

7 CHAPTER SEVEN

"Shit. *Fuck*." Sick to his stomach, Nikolai suddenly remembered Vivian's appointment with her doctor. Shame gutted him. How the hell had he forgotten that? Nothing that had happened today was more important than Vee and the baby, but their appointment hadn't registered even once.

"After she told me about the appointment, I left Boy and Ilya here. We took the Land Rover but ditched it at one of the parking garages in case we were followed. I switched to one of our decoy cars and took her to the doctor. I stayed in the hallway and didn't see anyone come on or off the elevator who looked out of place. After the appointment, we got the Land Rover, and I took her out for a late lunch at

Hugo's before bringing her home. We weren't followed. You can keep this a secret for a few more weeks."

The street captain Nikolai trusted the most proved yet again why he was always the one man who could be counted on in a tight situation. He had taken good care of Vivian.

Better than me. The thought caused a pang of guilt in his chest that threatened to stop his heart. He had promised Vee that he would do anything to make her happy. He had promised to protect her and love her and provide for her and their children, but he couldn't even remember one single doctor's appointment. He dreaded seeing her disappointed face. It would fucking kill him to see that he had let her down.

Artyom's gaze darted to the second floor. "No one even suspected that something was off with her. She's gotten very good at hiding what she thinks and feels. She's learning to build a better mask than yours. That was one part of you I was hoping wouldn't rub off on her."

There weren't many men who out there with balls big enough to censure him so the fact that his three-fingered captain had done it made Nikolai take notice. Was Vivian changing? Had he missed that?

"Did Ilya tell you about the judge's dog?"

Momentarily thrown by the question, Nikolai took a second to answer. "Yes."

"Do you want me to take some guys over to Pham's place?" Artyom didn't have to say the words. Nikolai understood what he was really asking. *Do you want me*

to bust down their front door and beat the shit out of
them until they get back into line?

"Not yet." There was something about the situation
that unsettled him. If he had to send the boys over to
knock some sense into Pham and his crew, it would be
better to know which team was propping up the fledg-
ling dealer.

"Do you need me to stay?"

"No. Go home."

Artyom headed for the front door. He wrenched it
open but paused on the threshold. Turning back, he
met Nikolai's gaze but hesitated to speak his mind.

Too tired to fight with an old friend, Nikolai
sighed. "Just say it."

"You dragged her into this life." He held up a hand
to stall the coming protest. "Sure. Okay. You warned
her what it would be like, but she loves you. All of
you. Even the ugly parts. I'm sure she thought she
understood what this life is like—but—*Jesus.*" Arty
blew out a noisy breath and lashed out with frustration. "This is your first child. Maybe your only child.
Don't fuck this up." Anguish twisted up his face, and
he swallowed hard. "You'll never forgive yourself."

Nikolai watched Artyom spin on his heel and leave
the house. For a long moment, he stared at the closed
door. Artyom was right, of course. About everything.

The pain on his friend's face forced Nikolai to think
of a tragedy that none of them ever mentioned. It was
the sort of thing no one wanted to remember. How
long had it been? Fourteen years? Fifteen? Another
lump of guilt piled onto his shoulders upon realizing he

couldn't even remember the date Artyom had buried his baby and his girlfriend Rozalina.

He scrubbed a hand down his face as those ugly memories assaulted him. God, they had all been so young then, barely out of their twenties and certain they had the whole fucking world figured out. They couldn't have been more wrong.

Everyone had warned Artyom about getting involved with a prostitute hooked on heroin but he couldn't be swayed. He had loved that woman and had stolen her away from the pimp who had owned her. Though Nikolai had thought it impossible, Artyom had gotten Rozalina clean a few months into the pregnancy. Their son had been a tiny little thing when he was born, but he was healthy.

For a few months, it had seemed like Artyom would get his happily ever after—but then the past came knocking at the front door with a fully-loaded Makarov. Rozalina had survived without taking a single hit, but Artyom had taken two gut shots. The baby...

With Artyom fighting for his life in the hospital and her baby dead, Rozalina had gone off the deep end. She had found her old dealer, traded her body for a bag of dope and had overdosed in some shit hole apartment, alone and afraid and drowning in her grief. Ivan had been the one who finally found her, half naked with a dirty sheet around her waist, a syringe dangling from her arm and the baby's photo clutched in her hand.

Nikolai's stomach lurched at those memories and of the bloody violence that had followed after the burials. They weren't memories he wanted to revisit, especially not before he went upstairs to make things right with Vivian. After locking the front door and setting the alarm, he shut off the lights and glanced out the closest window. He spotted Ilya talking to Danny as they handed off duties for the night.

A lumbering silhouette trudged across the yard to take up a spot out back. It was the first night Kir Petrov had guard duty. Ivan wasn't going to be pleased when he learned his best pro fighter was moonlighting as a guard to earn some extra cash. That was a conversation Nikolai didn't look forward to having. He had already made it abundantly clear to Kir that he was only allowed to watch the house at night and nothing more. That was it. If he put even a toe across the line, he would be bounced.

Already imagining the ringing ears that would result from talking to Ivan about Kir, Nikolai climbed the stairs and slowly made his way to the bedroom he shared with Vivian. He rested his hand on the door for a moment and tried to decide what he would say.

But what could he say? There was absolutely no excuse for what he had done. None. Zero.

Nikolai entered the bedroom. The lamp on his bedside table illuminated the room. His gaze moved along the Vivian-sized lump on the far right side of the bed. The covers were up around her ears. There was no mistaking that signal. She didn't move, and he wasn't sure if she was asleep or pretending. Should he wake her? Was it better to let her have a good night's rest before they argued in the morning?

"Where were you?" Her voice was thick with sadness and disappointment.

Sighing, he quietly shut the door and leaned back against it. "Corpus Christi."

"What was in Corpus?"

"Your father. There's a problem brewing between the cartel and Romero's outfit. It's not going to end well." He rubbed at his tired eyes. He had spent the entire day trying to keep her safe but what Vee had really needed was for him to be present. "But none of that shit matters. I should have been here."

She didn't argue with him. Her silence cut him worse than any blade ever had. Toeing off his shoes, he shoved them against the wall with his foot and bent down to rip off his socks. He balled them up and shot them toward his shoes. Tossing his jacket and tie onto the bench at the end of their bed, he unhooked his cufflinks, dropped them onto his jacket and rolled up his sleeves.

As he came around her side of the bed, Nikolai got his first look at Vee. The flush to her cheeks and the tip of her nose betrayed the fact that she had been crying. The usual luster to her blue eyes had dulled. She warily watched him, almost as if she were seeing him for the first time, really seeing him, and it terrified Nikolai. Because if she ever saw that darkness deep down inside him...

Crouching down next to the bed, Nikolai started to touch her face but withdrew his hand. He studied his palm for a moment and thought of all the filth he had touched today. The same hand that he yearned to stroke her face with had shaken the hands of a white supremacist and drug dealers. The same fingers that he wanted to trail along her cheekbones and her pouty lower lip had gripped Julio's throat. These were the same fingers that had pulled the trigger that nearly killed her all those years ago.

An invisible band squeezed his chest so hard, Nikolai couldn't breathe. Feeling so fucking dirty, he abruptly stood and took a step away from the bed. Vivian stared up at him with confusion. God, but she looked so impossibly young and innocent in his bed. A feeling he didn't want to name invaded his stomach.

Struck by the stark differences between them, by all the ways he could never be good enough for her and their child, he staggered away from their bedroom and into the bathroom. He ripped at his clothing, jerking it off his body and throwing it on the ground. Still struggling to breathe, he stepped into the shower and twisted the knob. The showerheads and jets mounted flush along the travertine ceiling and walls blasted him with cold water that shocked his system. Seconds later, the water burned hot. Resting his forehead against the tile, he didn't care if it scalded his tattooed skin. Nothing would ever wash away the stain of the terrible things he had done.

A small, soft hand touched his back and startled him. He instantly reached for the knob, adjusting the water temperature so Vivian wouldn't be hurt. Unable to look at her, he continued to press his forehead against the tile. He shut his eyes when she wrapped her arms around his waist and began dotting sweet little kisses across his back.

He had broken her trust. He had hurt her. He had made her cry. He had left her feeling forgotten and abandoned yet here she was comforting him. In some ways, her kindness and love made him feel even worse.

"I needed you today." Her cheek rested against his back now, and her arms embraced him tighter. "*We* needed you today."

He swallowed around the heavy lump in his throat. "I'm sorry, Vee."

It wasn't enough. It would never be enough. But it was all he could offer.

"Maybe we aren't ready to be parents."

The words stabbed through his heart like an ice pick. Was she having second thoughts about having his baby? "Don't say that."

"Why not? It's true. Look at us! I don't have the first clue about being a mother and you?"

He gritted his teeth at the unspoken implication. Those old bitter feelings of abandonment and worthlessness crept into his head and soured his stomach. "What? Say it, Vivian."

Her arms dropped from his waist. "I don't want to fight with you."

"It's too late for that." He couldn't bear to look at her so he kept his gaze fixed forward on the tile "Say it, Vivian. Say what you're really thinking about me. I'm sure it's nothing worse than I've thought about myself. I'm a violent criminal. I'm an ex-con who was such a bad seed that his real father left him to die on the streets rather than taking him in. I'm broken inside and all twisted up because I was pimped out to pedophiles and—"

"Stop." Vivian gripped his shoulder and tried to turn him around. "Stop it, Nikolai." She shoved hard on his shoulder, and he relented. Looking over her head, he tried to fight her as she cupped his face and tugged his head down, but it was futile. She peered into his face, her eyes searching his, and whispered "Enough."

For a long, heady moment, they simply stared at one another. She found the courage to speak first. Always his brave, beautiful Vee...

"I meant that your job isn't exactly the most stable. We never know when you're going to be here or when you're going to have to slip out of the house in the middle of the night." She trailed her fingertips down his cheek. "Today scared me. I started thinking about what it would be like to do this," her hand drifted to the gentle curve of her belly, "all alone."

"God, Vee." Shamed and feeling lower than dirt, he wrapped his arms around his wife and lovingly embraced her. "I fucked up today, but you aren't alone. You'll never be alone in this." He started to make promises but bit his tongue. He didn't want to break them. "I will try, Vee."

"I know you will." She brushed her fingers along his jaw. "You are broken and twisted inside, Nikolai, but so am I. The things we survived as kids?" She shook her head. "We're both lucky we're even alive today. It doesn't do us any good to dwell on all the mistakes we've made or the bad things that happened to us. It won't change anything. This is where we are in life— *our* shared life."

She grasped his hand and dragged it down to her stomach. She rested her palm atop his, their hands covering the small space where their child was growing. "We are all this baby has. It's you and me against a big, scary world. *Us. Together.* That's the only way this works."

With her words hanging in the air between them, she grabbed the bar of soap he preferred from the tile alcove where he kept it and lathered her hands. Gentle and thorough, Vivian spread her soapy palms all over his body. He suspected she had figured out the reason he had bolted from their bedroom to the shower. She took her time washing his skin and even scrubbed shampoo onto his hair, her short and neatly trimmed nails scratching at his scalp as he bent forward to make it easier for her to reach him.

The water rinsed away the soap and shampoo clinging to his skin, but one lone sudsy bubble rode the curve of Vivian's breast. He reached out to follow the path it had taken with his finger. Even after the bubble popped, Nikolai's finger continued its trek. Since Ivan's wedding, he had noticed the subtle changes to Vivian's body. Her breasts filled his hand now and felt firmer and heavier. He traced one of the more prominent veins that led to her nipple. The little peak was darker now, a deeper, duskier pink that enthralled him.

She exhaled a pleasured sigh when he dipped his head and tongued her nipple. He suckled her lightly, moving his mouth between breasts until she rose up on her toes and threaded her fingers through his hair. Concerned about the wet tile, he broke away from her just long enough to switch off the water. He didn't care about drying off or grabbing towels. He stepped out of the shower and onto the rug before swinging her up into his arms and carrying her into their bedroom.

After placing her on their bed, he crawled on top of her and ravished her mouth. He loved the feel of her hands roaming his body, gliding along his sides and gripping his shoulders. Their tongues danced, and she whimpered into his mouth. He turned his attention to the curve of her neck and nipped and licked at the spot that made her shiver and giggle.

Shoving her thighs apart, he clasped her ass in one hand and canted her hips up higher. His other hand snaked between her legs. Her eyes flashed when he dipped his fingers into her wet heat. She bucked her hips and boldly reached for him. Wrapping those elegant fingers around his cock, she stroked him a few times and bit her lower lip.

He kissed her hard, stabbing his tongue against hers before nibbling her lip. Lining up their bodies, he pressed forward and sought the slick slide of her pussy with the blunt head of his erection. He thrust inside her and groaned at the sensation of tight heat enveloping his cock.

Writhing and clutching, they moved together on the bed. Even after months as her husband, he still marveled in the intimacy they shared. He had never told Vee that she was the first—the only—woman he had ever made love to like this. With everyone else, face-to-face lovemaking had been too intimate and had made him feel too vulnerable. It was always rough and fast, from behind or facing away from him. The goal had always been simple—to get off and go home.

But not with Vee. He wanted to see her gorgeous face, and he wanted her to see him. He wanted her to see him vulnerable and unmasked. He wanted her to see a side of him that he showed no one else. He indulged his need for comfort with lingering touches and tenderness.

He loved watching the way her eyes widened and the way her pupils dilated. He had learned to read the twitch of her mouth and the flutter of her thick eyelashes. Judging by the way she clawed at his shoulders and gripped him between her thighs, she had learned to read him just as easily. She could see that he was close.

But first...

He changed the angle of his penetration and framed her clitoris between his fingers. He circled the little bud with quick flicks of his wrist all while driving into her cunt with deep, faster strokes that made her head fall back. Unable to help himself, he buried his face in her neck and nipped at the exposed line of her soft skin. Her pussy clenched him just before the fluttering waves of her climax gripped his cock.

"Kolya."

And there it was. His favorite sound. His name falling from her sweet mouth on a sigh of ecstasy.

Nikolai let go. He let those waves of pleasure crash over him and drag him down until he inhaled a shuddering, rough breath to refill his lungs. Not ready to be parted from her yet, he captured her mouth in a series of lazy, sensual kisses. He caressed her lush curves and smiled at the way she melted into his touch. Boneless beneath him, Vivian smiled sleepily.

Sliding his arms around her, he dragged her into a normal sleeping position on the bed. With their wet hair and bodies, they had made a mess of the comforter. He dragged it down the bed and tossed it in the corner of the room. It would have to go to dry cleaning with his suits. He could just imagine the *tsking* Anna would do in the morning when she collected the laundry—and the way Vivian would blush when the older woman made a ribald remark.

Turning off the lamp, he slid into bed beside her and tugged the sheet over their quickly cooling bodies. She burrowed into him, and he happily welcomed her into his arms and against his chest. Rubbing his face into her hair, he inhaled the sweet scent of her and felt the stress and the guilt of the day fade.

Vivian drifted off within seconds, but his mind wasn't so fast to settle. The words she had spoken to him in the shower rattled around in his head. Though he intended to do everything in his power to make sure that Vivian and the baby were safe, he accepted the odds of his personal safety weren't very good. He had a lot of enemies, and he blocked the path of many hungry, ambitious younger men. He wasn't as stupid as Lorenzo Guzman. The cartel boss thought himself untouchable but Nikolai didn't share that delusion. Someday, somewhere, someone would make a move against him.

Julio had seen that day coming. It was the reason why he had denied his son his name and sent the child's mother to Houston. It was the reason he had stood aside and allowed her to marry another man who would raise his son. None of that could have been easy for Julio to swallow, but he had done it with his son's best interests at heart.

It hadn't worked. He had lost his child to a senseless act of recklessness.

There had been a time when Nikolai had believed it might be possible to get out of the life. After the holiday attack on Vivian and the hell that broke loose in January, he had accepted the painful truth. He was never getting out of the mob. That door was closed, locked and barricaded. He was in this life until death.

He hoped—prayed, really—that he would have a long life with Vivian. He wanted it all with her, kids and grandkids. He intended to do everything in his power to make that possible, but he had to be realistic. If something happened to him, he needed to ensure that Vivian and the baby were safe.

Safe houses, stashed money, new identities—he had a lot of work to do.

8 CHAPTER EIGHT

The next morning, I came downstairs to find Nikolai in the kitchen. While I had barely found the energy to brush my teeth, wash my face and wrangle my hair into a messy bun, he had already showered and dressed for work. His wheat-colored suit jacket was slung over the back of a chair. He had a matching tie draped on top of it.

I didn't see anyone else in the house, but I was sure that his men were somewhere nearby, probably in the backyard or enjoying coffee on the front porch. Even though I was barefoot and made hardly any noise, he sensed my approach and greeted me with a playful smile on his handsome face. "Morning."

"Good morning." I embraced him from the side, careful to stay clear of the stove, and relished the strength of his arm around my shoulders. "I didn't realize you were already out of bed."

He brushed a loving kiss against my temple. "I woke early and slipped out quietly. You need your rest." He lowered his head and planted his lips on mine. Holding my gaze, he said, "I'm sorry about yesterday, Vee. It was terrible of me."

Even after making up last night, he still wore such an expression of pain on his face. I rubbed my hand across his chest. "I'm still annoyed with you about forgetting the appointment and not answering my texts or phone calls."

"I forgot to get my phone back from Kostya after the meeting. I turned it on and looked at it this morning. There were seven messages from you." His hand cupped the back of my neck, and his thumb gently massaged me. "It won't happen again. You can believe that."

"I do. So who did you meet with yesterday?"

He glanced down at me. "That's not happening."

"Touchy, touchy." I poked his side and disentangled myself from his arms to make a cup of tea. "Can you at least tell me about my father?"

"I don't think that's a good idea. Do you want green onions in your omelet this morning?"

"Not this morning." I wrinkled my nose and plucked one of the tiny cups of decaf green tea concentrate from the shelf near the one-cup brewer. Nikolai hated the contraption Lena had given us as a wedding gift and thought it was unnatural to drink coffee or tea that hadn't been properly brewed, but I was in love with it. "Why isn't it a good idea to tell me about my dad?"

"Because he's a fugitive, Vivian. He murdered a government witness, broke out of federal custody and ran to Mexico. You don't want to be the girl with any knowledge of his whereabouts. Telling you that he was in Corpus yesterday was a huge mistake." He shook his head. "I got rattled last night and slipped."

I popped the little cup of tea concentrate into place, chose my settings and leaned back against the countertop. "So the fact that he was in Corpus Christi yesterday means that something really, really bad is happening."

Nikolai plated my omelet alongside two slices of fluffy French toast. "Yes, and if anyone asks if you've seen him or heard from him, you say no."

"What about the call the other morning?" I brought my cup of tea to the island. "I can't lie about that."

"You can and you will." Nikolai plucked a banana from the fruit bowl, peeled it and cut thick slices that dropped onto the French toast, just the way I liked it. "Romero used a burner phone. No one can trace that call. If anyone comes and asks about him, you give them the party line. If they get difficult with you—"

"I call our lawyer and you."

"Exactly." He placed my plate in front of me. "The last thing we need are the Feds riding this perky little ass I love so much."

I gasped when he popped my bottom and planted a noisy kiss on my neck. "Not so little anymore," I reminded him as his caressed the spot he'd playfully swatted. "I tried on clothes yesterday evening and most of them were too tight."

"So we'll go shopping tomorrow," he promised. "You can get whatever you need for the trip." Now both of his hands were on my body, gliding over the silky fabric of my robe until he cupped my breasts. "I'm particularly enjoying this change."

"Kolya." I clasped his wrists to stop him from sliding his hands inside my camisole to fondle my bare breasts. "Anyone could walk in and see us."

"This is our home. We can do whatever the hell we'd like to do in our kitchen." He trailed ticklish kisses along the side of my throat. His hands moved down my sides and legs and turned up the inside of my thighs, forcing them apart slightly. His hands stopped at the tops of them, bunching up my sleep shorts. "If I want to toss you up on this counter and have you for breakfast, I will."

I let loose a disappointed noise when he pulled his hands away and left me throbbing and needy with only a lingering kiss on my cheek. "Tease."

He offered only a sexy grin before ducking into the refrigerator for the carton of orange juice. While I liked a big, delicious breakfast, he enjoyed simpler fare and rarely strayed from his usual bowl of oatmeal with a side of fruit plus coffee. The fact that he was having a glass of orange juice while I ate surprised me.

Before I sat down, I walked into the mud room and took down my purse from the shelf where I stored it. I unzipped one of the inner pouches and produced the ultrasound printout strip. Nikolai had taken his usual seat at the end of the island and leaned back against the bar-height chair while he flipped through the business section of the paper. I slipped onto the seat next to him and smiled when he reached out to stroke my back without looking up from the article he was reading.

"This isn't as good as seeing the baby in person but it's the next best thing." I unrolled the strip and flattened it on the milky white granite. "We won't have an ultrasound again until I'm sixteen weeks or so."

His face an unreadable mask, Nikolai set aside the paper and brushed the fingertips of his left hand down the strip of grainy images. He seemed almost afraid to touch them. Remembering the way he had gone to shower last night, I pieced together his hesitance. He wanted that ugly, viciously dirty side of his life never to touch me or the baby.

Reaching for his hand, I interlaced our fingers and held up the strip for him to examine. "The doctor says everything looks great. The baby is right on target. I had some bloodwork done yesterday. They're supposed to call me if anything is wrong."

Looking suddenly panicked, Nikolai asked, "Why would anything be wrong? Are you feeling unwell?"

I squeezed his hand. "I feel perfectly fine. I'm still really tired in the evenings, but my nausea seems to be fading. Except for last night," I added, glancing toward the sink I had barely reached before erupting. "Poor Boy! He thought it was his fault I got sick, but the pasta dish he made was so tasty."

"I told him you were nervous and stressed about the show." Nikolai finally took the strip from me and placed it on the counter in front of him. He traced the image of our baby with his fingertip. "Do you think about him? About the color his hair will be or if he'll have your blue eyes?"

"All the time," I admitted. "But he? You think it's a boy?"

Nikolai shrugged. "I have a feeling."

"Do you want a son first?" Personally, I wasn't concerned about the sex. Boy or girl, we would likely have our hands full. From what I knew of Nikolai's early years, he had been an absolute hellion as a little boy. I hadn't been much better.

"A daughter would be easier," he said, his mouth slanting with a smile as he touched the image of our baby kicking its legs.

"Easier? How?"

"It would be easier to keep her out of this life. My father, your father and me? We aren't the best role models for a little boy."

"Don't say that." I cupped his cheek and turned his face. Nikolai projected so much strength and confidence, but the prospect of fatherhood seemed to unsettle him. "If anyone in the world can help him understand why he shouldn't make the same mistakes, it's you."

Nikolai swallowed. "I'm trying so hard to build something for our children, Vee. Something real. Something legitimate. Something that will make them proud of me."

"I know you are." I didn't have all the nitty gritty details, but I believed he would find a way.

"I'm sorry I missed this." Nikolai leaned over and kissed me. The citrus burst that accompanied his mouth left me wanting more. Pulling back, he brushed his knuckles across my cheek. "Did you hear the heart-beat? Dima said that was his favorite part of going with Benny for her appointments."

"I did. It was very strong."

"That's good." Regret darkened his eyes. "Next time."

I nodded and captured his mouth in a tender kiss. "Next time."

Nikolai's cell phone beeped and vibrated. He leaned across the counter to grab it and the small glass bottle of maple syrup. "Eat."

I drizzled the sticky sweet syrup on my French toast and glanced at his phone. "Who is it?"

"Artyom." He tapped at the screen. "He wants to know if it's okay to come inside."

Nikolai walked around the corner of the island and retrieved a pair of kitchen shears from a drawer. He clipped the top ultrasound photo free and pushed the rest of the strip toward me. I carefully tucked them into the pocket of my robe and watched him place the small image of our baby into his wallet.

I was taking my first bite when the three-fingered captain strode into our kitchen with Ilya a few steps behind him. I didn't know Ilya very well. He hadn't spent much time around Samovar while I was waitressing. When he was there, he flirted outrageously with every other female employee but me. Ilya still made a point of standing far away from me and never being alone in a room with me. With his reputation as a Lothario, I suspected he didn't want to give Nikolai even the smallest reason to question his behavior.

"Good morning." I greeted the men who smiled and nodded at me. "There's coffee or tea if you'd like some."

Ilya took me up on the offer but Artyom strode closer. He removed the leather messenger bag he wore across his body, placed it on the counter, opened it up and retrieved five thick envelopes and one thin one. "I ran into Besian last night. He asked me to come over to his club and pick this up. He didn't want to hold it in his safe any longer."

"He doesn't owe me any money." Frowning, Nikolai extended his hand but Artyom shook his head.

"No, boss. These are Vivian's."

Nikolai froze. "Vivian's?"

Red-faced, I pulled the pile of envelopes toward me all while cursing Besian for being such a jerk. I could just imagine the mischievous laugh he had gotten out of this one. "Thank you, Arty."

Nikolai picked up one of the thick envelopes and thumbed through the stack of hundred dollar bills inside it. Seemingly taken aback, he asked, "Is there something you need to tell me?"

I sipped my tea and shrugged. "It was just a little bet on the soccer game yesterday and the fights you and Besian hosted earlier in the month."

"A little bet? This one maybe." He tapped the thin envelope. "But this one? Vivian, there's probably fifteen grand in that envelope."

"Sixteen-five," Arty corrected as he fixed a cup of coffee. "There's more in the bag. Apparently she got every single fight in the bracket right."

After digging through the bag and producing even more envelopes, Nikolai stared at me with a look of utter shock slackening his face. I realized I wasn't getting out of this uncomfortable situation. "Look, Papa used to bet a lot. Sometimes he would take me with him to see Afrim Barisha. I sort of, you know, learned how to place smart bets."

"Smart bets? Vivian, there's probably two hundred thousand dollars in this bag!"

The number left me dizzy. I couldn't believe three thousand hard-earned dollars had earned me that type of return. It was better than the stock market for sure. "Sergei had really good odds, and I had a pretty good feeling about Kelly so I pulled some money out of my emergency fund and...well..." I pointed to the bag. "That happened."

Staring at the piles of money on the counter, he asked, "How often are you placing bets?"

"It's not often. I've done this less than five times in the last four years. I only did it when I needed the money for something unexpected." I drew a tiny "X" over my heart. "Swear."

"How did I not know about this?" Nikolai sounded both extremely annoyed and uncommonly confounded.

"She's betting under the old man's name," Arty answered very unhelpfully.

"Is that true? You're betting under your grandfather's old account?""

I glared at Arty and then nodded contritely at Nikolai. "Basically."

"Basically?"

"Well I wasn't going to put my name on the Albanian's books!"

"How did this start? *When* did this start?"

Exhaling with frustration, I put down my fork. "Look, when I was a freshman in college, I needed some quick cash for art supplies. There was this girl in my dorm who dated one of the running backs at A&M so I knew he had this leg thing going on so I sort of scraped together my tips for the week and went to see Besian about placing a bet on the Saturday game."

"You went to one of his clubs?" Now Nikolai was aghast.

"No. Not one of *those* clubs." That was a bit of news that would have gotten straight back to Nikolai. "No, I waited on him during the lunch rush and just sort of, you know, casually asked about placing a bet. He took my money and came back with my winnings during the Monday dinner service."

My husband's eyes narrowed. "Those big tips weren't always tips."

"No."

"Vivian!"

"What? I paid taxes on the winnings because they came to me as tips. It's fine."

"It's not fine." He gestured to the bag in front of us. "You can't pay taxes on this."

I bit my lip. "I know. That's sort of why I hadn't gone to pick up my winnings yet."

"Jesus Christ, Vivian." He shook his head and huffed. "When were you going to tell me about this?"

"I was waiting for the right time." I nervously glanced at Arty and Ilya who were both looking anywhere but our direction. "That's not exactly a conversation starter that comes up easily. You've been busy lately."

He pinched the bridge of his nose and blew out a breath. I assumed he was thinking about the way he had totally screwed up yesterday by forgetting about our doctor's appointment. He couldn't get too angry with me, not after I had forgiven him for his mistake.

He lowered his hand and captured my gaze. I gulped at the sight of his serious expression. "No more bets, Vivian. This is the last one."

"Okay."

"I mean it, Vee. You can't get mixed up in this. You have to be spotless." Touching the envelopes, he added, "Gambling is all fun and games when you're on a hot streak, but it's easy to get burned, *solnyshka*. Think about your friend Kelly and all the trouble his father's gambling caused. We can't have any weaknesses for our enemies to exploit."

When he put it like that, the full weight of my action registered. "I understand."

He caressed my face and smiled. "I'm not angry
with you. Honestly I'm rather impressed and a little
jealous." He claimed my lips with a sweet, soft kiss
that assured me he really wasn't upset. "Now—what
do you want to do with this?"

"Well, um, that's the thing." I wrung my hands. "I
sort of planned to use the money to buy Sergei from
you. I figured that if I picked most of the right winners
I would have enough to clear his debt."

Nikolai's face slackened with shock. "How did you
know about his debt to the family?"

"I heard it somewhere."

"Somewhere?" he repeated dubiously.

"Yes."

I could tell he wanted to push for an answer but
didn't. He had to know there were only a handful of
possibilities. "Why?"

I frowned at him. "Why? Because Bianca loves him
and she's earned the right to some happiness. Because
Sergei didn't choose this life. Because it's not right
that you own someone like that."

Nikolai's jaw hardened and he broke our shared
gaze. I had hit a sore spot with that last remark, but I
wasn't going to apologize. The way Sergei had been
bought and sold by different branches of the Russian
mob was beyond wrong. Before he had made a deal to
save his family, he had been a man with a bright future. I wanted him to have that chance again.

"The debt has already been paid," Nikolai finally said.

"Nikolai," I said sadly. "Did you take money from Bianca?"

He avoided my stare. "We swapped for a piece of land I own."

"And you didn't tell me?"

His gaze flicked to the two men staring out the window and pretending not to listen to our conversation. "It was business, Vivian. That's all. It's done." He touched the bag of cash. "You'll have to find someone else to save with this." He started piling the envelopes back into the bag. The thin one he handed to me. "Do you want this one?"

Not at all satisfied with the abrupt end to the conversation I nevertheless nodded. "Sure. I could use some spending cash."

He frowned. "Vivian, if you need money, you only have to ask."

My lips parted, but I changed my mind. This wasn't a conversation I wanted to have with Arty and Ilya in the audience. We had already said too much. Instead, I replied, "I know."

Brow furrowed, Nikolai studied me for a moment. He turned his attention to Arty and Ilya. With a jerk of his head toward the door, the men silently took their order and left the kitchen. When we were alone, he reached for my hand. "Vee, what's wrong?" I hesitated, and he tipped my chin up. His thumb grazed my skin in the gentlest stroke. "Baby, tell me."

"I don't like asking you for money." I blurted out the words before I lost my nerve. "It makes me feel—"

"Like a child asking her father for an allowance?" he correctly guessed.

"That's an ugly way of putting it, but yes." Swallowing anxiously, I tried to explain myself better. "I don't have a problem using our household credit card when I'm buying groceries or shopping for us, but I'm used to having a job and having my own money. Sure, I made a nice chunk of cash from the show in January, but after gallery fees and taxes? I plow all of that back into supplies, framing, running my website, paying for Lena's PR services, the giclée print runs..."

"So there's nothing left for you to spend on things you want," he finished for me. His thumb traveled along my lip. "Vee, why didn't you tell me this earlier? We've been married for nearly six months. You should have said something."

"What could I say? You don't want me to work outside the home, and my paintings aren't producing enough profit."

"Yet," he said. "Your paintings aren't producing much profit *yet* but you are doing better than breaking even. You have money to invest in your business. That's a huge thing."

"I guess."

"It is." The slow caress of his thumb soothed my nerves and made this awkward conversation feel less daunting. "What do you think we should do about this? I'm open to any suggestion *except* you getting a job."

I rolled my eyes at him. "You are so old school."

"Yes," he agreed without hesitation. "I am what I am, Vivian. We had this discussion before we married. I explained my reasons for wanting you to work from home as a painter. Those haven't changed. If anything, I have more reasons." His other hand moved to my stomach. "It's hard enough to keep you guarded here at the house and your studio. Once the baby comes?"

"I actually like being home. I'm not like Lena. A high-powered career was never something I wanted. I always just wanted to raise children, keep a nice home and paint beautiful things." I ran my fingers through his hair and played with his earlobe. "You've given me that, and I love you for it."

He turned his head and kissed my palm. "What if we agree that you get a certain amount of discretionary income every month? It's yours to do with as you please. You can pull it out as cash at the bank or swipe the household card. You won't have to ask for money." He put a finger to my mouth when I started to argue. As if he could read my mind, he said, "It's not an allowance. We'll call it your salary for running our household."

It wasn't a perfect solution but it was palatable. I nipped at his finger, and his hand lowered. "I can live with that. But what does a household manager earn?"

"I have no idea. I suppose the fairest thing would be to go through my expenses for the last year. You should have the same amount of discretionary income."

My eyes nearly popped out of my head. "Kolya, do you have any idea how much money you spend every month? It's outrageous!"

Now he was the one rolling his eyes. "Hardly."

Not wanting to argue with him about his expenditures, I asked, "What if we just match my income from waitressing?"

"No. That's not even close to fair. You'll need more than that."

"How? I don't have rent, utilities, food or insurance costs anymore. A hundred bucks a week is fine."

Nikolai smirked. "You are a terrible negotiator, Vee. You're supposed to negotiate *up*, not down, *rybka*." He waved his hand. "We'll argue about this when we get back from London, all right? But I think you're worth far, far more than a hundred dollars a week."

Eyes narrowed and mouth quirked, I admitted, "I'm not sure if I should take that as a compliment or not."

"It's a compliment." He stood up and planted his hands on the arms of my chair. Nuzzling our noses together, he whispered, "You are more precious than rubies."

I laughed softly. "I never figured you for the type to use Proverbs to flirt."

"This isn't flirting." He pressed his forehead to mine. "It's the absolute truth."

Currents of warmth raced through me. "You're really good at that."

"At what?" He playfully avoided kissing me.

"Making my knees week and my belly tremble," I murmured before finally succeeding in capturing his mouth. The doorbell chime interrupted our loving kiss. Reluctantly, we parted.

Nikolai rested his chin atop my head. "I'll go see who that is. Finish your breakfast."

I hadn't taken two bites of the French toast before I heard Ivan's incredibly loud and always jovial voice echoing through the house. I grinned at the sound. Of all of Nikolai's friends, Ivan was my absolute favorite. He had a way of making everyone smile and laugh. It was so easy for me to understand why Erin utterly adored her great big beast of a husband.

Polishing off my breakfast, I glanced at the doorway at the sound of approaching footsteps. Nikolai entered the kitchen first and Ivan wasn't far behind. The strange man trailing Ivan surprised me, but I managed to hide my shock.

He was a big guy, almost as tall as Sergei and with shoulders as wide as Ivan's. He had a brawler's build and the rough, mean look of a man who used his fists to solve problems. The black polo shirt he wore brought out the reddish-brown tint to his hair. He had a short beard and so many tattoos. I suspected if I counted them up they would rival the number on Nikolai's body.

A quick inventory of his tattoos told me most of his story, but that tiger on his left arm interested me. It wasn't gang-related or prison work. It was expensive and gorgeously drawn. I didn't have to guess who had put that one on his skin: Tomi.

"Vee, this is Ten. He is your new bodyguard." Nikolai made a quick introduction and seemed completely oblivious to my discomfort at the idea of a man with Anton Vasiliev's reputation guarding me. This was a man who had just spent six years doing hard time. That was something I could deal with, but the infamous stories about The Shadow's propensity for violence worried me. The last thing I needed was a bodyguard who would fly off the handle at every slight, real or imagined.

"I see." I didn't want to be rude to Ten because this weird situation wasn't his fault. I had a feeling Nikolai had used his position to basically force him into taking my guard detail. Smiling warmly, I extended my hand. "It's nice to meet you, Ten."

The tall Russian's gaze dropped to my hand but he didn't move. "Yeah."

Surprised by his coldness, I tried not to let it show. "Right. Okay."

Nikolai exchanged a look with Ivan and stepped forward. "It will take time for the two of you to get comfortable."

A million years maybe...

"Ten, come with me." Nikolai gestured for my new bodyguard to follow him and picked up the leather messenger bag. "I'll show you the house."

Ten didn't offer me a second glance as he followed Nikolai out of the kitchen. Ivan plucked one of the Santa Rosa plums from the wooden bowl on the countertop. They were freshly picked from the trees out back. No doubt Nikolai had been out in the garden early this morning.

Ivan carried the stone fruit to the sink, rinsed and dried it before selecting a paring knife from the wooden block. Leaning back against the counter, he started to carve small slices. "Would you like a piece?"

"I'm good." Tapping my fork against my plate, I asked, "So...Ten?"

"I've known him since we were both kids. What you just saw isn't the real Ten. He just got popped from the pen and needs time to adjust. He's rough around the edges but he's a good guy." Ivan popped a plum slice into his mouth.

"Good guy? He was in prison for armed robbery."

Ivan swallowed and issued a harsh laugh. "Sweetheart, if we start comparing rap sheets, you aren't going to be very happy when we get to Nikolai's."

With a melodramatic glare, I tossed my cloth napkin at him, and Ivan laughingly dodged it. "I can see why Erin was so annoyed with you earlier this week."

His smile faded. "She was angry enough to call you?"

I nodded. "She didn't say what had her so riled up, but she was really frustrated with you."

"She had every right to be." Ivan finished up the plum and tossed the pit into the trash. "I decided to let Ten stay with us until he gets back on his feet. I should have asked her first."

It was bad enough that Nikolai had sprung a new bodyguard on me. I couldn't imagine how angry I would have been if he had announced a new house-guest. "Yeah, you should have."

Ivan picked up the napkin and placed the knife in the dishwasher. "It's not a mistake I'll make again."

Another thought occurred to me. "Is it the new sleeping arrangements that have her pissed off or is this about Ruby?"

Ivan moved closer and placed his big, scarred hands on the counter. I had seen those intimidating hands gently embrace Erin and stroke her cheek so softly. "It's always about Ruby. She'll get out of prison eventually, and if she comes into our home, she'll hurt Erin. She always hurts Erin. You and I both know the odds of Ruby staying clean are close to zero."

"That's true, but I also know the odds of a guy like Ten not re-offending are equally as small."

Ivan didn't speak for a long moment. Eventually, he turned toward me. "I stopped. Alexei stopped. It can be done."

"You got out. Alexei got out. Ten? He's still in."

"Yes, but he's on the outside. He'll be on probation for years. He'll have to walk the straight and narrow or risk going back inside. By the time he's free and clear, he'll have lost the taste for it."

Ivan wasn't the most loquacious man so when he spoke like this I made a point of listening. I stared at the platinum wedding band circling his ring finger. I had been at Kazimir's jewelry store the day Erin had chosen the design and the inscription on the inside. Reaching out, I tapped the wedding band. "That's a good look on you."

He smiled, his hard face lighting up and softening. "I'm luckier than I deserve."

"We make our own luck. You've earned Erin's love."

"And her forgiveness," he added quietly. "She isn't thrilled about Ten sharing our home, but she's agreed to give him a probationary period."

"Let me guess. You started calling her *angel moy* and she just melted?"

He snorted with laughter. "I wish! It's not that easy anymore."

"Sure it's not." I loved teasing this great big bear of a man, especially when it came to Erin.

Nikolai sauntered back into the kitchen with Ten and Arty on his heels. He picked up his tie and flipped his collar. Stepping toward him, I took the tie from his hand and looped it around his neck. "Pratt? Windsor?"

His sinfully sexy grin made my belly flutter. Was he remembering the morning he had taught me to tie the different knots he liked? What had started as a simple lesson in men's fashion had ended in Nikolai calling off work and us spending the day in bed...and on the couch and his desk and the shower. "Lady's choice."

While I expertly fixed his tie, he talked to the men surrounding us. The rapid-fire Russian being shot back and forth over my head was all above-board business. I caught a sly remark about Ten's welcome home party but one look from Nikolai silenced that talk. Considering Arty had brought me a payment from Besian, I didn't have to think too hard to fill in the blanks.

After making the final adjustments to the knot, I grabbed his jacket and helped him into it. He curled his fingers in my hair, cupping the back of my head, and kissed me tenderly. "I'll see you this evening."

"Bianca is coming by for a lesson later."

"With Sergei?"

"No, she's coming alone."

Nikolai's gaze briefly flicked in Ten's direction. There was something there I didn't like. A glimmer of apprehension maybe? As quickly as it appeared, it vanished. "I'll try to get home in time to see her. I always enjoy her company."

Of all of my friends, Bianca was the only one who showed the least amount of fear around him. I had a feeling there was more to the story about Sergei leaving Nikolai's employ. Bianca had those details but she was loyal to Sergei and loved him so much. She would do anything to protect him, even keep a dark secret about whatever leverage she had used to break Sergei free from the mob.

Nikolai, Ivan and Artyom left me alone with Ten. For a long moment, we simply stared at one another. "So," I said finally with a nervous smile, "I usually go running in the mornings."

"I don't run." Ten's gravelly, rough voice made my stomach clench. It reminded me of my father's voice and not in a good way.

"Okay," I dragged out the word. "Well, Boychenko likes to run so he'll go with me."

"Is that a good idea?" Ten crossed his massive arms.

"I run every weekday. It's my thing."

"But the boss said you're pregnant," he stated. "You shouldn't be exercising."

"Unless the Texas Department of Corrections has a med school program, I don't think you're qualified to make that judgment." I gathered up my dishes and carried them to the dishwasher. "Anna, our housekeeper, will be here in half an hour or so. She has her own key."

"That's not safe."

"She's sixty."

"It's not her I'm worried about," he countered. "She has sons."

"Who work at Samovar and one of Alexei Sarnov's dealerships," I reminded him.

"Which means they can be bought for the right price," he replied harshly. "They aren't part of this." He gestured to one of the tattoos on his hand. It was Nikolai's brand and a very hard mark to earn. "I'll take the key from her when she comes today. From now on, she knocks and comes in like every other visitor."

I gaped at him, agog. "You're not serious."

"As a fucking heart attack, sweetheart," he crudely replied. "The boss gave me one job, and I intend to do it. I don't particularly care if you like my methods. I'll keep you and the baby safe. That's all that matters."

Rattled by his harshness, I tried to remember what Ivan had said about Ten needing to adjust. "I understand that you have a job to do, and I won't interfere with that, but we don't have to be enemies."

"We aren't going to be friends either," he warned. "Sergei made the mistake of getting too close to you. I won't be making that same mistake. You're pretty, and you're sweet, but you aren't my type. Flirting and batting your eyelashes won't work on me."

"Wow." I shook my head. "You don't know Sergei half as well as you think you do. I'm not his type either. We didn't flirt. We're friends. *Real* friends. He's been there for me. We respect each other and care for each other."

"I don't need a friend. I don't need your respect. I'm here to work. That's it."

"Okay then." Putting up my hands, I signaled defeat. "Have it your way. I'm going upstairs to change. Tell Boy I'll be ready in twenty minutes."

"I'll get him to draw me the route so I can check it first."

"I'm just running around the neighborhood. It's safe."

"A judge's dog was poisoned yesterday. This neighborhood isn't safe."

That piece of news surprised me. "Roscoe? Someone poisoned him? Why didn't anyone tell me?"

"Because it's none of your business," Ten matter-of-factly replied.

"None of my business," I repeated, incredulous. "I live here. This is my home."

"This is Nikolai's home."

My jaw dropped. "You did not just say that to me."

"Is it yours? Is your name on the deed?"

"That's not—"

"You're his wife. That's it."

"And you're an asshole." Infuriated, I left the kitchen and headed upstairs. Safely inside our bedroom, I picked up my phone and texted Nikolai in a fit of rage.

This isn't going to work. I need a new guard. Now! Send Arty back.

Moments later, Nikolai called. I could hear road noise in the background. "Vee, it's been ten minutes. Give it some time."

"I don't need more time to know he's a bastard."

"Vee!"

"He said—"

Nikolai exhaled roughly. "I'm sure he said something stupid. I'll talk to him when I get home."

"So you expect me to spend all day with him?"

"Yes, I do. He's rough around the edges, but he'll keep you safe."

"Rough around the edges?" I scoffed. "He's a nightmare."

"He's good at his job."

"So was Sergei, but he didn't—"

"Sergei is gone. He chose Bianca over the family. That door is closed. He's not coming back."

It was the first time Nikolai had ever revealed that he was hurt by Sergei leaving.

"I chose Ten for a reason. You'll get used to him."

"And if I don't?"

"You will."

Gritting my teeth, I asked the other question that had been bothering me. "Why didn't you tell me about Roscoe?"

"Because I didn't want to worry you, Vee." Nikolai sounded exasperated. "We had a rough day and the last thing I wanted to do was frighten you. It's been taken care of so let it go."

"Just like that, huh? I'm just supposed to let it all go, right?"

Four long seconds of dead silence followed. "I'm not going to fight with you over the phone. We'll talk when I get home."

"Kolya—"

But the line went dead before I could get another word out of my mouth.

Like an angry child, I tossed my phone onto the bed and stormed into the closet. I jerked a T-shirt and a pair of running shorts out of a drawer. I slipped into a sports bra and my clothes and finger-combed my hair into a low ponytail that covered my neck tattoo.

Downstairs, I headed for the mud room where I stored my running shoes. I decided to use the older pair that had a few weeks of wear and tear left on them. When I bent down to grab them, my stomach lurched and I barely made it to the sink near the potting bench and garden tools before I promptly lost my breakfast.

I saw a blur of a tiger out of the corner of my eye. The faucet began to spew cold water. I heard a drawer open next to my hip. Moments later a dish cloth was dipped into the stream and wrung out. It was pressed against my neck.

"This will help." Ten's rumbling voice accompanied his surprisingly gentle gesture. He helped me stand up straight and plucked a glass from the cabinet closest to the sink. After filling it with cold water, he pushed it into my hands. "Rinse your mouth. Drink."

I did as instructed. Ten reached into the pocket of his jeans and withdrew a handful of small orange lozenges wrapped in clear plastic. They were the same ginger anti-nausea lozenges I kept in my purse.

"I bought them at the drugstore this morning. The pharmacist told me they were the best. They have good vitamins for pregnant women." He dropped one onto my palm. "Here."

I glanced up at him, mistrusting and confused. "Why?"

His light eyes, the color a strange combination of blue and green, sparked with regret. He seemed bothered by the way I looked at him. "Because I swore I would take care of you and the baby."

I tried to make sense of this harsh-tongued man. He had upset me so badly with his mean words, but he had also had the forethought to consider morning sickness and pregnancy. "I don't know what to think about you."

"Whatever you're thinking about me is probably true. I'm not a nice man, Vivian. Don't make the mistake of thinking I could ever be anything other than the mean bastard standing right in front of you."

Somehow I doubted that was true. I got the feeling this asshole act was all part of his emotional armor.

"You don't have to like me to trust me. I'll protect you and the baby until the day the boss tells me to stop. If that means taking a bullet to the chest or a knife to the gut, so be it."

"You don't even know me, Ten."

"I don't have to know you. I swore my loyalty to the boss. You are precious to him which means you're precious to every single one of us who wears this." He tapped that tattooed brand again. "You're carrying the heir to all of this." He waved his finger in a circle. "I'll die before I let anything happen to you."

The urge to deny that our child would inherit any of this was strong but I kept that to myself. "I don't want anyone to die for me."

"Then do what I tell you and we'll all be safe." Jaw tense, he held out his hand. "Let's try this again, yeah? Anton."

Realizing I had no other choice than to make the best of this situation, I accepted his hand. "Vivian."

"Nice to meet you, Vivian."

It wasn't much, but it was a start.

9 Chapter Nine

Tapping his phone against his leg, Nikolai stared out the window as Arty drove him to a meeting with Mr. Lu. After that business with the judge's dog, he wanted to get out in front of the problem and figure out a way to go in and get the girl without kicking off a fight or shootout. He also wanted to see the old man's face when they talked about Bobby Pham's side business.

If the old man really didn't know what the kid was doing, Nikolai would have to start making contingency plans. It would mean the old man was losing control of his people and that wasn't good for anyone. Mr. Lu would either have to be propped up or taken out. Neither option appealed to him much.

When they arrived at the dry cleaning shop, Artyom drove around back. Nikolai spotted one of Besian's cars parked in the employee spots. He hadn't expected to run into the Albanian boss today but he had a big fucking bone to pick with him. Glancing at his watch, he reached for the door handle. "Tell Kostya I want to see him in half an hour."

"Here?"

"Tell him to meet me at Kazimir's. I need to pick up Vivian's jewelry. It's supposed to be polished and ready to go."

"Okay. You want me to come in with you?"

Nikolai shook his head. "I've got this one." He slipped out of the SUV but didn't close the door. He hadn't been able to stop thinking about the argument he had had with Vivian over the phone. "Get in touch with Boychenko or Ilya. Ask them how Vee and Ten are working out."

"Sure, boss."

Feeling guilty for the way he had hung up on her that morning, Nikolai ran his fingers through his hair and crossed the parking lot. It had been stupid of him and childish. She had gotten under his skin with that remark about the way she was just supposed to let everything go.

A flutter of something that felt awfully similar to panic invaded his stomach. Was that really how she felt? There had always been friction between the two of them about the way he tended to be overbearing. When she had been his employee and the young woman he considered his ward, she had humored his overprotectiveness. Now that they were married, though, she seemed to be chafing under it.

He was so used to giving orders that it was second nature to him. He tried to remember that Vivian wasn't one of his soldiers. She was his wife. She was the woman he loved. He didn't want to be a controlling asshole. He didn't want her to feel trapped or ignored.

So why the hell didn't you ask her about Ten first?

Not wanting to think about all the reasons why he made decisions like that without involving her, he indulged in some equally as childish tit-for-tat thoughts. Why hadn't Vivian told him about the gambling? She had kept that secret for four years. In the great scheme of things, it wasn't a big one. She wasn't in debt, and she clearly had luck and strategy on her side, but she should have come clean after they were married. She sure as hell should have warned him about the massive payout Besian owed her.

And speaking of that Albanian devil...

"Nikolai!" Besian emerged from the building and slipped his sunglasses into place. "This is a happy surprise!"

"There's no such thing as a happy surprise." He shook Besian's hand but didn't let it go. Squeezing the other man's fingers, he jerked him forward. "Did you think it was funny to send a bag of money to my wife?"

"Honestly? I laughed my fucking ass off just imaging your face this morning."

"You're an asshole." He released Besian's hand. "You should have told me that my wife had a book with you."

"Technically—"

"Don't give me that technically bullshit. You rat on every single Russian on your books. You make damn sure I know who is up and who is down. You didn't think I needed to know that Vivian had bets with you?"

"I assumed you had your wife under control. How was I supposed to know she had a secret life she was keeping from you?"

Nikolai's eyes narrowed. "I'm feeling generous today so I'll forget you said that."

Besian shrugged. "Don't get pissed at me because your wife is keeping secrets."

Irritated with the situation, Nikolai marshaled his control and didn't punch him in the face for the insinuation that Vivian was a liar. If he blew up on Besian, the man would make sure everyone in Houston's underworld knew that he couldn't even keep order under his own roof. One rumor like that and it could all come crashing down around his ears.

"Hey, come on." Besian tapped his shoulder and grinned in that mischievous way of his. "I'm just fucking with you, Nikolai. Boss to boss," he added. "No one knows about the small bets she's placed but you, me and *daltë*." He held up three fingers and used the Albanian word for chisel. "She's never lost money and never owed anything. If she had ever gotten herself into trouble, I would have told you. It was all harmless fun."

Glancing away from Besian, he nodded. "Yeah. All right."

Besian changed the subject. "Listen, when you get back from London, we need to talk business." Nikolai nodded, and Besian clapped him on the back. "Go easy on the old man. He's not well."

Wondering what Besian meant by that, he entered the building and headed for the cramped, perpetually hot office where Mr. Lu liked to conduct private meetings. The door was open but he knocked on the frame before entering. Stepping into the office, he instantly understood what Besian had meant. The old man looked pale and tired.

Nikolai hesitated in the doorway. "Lu, I can come back tomorrow."

Mr. Lu gestured for him to shut the door. "I won't be any better tomorrow. It's that poison the doctors at MD Anderson are pumping into my veins."

MD Anderson? The cancer center. "You're sick."

The old man nodded. "They found it a few weeks ago. I started chemo last week. I'm feeling it this week."

"I'm sorry to hear that."

Mr. Lu waved his hand. "Shit happens. I've had a good run. Sixty-eight years? I survived *Việt Nam Cộng-sản*. I can beat this."

"Absolutely," Nikolai agreed and took the seat in front of the desk. He unbuttoned his suit jacket. "Look, Lu, we have a problem."

"Bobby." The old man leaned back in his worn leather chair and sighed. "He's always been a greedy little shit. He's too smart for his own good. It's always about the fast money." He tossed his pen onto his desk. "Kids these days! None of them want to work. Build slow and steady. That's the real way to make money."

"No arguments there."

"What has Bobby done?"

"He's tied up with a federal judge's daughter. The judge is my neighbor, and he's asked me to get her free."

"I told him to cut that girl loose."

"Well he didn't. That girl or Bobby or maybe both of them poisoned the judge's dog yesterday. With cocaine," Nikolai added gravely. "I can't have that in my backyard, Lu. If you won't deal with it, I will."

"Cocaine? You're sure?" Mr. Lu seemed surprised. "He moves counterfeits."

"He's been seen taking meetings with cartel players."

"The Houston crew? Julio? Lalo?"

Nikolai shook his head. "Hector Salas."

Lu cursed in Vietnamese. Reluctantly, he admitted, "I didn't know."

"I didn't think so. You're not stupid enough to try to go around Julio." Nikolai picked at the fabric of his trousers. "I don't have to tell you how this will play out when Julio figures out that the reason he's losing market share is because your nephew is trying to cut out the middleman to get his hands on product."

Mr. Lu turned even paler. "I'll take care of it."

"Soon."

"Before Sunday," he promised.

"If it's not done before I leave for London..." Nikolai didn't have to finish the rest of his warning.

"It will be done."

"Good." Nikolai stood up and headed for the door. He paused before leaving. "Good luck, Lu."

Back outside, Nikolai grimaced at the suffocating heat that slapped him in the face. The humidity was off the charts, and the three-digit temperature made the heat nearly unbearable. He couldn't wait to get out of Texas for a week. The prospect of visiting London and getting that close to his old life in Moscow hadn't thrilled him. He could think of a dozen reasons why getting within thumping distance of Maksim was a bad idea, but he had set them aside and focused on supporting Vivian's career. She had earned this chance. She deserved it.

As Arty navigated the rush hour traffic, Nikolai allowed his thoughts to wander. He didn't want to dwell on the fact that he had fought with Vivian two days in a row. He really didn't want to think about other arguments that had cropped up between them. Rolling through his mental calendar, he tried to narrow down the start of the problems.

Worry speared his heart when he arrived at the date. All the friction had started after they had discovered they were pregnant. What had Vivian said last night? That they weren't ready to be parents...

Was this normal? Did other couples argue more when there was a new baby in the picture? It seemed likely. He had rushed Vivian into marrying him and had gotten her pregnant only three months later. Was it too fast? Was it too much too soon?

He thought about Dimitri and Benny. The pair had been friends for five years before one night together had changed their relationship forever. They had gone from dating to pregnant to married to parents within nine very quick months. They had weathered an assault and an arson plus the usual problems that cropped up when running two small businesses. They seemed even stronger together.

But Dimitri was always talking about Benny as his partner. The couple discussed everything and made decisions together about each other's businesses. He couldn't do that with Vivian. They weren't ever going to be equal partners. There were always going to be imbalances.

Like money. Vivian's admission about asking for money added to his guilt. He should have seen that one coming. She had been standing on her own two feet for years. He had asked her to stop working at Samovar because it would have been unseemly for his wife to wait tables. He was the one who had cut off her income, and he hadn't even considered that she might feel uncomfortable about having to rely on him for everything. In his mind, she was his wife so that meant everything that belonged to him belonged to her. *So why didn't you tell her that?*

"You okay, boss?" Arty glanced at him as they idled at a street light.

He ignored the question and asked one of his own. "Did you talk to Ilya or Boychenko?"

"Ilya says that there's been some tension."

"Tension?"

"That's all he said." He accelerated through the intersection. "Are we going to have trouble with Mr. Lu?"

"Lu has cancer."

"Shit. Is it bad?"

"He's nearly seventy years old. Everything is bad at that age."

"What happens if he dies? Who is the heir?"

Artyom hit the nail right on the head, as usual. "The son is straight as an arrow. He's in Austin, and I don't see him coming back to take over the business."

"What about the daughter? She's his right-hand girl, right? She's the one who runs the legit businesses."

"An? She's pretty straight. I don't think she's ever handled any of the smuggling or counterfeit work. I see her at Chamber of Commerce meetings and other business functions around the city."

"She's his daughter. She knows the score."

"The men in the family might not like answering to a woman."

"She doesn't need a dick to make them money."

Nikolai laughed at that astute observation. "True."

"It will get messy if they start fighting among themselves," Artyom warned. "I don't have enough soldiers to referee an internal disagreement among the Asians and keep the peace with the Albanians, the Hermanos and whatever the fuck is going on with the cartel. We need to bring in reinforcements."

Nikolai wiped a hand down his face. "Even if they're legal, we'll have immigration up our asses. Once ICE is done with us, Santos and his gang task force friends will start shaking us down. Besian and Nickel Jackson will start to complain that there are too many of us in the city. Lorenzo and the rest of the cartel will get nervous that we're planning something."

"Which we are," Artyom cut in. "We're planning to protect ourselves and our business interests."

"The others won't see it that way. They'll think we're building up our numbers to force new terms and take territory. This city is already a powder keg. I won't be the one who sets off the first spark."

"I don't think you have to worry about that, boss. There's a long line in front of you with lighters in hand."

Artyom had a good feel for the pulse on the streets so Nikolai took his warning to heart. He didn't want the added headache of dancing with ICE or fending off Vivian's cousin and his gang squad, but he refused to leave his men exposed. Like Artyom, he could feel something coming. There was a shift in the air, an electrified sensation that prickled the skin, and a foreboding darkness that settled in the back of his mind. His very bones ached with a pulsing hum of warning.

He had to be ready. He could not fail.

When they reached the jewelry store, he hopped out of the SUV and left Artyom sitting in a curb-side parking spot. He stepped into the shop and spotted Kostya at one of the counters. The cleaner swiftly pocketed a small box and turned toward the main entrance as if nothing had happened. Kostya's love life was none of his business so he pretended not to notice.

A flash of white-blonde hair caught his attention. Dressed in a very conservative dove gray skirt with pink blouse, Zoya emerged from a back room with three slim Prussian blue boxes embossed with the gold seal of the company in her hand. The only child of the store's owner, she had followed in her father's footsteps as a gemologist and jewelry designer. She had big dreams and the talent to make them happen. There was no doubt in Nikolai's mind that his investment in Abramov's would continue to bear fruit for years to come.

"Mr. Kalasnikov, how are you today?" She retrieved a black velvet tray from behind the counter and placed the boxes on top of it.

"I'm fine. How are you, Zoya?" He made a point of replying to her in Russian

"Busy, busy, busy," she said with a little laugh. "It's wedding season so that door chime is ringing non-stop."

Her Russian was technically perfect, but she had that same habit of coloring the syllables with a hint of Texas twang just like Vivian and Boychenko. Would his Houston-born child do the same thing?

Opening the boxes, she revealed the beautifully feminine jewelry that she had designed for Vivian. The gold and diamonds of the necklace, bracelet and earrings glittered under the lighting and made the sunbursts look brilliantly bright. "I handled this one myself this morning."

"It's perfect." He fought the urge to stroke the polished gold and twinkling diamonds. "The insurance paperwork?"

"Right here." She lifted the jeweler's loupe from her neck and used the key dangling from the chain to unlock a drawer beneath the register. She retrieved an envelope and handed it to him. "It's all in order. If anything happens, you come back to see us, and we'll take care of everything." She placed the lid back on the box. "Would you like me to wrap this with ribbon?"

"Please," he said with a nod. While Zoya artfully decorated the boxes with gold ribbon, he skimmed the insurance paperwork.

Kostya had worked his way over to his side and waited for the transaction to be completed. He leaned against the counter and asked, "Did Sergei find the perfect diamond?"

Nikolai glanced up from the paperwork upon hearing the question. Earlier in the week, he had visited the store to make the final approval on the celebratory jewelry he had ordered for Vivian. He had run into Sergei on his visit and had learned his former prize fighter was going to propose to Bianca. He had his suspicions about why the two would rush into a marriage, but it wasn't any of his business. Unless he was specifically asked for his opinion, he was staying out of it.

"He did." Zoya smiled at them. "Abram set the stone this morning. It's gorgeous. I think he'll be very pleased, and Bianca will love it." She finished tying the ribbons and carefully placed the boxes into a bag that matched the boxes and decorated it with a few sheets of gold tissue paper. "All done. Here you go."

"Thank you." He took the bag from her and retrieved his wallet. He plucked one of the credit cards free and handed it to her. After signing the receipt and pocketing his wallet, he wished her a good day and left the store with Kostya at his side.

"How was the meeting with Mr. Lu?" Kostya asked as soon as they were outside.

"He didn't know about his nephew's side deal. I've given him until Sunday to turn the girl over to the judge. If he doesn't..."

"I'll handle it."

Nikolai put on his sunglasses. "Did you know he has cancer?"

Kostya nodded. "I found out last week. I didn't think it mattered. Cancer or old age, that guy is headed out the door soon enough."

"It matters. Don't keep shit like that from me again."

A few seconds of silence stretched between them. "Yeah. Okay."

"What do you know about An?"

Kostya glanced at him in surprise. "You think she'll inherit the old man's kingdom?"

"Who else is there? Bobby might make a play for it, but he's weak and stupid."

"I'll dig up what I can on her."

"What about Mando?"

Kostya shook his head. "Nothing yet. I'm digging, boss. I'll find him."

"I don't care who you have to pay or turn. We need to get to him. Handing him over to Julio and letting the cartel mete out their own brand of justice is the only way we hold off a war."

"And when the MC finds out we gave their sergeant-at-arms to the cartel?"

"They'll understand that actions have consequences. They'll learn that my connection to Romero doesn't give them a free pass to kill kids in my city." Nikolai put his hand on the door of the SUV but didn't open it yet. "Did you know Vivian was gambling?"

Kostya betrayed himself by flashing his tell. "Look, it was only a little bit of money here and there. If she had gotten into trouble, I would have taken care of it."

The idea of another man, even one he trusted and loved as much as Kostya, coming to her rescue burned him up with jealousy. It wasn't a reaction that he was proud of, but there it was.

"When I found out, she was just a kid, boss. She was working for the restaurant part-time, and I could tell she needed the extra money. They were small bets, and she was careful about it. She wasn't yours yet so I didn't see the point of bringing it to your attention."

He rubbed his thumb over his key ring. "I thought she had earned the right to a little fun. It wasn't hurting anyone."

Nikolai started to tell Kostya that he should have come clean after he had married Vivian, but that wasn't on Kostya, was it? It was on her.

"The last bet, the one she put on the fights? I figured that was her way of making sure that Sergei and Bianca could be together. You know how she is about her friends. I didn't realize you were going to sell him to Bianca until after that deal was made."

The harshness of the way Kostya described that particular transaction almost made him flinch. For all his righteous indignation about staying out of the skin trade, Nikolai hadn't hesitated at the chance to buy Sergei's contract from Maksim. He might not have been forcing Sergei to live in a ramshackle whorehouse or service dozens of men a night, but he had forced the man to break bones and spirits. He had forced Sergei into a cage to fight other violent men with the unspoken threat that if he didn't do as he was told Maksim would find a way to extract payment from Sergei's mother and brother. How was he any different than the madams and pimps he sneered at?

"Boss?"

Shoving aside thoughts of Sergei, he looked at Kostya. "If you need me tonight, I'll be at the house."

"How is Ten working out?"

"He's fine." *He will be, once I've had a chance to straighten him out.*

"Good." Kostya took a step back and reached into his pocket for his lighter. "I'll let you know if I have any luck smoking out Mando."

Nodding, Nikolai slid back into the SUV and buckled his belt. He gestured for Artyom to drive. His mind raced in a thousand different directions. There were so many variables to plug in to the various equations. Very few of the outcomes pleased him.

When they arrived at the house, he sent Artyom home for the night and hoped the captain would use the time off wisely. Come Sunday evening, Kostya and Artyom would be holding down the city for him. If anyone was going to be stupid enough to make a move, it would be done the moment he was out of town. To outsiders, the family would be in a weakened position. That assumption couldn't be more wrong. His men would bloody the streets before they lost even an inch of territory while their boss was away.

"Boss." Ilya greeted him from the back porch. "Your wife and her friend are inside with Ten. I sent Boychenko home. He has to be at the gym early in the morning."

"That's fine." Remembering what Arytom had said, he asked, "So...tension?"

Ilya shrugged. "It's the first day. It will get easier for both of them."

Hoping that was the case, he entered the house and hid the gift bag for Vivian in the mud room closet where their heavy winter coats were stored. Certain the two women would be in the library, he made his way across the house. His lips drew tight when he spotted Ten leaning against the wall with his arms crossed and a scowl on his face. "What's wrong?"

Not moving off the wall, Ten jerked his head toward the door. "She locked me out."

"What do you mean?" He tested the door handle and found it locked. Irritated by the discovery of a locked door, he rapped his knuckles on the door. "Vee!"

She took her sweet time unlocking it. The fact that she opened the door only far enough to peek out riled him up even more. Addressing him in Russian, probably to spare Bianca the inevitable uncomfortable urge to eavesdrop, she asked, "Yes?"

"You know how I feel about locked doors." He hated the panic that gripped him when he heard a door lock. It was a holdover from his early years in that horror house of an orphanage. The irrational reaction was one he couldn't control and one that embarrassed him to even admit. Vivian knew that. He had told her that in their first weeks together living in this house as man and wife. She had promised not to put locked doors between them.

Her frustrated expression softened. "I wasn't locking you out." She opened the door wide enough to peek out and glare at Ten. "I locked him out."

"Why?"

"Because he's a jerk."

"So?" Nikolai wasn't going to argue that point. "He's not here to be your friend, Vivian. He's here to be your bodyguard. He can't do that if he's out here in the hallway."

"He doesn't need to be attached to me like a para-
site when we're here in the house."

"That's his call to make. He's the one with his ass
on the line if something happens to you."

"Like what? A paper cut? That's the worst thing
that might have happened to me in the library." Her
eyes narrowed, and she studied him with a suspicious
stare. "What are you hiding from me? Why are you so
worried about my safety all of a sudden?"

"You know why I'm worried about you." He cast a
pointed look at her stomach.

"No," she argued. "That's not it. Not all of it, at
least. What aren't you telling me?"

His patience thin, he hissed harshly, "Are you sure
you want to open that door, Vivian? Do I need to remind you about the bag of money that was dropped in
our kitchen this morning? You're the one who wants
truth and honesty—but only from me. What happened
to no secrets, Vee? Huh? So much for us being partners."

She blinked a few times. He realized a moment too
late that he had never snapped at her like this. Never.
Not once. The fact that he had chosen to do it in front
of two other people made him feel worse.

"Vee, I—"

"It's all right." She smiled weakly. "You're right."
Glancing over her shoulder, she seemed to remember
that Bianca was waiting. As if nothing had happened,
she opened the door and gestured for him to come inside. For a moment, he lingered there in the doorway

and simply studied her face. Artyom was right. Vivian was changing. She was learning to use masks.

And it killed him. It fucking slayed him.

All the things he loved about her were the things that made it so difficult for her to play the role of perfect little mob wife. If he wasn't careful, he was going to lose her. He was going to push her and squeeze her and mold her into someone he didn't even recognize.

He slid his arms around her waist, kissed the top of her head and prayed she would let him make this right later. She had made a mistake keeping the gambling from him, but Kostya and Besian were right. In the great scheme of things, it was a tiny indiscretion. She hadn't hurt anyone. She hadn't gotten into trouble. She had placed a handful of bets over the span of four years.

Deep down inside, he knew exactly why this bothered him so much. She wasn't supposed to be the one with secrets. He was supposed to know everything about her. She was supposed to be the one constant source of light and goodness in his life. There were no dark corners or closed doors in her life.

He wanted to have zero reasons to mistrust her. All while he kept secrets and told white lies and did terrible, horrible things right under her nose. The hypocrisy of it turned his stomach.

He turned his attention to Vivian's friend. Bianca sat at the small table in the library where Vivian sometimes sketched while he read in one of the comfortable chairs. She had her back to the door and seemed to be putting an awful lot of thought into copying the Russian phrases on her notepad. "Bianca, it's good to see you."

She twisted in her seat and smiled. "It's nice to see you too." She gathered up her notepad and her oversized purse. The buttery yellow leather seemed impossibly bright against her rich, dark skin. As usual, she was dressed to sheer perfection. The girl had style and a smile that made a man think of sinful things. It was easy enough to see why Sergei loved and adored her.

Making a show of glancing at her watch, she said, "I need to run. Sergei will be home soon. I promised to handle dinner tonight."

Still holding Vivian close, he asked, "What time are you two heading to the airport on Sunday?"

"I think Sergei said eight?" She tucked her notepad into her purse along with the capped pen. "What about you two?"

"Eight. You're staying at the same hotel as Erin and Ivan?"

"Yes."

"And Sergei's mother and brother are joining us on Tuesday evening?"

She nodded. "They'll be with us until Sunday morning when they fly back to Russia."

"I haven't had a chance to talk with Sergei about the immigration situation. It's going well?" He had recommended a better, more expensive lawyer earlier in the month. The attorney had useful connections and could speed up the process.

"He had a meeting with his new lawyer earlier this week. It seems promising so far."

"I'm glad to hear that. It will be good for the entire family to be here together."

"Yes, it will."

Moving his arms to Vivian's shoulders, he guided her to one side of the doorway. "Ten?" The man stepped forward but said nothing. "Walk Bianca out to her car.

"*Da.*"

"Oh, I don't need an escort," Bianca hurriedly replied with a slightly nervous laugh. "I'm a big girl."

"It's no trouble." Just to ensure that she understood this wasn't up for debate, he added, "I insist."

Vivian stepped away from him and walked Bianca out of the house with Ten a few steps behind them. He moved to the window overlooking the front yard and watched Ten escort Bianca to her car. When Ten boxed her in with his larger body, Nikolai curled his hands at his sides. Ten had never been violent or inappropriate with a woman, but prison had a way of changing a man and never for the better.

Ready to intervene, he closely watched the pair and relaxed when Ten behaved himself. He was trying to flirt with her, that much was clear even from this distance, but he didn't cross any lines. Bianca was a strong woman and more than capable of putting even a man as intimidating and huge as Ten in his place.

He watched Ten take Bianca's hand and hold it up to the light from the antique-style street lamps. It was easy enough to deduce the topic of their conversation.

"If Sergei catches Ten leering at Bianca like that, he'll shatter Ten's jaw." Vivian had returned to the library but didn't come closer to him. She hovered near the doorway. He didn't want to dwell on the reasons why she was distancing herself from him.

Not taking his eyes off Bianca and Ten, Nikolai nodded in agreement with Vivian's statement. "A shattered jaw will be the least of Ten's worries if he tries to seduce Bianca."

"Even if he tries, he won't succeed. Bianca is committed to Sergei, and he to her. They're unbreakable."

"No couple is truly unbreakable," he murmured without thinking. A moment too late, he realized what he had said. He spun to face Vivian, but she was already gone. Her habit of traipsing barefoot around the house allowed her to move so quietly. Kostya would be so proud of her stealth.

Searching her out, he left the library and came face-to-face with Ten in the entryway. He put a hand on the larger man's chest. Ten's eyebrows raised at the rough touch, but he didn't pull away. "Yes?"

"Leave Bianca Bradshaw alone. She belongs to Sergei, and I will let him break you if you put another hand on her."

Ten's jaw clenched and unclenched. "I didn't hurt her. I was warning her."

"About?"

"You know."

Nikolai replayed the scene he had watched play out in front of his house. "You warned her about Sergei's mother."

"Someone had to."

"She's a good woman. Sergei's family will learn to love her when they see how kind and gentle she is. She'll make him a better man. That's all any mother wants for her son." He flicked Ten's chest. "There are plenty of other big, beautiful girls like Bianca in Houston. Go find one of them—or two or three," he added with a wry smile, thinking of Ten's appetites. "But leave this one alone. She's taken, and she's one of us."

Ten nodded. "I'll stay away from Bianca."

"Now, let's talk about Vivian."

Ten rubbed the back of his neck. "It could have gone better. We had good moments and bad ones." He dropped his hand. "It will get easier." He swallowed and glanced away for a second. "I'll try harder."

Nikolai figured that was the most he could ask for and smacked Ten's arm. "Go home. We'll see you in the morning."

After Ten had lumbered away and out the back door to catch a ride with Ilya, Nikolai made sure the night guard was in place before locking up and setting the alarm. He followed the low thump of music to Vivian's home studio. She never painted late when he was home early. The fact that she had chosen to do so tonight didn't bode well for him.

He lingered outside the closed French doors that led to the sunroom-slash-studio. Even from here, he could smell the oil paints and canvas. He worried about her exposure to the paints, but he trusted that she was being careful. The music thrummed at a level that was just loud enough to drown out the noise of the house.

Nikolai reached out to open the door. He grasped the handle but stopped. The last thing he wanted was to fight with her. He didn't trust himself to get it right tonight. Maybe she needed some space. She had closed the doors for a reason. He decided to respect that and let her come to him when she was ready.

Unable to help himself, he tested the handle. It moved freely. The door was unlocked. Tonight that was enough.

He pivoted on his heel and headed to the kitchen to find something for dinner. After poking through the refrigerator, he settled on a sandwich and a beer. As he opened the drawer to search for the bottle opener, his pocket started to vibrate. He fished out his phone and spotted Kostya's number.

"Yes?" He clamped the phone between his ear and shoulder and popped the cap off his beer.

"Boss, we have a problem."

Tossing the bottle opener into the drawer, he bumped it closed with his hip. "What kind of problem?"

"I had a tip about a guest checking into a hotel downtown. A maid who dates one of your soldiers recognized the face. I decided to check it out."

"And? Is it Mando or his stripper girlfriend?" He took a long pull from the ice cold bottle.

"No, boss." Kostya hesitated. "It's Tatiana. She's back in Houston."

Nikolai choked on his mouthful of beer and barely managed to get it down his throat. Tatiana? Back in

Houston? Was she trying to get both of them killed? "Are you at the hotel?"

"Yes."

"Deal with her. *Now.*"

"It's done." Kostya cleared his throat. "What should I do about Santos?"

Kostya had named the one person Nikolai did not want to deal with tonight or any other. Vivian's cousin, the Houston detective, was a perennial pain in his fucking ass, and if he found out Tatiana was alive and back in Houston? *Fuck.*

"Leave it to me."

"*Da.*"

The line went dead. Awash in anger and frustration that Tatiana had dared to come back, he scrolled through his contacts until he found Ilya's name. He needed a diversion to keep Santos and his gang task force buddies busy.

"Boss? What's wrong?" Ilya answered promptly. It was quiet in the background which meant Ilya had gone straight home instead of out to drink or carouse. That was good because he needed a clear head for the task he was about to be assigned. It was going to be a very long night for Ilya and his crew as they stirred up trouble on the streets to keep Eric and his men busy.

"Ilya, I need you to do something for me..."

10 CHAPTER TEN

"What's next on the list?" Erin glanced around the busy Starbucks and sipped the last bit of her iced blackberry mojito tea. The noise of the Galleria crowd echoed like a dull roar in the mega-sized mall. Like Bianca, Erin lived for fashion and had practically squealed with delight when I had asked her to come shopping with me after Nikolai had ducked out of the house early to deal with some business.

The secret kind of business, of course.

I tried not to dwell on my confused emotions. After spending the evening painting and trying to give Nikolai some space, I had gone up to our bedroom to find him already asleep. That had never happened. I had showered and slipped quietly into bed. I had expected him to roll toward me or wrap his arms around me in that possessive, comforting way I loved so much, but he hadn't moved at all.

Honestly, I had suspected he was actually awake. His breathing had been too even and too controlled for sleep. The fact that he was pretending to sleep rather than talk to me had cut deeply, but I had decided to let it go. I couldn't bear the thought of fighting with him while we were in our bed. In the end, I had turned on my side, facing away from him, hugged the covers up to my chin and closed my eyes.

Pushing aside that troubling memory, I pulled the small pink notepad from my purse and looked at the list. Erin had helped me choose a few new tops and some bottoms in a slightly larger size than I normally wore. By the time I returned from London, I would have no choice but to hit up the maternity stores and boutiques around town. "I still need a dress for the actual gallery show."

"What kind of dress? Evening? Cocktail? Red? Blue? Gold and glittery? Empire waist? Bandage? Long hem? Short hem?"

From his seat at the table directly behind Erin, Ten smirked and polished off his iced coffee. He seemed to find Erin terribly amusing. Despite her frustrations with the way Ivan had moved him into their home without warning, she appeared to have warmed toward Ten.

"I spoke to Lena this morning, and she told me to wear something black. Apparently it will photograph better. I'm supposed to make sure that Nikolai wears a black suit, too."

"Well, she is the PR guru so I would take that suggestion to heart." Erin glanced around the busy mall. "BCBG is back that way, and bebe is down there, right across from GAP. They both have really sexy and fun little black dresses. I'm sure we can find something for you there."

"Okay. And you? Do you have anything else on your list?"

"I still need to grab a new belt for Ivan. Apparently it has to come from Gucci." Rolling her eyes, she laughed softly and started digging through her purse in search of lipstick and her compact. "I promised Ivan I would take this guy," she gestured behind her with the black tube, "to get some polos and tees. I figured we'd try Express or Kenneth Cole maybe. If they have shirts that will fit my big man-beast, they'll have shirts that fit Ten."

Behind her, Ten snorted with amusement and lifted the lid on his drink to get to the ice cubes inside. He shook some into his mouth and crunched on them. Erin swiveled in her seat at the loud noise and playfully chastised him. "Hey, comrade, were you raised in a barn?"

Ten noisily smashed another cube between his teeth. "Keep that up, and I might accidentally let it slip that you went on a binge in that makeup store. I'm pretty sure I heard Ivan complaining about the counter space in your bathroom."

She stuck out her tongue at him, and Ten made a circling motion with his finger, silently instructing her to turn around. She touched up her lips and dropped her makeup back into her bag. Her gaze landed on my half-full peach green tea. "You didn't finish your tea, and you always finish your tea. Was it mixed wrong? I'll take it back up to the counter for you."

"No, it's fine. I'm not that thirsty." My stomach was swirling with nausea, and I had forgotten to toss the ginger lozenges and gum into my purse before leaving the house.

"It's like a hundred degrees outside, Vivi. You need to drink up."

"I'll take it with me." I wrapped a napkin around the plastic cup to shield my hands from the condensation.

"Okay." Erin continued to eye me with concern as she gathered up her empty cup, napkins and wrapped the leftover half of her brightly iced sugar cookie in the crinkly paper bag. She stowed the cookie in her purse and tossed her trash.

While her back was turned, Ten touched my hand. I glanced down and caught him trying to press an unwrapped ginger lozenge into my hand. He winked at me and dropped it onto my upturned palm. I thanked him with a smile and popped it into my mouth.

Erin looped her arm through mine and guided me into the bustling crowd. She veered toward the left, and I correctly assumed we were going to tackle the men's shopping first. Picking out a belt for Ivan took longer than I had expected. Eventually, she settled on two different belts, one black with a spur buckle and the other a dark brown leather with a square buckle.

Picking out shirts with Ten brought back memories of prom dress hunting with Erin and Lena. This shirt was too heavy, but that one was too thin. The fabric on this one was scratchy, but the fabric on that one was too stiff. He didn't like bright colors, but he didn't want all black.

"What about this one?" Erin held up an orange polo, and I thought Ten was going to blow a pupil. She realized her mistake too late. The man had just gotten out of prison, and she was trying to put him back in convict orange.

"*Nyet.*"

"Yeah. Sorry." She hastily stuck it back on the rack. "My bad. How about something more cheerful?" She plucked a purple one off the rack but quickly put it back when Ten's eyebrows shot toward his hairline. "So, um, gray?"

With a grim expression, he stepped forward and selected four different shirts, each in shades of dark blue and gray. "These will do."

I took them from his arms before he could react. "Anything else?"

"No. That's it."

"Okay." I headed for the cashier but Erin lightly smacked my arm to get my attention. "What?"

"Ivan told me to pick up the tab." She tried to take the shirts from me, but I held firm.

"No. I've got this. My treat," I said and smiled at Ten.

"Ladies," he said with a deep laugh. "I'm flattered to have you fighting over me, but let's not throw down in the middle of this store. Getting tossed out of the Galleria because of a cat fight won't go over well with my P.O."

Erin rolled her eyes. "Boy, you really are a charmer."

After paying for Ten's shirts, I handed him the bag. He was already carrying my other shopping bags. I almost felt sorry for him. Almost.

We started the search for a dress and found three possibilities at the first shop we visited. Erin followed me to the dressing room and plopped down on a flat, round black leather chair to wait for me. She held my cup of tea in her hand and crossed her legs. "Go on. Dazzle me."

Shaking my head and smiling, I closed the door and stripped out of my skirt and top. The first dress was lovely, but it clung to the swell of my belly in a way I hadn't expected.

"Well?"

"No," I answered. "This one is definitely a no."

Standing there in front of the mirrors, I stared at my reflection. My hands glided over my belly and the subtle but noticeable curve to my stomach. With each passing week, it became more and more prominent. For the last five weeks, I had been secretly snapping photos of my ever-changing abdomen. I wasn't sure what I would do with all the photos when I reached the end of my pregnancy. I had almost twenty-eight weeks to think of something.

"Try the one-shoulder drapey-like dress," Erin suggested through the door.

I shrugged out of the curve hugging dress and into the one-shoulder number. It had a nice fit, but I wasn't sold on the asymmetrical top and the bared shoulder. The dress would have looked phenomenal on Lena. I snapped a quick photo and texted it to her.

V: Shopping with Erin. Tried this one on and thought of you. Want?

"Who are you texting?" Erin nosily asked. "I can hear you taking pictures in there. Are you spicing it up with Nikolai?"

"No," I answered with a laugh and shimmied out of the dress. I could just imagine the look on his face if he received a half-naked snapshot of me.

"Why not?" She had moved closer to the door and whispered conspiratorially through it. "Ivan goes crazy when I send him pics during the day. Like—holy shit. You can't even imagine what he's like when he gets home."

"Oh my God," I replied with shocked laughter. "Will you calm down? TMI, much?"

"I'm just saying—"

"No!"

"Fine."

Imagining her pout, I wiggled into the strapless dress. It was the simplest of the three I had taken into the fitting room. The high, contoured waist and the loose, fluttery skirt camouflaged my problem areas. With a smile on my face, I unlocked and opened the door and stepped out for Erin to give her opinion. "Well?"

Her mouth curved in a broad grin. "It's perfect! It's flirty and sexy but simple." She held up her phone. "Let's see how it photographs." She snapped a quick photo. "Turn sideways. Got it."

Uncrossing her legs, she stood up and walked toward me. Standing beside me, she peered at my reflection in the mirror. Her head tilted to the side. "You look different."

"Different? How?" I pretended I didn't know what she meant.

She shrugged and fluffed the ends of my hair so that they curled around my bare shoulders. "Brighter? Warmer? I don't know. It's hard to explain." Her smile turned mischievous. She gestured to the swell of cleavage the structure of the dress emphasized. "And look at these!"

"What about them?" I self-consciously tugged up the front of the dress, but Erin clicked her teeth and tugged it right back down.

"They're magnificent." She grinned impishly. "I think it's good that you're filling out a little. You're not running as much so it's probably hard for you to burn off all that caviar and those ridiculously delicious, calorie heavy desserts you're eating during Sunday dinner at Samovar."

"Something like that," I agreed.

My phone started to ring, and Erin stepped into the dressing room to pick it up. A photo of Lena and Yuri from their recent trip to Disney World lit up the

screen. The pair were wearing mouse ears and ham-
ming it up for the camera. Erin swiped her finger
across the screen and answered. "Erin Markovic, fash-
ionista, party planner and accountant extraordinaire
speaking. How may I direct your call?"

Smiling at Erin's silliness, I studied my reflection
and decided I would need to pair the dress with pretty
jewelry. I had a pair of heels in my closet that would
look nice. Knowing Erin, she would try to pressure me
into the closest shoe department regardless.

"No, no, I got her into a black dress. It's gorgeous.
No. Strapless. Mmmhmm." Erin picked up the one-
shouldered dress. "No, this store runs true to size. This
one fits Vivi so it's Thumbelina tiny, but I saw a size
eight and a size ten on the rack. I can grab either one
for you. The ten? Okay. Yeah. Here she is."

I accepted my phone from Erin who whisked away
the one-shouldered dress and gestured toward the front
of the store. I nodded at her and slipped back into the
fitting room to change back into my skirt and top.
"Hey, Lena! How is Austin?"

"Hot," she replied matter-of-factly. "But the hotel is
nice and the offices we're working out of are in an interesting area. This new fracking client Ty recently
acquired is in all sorts of trouble. I had hoped this
would be a one day deal, but I'm going to be lucky to
get out of here by Sunday afternoon."

I winced in sympathy. "That sounds stressful."

"I keep reminding myself that it's better to be
stressed and busy than sitting around in our Houston
offices without new clients or work. Hang on a second."

A chair squeaked and high heels tapped against wooden floors. A door whined as it closed. "Speaking of clients," she said, "I was going to touch base with you tomorrow, but I had a weird phone call this morning. I think it's something we should discuss now."

"Oh?" I put the dress back on its hanger.

"Are you alone?"

"Yes. Why?"

Lena hesitated, and my stomach knotted with anxiety. She never hesitated. Ever. "Look, I know we've talked a little bit about the...complications...of your personal life. You know I've done everything I can to make sure that you aren't bombarded with questions about your dad, your juvie history or Nikolai."

"I know you've tried," I assured her. "And I've accepted that some parts of my history were going to be too juicy for journalists to ignore."

"Which is exactly why I was up front about some of the bigger, juicier parts to shield more sensitive aspects." She didn't have to elaborate on what those sensitive aspects might be. She meant Nikolai and his rumored *bratva* connections. "I've been upfront about your dad's, you know, shenanigans and his fugitive status, but this is different. I don't want to cause problems between you and your husband—"

I stopped dressing and pressed the phone against my ear. My heart fluttered in my chest. "Lena, whatever it is, just say it."

"Last week, I had a question from a journalist about a woman named Tatiana Filiopova."

My breath caught in my throat.

"Her name sounded familiar so I checked the invite request sheet. There's a Tatiana *Melnikova* on the list twice. I thought the reporter had gotten the name wrong until I spoke with Yuri last night. I had to pry it out of him, but he finally told me that Tatiana Filipova was Nikolai's fiancée. He told me that she disappeared eight years ago and that everyone assumed she was dead."

Lena seemed to be holding her breath. "But I think that's a lie. I think Tatiana Filipova and Tatiana Melnikoa are the same woman. I think she just ran away from Houston, changed her name and started a new career in Hong Kong. That's where I tracked Tatiana Melnikova to," she clarified. "She's in finance there."

"Lena, please be careful with this." I wasn't going to insult her intelligence by insisting she was wrong. "There's a lot of sticky history here. I don't know all the minute details, but Nikolai was very clear that Tatiana is dead to him. He wants nothing to do with her, and she's not supposed to have anything to do with him."

"I understand," she assured me. "Frankly, this isn't even the worst or craziest client secret I've had to keep quiet. I hesitated to bring all this up, but I didn't want you to be blindsided by some crazy lady barging into your show claiming to be Nikolai's old flame, you know?"

"Do you think that's what she plans to do? Show up at the gallery, I mean."

"I don't know. She submitted a request for an invite through me *and* Niels, but neither of us gave her one. She has no art connections or press credentials so she wasn't a priority approval. She's on the blacklist now." Lena exhaled noisily. "Vivian, it sounds like she has unfinished business with your husband. Yuri was tight-lipped about their history, and it made me nervous. I got the feeling there's more to that story than he wants me—or you—to know."

A knock echoed in the background on her end of the call. A moment later I heard the voice of her business partner, Ty Weston, drifting over the line. "Hey, sugar, we need to get moving if we're going to make it out to that location. And, honey, I hope you brought those sneakers I recommended. Those Manolos weren't made for a seventy-six stage frack job."

"They're Mary Katrantzous, and I don't plan to get out of the car."

"Really? They're not Manolos? They're gorgeous. Are they comfortable? Because I think Cait would look cute in a pair, but you know how she is about her feet."

"Ty, can we talk about my shoes and your sister's feet later? I'm sort of on a call here."

"Oh! Right! Sorry. I'll wait for you in the lobby."

"Vivi? You still there?"

"Yes." I adjusted the waistband of my skirt and fluffed the bottom of my blouse.

"Sorry about that. Look, there's something else you need to know."

"Okay," I nervously replied at her ominous tone.

"That journalist who first contacted me about Tatiana called me back this morning. He had some very pointed questions about her, Nikolai and some guy named Evgeni Zhukov. This guy is not a reporter that follows the arts and society scene, Vivi. He's into hard news, financial stuff. I think he's going to dig, and I'm worried you might not like what he finds."

Refusing to be cowed by a nosy reporter, I mentally shrugged. "I'm not worried. There's nothing for him to find."

"Are you sure?"

No, I thought even as I staunchly replied, "Yes."

"Positive?"

"Yes." I wasn't. I had no freaking idea what this journalist wanted or how complicated the history was between Nikolai and Tatiana. The addition of a third person to the mix made me extremely nervous. What, exactly, was Nikolai hiding?

"Well, if you need my help, you call me, Vivian. I'll do whatever I can to protect you."

"I know you will," I said softly. "You're the best almost-sister a girl could ask for, Lena."

"Butter me up all you want, but I'm still charging you for my services," she teased with a laugh. "All right. I'll see you on Sunday."

"Be safe at that frack site."

"I will."

We ended our call, and I dropped my phone back into my purse. I didn't want to dwell on the what-ifs and maybes. I wanted to enjoy my day with Erin. Everything else could wait.

"I found the size Lena wanted," Erin said when I emerged from the dressing room. "Do you want to look at anything else in the store?"

I shook my head. "I'm good."

"Then let's check out and go find some lunch."

"Sure. Any ideas where you'd like to go?" I walked beside her toward the cashier.

She glanced at her watch and made a face. "Well, every place in town is going to be packed, but that new last name of yours should get us a table anywhere we'd like."

"Maybe." I wasn't comfortable pulling the "Do You Know Who I Am?" card just to hop a line.

"What about Quattro?"

"At the Four Seasons? Their dinner service is nice, especially in the private rooms," I added, thinking of the delicious meal I had shared with Nikolai in the exclusive wine cellar dining room.

She stepped up to the cashier and handed over Lena's dress. "Ivan and I had lunch there a couple of times when we were planning the wedding. We really enjoyed it."

With our bags in hand, we headed for the store's entrance where Ten patiently waited for us. "Where to next, ladies?"

"We thought we'd have lunch."

"Okay." He gestured for us to walk in front of him. "Where am I taking you?"

"The Four Seasons," Erin answered over her shoulder. "Do you remember how to get there? Or do I need to teach you how to use GPS?"

Ten narrowed his eyes at her. "I was inside for six years, not sixty." His gaze flicked toward me. "Are you sure you want to go downtown? Traffic and parking will be a nightmare."

"Traffic is a nightmare everywhere during lunch," Erin countered. "Besides you can just valet. I'm sure your boss will reimburse you."

"That's not the problem," he grumbled in Russian.

I started to ask him what the problem was, but he suddenly clamped one of his massive hands on my shoulders. He gently but forcefully steered me to the left before reaching out and putting his hand between Erin's shoulders to make sure she followed. His hand returned to my shoulder, and he stepped to my side as if to shield me.

I leaned back and caught sight of four guys, Latinos close to my age with the Hermanos gang tat emblazoned on their necks, standing off to the left. As far as I knew, the street gang was still relatively tight with Nikolai's crews, but Ten clearly didn't want me getting close to them. He glared at the four men with a terrifying scowl that he had obviously perfected during his six years on the prison yard. The leader of the men inclined his head in a respectful way before retreating to a different part of the mall with his friends.

With an ever-vigilant Ten at my side, I finally acknowledged the niggling suspicion that had been troubling me for weeks. Alliances were shifting. The city was changing, and I had never been more afraid.

11 CHAPTER ELEVEN

"Hey, I'm going to powder my nose," Erin quietly announced when we reached the restaurant. "Get us a table?"

"Sure." I turned to the side to avoid being whacked by a tall and impeccably dressed man carrying a briefcase. The downtown finance and energy crowd seemed to have descended upon the restaurant for their popular lunch service. Ten's suggestion that we go elsewhere seemed terribly prescient now.

My shadow stood a few feet behind me. I glanced back at him and instantly noticed his tense posture. A pang of guilt struck me. Ten's time on the inside probably made loud, noisy places like this difficult to handle. His hard-edged gaze jumped around the busy, bustling room. No doubt he saw potential threats in every face.

The hostess smiled at me. "How many in your party?"

"Three," I said, stepping up to her station.

"The wait time is forty-five minutes to an hour," she replied with an apologetic expression. "I'd offer to seat you at the bar until a table opens but..."

"That's fine. We'll wait." I moved away from the hostess and lifted on tiptoes to see if I could spot Erin. I turned toward Ten. "I'm going to find Erin. I'll be back in a few minutes."

He took a step forward, almost as if he intended to follow me to the restroom, and then stopped. With a stiff nod, he gave his consent. Lowering his head, he warned in Russian, "You go to the bathroom and you come right back here. If you aren't back in five minutes—"

"Yeah, yeah, yeah," I replied with a roll of my eyes. "You'll come find me."

"Vivian." The gruff way he spoke my name got my attention.

Placing a hand on his arm, I made sure he could see my face. "I'll be careful."

Hiking my purse straps a bit higher on my shoulder, I left Ten. As I weaved in and out of the crowd, I scanned the busy floor for a glimpse of Erin. Quite unexpectedly, a familiar waiter stepped into my path and grinned at me. "Mrs. Kalasnikov! How nice to see you again! Are you looking for your husband?"

"Nikolai?" The question surprised me. I finally placed the familiar face of the waiter. He had been our server the night Nikolai had brought me here. "Is he having lunch here?"

"Yes, he's in the cellar. They were just seated. I can take you to see him."

I wasn't sure whether it was a good idea to interrupt a business meeting. I doubted that he would bring a business contact of the illegal sort to such a public place so the risk of meeting someone or overhearing something I shouldn't was low. Certain he wouldn't mind if I popped in to say hello, I smiled at the waiter and glanced at his nametag. "Would you mind, Rob?"

"Not at all, ma'am." He gestured toward the wine room. "This way."

We shared some friendly chit-chat as he led me across the main floor to the tucked away wine room and the private dining area hidden away there. When we neared the entrance, he smiled at me and gestured for me to go ahead before pivoting on his heel and heading back to the floor to serve his guests. I walked toward the doorway but stopped abruptly at the sound of a woman's sultry voice and Nikolai's laughter.

With hand on the wall to steady myself, I gripped the straps of my purse in the other and listened intently to the familiar tenor of Nikolai's voice. The string of Russian that left his mouth sounded unhurried and easy, his comfort with the unknown woman evident in the gentle way he spoke with her.

"So when do I get to meet your wife?" she asked, her Russian as languid and soft as his.

Nikolai issued an amused snort. "Never."

Feminine laughter filled the air. "I never took you for the type to marry a jealous woman."

"That's not—it's complicated, Tanya."

Tanya? My stomach dropped. *Tatiana.* He was having a secret lunch with Tatiana, the woman he had sworn he hadn't seen in years and wouldn't ever see again. So much for being dead to him!

"Does she know?"

"About us?" he asked. "Yes, I told her."

"You told her everything?"

My head throbbed with every pulse of my heart-beat. I held my breath and waited for his answer.

"No," he conceded. "Not everything."

"You didn't tell her about the baby." It was a statement. Not a question.

Baby? What baby?

"No," he answered quickly. "She doesn't need to know about any of that. It will open up too may old wounds—for everyone."

"Far be it from me to tell you how to run your marriage—"

"Then don't," Nikolai replied, a warning edge to his voice. "I didn't come here for marriage advice."

"Why did you come?"

"Don't play coy, Tanya. You know why I'm here."

"Then why are we wasting time with lunch? Surely our business is better conducted upstairs in my suite." The teasing, flirtatious tone to her voice clawed at my heart.

"Because this little stunt of yours dragged me out of bed before I had my breakfast and the striped bass here is one of the best in town," he replied matter-of-factly. "Our business can wait..."

He didn't mean...? He wouldn't. He simply wouldn't.

Except...

He was here with her now, wasn't he? What was to stop him from going upstairs with her?

He loves me. It's me. It's only ever been me. I'm his sun.

"For dessert," he added almost playfully. "In the suite."

An ice-cold current raced through my body. My brain couldn't process what my ears had just heard. I didn't know what to do. My courage fled in that moment. All I wanted to do was run. I wanted to get the hell out of here.

Stomach swirling, heart racing and mouth dry, I retreated from the private dining room with the smallest, quietest footsteps possible. The soft soles of my ballet flats made not even a whisper of noise as I backed down the hall. Clutching my purse and fighting the nausea that overwhelmed me, I emerged into the main dining room—and slammed right into Ten's brawny chest.

Two massive hands carefully clasped my shoulders. Ten peered down at me with concern. "Are you okay? Erin said she didn't see you. I was worried."

Still in shock and feeling sick, I sputtered a lie. "I...I...got lost." I sucked in a harsh breath. "I got lost."

"Vivian," Ten said forcefully. "Are you okay? You look pale."

"It's the noise and the smells." I had already lied to him once so the next one came so easily. "Can we go?"

"Yes. Of course." He placed his hand against my upper back and guided me toward the front of the restaurant where Erin was tapping her foot and anxiously scanning for me.

When she spotted us, her brow furrowed. "What's wrong?"

"She's not feeling well. I think she's been pushing herself too hard for the show and the trip to London." Like a true bodyguard, he shielded me both physically and emotionally. He didn't need me to tell him the truth. He could tell I had been badly rattled by something and needed protecting.

Embracing her inner mother, Erin clucked her teeth and sidled close to me. "Why don't we get you home, okay? We have a dozen chances for lunch or dinner while we're in London next week, right?"

"Right," I answered with a slight nod. The shock of overhearing Nikolai and Tatiana and the uncertainty of what, exactly, I had overheard rendered me nearly mute. I let Erin guide me toward the elevators and out of the hotel. Like a robot, I participated in the conversation swirling around me on the ride back to the house. Somehow I managed to keep my answers from sounding mechanic and cold. Somehow I managed not to break down.

After a warm, lingering hug from Erin and a promise to call her if I needed anything, I sat in the front passenger seat and watched Ten walk her inside the Tanglewood mansion she shared with Ivan. Ten returned quickly and slid behind the wheel. He shot me a concerned look as he followed the horseshoe driveway to the street. "Vivian, are you all right? Do I need to take you to the hospital?"

"No, I'm fine. It's nothing like that."

"You're sure?" He glanced at my stomach. "The baby?"

"Is fine," I assured him. "The baby is just fine."

Ten wasn't convinced. When we reached the first stop sign, he expelled a rough breath. "Do you want me to call the boss? He'll come home if you need him."

"No!" The word came out too harshly. Softening my voice, I repeated myself. "No. I'm fine. We don't—I don't want to bother him."

Scowling, Ten shook his head. "What happened back there? You look like you saw a ghost."

"I didn't see anything. I just got lost and then I didn't feel well." He had no idea how close he had come to hitting the mark, but I didn't want to say anything until I could ascertain how much he knew about Nikolai's schedule today. Stomach wobbling dangerously, I projected calmness and asked, "Where is Nikolai today?"

He shrugged nonchalantly. "Samovar, I expect. If he's not at the restaurant, he's taking meetings around town." His gaze skipped from the road to me. "I can get him for you. It won't be a problem. One phone call—and he'll come for you."

The sincerity on Ten's face convinced me. He knew nothing of the secret meeting. There was no way he would have let us go to the Four Seasons for lunch if he had known there was even the slightest chance we could have a run-in with Nikolai and Tatiana.

That left me wondering what he knew of Tatiana. But how the hell was I supposed to ask a question like that without rousing too much suspicion?

Thinking of Lena's phone call, I had a better idea of how to do it. "Ten?"

"Yeah?"

"You know my friend Lena?"

"The one who dates Yuri? I don't know her, but I know who she is. Why?"

"She called me earlier and said that there were some reporters poking around and asking questions."

His jaw hardened, and his eyes glinted fiercely when his gaze shifted toward me. "What types of questions?"

"They wanted to know about our ties to different people."

"Like?"

Glad he had taken the bait, I said, "Well, there were two names. One was Evgeni Zhukov."

"Ev?" He used the nickname with enough familiarity and a ghost of a smile that I assumed they were more than mere acquaintances. "He's from the old country." Ten grinned at the joke he had made. "We grew up together. Me, Ev, Artyom, Ilya," he clarified. "Three of us went bad but not Ev. His mama made sure that he went to university. He went off to London and made a fortune in finance. Now he's like Yuri."

"So why would a reporter be asking about him?"

"He's Russian. He's rich. Nikolai is connected to lots of rich Russians."

"And is he connected to Evgeni?"

Ten kept his gaze fixed forward. "That's not a question for me to answer."

I huffed and leaned back in my seat. Deciding it was now or never, I asked, "What about Tatiana Melnikova?"

He shrugged. "I don't know that name."

"Lena said that she thinks she might have gone by a different name when she lived in Houston a while ago. She was Tatiana Filipova then."

The only clue that he recognized her name was the clench of his hands on the steering wheel. "What about her?"

"Are we really going to sit here and play this game?"

He didn't look at me. "Whatever you know about her is what you're supposed to know about her. You won't get anything else out of me."

His reply frustrated me, but I didn't push. It wasn't fair of me to put him in this position. His loyalties to Nikolai trumped his loyalties to me. That much was clear. I couldn't be angry or upset with him for that. I could only imagine what the two men had been through together.

"Listen," Ten said in a surprisingly gentle voice. "Tatiana was the past. She's dead. I was with Kostya when he found her body. No one could have survived that car wreck. No one." His hand cut through the air like a knife. "This Tatiana Melnikova woman? She's not Tanya Filipova. It's impossible. So there's nothing that you or a reporter need to worry about, okay?"

I nodded in silent reply and turned to look out the window. The fact that Ten believed Tatiana was dead and that she couldn't possibly be alive or living under a different name left me with even more questions. Knowing Kostya's reputation, he could have manufactured a fake death for her. Having Ten with him to discover the body would have given the lie a strong foundation.

But if Nikolai had gone to all that trouble to help her disappear, why was she back now? If she had been in trouble, there were easier ways to contact him than flying halfway around the world to see him in person. No, if she had come here, she wanted something important.

Why had he agreed to meet her? Why were they having lunch? In a hotel? I recalled the conversation I had overheard. They hadn't sound like two people who disliked each other. They had sounded friendly, *too* friendly.

My stomach threatened to revolt at any minute. I breathed slowly and calmly and kept a tight handle on my seat belt strap. Images of Nikolai alone with Tatiana tormented me. I didn't know what she looked like so my mind created a vision of her from the clues I had. I thought of the Russian-born women who often frequented Samovar to create a picture of a woman who was tall, blonde and beautiful with a keen eye for fashion.

What were they doing right now? Were they still tucked away in that cozy, quiet dining area of the wine cellar or was it even worse? Had they gone up to her suite? I brought a hand to my mouth and closed my eyes as my stomach churned violently.

Ten reacted before I even knew that I was about to be sick. We had just crossed the 610 Loop and were barreling down busy San Felipe Street. He crushed the brake beneath his boot, signaled for a right turn and whipped into the parking lot of the Starbucks. He pulled into a corner spot and reached over to unbuckle my belt. I scrambled from the SUV and barely made it to the grass. Ten was there a moment later, his strong arms bracing me as I heaved pitifully.

When I was done, I sagged against him. He got me out of the sweltering, suffocating heat and back into our idling vehicle. I sat there like a child while he retrieved a travel-sized package of wipes from the glove box. He carefully cleaned my hands and face and then offered me a stick of cinnamon-flavored gum. Touching my shoulder, he captured my gaze. "Stay here. Lock the door. I'll be right back."

He waited outside the closed door until he heard it lock before hurrying across the parking lot. Embarrassed but grateful for my complicated, grouchy bodyguard, I began to understand what Ivan had been trying to tell me about Ten. The former enforcer had done *terrible* things, but he had a softness inside him that was proving to be exactly what I needed.

When Ten returned, he had a plain iced tea and a chocolate smoothie for me. "Drink this. All of it," he ordered. "If you keep getting sick like this, I'm calling the boss and taking you to the hospital."

It wasn't a threat or a warning. True concern radiated off of him in waves. I accepted the smoothie from him and put the iced tea in the cup holder. "I'll be fine. It's just morning sickness."

He didn't believe me. As he buckled his belt, he grumbled, "One of these days you'll learn to trust me."

"One of these days," I murmured. "Yes."

We drove home in silence, and I went straight for the library while he carried my bags upstairs. I started to close the door but stopped. The last thing I wanted was another argument with him. I walked to the desk I had set up as my work station and opened my laptop. After logging in, I went straight to my internet browser and hit up Google. Unable to help myself, I typed in Tatiana's assumed name and hit enter.

The results appeared in a flash. I scanned the page and felt my heart sinking. There, in full color, in glossy image after glossy image was the stunningly gorgeous blonde who had once been engaged to Nikolai. Her perfectly styled hair and artfully applied makeup complemented an extraordinary body with killer curves. She projected such confidence in her photographs. The Hong Kong skyline visible through the glass wall of her office gave off the impression of power and success. There was no doubt that she was the financial prodigy all of these articles claimed her to be.

Glancing over her resume, I slumped in the chair. She was perfect—on paper and in pictures. She might be living under a new identity, but I could tell Kostya had allowed her to keep her educational history when he built her new life. I understood now why Maksim had tried to force a marriage of convenience between Nikolai and Tatiana. Who wouldn't want a daughter-in-law like that?

From a purely financial standpoint, she would have been absolutely perfect. Even now, living halfway around the world under an assumed identity, she was a much better match for him. She possessed exactly the sort of connection a man like Nikolai needed. With her brains and skills and her international network of contacts, she would have been a huge help to him when it came to the shadier side of his life.

In short, Tatiana was everything I could never be. I was just a flighty artist with a dead mother and a fugitive ex-con father who was probably going to tip off the cartel version of World War III, if the newspaper articles I read every morning were to be believed. I was a heavy weight on Nikolai's shoulders and a burden I feared he was starting to regret taking on.

"You forgot this one." Ten entered the library with my iced tea. I closed the window as inconspicuously as possible and took the tea from his hand when he reached the desk. "Do you think you can eat? Maybe some soup and crackers?"

Wanting to be anywhere but the library where I would be tempted to keep digging into Tatiana's life, I stood up slowly. "I'll go make some toast."

"No. I'll make it. Go get comfortable in the living room or the media room. I'll find you."

"I don't need—"

"Go." He pointed to the doorway. "You need to rest."

I started to roll my eyes at his alpha caveman routine but then it occurred to me that this was his way of making sure I was okay. This was his way of taking care of me. He had promised to do this one job, and he clearly had every intention of doing it.

"I'll be in the media room."

"I'll bring your lunch. Take these." He handed me the rest of the smoothie and the cold tea. "Drink them."

I wandered into the media room and got comfy on the sectional in there. I was still trying to decide on a movie when Ten walked in with a large tray. He set it on the big square ottoman that doubled as a coffee table. One glance told me that the peanut butter toast, banana and glass of milk were for me while that stack of outrageously thick sandwiches, the bag of chips and the sodas were his.

"How can you eat like that and still have muscles like those?" I picked up my plate of toast and fruit and settled back into the corner I had chosen.

"I work out." He popped the tab on a can of soda. "A lot."

"Because?"

"It's good for me." He took a sip and stared at the television screen. "It helps me stay out of trouble. I feel...calmer."

"That's good, right?"

Ten nodded. "Now? Yes. Before, when I was on the street, it was better for me to be angry all the time. Hot-headed," he added. "It was useful. Now? Now I need to be calm. I need to simmer instead of boil."

I chewed a bite of my crisp toast and washed down the peanut butter and bread with some cold milk. Thinking of his reputation and the way he had described himself, I admitted, "I don't think I would have liked you very much back then."

Ten snorted and crunched chips between his teeth. "You don't like me very much now."

"That's not true."

"Isn't it?"

"You're growing on me."

Ten smiled, and I understood why he had such a reputation with women. He had perfected that flirtatious smile that hinted at danger and something more primal. "You're only saying that because I went shopping with you and carried your bags from one end of the Galleria to the other."

"Don't forget holding my hair while I tossed my cookies in a Starbucks parking lot," I added with an embarrassed blush.

He chuckled. "No, I don't think I'll be forgetting that anytime soon. It sure as hell wasn't in the job description. I'll be asking Nikolai for hazard pay tonight."

The mention of Nikolai dashed my spirits, but I managed to keep a smile in place for Ten. We settled on a sci-fi film and its sequel and lapsed into a comfortable silence. My mind strayed from the juicy plot of the movie. What was Nikolai doing right now? Was he still with her? Were they...?

I couldn't even bring myself to think the words. Hugging my waist, I stared at the screen and tried to lose myself in the films. The carbohydrate heavy lunch plus the smoothie and the normal exhaustion of pregnancy hit me hard as we were starting the second film. Not even the explosions and slick graphics could maintain my interest. My eyelids drifted together, and I surrendered to the heavy pull of sleep.

"Vee?" Fingertips trailed down my cheek. "*Zolota.*"

Inhaling deeply, I blinked rapidly and came awake to the sight of Nikolai crouched down beside me. He wore a tender expression and gently stroked my face. "How are you feeling?"

His simple question caused a rush of emotions that left me feeling twisted and angry inside. Batting away his hand, I struggled to sit up on my own. "Where is Ten?"

Nikolai frowned and sat back on his heels. "He stayed here with you until I came home. He's gone, but I can get him back if you needed something."

"I'm fine."

"Are you?" He tilted his head as if to study me. "You don't look well."

"I'm fine." I repeated the words tersely and finally found the strength to shove off the sectional.

"No, you're not." Crouched in front of me again, he clasped my shoulders and peered at my face. "You look terrible."

"Gee, thanks." I pushed away his hands and struggled to my feet.

"Stop." He clutched at my waist but I was faster and got away from him. "Vee! Wait. What's wrong?"

"Nothing." *Everything.* My chest ached, and my stomach swirled. I didn't want to do this right now. I didn't want to hear him say what I feared most. Would he even tell me the truth?

"*Solnyshka.*" He caught up with me at the door. His hand settled on my hip and he expertly spun me around until my back was against the wall. One hand cupped my face, and his thumb glided along my skin. The scent of his cologne and soap filled my nose. It was a smell that usually made my heart race and caused such primitive, lustful urges. Right now, I inhaled the smell but for all the wrong reasons. I wasn't try to breathe him in. No, I was searching for a hint of *her.*

"Vee," he whispered. "What's wrong?"

My head cleared, and I took a good, long look at him. The color of his tie and shirt caught my attention. Last night, when I had come to bed after him, I had seen the suit, tie and shirt he had selected for today hanging in the closet. He had chosen a grey suit, white shirt, and a navy tie with pale blue diagonal stripes.

But he was wearing the steel blue tie with the delicate silver circle pattern that he kept in the office at Samovar with his backup white shirt.

"What happened to your other shirt and tie?"

His hand dropped from my face, and he glanced down at his chest. "There was a spill at the restaurant."

"At Samovar?" I couldn't help the suspicious tone that invaded my voice.

He nodded. "Lidia didn't see me coming across the floor. You know how clumsy she can be."

It was the perfect cover story. I had been there the night Lidia had *accidentally* spilled a glass of red wine all over Bianca. Maybe he was telling the truth. Maybe it really had happened that way.

Or maybe he had dumped the shirt and tie because they were saturated in her perfume or stained with her lipstick.

"Did you get everything you needed at the mall?" He tucked stray strands of my hair behind my ear. Had he done the same thing for Tatiana? Had the hands that I loved so much touched her intimately? Lovingly?

"Yes." My voice was soft and small. It was all I could do to stand there and not break down in front of him. I wasn't sure where the strength that welled inside me came from but I embraced it. I wasn't going to cry. Not now. "And you? How was your day?"

He shrugged. "It was the same as every other day. Business as usual."

There wasn't a trace of anything suspicious on his face. If I hadn't overheard him with Tatiana today, I never would have even suspected anything was wrong. The wrongness of this whole fucking mess hit me like a punch to the gut.

Nikolai, my husband and the only man I had ever loved, was standing in front of me, had me pressed between a wall and his hard, hot body while his possessive hands cupped and caressed my skin—and he was lying to me. He was lying right through his teeth.

The realization that I had been so easily fooled by him took me out at the knees. My entire world started to tilt, and only his arms kept me from hitting the ground. I crumpled against him. The feel of his powerful arms scooping me up was a sensation I loved and hated in the same moment. Unbidden images of Nikolai, *my* Nikolai, sweeping up Tatiana and tossing her on a messy hotel bed flashed in front of me.

Not mine, I glumly acknowledged. Maybe he was never mine. She had a claim on him first, didn't she? In reality, I was the interloper.

"You need to rest," Nikolai urged as he carried me upstairs and into our bedroom. "Pregnancy, stress and the heat aren't a good mix for you."

I bit back a bitter laugh. *Stress? The stress you're causing me, you mean?*

But I didn't say the words. I wasn't brave enough, and I was tired. I was so damn tired.

He tugged back the comforter and top sheet with one hand and placed me onto my side of the bed. I didn't move and avoided looking at his face as he removed all of my clothing. He ducked into the closet and returned with one of my loose cotton nightgowns. Once I was clothed again, he pressed me back to the bed and covered me with the sheet.

His hip touched mine as he stroked my face. "Are you hungry? Would you like me to bring you dinner?"

The thought of eating made my stomach clench. "No. I just...I want to sleep."

His face tight with worry, Nikolai studied me for a long, unnerving moment. Finally, he leaned forward and kissed my forehead. His lips lingered on my skin, and he caressed my cheek. "Goodnight."

"Goodnight."

He sat there for a few seconds, and I wondered if he was trying to work up the courage to tell me the truth about where he had been today and about Tatiana. My heartbeat ticked up a few notches as I waited and wondered, but in the end, he simply stood up and left the bedroom.

Curled on my side, I tugged the sheet over my head. I tried to stop the hot tears that erupted from the corners of my eyes, but it was impossible. There was no stopping them. Betrayed and heartbroken, I cried quietly in the darkness as one question rattled round and round in my head.

What else wasn't he telling me?

12 Chapter Twelve

Nikolai didn't come clean with me the next day or the next. We were leaving for London tomorrow evening, and I didn't know how much more of the lies I could take. He wasn't around the house very much because he was so busy trying to get everything situated before we left on our short holiday. I wasn't sure if that was a good or bad thing.

After the shock had worn off, I wanted to confront him, but he had to be present for that to happen. Some part of me still believed there was an innocent explanation for Tatiana's return to Houston and the lunch date I had stumbled across. It was the silly, naïve part of me that desperately wanted everything to be smoothed over easily. It was the side of me that was going to be slain and broken, left bleeding on the floor and writhing in agony when the ugly, painful truth finally came spilling out of Nikolai's mouth.

"Miss Vivian?" Roman Boychenko popped his head into the sunroom-slash-studio. Not long out of high school, he still had a sweetness about him that the other men who ran with Nikolai had long ago lost.

"Yes?" I swirled one of my brushes in the small pool of mineral spirits in the Mason jar near the sink that had been installed in my home studio. The scent of paint thinner had been too much for me to handle in the earliest days of my pregnancy so I had switched to the less smelly but more expensive spirits for cleanup.

"You have a visitor."

"You can send them back here." I watched the thin streaks of brick red pigment blossom in the jar. "I'm cleaning brushes."

"I don't think he wants to come back here." Boychenko took a step into the room. "I can do that for you. I remember the steps you taught me." As if ticking them off for a test, he said, "First I use news-paper to squeeze the excess paint off the bristles. I swish them in the paint thinner and then I use the newspaper again. Then I use that pink bottle of soap. I squirt it into the palm of my hand and clean the bris-tles until the foam is white."

Satisfied that Boychenko wouldn't damage himself or the brushes, I nodded and invited him closer with a wave of my hand. "You don't mind?"

"No, ma'am." I had asked him a dozen times not to use ma'am with me, but his manners simply wouldn't allow it. There were less than four years between us, but I was his boss's wife and that meant something to him.

"Okay." I handed him the brush I had been rinsing and a piece of newspaper before untying my smock and hanging it on the closest peg. It occurred to me that I hadn't even asked who was at the door. "Who came to see me?"

"The detective," he said glumly. "Your cousin."

Shit. The thought of Ten and Eric alone together scared me. I practically ran across the house toward the front door where I found the two facing off in the foyer. The way they stood across from each other, glaring viciously with their shoulders squared, reminded me of the fights I had watched at the meatpacking warehouse. It was like watching Sergei facing off with Kelly Connolly all over again.

"Eric!" I said a bit too brightly.

He broke his standoff with Ten to smile at me. "Vivi." Glancing back at my bodyguard, he said, "I'm just waiting for your new gorilla to frisk me for weapons."

"Don't be ridiculous. He's not going to frisk you for a weapon!" Even as I denied that would ever happen in the entryway of my home, I had the distinct feeling Ten had been preparing to do just that.

"It's not his guns that worry me. It's the wires," Ten grumbled in Russian, his voice so low I barely made out the words.

I shot him a pleading look, silently begging him to behave, and turned my attention to Eric. "You should have called me. We could have made plans for dinner."

"I didn't want to give you a chance to blow me off."

I poked his chest. "I wouldn't have done that."

"No, you wouldn't." His gaze slid to Ten as if it to wordlessly say, "But he would."

Opening his arms, Eric beckoned me closer. My cousin, one of Houston's toughest detectives, embraced me warmly and tightly. We hadn't always been close, and we didn't always see eye-to-eye, but we cared about each other. For the longest time, he had been the only blood family connection in my life. Now my father was sort of in the picture again, but it was Eric who had been there for me in the worst and most difficult times.

But he and Nikolai had bad blood between them that went back years and years. Neither had ever told me the source, but it wasn't hard to fill in those blanks. Though Nikolai's links to organized crime in Houston had never been proven, Eric wasn't stupid. He knew exactly who yanked the invisible chains attached to every member of the local *bratva*.

"I've missed you, Eric." My words were muffled by his chest. The hard plank of his cleverly concealed bulletproof vest was probably the only thing that kept him from feeling the swell of my pregnant belly. The loose T-shirt with the Eiffel Tower graphic on the front and the too-big plaid shirt with the arms rolled up to my elbows helped.

"I've missed you, too, kiddo." He pressed a quick kiss to my temple. "I'll try harder to keep in touch."

We both knew that he wouldn't but neither of us said a word. My marriage to Nikolai complicated things so badly. Even coming to the house to see me now put him in such an awkward position professionally.

"We should set up a standing lunch date or something," I suggested, hoping that if we were meeting away from the house it wouldn't be such a big deal.

Before Eric could answer, Ten growled at me in Russian. "That's not happening."

Glancing back at him, I frowned and replied in the same language. "Why not?"

"Are you serious?" Ten looked at me as if I might be going soft in the head. "He's a fucking police officer. You're the wife of a boss. Why don't I just paint a big red target on your back, huh? It will make it easier for the cartel snipers to pick you and your cousin off like Coke cans on a fence."

Cartel snipers? Were the problems in Mexico finally crossing the border? Was Houston safe anymore? "Do you always have to be so negative?"

"It's my job to be negative."

"What's wrong now?" Eric warily eyed Ten.

"Nothing," I lied in English and tried to lead him out of the entryway. "Let's go to the kitchen and have some iced tea or lemonade. It's pink. I made it this morning."

Eric resisted my attempts to tug him along after me. Toe to toe with Ten, he asked, "Do you have a problem with me having lunch with my cousin? Because if you do, you should take it up with me and stop bullying her."

"You think I'm bullying her?" Frustration deepened Ten's voice. "I'm trying to keep her safe."

"I'm a cop. I don't need a con riding shotgun to a lunch date to keep my cousin safe."

"Ex-con," Ten testily countered. "I did my fucking time."

"Not enough if you ask me," Eric snarled. "I saw the crime scene photos. I know what happened that night you knocked off that convenience store. Six years for that? Four years of probation? A fine? It's a goddamned joke."

Fists clenched, Ten took a menacing step forward. "You don't know shit about what happened that night."

"I know plenty about you, Anton." Eric stepped into Ten and daringly invaded the other man's personal space. After six years on the inside, Ten was understandably peculiar when it came to his personal space. Eric's behavior was a blatant provocation. "I know exactly what sort of fucking lowlife scum Nikolai has hired to guard my cousin."

The scum remark was too much for Ten. He raised a clenched fist, and I reacted without thinking, throwing myself between the two men. "No!"

Eric shoved me out of the way at the last possible moment, and Ten threw his weight to the side, slamming his hand into the entryway lamp instead. Glass and ceramic shards exploded everywhere. Eric pushed me behind him, knocking me into the wall on accident, and jumped on Ten. I lost my balance and crumpled to the floor.

Scrambling backward like a crab, I managed to narrowly escape being kicked by one of them. I couldn't tell who the foot belonged to as I scurried out of the way. The demi-lune table crashed to the floor, taking the photographs and the vase of flowers with it. Water splashed onto the walls. Glass and metal crunched beneath boots.

In a flash of movement, Boychenko suddenly appeared. He hauled me up off the floor and swung me out of the way. He carefully deposited me in the living room before rushing out to break up the fight. The shouting and cursing intensified but the physical blows had stopped.

Hands shaking and legs wobbly, I emerged from the living room to find Eric leaning against the front door. He had a swollen cheek and busted lip and roughly wiped blood off his chin. Ten was slumped against the wall and dabbed at his nose. A red trickle made its way down his neck and stained the collar of his shirt. Boychenko winced and picked a shard of glass from his palm.

Panting and flexing his already swelling hand, Eric shook his head. "I knew this was a bad idea." He turned toward the front door and yanked it open. "When you get rid of the bulldog, call me, Vivian. We need to talk."

"Wait! Eric! Don't—"

The door slammed behind him, rattling the paintings on the walls.

"Fucking dick cop almost broke my nose," Ten huffed.

Infuriated, I spun around and thumped his chest with a closed fist. "I should finish what he started!"

Ten gripped my wrist, not hard enough to bruise or hurt me but with enough force that I didn't dare try to jerk free. "Do. Not. Hit. Me."

"Ten! What the fuck, man?" Boychenko shoved at Ten's shoulder but the larger man didn't even move.

"Let go of me. *Now*." His fingers straightened, and my wrist dropped from his hold. Gritting my teeth, I pointed a finger toward his bruised, bloodied face. "Don't ever touch me like that again. Do you understand?"

Jaw clenched, Ten nodded.

"Get this cleaned up. *Now*." Trembling inside, I left the entryway of the house and stormed toward the sunroom. I could hear Ten and Boy arguing behind me, but I didn't stick around to hear what they were saying. I picked up my cell phone from the table where I had left it in the studio and immediately called Eric.

It went straight to voicemail.

"Eric, I'm so sorry. Please call me back. We can meet wherever you would like. I'm just...I'm sorry. So, so sorry."

After hanging up the phone, I tucked it into the pocket of my jeans. They were my loosest pair but I had been forced to leave them unbuttoned that morning. I had resorted to using one of those wide elastic maternity bands that I had ordered off the internet to cover up my questionable fashion choice.

Running my fingers through my hair, I felt suddenly claustrophobic. I needed some fresh air. I needed to get away from Ten and Boychenko, even if it was only a few steps into the garden. I left the sunroom through the French doors on the side and walked toward the pergola.

"Vivian! How are you?" Judge Walker leaned against the low back fence that allowed entrance to the rear of our property.

Forcing a smile, I crossed the yard to talk with him. "I'm good. How are you?"

"I'm all right." A flicker of sadness darkened his face. "I had Roscoe put to sleep yesterday. I'm still trying to adjust to the quiet house."

"I'm so sorry." I thought of the big, slobbering but sweet dog who was such a familiar sight in our neighborhood. Nikolai and Ten had said the dog was poisoned, but neither had offered any suggestions as to the culprit. It worried me to think some psycho was running around our neighborhood throwing poisoned food over fences. "That must be so difficult for you."

The judge nodded sadly. "It will get better, but for now, the grief is very real." He patted my hand where it rested on the wrought iron scrollwork adorning the gate. "Do you have plans?"

"When?"

"Now."

"Oh. Um...no." I couldn't quite face going back inside the house yet. "Why?"

"Let's have dinner. I know a great little barbecue joint. It's quiet and a good place to relax." He must have known I was wavering on the inside because he added, "It's a favorite hangout for law enforcement and fire and EMS."

In other words, it was safe. The thought of escaping, even for something as simple as smoked brisket smothered in a sweet, spicy sauce and creamy potato salad, was too tempting. Ten would blow a gasket, and Nikolai was definitely going to be annoyed when I finally came back, but I just didn't care. I really didn't. Not anymore.

This week had been absolute hell—the forgotten prenatal appointment, springing Ten on me, finding Nikolai with Tatiana at the hotel and having him lie to me about it to my face, watching Ten and Eric beat the shit out of each other in my entryway—and I couldn't take it anymore. I wanted to run away, even if only for a couple of hours.

"Barbecue sounds like a delicious way to end the day." I unlatched the gate and stepped out of the backyard. "Let's go."

The judge gestured toward his property. "After you..."

Within five minutes, we had left the neighborhood and were on our way. My cell phone started to ring, but I silenced it without even looking at the screen, switched to vibrate and stuffed it back into my pocket.

"Your shadow?"

Did he know that was Ten's nickname or was he just making a joke? "Probably."

"I heard the ruckus earlier. Is everything all right?"

"It was just a disagreement between Eric and Ten that got out of hand."

"Boys will be boys," he sagely replied.

"That may be, but I would rather they not turn my hallway into one of Ivan's sparring cages, you know?"

"I bet." Judge Walker tapped the touchscreen console to switch stations and landed on a classic country one. He turned down the volume. "Do you mind if I swing by and pick up my daughter on our way?"

"Not at all."

"Good." He smiled at me. "Have you ever met Julie?"

"No." I had heard from our neighbors that she was a wild drug addict, but I also knew how our neighbors liked to embellish tales.

"I think you'll like her. I know she'll like you. Julie has always wanted to be an artist."

"Does she paint or draw?"

"She prefers pastels and charcoals," he said. "Her art won awards in high school. I had hoped that she would go to art school, but she met a boy—and—well. You know how that goes."

"Yes," I said quietly. "There are art classes around town that she might enjoy. Hadley's center mainly hosts courses for special needs kids and adults, but they also have some evening classes that are open to anyone. She gets some really great visiting artists. I've enjoyed the workshops I've attended."

"I'll have to pass that along to Julie." He merged onto the loop headed south. "We aren't far from her boyfriend's house. Maybe twenty minutes."

"I'm in no rush." I inhaled a relaxing breath and settled back against the leather seat. We talked about the neighborhood while he drove. It was a nice, quiet conversation that I rather enjoyed.

He turned into an upper middle class neighborhood that had quite a few FOR SALE signs with FORE-CLOSURE stickers slapped across them. It wasn't an uncommon sight in this type of neighborhood. A few years ago, people had purchased way more house than they could afford on shaky mortgages and this was the result.

He pulled into the curved driveway of the large house at the center of the cul-de-sac. It had a Spanish feel about it with white stucco walls and red clay roof tiles. I took a long look and guessed it was in the four or five thousand square foot range. After spending time in large homes like Yuri's and Ivan's and ours, I had gotten better at guessing the sizes of homes. This one looked similar in size to the home Benny and Di-mitri shared.

The houses on either side of it were empty. The yards were slightly overgrown and the flowerbeds had been scorched by the summer sun. The houses next to those were for sale. No wonder the neighborhood was so quiet.

"Would you like to come in? Julie tends to take forever to get ready. If you're with me, she'll be quick about it."

"Sure." I unlatched my seatbelt and stepped out of his car. Trailing him to the front door, I glanced at my surroundings. I stood beside the judge as he knocked and waited for someone to answer. The door opened suddenly and noisily as if someone had jerked on it.

An Asian man close to my age appeared in the doorway. He wore skinny jeans and a tight red shirt that bared a stripe of tanned skin. Vividly colored tattoos swirled along his arms. He ran bony fingers through dirty, disheveled hair. I noticed his blown pupils and took a nervous step back. This guy was high as a kite.

"The store's closed, Grandpa. Go find of our slingers."

Slingers? Was this a stash house? Or a dope dealer's house? I glanced at the judge and wondered if he had any idea what sort of place this was. Surely not. He wouldn't have brought me here if he'd known.

Before the other guy could slam the door in our face, Judge Walker gripped it with one hand and stunned me speechless by whipping out the pistol he had concealed in a holster hidden beneath the back of his shirt. He expertly flicked off the safety and pointed it right in Mr. Skinny Jeans' face. "Let go of the door and back up. Now."

Eyes wide, I glanced from the man who was clearly a dealer and the judge. "What are you doing?"

Judge Walker kicked the door open, forcing the man to stumble backward into the house, and grabbed my arm. "Come with me."

"What?" I tried to jerk away from him, but the sight of his gun and the determined, grim look on his face stopped me. "What are you doing, Judge?"

"I'm getting my daughter back," he stated and shoved me into the house. "They won't let me see her, but they can't stop me if I have you with me."

"Are you crazy?"

"A father's love makes a man do crazy things." He gave me another shove, stepped into the house after me and shut the door behind us. He pushed me toward the dealer and pointed the gun at him. "Pat him down."

I did exactly as he told me. Worried I might be stabbed by a needle or worse, I was careful in touching this stranger. The noise of music coming from somewhere else in the house covered up the sounds coming from the entryway. There had to be other people here. What if they came looking for this guy? Would they shoot us? How the hell was I going to get out of here?

Hands shaking and thinking of the baby depending on me to survive, I finished frisking the dealer and handed over the knife and small revolver I had taken from him. The judge shoved the knife into his pocket but kept the revolver in his hand.

Armed with two guns, he motioned for us to head into the house. "Walk. Now."

Standing beside the dealer, I matched his steps. We crossed a living room filled with crates and boxes of supplies like plastic bags, mannitol and caffeine powder. I didn't have to be a genius to figure out was going on in this house. I wrinkled my nose in the filthy dining room where empty takeout and pizza boxes covered every flat surface. There were energy drink cans stacked nearly to the ceiling in one corner.

We finally entered the kitchen, except it wasn't being used as a kitchen. This was the center of their drug dealing operation. Everywhere I looked, there was lab equipment. Two long tables draped in clear plastic supported piles of tightly wrapped bricks of white powder. The bright red stamp on the brown packing tape sealing them shut was a symbol I knew only too well. It belonged to the Guzman cartel, the same cartel my father had worked for most of his life. The same cartel he had given the finger and fled after killing that cartel witness in January.

A woman a few years older than me with stringy brown hair stood next to another Asian guy. They were both high and working like fiends to bag up the mound of loose powder in the center of the kitchen island. Judging by the empty bottles of caffeine and mannitol powder, the duo had cut the pure product to make cheaper blow that low-end users could afford. They filled tiny bags, weighed them, sealed them and tossed them into a waiting box. Neither of them noticed us at first, not until the judge finally spoke.

"Julie, honey, it's time to come home."

Her head popped up, and she blinked three times, almost as if she couldn't believe her eyes. The briefest flash of a smile curved her mouth before her expression turned angry and dark. "What the hell are you doing here?"

"I'm here to take you home." He kept his guns trained on the two men in the room. "Come on, sweetheart. Let's go."

"I don't want to go with you."

"Yes, you do." He swallowed loudly and tried to reason with her. "Honey, you're sick. You need to come home and rest. Let me take care of you."

Like an irritated child, she stomped her foot and slapped at the white mountain in front of her. "I don't want your help! I'm not sick!"

I held my breath, suddenly afraid to inhale the air for fear of ingesting even a single particle of cocaine. I lifted my shirt to cover my face and prayed none of the drugs would make it into my system. Anxious and desperate to escape this rapidly deteriorating situation, I glanced around the kitchen and then back at the door we had used.

Was I fast enough to get away from the judge? Probably. But then what? He had the keys in his pocket. All of the houses around here were empty. I could run, hide and call Nikolai, but it would take him time to reach me.

"You need my help, honey. You need to come home."

"I don't want your help! I'm fine."

"Fine?" The judge repeated in disbelief. "Julie, look at yourself. You're wasting away. Your skin is a mess. Your hair is falling out. When was the last time you had a real meal? When was the last time you showered? When was the last time you saw a doctor?"

"I don't need a doctor!" Like a dog trying to get the last few dregs of gravy from its bow, she licked at the white powder coating her hand. It wasn't enough to satisfy her craving. She picked up a small plate that held her own private supply and scooped up half of a line with the corner of a credit card. She dotted the tiny mound on the skin stretched between her thumb and forefinger and then brought it to her nose. After inhaling a noisy bump, she rubbed at her nose and licked her top lip. "Bobby takes real good care of me."

Judge Walker looked like he was about to shatter right in front of me. Distraught, he shouted, "Bobby Pham doesn't give a shit about you! He's using you, Julie. Don't you see that?"

I didn't know who the hell Bobby Pham was, but I assumed he was the boyfriend. This wasn't a very good tactic. Trying to turn her against her dealer and boyfriend? It was never going to work.

"Bobby loves me! He loves me! He takes care of me. You don't know anything. Just leave!"

"No! I'm not leaving without you, Julie."

"Get out!" she screamed like a banshee.

"What the hell is going on in here?"

With all of the shouting between father and daughter and the music blaring in the background, none of us had heard the front door open. Two men appeared in the doorway behind us, one of them Asian and the other Latino. I assumed the Asian guy was Bobby Pham, but there was something vaguely familiar about the dark-haired, brown-skinned man at his side. I had seen his face somewhere, but I couldn't quite place it.

Guns were drawn in a flash, and Judge Walker was quickly overtaken by the two men who were part of the Vietnamese crew. His guns were stripped, and he was shoved down to his knees. I hastily flattened myself against the closest wall. The Latino man glanced at me and then jerked his head back in my direction. He looked me up and down and narrowed his eyes as if he recognized me.

"Bobby, it's just my dad and some girl. They're leaving." Julie hurried to Bobby's side, her bare and dirty feet slapping against the tile, and slid her arm around her boyfriend's waist. "They're going. It's no big deal."

"No big deal?" Bobby thundered angrily. "He has guns on me and my boys. He's disrespecting me in my home."

"Respect? You want my respect?" The judge actually spit at Bobby. "You stole my daughter, you little bastard. I'm here to take her home."   '

"The hell you are. She loves it here. She's mine." As if to prove his point, Bobby cupped Julie's bottom and gave it a lewd squeeze before kissing her noisily on the cheek. "Julie is happy here. Right, baby?"

"Right," she said, her eyes devoid of any emotion. Still she clung to Bobby as if he were her lifeline. As her dealer, he very likely was the only thing keeping her alive.

"Julie." The anguish in the judge's voice made my heart ache. "Come home, honey. Come home with me."

For a moment, I thought she would break, but in the end, she shook her head. "I love, Bobby. I'm staying."

"You'll die here," her father warned. "You'll die in this godforsaken drug den."

She didn't have a reply ready for that one.

"And who the fuck is this?" Bobby pushed away Julie and sauntered toward me. He waved the gun at me, and I blanched. My hands flew to my stomach in a futile attempt to shield the baby.

"No." The Latino guy stepped in front of Bobby and put his body between mine and his cohort's. "Don't touch her."

"Jesus, you're hot on her already, Hector?" Bobby leaned to the side for a better look at me. "She's too short and scrawny for my tastes, but if that's your thing—"

Hector? Oh God. I finally remembered why his face was so familiar. I had seen it in Mexican newspapers and on the blogs that followed the Mexican underworld. This was Hector Salas, the cartel's top enforcer. If anyone in this room had bad blood with my father, it was going to be Hector.

"Shut the fuck up, Bobby," Hector snapped. "Do you know who the hell this woman is?"

Bobby shrugged. "Some tramp that the old man is banging?"

"No, you fucking idiot. This is Nikolai Kalasnikov's wife."

The entire room went still. Everyone looked at me, and my skin prickled as a nervous heat raced through me. I wasn't sure what would happen now. In some circle's Nikolai's name would get me a free pass. In others...

Bobby lowered his gun away from me but whirled around on the judge. He hauled the older man up by his shirt and slammed him into the island. Judge Walker cried out in pain as the thick marble slab cut into his hip. Bobby shook him like a ragdoll. "What the fuck is wrong with you, old man? Bringing the Russian's wife to my house? Do have any idea what you've done?"

"Bobby, stop!" Julie tried to intervene. Despite her earlier protests, it was clear she still loved her father a great deal. "Stop! He just wanted to help me."

"Help you? He's just signed our fucking death warrants! Do you know what Nikolai is going to do when he finds out that I waved a gun at his wife? Do you have any idea what Romero will do if he gets his hands on me?"

Judge Walker laughed right in Bobby's face. "I'm counting on it, you miserable little shit."

Bobby growled with anger and pistol-whipped the judge so hard that blood splattered across the kitchen. The droplets landed on the refrigerator and dotted the mountains of white powder sitting on the island.

"NO! Bobby, leave him alone!" Julie attacked her boyfriend, but she was too weak and strung out to be effective. He backhanded her with so much force that she was thrown to the ground. I watched in horror as the judge launched himself at Bobby. The pair started to fight viciously. Bobby's crew rushed in to help him—and in the ensuing scuffle, a gun discharged.

The blast ricocheted in the kitchen, and I screamed. The memories of the blitz attack where Nikolai had been so badly beaten and where I had been kidnapped overwhelmed me. Panicked, I thought only of the baby and ran.

Hands clutched at me, but I shook them off and kicked out hard, catching my attacker right in the balls. I managed to get free of the kitchen just as another round was fired and then another. The bullets ripped through the drywall. Glass shattered behind me. I scrambled for the closest piece of cover I could find and dove behind a heavy couch.

Crawling on hands and knees, I scurried across the dirty living room floor and desperately tried to reach the entryway. The fighting and shooting continued in the kitchen behind me. Julie's screams and the judge's bellowing voice sent a pang of guilt through me, but I didn't dare go back for them. I had to stay alive for the baby.

Just as I made it to the entryway, the front door was violently kicked open. I curled up into a ball and covered my face and neck with my arms. Tears sprang to my eyes. I was going to die here. My baby was going to die in this terrible, disgusting drug hellhole because I had made a stupid, stupid decision.

"Vee!"

My head popped up as Nikolai's deep, loud voice registered. I couldn't believe what I was seeing. I blinked my watery eyes and nearly fainted with relief as he rushed through the door he had just kicked open and into the house. He dropped to his knees with enough momentum that he slid across the hardwood. Wrapping his arms around me, he pulled me in front of him and shielded my body with his own.

All hell broke loose in the house. Men ran through the front door and into the kitchen. There weren't any more shots fired, but the smack of skin on skin told me that the fighting was still at a fever pitch. Finally, Kostya's voice filled the house as he called out to Nikolai in Russian, telling him it was all clear.

Nikolai's arms relaxed around me, and he slowly stood. Grasping my shoulders, he guided me to my feet. I found the courage to stare up at him, but the expression on his handsome face made my stomach drop like a runaway elevator. The softness and tender heat that always warmed his eyes had vanished. He looked at me with the same cold indifference that he showed everyone else. That icy wall he used to keep others out had suddenly appeared between us.

Ten walked up behind Nikolai. The bruises on his face from his fight with Eric were even darker and more pronounced now. There were fresh blood stains on his shirt and jeans. I didn't even want to think about the ways he had earned those. "The judge is alive. So is the girl. The Pham crew is dead. Hector Salas took a bullet to the shoulder, but it's nothing our doctor can't fix." He glanced at me and winced. "There's fucking *llelo* everywhere, boss. It's not safe for her to be here."

His business-like rundown of the mayhem didn't surprise me. This was Ten's element. This was what he did best.

Turning away from me, Nikolai clenched his jaw together so tightly I could see the muscles flexing in his cheek. He stared at Ten for a moment before finally speaking. "Get her out here."

"*Da.*" Ten stepped toward me as Nikolai pivoted toward the living room.

"Kolya." I reached for my husband in a desperate attempt to make him stop, to make him come back and talk to me. Shaken up and in shock, I needed his strength. I needed to feel his arms around me. I needed to hear him whispering gently in my ear, reassuring me that everything would be all right.

But he didn't stop or slow down. He just kept walking—away from me.

I tried to follow him, but Ten stopped me. "No, Vivian. He doesn't want you now."

Ten didn't speak with malice or cruelty. He was speaking matter-of-factly. Nikolai didn't want me.

"*Dorogaya moya.*" He wrapped a brawny arm around my shoulders and carefully held me back. Lowering his head, he spoke in a low tone only I could hear. "Leave him. Give him some space. He'll come around."

I stumbled out of the house with Ten guiding the way. By the time we reached an idling SUV, he was practically carrying me. I could hardly stand. He lifted me into the front seat and fastened my seatbelt. Not a word was spoken between us as we drove. There wasn't anything to say anymore.

With my forehead against the hot glass of my window, I closed my eyes and let the tears come. Ten's voice raced around my head. *He doesn't want you now.*

No, I thought sadly, *he doesn't.*

13 CHAPTER THIRTEEN

Sick to his stomach, Nikolai gritted his teeth and fought the urge to run after Vivian. The urge to shout at her for being so reckless, and the maddening desire to sweep her into his arms and kiss her until she was limp with pleasure gripped him like a vise. Somehow he managed to muscle control over his baser needs. He kept his back to her and his feet moving toward the kitchen. Ten would take care of her. Right now, he had more pressing matters to attend.

The kitchen looked like a fucking war zone. He stopped abruptly after two steps because of the growing blood pool and the haze of white powder in the air. His expert gaze took in the sealed bricks of product and the piles of cocaine on the counter. He hazarded a guess at the weight and wondered how the fuck a low-end counterfeiter like Bobby Pham had scraped together enough cash to make the initial buy. This was millions of dollars in weight in pure Colombian candy. After cutting it, adding a premium to every gram and pushing it out onto the street, there was still a tidy profit in it for Bobby and his crew.

Or, at least, there had been.

He looked at the three bodies on the floor. Two of the faces he didn't recognize but the third he did. He would have to visit Mr. Lu personally to let him know what had happened here. It was a visit he didn't look forward to making tonight.

Judge Walker sat in a chair while his daughter knelt next to him and wept over the body of her boyfriend. Miraculously neither had been shot, but the daughter made Nikolai nervous. A coke addict with an axe to grind was a loose end he didn't like. He silently added her to the list he would be giving to Kostya. At the first indication that she might break, he would have to give the order. Vivian had been here, and he refused to put her at risk.

But what the hell had Vee been doing in this house? Why would she do something so stupid? Did she think of the baby even once? The bullet holes in the walls made him sick. He couldn't help but imagine the burning hot projectiles ripping through her soft flesh.

Finding her curled in a ball and unharmed in the entryway had been nothing but sheer dumb luck. He had fully expected to find her shot and bleeding on the floor. His heart threatened to burst as pain unlike any he had ever known struck him. He could have lost Vee and the baby.

A grunt of pain dragged his attention away from the trouble that would follow him home. Hector Salas sat in a chair and pressed a wad of paper towels against his bleeding shoulder. From the looks of the wound, it wasn't too bad. He would live.

As if sensing that he needed to explain what had happened, the judge raised a hand in front of him. The gesture was one that pleaded for understanding. "Listen, Nikolai, I didn't think it would go like this."

"Not another fucking word out of you," Nikolai warned. His anger toward the judge threatened to erupt in a fit of violence. "I told you to leave this alone. I warned you that something like this would happen if you got involved, but you didn't listen. Now I have three dealers dead at my feet, and a crime scene that has to be cleaned up. Unless you plan to take credit for this fucking nightmare," he added meanly.

Judge Walker had the decency to glance away and look chagrined. He didn't say another word. He kept his gaze glued to the bloody, dirty floor.

Speaking in Russian so the judge, his daughter and Hector wouldn't get involved, Nikolai started giving orders. "Kostya, call the Liquidator. Get his cleaner in here tonight. I want this place gone over with a fine tooth comb, and I want us out of it."

Kostya looked relieved to not be in charge of cleaning up this mess. "What about the drugs?"

"Call Zec. He'll take care of it for us. We'll consider it payment for all this trouble."

"And the bodies?" Kostya used the toe of his boot to lift the head of one man.

"We'll take them to Mr. Lu after they've been cleaned." The old man would want to bury his nephew appropriately. Nikolai couldn't be sure about his degree of relationship to the other two dead men. If they were close relations, they had to be returned.

Nikolai motioned to Hector. "Take him to see the doctor after you make that call."

Kostya nodded, and Nikolai switched to Spanish as he addressed Hector. "You and I are going to talk later tonight so go easy on the painkillers when they patch you back together."

Hector's gaze fell to the dead men on the floor. He didn't seem the least bit fazed by the sight of three sprawling, bleeding bodies. "This alliance wasn't working out. It was time for a change."

The cartel man's reply didn't surprise Nikolai. A man like Hector didn't reach the pinnacle of power he had attained without being a cold son of a bitch.

Turning to Ilya, Nikolai pointed to the judge and his daughter. "Get them out of town tonight. They can come back on Tuesday or Wednesday."

"I'll take care of it," Ilya assured him.

Nikolai fixed the judge with a furious glare. "You're taking your daughter and you're leaving. Tonight. You aren't going back to your house or making any stops. You're getting in Ilya's truck, and you're going wherever the hell he tells you to go. Understood?"

The judge nodded tersely. "I get it."

"We'll talk about this," Nikolai gestured to the mess on the floor, "when I get back from London." He didn't have to say that he expected to be owed a huge fucking favor for taking care of everything. Studying the judge, he sensed the older man finally understood what Nikolai had been trying to tell him that night in his backyard. There was a way to go about these things and barging into the lion's den with a gun wasn't one of them.

Spinning on his heel, Nikolai left the kitchen and made his way across the house. He tapped Artyom's shoulder to let him know that he was needed. They left the house with their heads down, and he prayed all of these houses around them were truly empty. If not, the homeless squatters who liked to hide out in them would be easy to silence with money or a visit from an enforcer.

The ride to the house was one of the longest of his life. The image of Vivian curled into a tight little ball in the entryway while gunfire popped around her tormented him. He had come *this close* to losing her and the baby. He couldn't even comprehend a future without her or their child.

He scrubbed a hand down his face and thanked God he had found her so quickly. His anger toward Ten and Eric Santos would manifest soon enough. After two days of nonstop tension with Vee, he had cut out of Samovar early with the full intention of devoting the entire evening to her. The guilt of hiding his meeting with Tatiana was eating a hole in him. He needed to come clean with her about everything that had happened and why Tatiana had come back. Vee deserved to know the truth, even if it meant admitting that he had lied to her.

But he had walked into the house with Artyom trailing him to find Ten and Boychenko arguing in the kitchen. The sight of Ten's battered face had surprised him. Learning that Ten had attacked Eric, a damned Houston detective, in his home had infuriated him beyond belief. Didn't Ten understand that he had just given Eric the evidence necessary to have his probation revoked? The last thing he needed was Eric sniffing around in their business, especially while Tatiana was still hiding out at the Four Seasons.

When Ten had confessed that Vivian was missing, Nikolai had nearly strangled him. He had rushed the larger man but had refrained from hitting him. It wasn't necessary. Ten had instantly told him what they knew. Vivian had gone outside to get some space. Boychenko had spotted her talking to the judge while he was on his way to dump a dustpan filled with glass and ceramic shards. Not long after, he had passed the window on another trip to the trashcan and had discovered the backyard empty.

Nikolai had instantly known where she had gone with the judge. He didn't know what fucking sob story the old man had used to get Vivian to go with him on such a fool's errand, but it must have been a good one. She wouldn't have put herself at risk without a good, convincing story to get her out of the yard and into the judge's vehicle.

Artyom stopped in front of the house, and Nikolai was out of the SUV before the street captain even had the vehicle in park. He ate up the sidewalk in long, determined strides and took the porch steps two at a time. When he opened the front door and entered the house, he saw the destruction caused by Eric and Ten's fight. The debris had been cleaned away, but the ruined picture frames, the broken table and the water stain on the hardwood were evidence of what had happened here.

Ready to tear into Ten, he stormed through the house and followed the sound of voices into the kitchen. Vivian stood on one side of the island, a cup of hot tea clamped in her hands, while Ten was at the sink washing his. His gaze skipped from his wife's blotchy face, her eyes red from crying, to Ten's as the enforcer turned toward the sound of footsteps.

He hooked his thumb over his shoulder. "Get the fuck out. Now."

Ten didn't even bother to dry his hands. He left the kitchen without a single word.

Standing across the island from Vivian, he stared at her for a long time. The distance between them was only five feet in reality, but it felt so much wider. They were drifting farther and farther apart, and he didn't know how to pull her back. He was losing her.

His chest heaved as he tried to control his breaths with measured inhalations. Even though he tried to remain calm, he couldn't keep the anger out of his voice as he demanded to know, "What the hell were you thinking, Vivian?"

She went rigid at that and glared at him. "Are you serious? That's the first question you ask me? You're not going to ask me if I'm okay? You're not going to ask me if I need to go to the hospital? You're not going to ask me about the baby?"

"Are you all right? Do you need me to take you to the hospital?"

"Would you let me go if I wanted to? Aren't you worried someone will find out what happened back there?"

He couldn't believe she would even ask that. "Of course I would let you go! Jesus Christ, Vivian, I'm not a fucking ogre. *I* wouldn't put *my* baby at risk."

She flinched at his cruelly flung words. "This isn't my fault."

"Not your fault?" He repeated harshly and incredulously. "You ran off with the judge, busted into a stash house and escaped a shootout. Do you have any fucking idea how lucky you are? Do you have any clue how close you came to being shot?"

"Yes! I am *painfully* aware of how close I came to taking another bullet or two."

That barb hit its mark. The only scars on her body were the ones he had given her, after all.

"Why are you badgering me like this? Why are you interrogating me like some criminal?"

"Are you serious?" He curled his fingers at his sides as the image of her broken and bloodied and surrounded by clouds of cocaine flashed in front of his eyes. He had done everything he could to keep her safe, and she had stupidly and recklessly risked her life. Panic and fury and fear surged with him. For the first time ever in her presence, he lost control. "I wouldn't have to ask any of these questions if you would just remember your fucking place!"

The nasty, ugly words he had just shouted at his wife, at the woman he loved, at his sun, echoed in the kitchen like a gunshot. He regretted them instantly. Self-hatred burned through him. *Why the fuck did you say that? What the hell is wrong with you? Apologize. Get on your knees and grovel.*

Vivian reared back as if he had slapped her. The color drained from her face. "My place? And where is that, exactly, Nikolai? Hmm? Here? Locked up in the house with a bunch of street soldiers to keep me company? Is that my place? Or maybe my place is in the kitchen and in your bed." A fiery glint brightened her blue eyes. "Is that what you want from me? You want me to look pretty and keep house and fuck you and give you babies and never ask for anything else from you?"

The situation was spiraling out of control. He needed to call a timeout. He needed to walk away and cool off, but he just kept fighting with her. He was like a rabid dog that had chomped down on its prey and refused to let go. "Don't even start that with me, Vivian. I don't want to hear it."

"You know what? I don't want to hear anything else come out of your mouth." She pushed away her mug of tea. "I don't even know what is or isn't true anymore." He could tell that she was trying to be strong, but her wobbling lower lip betrayed her struggle. "I feel like I don't even know you anymore."

Her words stabbed at him. Was that really how she felt? Was she even happy with him anymore? He had watched enough relationships crumble to know that statements like those usually preceded life-altering events like separations or worse.

A desperate feeling invaded his chest. Like a wounded animal, he lashed out at her. "Well I know exactly who you are, Vivian Valero. You're the woman who just put our baby at risk by leaving her bodyguards and driving off with a judge who sold her on a sob story. Were you trying to get yourself killed? Were you trying to hurt the baby?"

Her face slackened, and he loathed himself for being so petty and childish and cruel. She gulped and bit her lower lip. On the verge of tears, she said, "You know what they say, Kolya. The apple doesn't fall very far from the tree. Maybe I'm more like my mother than I ever suspected."

His heart was ripped in two as her painfully spoken words hit him. God, what the hell was he thinking saying something like that to her? She carried so much fear about turning into her mother and about hurting their child. Why had he said that? Of all the nasty, ugly things he could have said, why had he gone *there*?

Because you're a miserable fucking bastard, that's why.

Without another word, Vivian abandoned her mug of tea and left the kitchen. She gave him a wide berth and disappeared from sight with footsteps so soft they didn't make even a whisper of sound. Overwhelmed by anger at his own stupidity and callousness, he picked up her mug of tea and threw it. Hot tea spilled down his arm and on the floor. The mug hit the sink and exploded loudly. He didn't even bother to clean up the mess.

Pivoting on his heel, he strode out of the kitchen and came face-to-face with Ten and Arytom in the entryway. Both men stared at him. Ten looked guilty and agitated. Artyom's expression was one of pure disappointment.

In me, Nikolai thought. *He's disappointed in me.*

"Get your keys," he ordered with a flick of his wrist. "We're leaving."

Wordlessly, Artyom followed him out of the house and out to his vehicle. His captain started the engine but didn't put the SUV into drive. Hands on the wheel, he said, "Boss, I can handle all of this tonight. You can go back inside and—"

"Don't," Nikolai warned. "Just fucking drive."

Artyom grabbed the gear shift. "Yes, sir."

As ice hardened his heart, Nikolai stared out the window and tried to keep it together. After so many months of happiness with Vivian, he should have expected this to happen. He had tasted sunshine. He had felt the bright, pure burn of it on his skin. He had inhaled the sweet scent of it and let it warm his heart.

But that was all gone now. He had fucked it up, probably irrevocably.

Everything was falling apart.

14 CHAPTER FOURTEEN

"It's time to go." Ten ducked his head into the living room where I was curled up on the couch watching a twenty-four hour news channel. It was the most he had spoken to me since returning to the house after the shootout at Bobby Pham's place. "I've already loaded all the luggage. Boychenko is driving us." He seemed uneasy and uncertain. "If you're ready to go, I mean."

"I'm ready." I glanced at my watch and noted the time. There was nearly an hour before Yuri's jet was scheduled to leave. Nikolai had plenty of time to meet us at the small, private airport Yuri preferred.

It had been a long night. *The worst night.* Nikolai hadn't come home as far as I could tell, but Ten had never left. He had been asleep in a chair outside our bedroom door that morning. Boychenko had been downstairs, making a breakfast I didn't have the appetite to eat. In the end, Ten convinced me to shovel down the oatmeal and peaches by reminding me that I had to think of the baby.

The baby that Nikolai had meanly accused me of trying to hurt. Just the memory of those viciously spoken words made my heart stutter and my stomach flop. Did I think he meant it? No, not at all. He had been angry and scared, and he had stupidly lashed out at me. His childhood hadn't exactly prepared him for learning to fight fair, even with his wife.

But he had walked away instead of apologizing. That had hurt the most. Instead of trying to make things right, he had piled more bricks on top of that wall between us and had completely shut me out. I didn't have the strength to pick up a sledgehammer and tear it down. I was tired. I was just so tired.

For the first time in years, I had skipped church without a valid reason. St. Vladimir's was usually the one place I always felt safe and protected and happy. This morning I couldn't face the social aspect of it. All those people expecting me to smile and chat? All those people who would ask about Nikolai? The old women who loved to ask me when we were going to start a family and the ones who loved to tell me how lucky I was to have a husband like him? I couldn't deal with it. I just couldn't.

My joy at finally traveling abroad and seeing London had been dashed and stomped on by the terrible, nasty fight that had taken place in the kitchen last night. I couldn't stop replaying everything that had gone wrong, from the brawl between Ten and Eric, to the moment I had agreed to have dinner with the judge, to the first bullet exploding in that kitchen filled with drugs, to the horrible things I had said to Nikolai and he had said to me.

I didn't know where I stood anymore. I couldn't make sense of what was happening to our relationship. That old fear of mine about the foundation of our marriage seemed to be coming true. Those cracks were growing, and I didn't know if we could patch them before the whole damned thing came crashing down onto us.

"Hey," Ten said just before we reached the idling SUV waiting out back. He gently touched my shoulder in a silent bid for me to stop and then exhaled roughly as he scratched his fingers through his short hair. "I know it's too late, but I need to apologize for yesterday. That was so fucking out of line. It's my fault you ended up in that mess. I was hired to protect you, and I failed. Big time."

I had already let go of my anger toward Ten so I forgave him without hesitation. "We both screwed up yesterday. It's not fair for you to take all the blame. I shouldn't have gone with the judge."

Ten tilted his head. "Why did you go with the judge?"

"He asked me out to dinner."

"And?"

"And that's it. He seemed sad about his dog, and I needed to get away from the house—"

"And me," Ten grunted.

"And you," I repeated with a nod.

"So he lied to you about what he really wanted."

Thinking of Nikolai and Tatiana all I could do was shrug. "There seems to be a lot of that going around this house."

Ten frowned. "Who else is lying to you?"

"It doesn't matter."

"It does. It matters to me. *You* matter to me."

"You hardly know me."

"I know enough," he said matter-of-factly. "I know that anyone else would have demanded I be thrown out on my ass that first day. Anyone else would have fired me yesterday." Looking decidedly uncomfortable, he gruffly insisted, "You're a good person, Vivian. You're a better woman than I'll ever deserve, and I'm lucky to work for you. So if someone is lying to you, if someone is hurting you, I want to know about it. I'll take care of them."

Stunned into silence by Ten's strident declaration of his loyalty to me, I stared up at him. My eyes prickled, and I blinked away the tears. Overly emotional because of the pregnancy and the stress, I seemed to be crying over everything these days.

"Tell me, Vivian," Ten urged. "Let me do something nice for you. Let me help you."

My mouth slanted with a sad little smile. "You can't help me, Ten. Not with this problem."

His eyes widened as he finally understood what I meant. "The boss? Why would he lie to you? If it's business—"

"Tatiana Filipova." I couldn't hold the truth in a moment longer. I needed to get it off my chest before it turned me rotten from the inside out.

Ten stiffened. "She's gone. She's history."

"She's alive. She's in Houston."

"What? That's not possible. She's dead."

I shook my head. "Nikolai faked her death. He told me himself. Whatever you saw with Kostya? It wasn't real."

Ten looked as if he wanted to argue, but I could see the realization dawn upon his face. He narrowed his eyes suspiciously. "When did you see her?"

"Thursday."

"Thursday? Where? At the mall? At..." His voice trailed off, and his gaze jumped to the house. I could see the wheels turning in his head. With a vicious snarl, he dropped a string of Russian and English curse words that actually made me blush. "You saw her at the hotel restaurant, didn't you? That's why you were so upset. Why didn't you tell me she was there? I would have run her off. If the boss faked her death, he wanted her gone, not hanging around here like a fucking ghost."

"She was with Nikolai." There was no point in holding back now.

Ten's lips parted but no sound issued forth. Was he thinking the same thoughts I had when I'd discovered the pair together? Was he wondering if Nikolai had ever truly ended things with her? Was he wondering what was so important that she had come back here? Was he imaging them alone in a hotel room?

Shocked speechless, Ten put his hand on my back and urged me forward. We said nothing as we climbed into the SUV. If Boychenko noticed our strange behavior, he didn't comment. He drove us to the airport and helped Ten with all of the luggage that had been stowed in the cargo area.

After the luggage was handed off to a skycap, Ten trailed me into the airport. The luxurious lobby was small and quiet and hosted only one other party of travelers preparing to embark in a different private jet. Yuri, Lena, Ivan and Erin were already waiting. Sergei and Bianca hadn't arrived yet, and unfortunately, Dimitri and Benny couldn't travel with baby Sofia yet.

Ten hung back as Erin and Lena squashed me with their hugs and dragged me over to a sitting area to talk about all the places they wanted to visit in London. I glanced back at him a couple of times but he seemed to be deep in thought. Even when Ivan wandered over to talk to him, he kept his attention focused solely on me. After last night's scare, he wasn't going to take any chances it seemed.

It felt incredibly bizarre and surreal to sit on the plush leather seating and chat with Lena and Erin about dresses and tourist hotspots and Michelin-starred restaurants when twenty-four hours earlier I had been crawling on hands and knees through a stash house while bullets whizzed by my ears. I didn't even want to think about what Kostya or men like him had done to keep that shooting and the deaths of the Pham crew quiet.

Obviously it had worked. There hadn't been even a hint of coverage on the local news or in the papers. Not even Ivan seemed to suspect anything, and with his fingers still on the pulse of Houston's underworld, he usually had the good gossip fairly quickly.

When Bianca and Sergei arrived, I couldn't help but smile. They made such a beautiful couple, and I was absolutely thrilled they had finally gotten together. Sergei wasn't like the other men in Nikolai's family of thieves and criminals. He had been forced into an unholy alliance with the Prokhorov family to save his family. Bianca had freed him from that hell, and I prayed they would have a long, happy life together.

Bianca engulfed me in one of her trademark hugs and air-kissed my cheeks before squeezing onto the loveseat with me. As always, she looked as if she had just stepped off the pages of a high-end plus-sized fashion magazine. There was a reason her wedding dress designs were so popular. She had an eye for style that not even Lena could beat.

"Are you all right?" Bianca asked quietly. "You seem…distant."

"It's nerves." I played it off with a wave of my hand. "You look really happy. You're, like, glowing, and I bet you haven't stopped smiling since the last time I saw you."

Bianca lowered her gaze in a demure way. "I'm a very lucky girl."

I glanced at Sergei who stood shoulder-to-shoulder with Ivan and Yuri. The handsome behemoth had been the one guy every waitress at Samovar had wanted to date for a reason. He wasn't just good-looking. He was the perfect package. He balanced that alpha personality of his with kindness and respect and such sweetness.

Of course, if the rumors were to be believed he was something of a god between the sheets. Realizing Sergei was headed my way, I quickly cleared *that* salacious thought from my mind. I hoped he wouldn't able to tell that I had been thinking of him in that way. He would never stop teasing me if he suspected for one second that I wondered if the tales of his virility and sexual prowess were true. Then again, judging by the elated smile permanently plastered on Bianca's face these days, those stories were probably understated.

But Sergei wasn't smiling when he sat down in the spot Bianca had vacated a few seconds earlier so she could get a better look at the photos Lena was showing off on her phone. His sad, apologetic expression took me back to a morning so many months earlier. It was the morning I had come downstairs after spending my wedding night alone to find Nikolai still gone and only Sergei waiting for me. It had been a morning filled with disappointment and heartache.

Something told me we were about to relive the awfulness of that morning.

As I stared at Sergei's face, I guessed what he was about to say. It wasn't hard to piece together the clues. Slipping into Russian, I whispered, "He's not coming."

Sergei's eyes closed briefly. He shook his head and then reached for my hand. His massive paw engulfed my fingers. "If he could be here—"

"I know." Resigned and heartbroken, I refused to cry. I had done enough of that over the last week to last me a lifetime. I was finished feeling sorry for myself. I had earned this trip with my hard work and talent, and I was going to make the most of it.

Even if I had to do it alone.

I smiled broadly and pretended that I wasn't the least bit bothered. If I wasn't a priority for Nikolai, then he wasn't going to be one of mine. I shoved him out of my thoughts and concentrated only on my friends and the trip ahead of me. Grabbing my messenger bag, I stood up. "Tell Yuri we're ready to go. London's calling."

Sergei nodded slowly and rose to his feet with obvious hesitation. He wanted to say something, but he didn't. He did as I had asked and soon we were boarding the plane. Ten followed us out to the tarmac and waited until I had gotten safely onboard to leave. Whatever his faults, he was trying to do right by me as my bodyguard.

I didn't pay any attention to the couples sitting down together on the plane. I chose a seat in an empty row and opened the window. I didn't get the chance to fly much, and I had never flown overseas. I doubted I would ever again fly on a private jet like this one.

Like everything else Yuri did, he had gone overboard with his plane. The seats were luxurious and roomy. The gleaming walnut accents in the main cabin were gorgeous. Farther back in the plane, there was a dining area and a media room. I could just imagine what the bathrooms were like.

Soon, we were in the air and rocketing toward London. A gourmet meal was served about an hour into the flight. I found myself seated between Yuri and Bianca. They kept me entertained and in good spirits. No one mentioned Nikolai's absence, but I sensed Yuri and Ivan were angry on my behalf.

Somehow Lena and Erin wrangled me into joining a game of poker. We hadn't played in almost a year. Lena had an uncanny knack for the game so I was glad we were only playing for fun.

"I'm not very good at poker," Bianca apologized as she set up her small stack of chips.

"It doesn't matter," Erin reassured her. "We don't stand a chance against Vivian or Lena." She sipped her glass of moscato and then laughed. "When we were in college, I watched these two clean out an entire frat house the week before Spring Break started. They used their ill-gotten gains for a wild vacation to Punta Cana."

My memories of that trip were hazy at best. It had been the one and only time I had thrown caution to the wind. I cringed as Erin recounted some of our more embarrassing moments on the beautiful sun-soaked beaches of the Dominican Republic. Before I knew it, we were reminiscing about high school and college and marveling at how far we had come in our short lives. The four of us had accomplished so much, both professionally and personally. More and more, I believed it was the support and love we had for each other that had made those successes possible.

As predicted, Lena and I beat the pants off of Erin and Bianca. It was all in good fun, and we were all smiling and laughing as we cleaned up the cards and chips and moved to our seats to settle in for the night. I reclined mine fully and cuddled up under a blanket. Sleep didn't come easily though. Every little noise on the plane got my attention.

Yuri stayed up late somewhere in rear of the plane making phone calls. When he had wrapped up his business, he returned to the seats he and Lena had claimed in front of me. A moment after he had reclined and gotten comfortable, Lena scooted toward him. I heard him whisper sweetly to her before dragging her into his arms and making room for her in the wide, cushy seat. She draped herself over him, and he kissed the top of her head while telling her how much he loved her.

I tugged the blanket over my head to give the couple some privacy. Not far from me, Bianca and Sergei were undoubtedly curled up together in a similar fashion. I didn't dare glance back at the corner seats Erin and Ivan had taken. Those two were insatiable, so wildly hungry for each other that I wasn't the least bit surprised when I heard Erin get up and disappear toward the rear of the plane. Ivan followed a few minutes later.

I was simultaneously amused and envious. It was hard not to feel out of place among all these happy, loving couples. Glad for the exhaustion that finally overwhelmed me, I closed my eyes and drifted off to sleep. I woke a long time later with a painful ache in my neck and the worst case of heartburn. I reached for my cell phone in the cup holder where I had stored it earlier and pulled it under the blanket so I could glance at the screen without waking everyone else on the plane with the bright light.

We were still four hours away from London by my calculation. Not wanting to bother my friends by calling for one of the attendants, I quietly slipped out of my seat and walked back to the rear of the plane. I had seen a first aid kit attached to the wall near the bathroom. Hopefully it had some antacids in it.

I managed to detach the heavy box from the wall and carried it to the dining table. The dimmed lights made the task more difficult than it should have been. I was sorting through the compartments when the door to this section of the plane opened quietly and Yuri appeared. He wore an expression of concern. "Are you all right?"

I rubbed at my burning chest and grimaced at the sour taste invading my mouth. "I have heartburn. I didn't pack any antacids in my purse or carryon."

"Oh." He walked to a cabinet near the small wet bar, opened the door and retrieved a bottle of fruit-flavored tablets and a bottle of liquid medication. "The stress and travel plus the food and strange meal times kills me," he explained as he placed them on the table. "If it's really bad, I would use this one." He shook the liquid. "It tastes terrible, but it works fast."

"Terrible it is, then," I decided as I gulped in agony. The burning sensation was spreading, and I swore I would never, ever eat curry again. I didn't care how delicious it had been. This was sheer torture.

"Here." Yuri handed me a soup spoon from the closest drawer. "I lost the cup that comes with it. One spoon usually does the trick for me."

I unscrewed the cap and sniffed the liquid. It had a bizarrely strong cherry scent. After measuring out what looked like two or three teaspoons of the thick fluid, I knocked it back before I lost my nerve. I managed not to gag as I swallowed it down, but the taste clinging to my tongue was too much for me to handle.

Yuri must have read my mind. He grabbed a bottle of water from the counter, yanked off the cap and pressed it into my hand. I took a drink, swished it around my mouth and leaned forward to spit it into the sink. The movement parted my hair and gave Yuri his first glimpse of my tattoo.

He stepped close to me and ran his fingers over my skin. I jumped at the sensation of his unexpected touch and nearly knocked him over when I straightened up. He immediately stepped back and held up his hands. "I'm sorry, Vivian. That was over the line."

"It's okay. I just didn't expect it."

"No, I should have asked before touching you. I'm sorry."

"Apology accepted," I assured him with a smile. The antacid was already soothing the raging fire consuming my throat and stomach, and I relaxed against the counter. I sensed Yuri wanted to know the story behind the tattoo. "You can ask."

The corners of his mouth lifted. "When?"

"We had them done in April."

"We? So Nikolai has a matching one?"

"Yes. In the same place," I said, reaching back to touch the mark on my neck.

"I suppose I shouldn't be surprised. Nikolai's entire life is told in the tattoos on his body. They're a roadmap of all the things he's survived and all the bad things he's done. It's about time he put something good on his body. He needs to remember how lucky he is to have you as his wife."

I didn't know what to say to that, not after the awful week that had battered our marriage from all sides.

"Can I give you some advice?"

I eyed him wearily but nodded. "Sure."

"When he finally gets to London, you need to put Kolya in his place."

Yuri's phrase surprised me—and left me very suspicious. "How did—?"

"I've known Artyom since we were teenagers."

That was all he had to say. Arty had been there last night. He had heard every single ugly word.

"Kolya is my best friend. I love him. He's a brother to me—but he's a difficult man. He's complicated in the extreme."

"I know," I quietly agreed.

"That doesn't give him the right to talk to you that way." Yuri shook his head. "Vivian, you're just too damned sweet. You're too loving and forgiving. He needs your love. It's healing him, but he also needs a firm hand."

"A firm hand?"

"He may be the boss of Houston, but *you* are the boss of your home. He should come home every night, drop down to his fucking knees, kiss your feet and thank you for the privilege of groveling."

Eyes wide, I chortled at his description. "That's never going to happen."

He shot me a mischievous look. "Never say never, Vivian."

Now I was blushing. "No. Never."

"That was a bit of hyperbole, but you understand what I'm trying to say, right? He married *up*. You are too fucking good for him. He needs to remember how lucky he is that you love him. If he can't take care of you the way he promised, then someone else will."

Yuri's advice kept me awake long after we had returned to our seats. Curled on my side facing the open window, I burrowed deep under the blanket and resolved to do exactly as Yuri had suggested. When Nikolai finally made it to London, I was taking control. Not in that weirdly kinky way that Yuri had suggested, though. That was too far outside my comfort zone. I didn't think I could even deliver a command like that with a straight face.

Tired from two nights with little sleep and the emotional rollercoaster I had been riding, I walked like a zombie out of the airport and fumbled for my sunglasses as I squinted against the bright morning sun. I made it into one of the cars waiting to take us to

Yuri's penthouse. Like the plane, his Knightsbridge property was opulent and included the entire top floor of a historic mansion that had been converted to private luxury apartments. It was clear that Yuri had spared no expense in the renovation of his space.

Breakfast on the rooftop terrace was lovely, but my sagging eyelids didn't go unnoticed. Not long after Bianca and Sergei left, I excused myself for a much-needed nap. Lena showed me to my room. It was on the opposite end of the penthouse from their master suite and provided me with plenty of privacy. After a quick hug and instructions to make myself at home, Lena left me in peace.

I headed straight for the lavishly decorated bathroom, stripped out of my clothes and stepped into a steamy shower. Because I was so out of it with exhaustion, I didn't even remember to grab my toiletry bag from suitcase. Luckily, there was a selection of travel-sized toiletries in one of the tiled alcoves of the walk-in shower.

Squeaky clean and bright pink from the warm water, I emerged from the bathroom feeling refreshed but just as tired. I almost climbed right into bed, but the thought of waking to knotted, tangled hair stopped me. My luggage and Nikolai's had been set up in the corner of the room. I ignored the pang of sadness that reverberated in my chest when I touched his suitcase and forced my feet to keep moving to my own over-sized piece of luggage.

When I unzipped the bag, I immediately noticed something wrong. There was an extra soft-sided toiletry case tucked under the stretchy straps that held my clothing in place. Confused, I picked it up and noticed how heavy it was. The hot pink and lime green polka dots reminded me of something Erin would buy. Had our luggage spilled open during the flight? Had an attendant jammed this one into my bag thinking it was mine?

I unzipped the toiletry case and found a folded note and six burner cell phones. *What in the hell?*

Wrapped in my towel, with my wet hair dripping onto my shoulders and back, I sat down on the bench at the end of the bed and dumped the phones onto the duvet. I opened the note and tried to decipher the terrible handwriting. The Cyrillic letters ran into and over each other, making it difficult to read on the first pass. Whoever had written it was more comfortable writing in Russian than English and wasn't a very good speller.

My gaze drifted to the bottom. A grin tugged at my lips. The writer had signed his name in the most peculiar but fitting way.

V, I saved the numbers you'll need if shit goes bad. Memorize the address at the bottom of this note. If you can't get to one of these phones, take a cab to that address. Use my real name. You'll be safe there until someone we trust can get you. Just don't sit on the bed if they give you a room. ~ 10

Don't sit on the bed? I stared at the address and wondered where exactly he wanted me to hideout. Of course, if I was on the run, I couldn't exactly be picky about whatever spot would offer me sanctuary.

Did Ten think I was in that much danger here? After what had happened with Judge Walker, I suspected he was using an abundance of caution. Even so, I decided to keep two of the burner phones in my purse at all times. If I had to use one, I would still have the other as a backup.

I stowed two of the phones in my purse and hid the toiletry case in my suitcase. After I squeezed the excess water from my hair, I combed and braided it before finally collapsing on the bed. As I drifted off to sleep, I kept thinking about those phones and what they meant. This London getaway was supposed to be an easy, fun trip. Sure, there were mob problems in every city in the world, but the branch of Maksim Prokhorov's family that operated here had given Nikolai safe passage. We were under their protection while in the city.

But as I succumbed to my exhaustion, I couldn't shake the feeling that I would never again be truly safe.

15 CHAPTER FIFTEEN

Sitting next to Mr. Lu on the sky-high observation deck on the MD Anderson hospital campus, Nikolai fought the urge to glance at his watch. He could tell by the position of the sun that he was running out of time to meet Vivian at the airport. Even so, he refused to disrespect the old, grieving man who seemed even thinner and sicker since the last time he had seen him.

This was a meeting he had tried to have yesterday, right after his blowup with Vivian, but Lu had been admitted earlier that afternoon for a fainting spell. This was the first time they had been able to speak. Telling Lu that his nephew had been shot, probably by one of his own men during the melee that ensued, hadn't been easy. Now he waited for the old man's reaction.

With a sad sigh, he shook his head. "Bobby was a good boy, but he didn't have the patience or the discipline needed. He could have worked hard and climbed the ranks, but he wanted that easy money, that fast money."

Nikolai understood that type of man all too well. He had come up against them time and again—and beat them every single time.

"I'm glad his mother his gone. This would have broken her heart." Lowering his voice, Mr. Lu asked, "Where is his body?"

Nikolai glanced around the observation deck to make sure they were still alone. "He and his two friends are at a funeral home that we own. We staged an overdose in an abandoned house. A Justice of the Peace that Besian has in his pocket took care of the paperwork." He paused to let that information sink in. "Bobby's friends? Do they have family?"

"No. The other two boys—Jake Tran and Minh Jackson—don't have any family. No one will poke around for answers. If they do, we'll take care of it." Mr. Lu grimaced and rubbed at his throat.

"Are you all right? Should I get a doctor or a nurse?"

"I'm fine. It's this damn reflux." His shaky hand brought the bottle of water he was carrying to his mouth, and he took a long drink. While his trembling fingers fumbled with the lid, he asked, "What do I owe you?"

"Nothing." Nikolai couldn't stomach the thought of extracting money over this fiasco, not when Mr. Lu was in such bad shape. Whatever their disagreements, he wouldn't disrespect another boss like that. "It's been handled."

"And the repercussions?"

"Your family paid that debt with blood. We're good."

"What about the cartel?"

"I'll fucking bury Lorenzo Guzman myself if he even tries to come after you in retaliation. He's lost control of his own men. If he want to start making cuts, he should make them on his own arms first."

"Do you think he's going to fall?" Concern darkened the old man's face. "Because it feels the way it did before the coup that took out his father. Now that Romero is out of prison and hiding out in Mexico, he's a threat to Lorenzo. He has the loyalty and respect of the hard men in the cartel. He could break them away from Lorenzo and then what? Who fills that vacuum?"

"I don't know," Nikolai admitted. "That's what keeps me awake at night."

Mr. Lu nodded in agreement. "Things change, Russian. We have to change with them, or we get it in the neck." He inhaled noisily. "I'm not going to beat this. I can feel it in my bones. My change is coming soon." Lu turned to face him. "I need assurances from you that when I'm gone you'll support An. She's smart. She's strong. She has ideas and plans for my people."

Nikolai found the idea of a female boss in the city refreshing. "I'll work with her."

"She won't disappoint you." Mr. Lu grimaced again and coughed. "I should go back to my room now. I'm tired."

Nikolai reached out to help the older man to his feet and walked beside him back to the elevator and down to his room where his daughter waited for him. Thin with an angular face that was emphasized by her sharp short haircut, An sat in a chair by the window and read a magazine. She didn't smile at him when he entered the room at her father's side. She sized him up and didn't seem the least bit impressed.

He liked her instantly.

Leaving Mr. Lu in the care of his daughter, Nikolai headed out of the hospital and used the sky bridge to reach the garage where Kostya waited for him. He used the stairs rather than waiting for an elevator and checked his watch. He was cutting it close, but he still had time to make it.

He crossed the parking garage toward the black SUV Kostya had driven that morning and jerked open the front passenger door. "We need to hurry if we're going to make it."

"You're not going to make it, boss."

"What?" Nikolai spun toward his right-hand man and caught the flash of movement in the backseat. He started to reach for the sheathed knife he wore every-day but recognized the harsh face staring back at him at the last second.

Romero Valero laughed, the raspy, rattling sound filling the Escalade's interior. "You can let go of the knife. We're family, remember?"

"Don't remind me," Nikolai grumbled. "What the hell are you doing here?"

"Hector Salas. Bobby Pham. My daughter and grandbaby nearly getting shot. Why the hell else would I be here?"

Nikolai glanced at Kostya who exited the SUV without having to be asked. When they were alone, he said, "Vivian is fine. She wasn't hurt."

"Why the fuck was she there in the first place? I thought you had guards on her? You're damned lucky it wasn't Julio who got his hands on her."

Not in the mood for a recounting of his failures, he snapped, "Julio wouldn't be gunning for my family if you had given him Mando."

"I've made mistakes, but you married my daughter. You swore to fucking keep her safe. Last night you failed."

"I was there, Romero. I don't need the play-by-play." Irritated, he growled, "I don't have time for this. I've got to get to the airport. Vivian is waiting for me."

"Your rich friend's plane isn't the only one that goes to London, you know. There's a big, fucking airport that has planes that fly all night. Vivian will just have to wait." Romero leaned forward. "From what I've heard, a little distance between the two of you might be a good thing."

"What the fuck is that supposed to mean?"

"It means that if you ever go to a hotel with that blonde whore or any other woman again, I'll cut your worthless dick off and let you bleed to death in a Mexican desert."

Nikolai twisted in his seat to tell Romero to go to hell, but Romero's ink black eyes stopped him. They were so dark and flashed with such violent anger that Nikolai briefly entertained the thought that Vivian's father might actually be a demon. "Are you having me followed?"

"You think you're the only one with eyes and ears all over this city?" Romero snorted. "Every housekeeper, busboy, dishwasher and janitor in this city knows they can come to me with information, and I'll pay good money for it."

"You should ask for a refund because you got bad information."

"Bullshit. You were at that hotel with that blonde tramp we all thought you had killed for stepping out on you."

"We had lunch. Yes, we spoke privately in her suite, but I didn't fuck Tatiana. I haven't been with another woman in nearly two years. Whatever my mistakes—and Christ knows I'm piling them up this week—I've never betrayed Vivian. I fucking love her. She's my wife. I made a vow to her and only her."

"Then start acting like it!" Romero punctuated every word with a stab of his finger. "That girl of mine has been hurt enough. Her mother hurt her. I hurt her. Now you're hurting her. If you don't stop, I'm going to hurt you."

Nikolai would have scoffed and laughed in any other man's face at that threat, but Romero meant it.

Feeling uncomfortably exposed but knowing he deserved every bit of her father's anger, Nikolai looked his father-in-law in the eyes and promised, "I'm going to make it right."

"You fucking better. I've taken out a boss before, Nikolai. I have no problem doing it again."

"Understood."

"Good." He sat back and stretched out his legs. "Why is the judge still alive? Why didn't you slit that junkie's throat?"

"Leaving the daughter alive wasn't my first choice," Nikolai admitted. "She's a liability, but she can be managed. The judge is more valuable to me alive. He owes me a debt."

"A big fucking debt," Romero grumbled. "Get your spy back in here. We need to drive and talk."

"About?"

"Moving up my timetable," Romero said matter-of-factly.

"Your timetable for what?"

Romero betrayed his nervousness by glancing out the rear window. "We've been sitting here too long. Get on the road, and I'll tell you exactly why Hector Salas was working with Bobby Pham."

Hector had been so doped up after his surgery that Nikolai hadn't been able to interrogate him at all. If he wanted to know what was coming, and if he was going to have time to make plans to keep his family safe, he had to stay and hear what Romero had to say.

He gestured for Kostya to rejoin them and pulled his phone out of his pocket. Not wanting their first discussion since that terrible fight to be yet another disappointment, Nikolai chose not to call Vivian but settled on Yuri instead. As he waited for Yuri to pick up, Nikolai wiped a hand down his face. It was going to be another long night.

"You've got your passport? Your ID?" Kostya asked as they followed the winding route to the airport curbside drop-off spot for the airline he was flying.

"Yes." He still patted his pockets to double check. "My luggage is already on its way with Vee."

"It's late so the lines at the security checkpoints should be short. I got you a first class seat so you should fly right through them."

"I hate going through security," he admitted. "I swear to God I have flashbacks of Krasnoyarsk."

Kostya laughed darkly and merged into the far right lane where a line of cars queued up. He slowed to a stop, and Nikolai reached for the door handle. Kostya's hand settled on his arm. "Boss, wait."

"What is it?"

Kostya put the SUV in park and turned in his seat so they were looking eye-to-eye. "Ilya called to give me a report on the judge and the cocaine princess while you were talking with Romero and Hector at the safe house."

"And?"

"Ilya says that the judge told him that he lied to Vivian to get her to come with him. He told Ilya that he was coming over to the house to talk with Vivian, to see if he could get her to intervene, but then he heard the fighting between Ten and Eric. He saw her outside, and she looked upset so he decided it was the perfect opening. He told her about losing his dog and then asked her if she'd like to have dinner with him. He told her that he was taking her to a barbecue joint that all the cops around town like so she would feel safe."

Kostya paused, and Nikolai had a feeling he wasn't going to like whatever was said next. "He told her he wanted to pick his daughter up to join them. When they got to the door, he pulled his gun, and he forced Vivian in to the house. He made her frisk the guy who had answered and then basically held them both at gunpoint. He used her as a shield because he knew that Bobby Pham would never allow anything bad to happen with your wife there."

Nikolai turned his head and closed his eyes. He remembered every cruel word that had come out his hateful mouth. He remembered the cold way he had treated her after the shooting, the way he had punished her with his silence and sent her away with Ten rather than comforting her. At the time, he hadn't wanted to reward her reckless behavior.

But she had been a victim.

And he had treated her terribly.

"There's something else," Kostya reluctantly added.

"Just fucking tell me."

"Ten and I had a chance to speak while you were in the hospital with Mr. Lu. He came to the parking garage to find me because he didn't want to do it over the phone."

"What did he want?"

Kostya tapped his fingertips on the steering wheel. "Vivian knows about Tatiana."

"I know. I told her. A reporter was poking around and asking questions about Tatiana's new identity. I told Vivian what she needed to know."

Kostya shook his head. "That's not what I meant. Vivian saw you."

"Saw me? Where?"

"At the Four Seasons," Kostya finally said. "She and Erin went to Quattro for lunch. You hadn't told Ten that you were meeting with Tatiana there so he didn't stop them. Somehow she wandered back to the cellar—and she saw you with Tatiana."

Nikolai's heart fucking stopped. He tried to breathe, but his lungs refused to work. Memories of the last week flashed before his eyes. Vivian had been sick on Thursday. She had seemed so sad and fragile when he had returned home that evening.

And no fucking wonder! He replayed the conversation he had shared with Tatiana. It had been tense at first, but once they were down in the restaurant, they had warmed to one another and had remembered their fondness for teasing. The flirtatious remarks between them were harmless.

But Vivian didn't know that. If she had overheard them, she would have gotten the wrong idea. It would have been painful and confusing for her. He could only imagine the heartache she had suffered because of him. His own chest hurt so badly now he could hardly breathe.

"I can't get it right anymore," he muttered. "Everything I do is wrong. Everything I touch turns to shit. Everyone I have ever cared about gets hurt because of me."

"Nikolai." Kostya rarely spoke his name so it drew him out of his self-pitying wallow quickly. "Look at me."

He did. "What?"

"Don't come back next week."

He frowned. "What do you mean?"

"I mean that I'll take care of Houston. I've got Artyom and Ilya. Ten is back, and if shit goes bad, he'll step up and help."

"No, Ten is on parole."

"Ten is a grown man. He can make his own decisions." Kostya gripped his shoulder and squeezed. "We can hold the city, but we can't help you save your marriage. You have to do that hard work yourself." Kostya's grip tightened. "You love her. You've risked everything for her. *Fight* for her."

A pent-up breath that he hadn't realized he had been carrying rushed out of Nikolai's lungs. He felt the stress and tension roll out of his shoulders and back. Kostya was right. He had that uncanny knack for always knowing the right thing to say. "I will."

"Good."

Old habits were hard to break so he quickly gave his last orders before climbing out of the SUV and entering the airport. He made his way to the ticket counter for his airline and waited patiently behind a family of seven who were taking the late-night Houston to London flight. The parents seemed to be in their mid-to-late thirties, and their children ranged from nine or ten to less than a year.

Nikolai's gaze settled on the chubby baby chewing on her fist and drooling all over her father's shoulder. He hadn't been around babies much. Holding Dimitri's daughter had been a strangely eye-opening experience for him. She was the tiniest little thing with big, beautiful eyes and the sweetest smell. He had been struck by the realization that in a few short months he would be holding his own child like that every single day.

But mixed in with the happiness and the excitement was dread. He feared the sins of his past would come back to haunt his family. The sins of his father and Vivian's had fucked with their lives more than once. He didn't want that for his child. He wanted his son or daughter to have a good life.

More and more, he thought of Romero's statement that day in Corpus Christi about cutting their leashes. Was that the answer? Was it time to break away from Maksim? The complications and repercussions would be heavy, maybe too heavy, for him to bear.

Armed with their tickets and relieved of their checked baggage, the family left the counter and headed for the nearby security line. Nikolai stepped forward

and smiled at the woman behind the computer termi-
nal. "Hello." He pushed his driver's license and passport across the counter. "I'm checking in for my flight
to London."

She picked up his license and glanced at his information before tapping at her keyboard. "How are you
tonight, Mr. Kalasnikov?"

"Fine. How is your night shaping up?"

"Busy." She flashed him a smile and then concentrated on her screen. A flicker of a frown crossed her
face. "You've flown with our airline before, sir?"

"Yes." He tried to think back to the last time he
had gone overseas. "Four years ago, I think."

"Hmmm," she hummed aloud. "Did you have any
trouble boarding your flight?"

"No." He didn't like the tone of that question at all.
"Why?"

"Well, Mr. Kalasnikov, it seems that you've been
put on the No-Fly List."

He blinked. "Excuse me?"

"Your name is on the list. It means we can't allow
you to board our flight. In fact, it means you can't
board any flight in the United States."

He couldn't believe what he was hearing. "That's a
list for terrorists."

"Yes." She eyed him warily now and pushed his
driver's license and passport back toward him with one
finger. Her gaze flicked to the left, just behind him,
and he glanced back to see a pair of TSA agents and a
police officer coming closer. "Sir, I'm sorry, but you'll
have to go with these men."

It took every ounce of his self-control not to blow up with anger. The last fucking thing he needed was to spend the night sweating in some interrogation room. "Sure," he ground out between clenched teeth. "I'll go with them."

He jammed his driver's license back into his wallet and his passport back into his jacket pocket and allowed the TSA agents to surround him. Without saying a word, he followed the police officer to the nearest station. On edge and feeling his fight-or-flight response kicking in, Nikolai clenched his fingers at his side. He dropped down in the empty seat offered to him and glanced around the cold, stark room.

Could this night get any fucking worse?

16 CHAPTER SIXTEEN

The night got worse.

In fact, it went downhill quickly, and Nikolai resorted to waking up his lawyer and dragging his overpaid ass out of his mansion in The Woodlands to the airport holding cell where he had been corralled. The sun was rising, turning the Houston skyline a hazy pink, when David finally popped him from the TSA's custody.

"This is a mistake," David assured him as they drove away from the airport in a private car with darkly tinted windows. "You have no criminal convictions or arrests in this country. On paper, you've been a model citizen here."

"Here, yes," Nikolai agreed, "but back home?" He shook his head. "I was in deep, dirty shit, and it was all out in the open. You saw the printouts they were waving in front of my face. Those records were supposed to have been destroyed when I came over here."

When he had agreed to come to Houston to help Maksim expand the family's control, the old man had used his government connections to destroy their criminal records and convictions. They came halfway across the world on clean papers and with clean passports. So how the hell had the TSA gotten their hands on records that weren't supposed to exist anymore?

"Obviously some of those records exist." David stated the obvious. "If you want to be able to board a flight or re-enter the US anytime in the near future, I would highly suggest you get one of your friends with useful contacts to take care of that. I'll do what I can from here, but you need to be realistic, Nikolai. Publicly, you've kept your nose clean. You've stayed out trouble."

"Yes, but the government knows everything about me." It was his turn to state the obvious. An alphabet soup of government agencies kept a close eye on him—DEA, ATF, FBI, CIA. There was a reason his home, cars, Samovar and his favorite meeting spots were swept by Kostya every week. He tried to keep his cell and landline use to a minimum and gave orders of a sensitive nature directly to the two or three men he trusted most.

But he was going to have to be more careful now. It was clear that he was on the government's radar.

Nikolai sat forward and tapped on the glass divider between the rear and front seats. The driver lowered the partition, and he ordered, "Drop me off at the convenience store on the next corner."

"Yes, sir."

"I can take you home." David seemed surprised by the instruction he had given their driver. "It's not a problem."

"I'm not going home."

David's eyes narrowed. "Where are you going?"

"To see my wife," he replied matter-of-factly.

"Your wife? Vivian is in London. Unless you plan to sprout wings—"

"There is more than one way to get across that fucking ocean, and I'm going to find one." The car slowed to a stop, and he unbuckled his belt. "I'll fucking swim if I have to because I'm not missing her show."

"Nikolai." David grabbed his arm. "As your lawyer—"

"I know, David." He shrugged off the other man's hand. "I'll be careful. If not, I'm sure you can point me in the right direction for a good attorney overseas."

To his credit, David didn't seem flustered by the realization that a client was about to do something stupid. Instead, he muttered, "If I have to fly to London, I'm going first class and staying at a five-star hotel and eating at the best restaurants, and I'm charging it all to your account."

Nikolai laughed. "I'd expect nothing else from you."

David smiled at him. "Good luck, Nikolai."

Nodding, he stepped out of the car and closed the door. He went inside and bought a cup of coffee and three prepaid cell phones. He made sure to get his change in quarters and dimes so he could use the ancient payphone along the side of the building. Trying not to think about the grime coating the handset, Nikolai inserted his change and punched in Kostya's number.

From the gruff, heavy sound of Kosyta's voice when he answered, he had been asleep. "Yeah?"

"Kostya, I need you to come get me."

"Nikolai? What's wrong? Where are you?" Fully alert now, he asked questions quickly in Russian.

"It's a long story." He sipped the too hot but surprisingly good coffee. "I'm at the Shell station on the corner of JFK and Greens."

"I'll send Boychenko. He goes to see his grandmother at the nursing home every morning. It's right there next to the airport."

Knowing how close the kid was to his grandmother, he didn't want to keep him from her for long. "I only need him to drop me off somewhere."

Kostya didn't ask where. "Be careful, boss."

"Yeah."

After hanging up, he activated two cell phones and placed a call to a private number that went straight to a voicemail box for a travel agency. The line beeped, and he left his message. "I'm following up on a lost piece of luggage. The ticket number was..." He glanced at the other cell phone and rattled off its number. "Thank you."

When the call was finished, he broke the phone into pieces and retrieved the SIM card before tossing the rest into the trash can. Not long after, Boychenko arrived at the gas station in his '67 Chevy Impala. The kid had put hours of work into restoring the muscle car, and it showed.

"Boss," Boychenko greeted as he slid into the front passenger seat. "Is everything okay?"

"No." He closed the door and enjoyed the cold blast from the air conditioner. The hot, muggy morning air made his rumpled suit feel heavy and uncomfortable. "I know that you're on your way to see your grandmother so I'll make it quick."

"It's fine, boss. She'll understand, and she won't mind, not after everything you've done for her."

When Agnessa had first started to have complications with her diabetes and heart condition, she had come to him for help. Nikolai had gladly given it. She had been one of the first people to welcome him to Houston. Her door had always been open to him. If he had needed a hot meal or a place to do laundry, she had always obliged. When he had opened Samovar, she had helped him staff the place by suggesting cooks and servers and other people she knew and trusted.

So he had purchased the small grocery store she owned, paying more than it was worth, to ensure that she would be able to get the medical care she would need. Without insurance, she had gone through the money quickly. Once he had learned that she was facing the prospect of spending her final years in a state-run facility, Nikolai had made arrangements for her care and paid the bill personally.

"That's not a debt your family owes," he told Boychenko and not for the first time. "Everything I've done for Agnessa was because of her kindness to me."

"And everything I've done for you, boss, is because of the kindness you showed her," Boychenko replied.

Certain he could trust the kid, he said, "I need you to take me to one of my bolt-holes."

Boy's eyes widened. He understood that he was being trusted with a location that no one else had, not even Kostya. "Yes, sir." He put the car in drive. "Which way?"

"Head toward Spring. I'll give you the directions as we get closer."

They didn't speak as they drove north on I-45. Rock music played in the background, just loud enough that the silence wasn't grating. He rolled down the window as they flew down the interstate and tossed out the SIM card. The wind caught it up and carried it away.

Nikolai stared out the window, but he didn't actually see any of the scenery whizzing by them. He was consumed by thoughts of Vivian, of the ways he had failed her and of the ways he might make things right between them again. It was clear to him that his policy of shielding her and keeping secrets had to end. All the little lies and the omissions were adding up. He wanted to settle that tab and be done with it.

If she still wants me...

That was the heart of it, wasn't it? What if he had pushed too far? What if she had finally realized that she could do better? Because she could. She deserved so much better than a mobbed-up ex-con with a shady past that would never leave him. Their child deserved better.

But no matter how hard he tried, Nikolai didn't see a way out. He wasn't Sergei. He wasn't Ivan or Alexei. He was in this life forever. Even if he tried to leave and make a clean break, Maksim's men would hunt him down and end him. If it wasn't Maksim, it would be the cartel or Liam, his Irish gun-runner, or one of a dozen different underworld contacts who might be afraid he would snitch. He knew too much to get out.

He gave Boy a series of directions that took them to a rundown apartment complex. He had the kid park in one of the guest spots along the back wall and asked him to come inside. Boy didn't dare refuse. He trailed Nikolai to the covered parking spot near the garbage cans where he kept a dark blue late model Toyota with fender damage. Crouching down, Nikolai unhooked the magnetic box keeping the key to his apartment securely attached to the underside of the vehicle. Boy stayed close as they walked to a ground-floor corner apartment.

When they were safely inside, he locked the door behind them and tossed the spare key from the empty bookshelf to Boychenko who showed those quick reflexes by catching it. "This is yours now."

"Mine?" He glanced around the sparsely furnished, dusty apartment. "Are you serious?"

Nikolai's brow arched. "Have I ever joked with you?"

"No, sir."

"You've seen this location so it's no good for me anymore. Now it's your secret to keep."

Boychenko pocketed the key. "How do I pay for it?"

"You don't. It's taken care of for the next seven years. By the time another payment is due, you'll have your own hidey hole somewhere else. This will be another man's problem."

Boychenko seemed hesitant to ask, but he did anyway. "Why?"

"Because I like you," Nikolai said simply. "You're a good kid. You work hard. You deserve a safe place to retreat."

"Thank you."

"Come on. I'll give you the grand tour." Nikolai led him around the one-bedroom space and showed him where he had hidden things like cash, weapons and other supplies. Nikolai opened the closet and took out a backpack that he unzipped to show Boychenko the contents. "This is ready to grab and run, you understand?"

"Yes, sir."

"You need to get a backpack. Stuff it with a change of clothing, good shoes for running, a burner phone and a charger, cash and guns." He picked up the second backpack that he kept at the apartment. It was heavier than the other one and crammed with wrapped stacks of hundred and twenty dollar bills. He tossed two banded stacks of bills at Boychenko. "Take these. They can be your emergency fund starter."

The kid gaped at the money tossed his way. "This is, like, twenty thousand dollars, boss."

"Roman," he used the kid's first name, "if you ever have to run, twenty thousand won't get you very far." He motioned to the shoeboxes of guns and ammo. "You can have those too. They're clean steel. They went straight from Liam's hand to mine." He tapped the kid's chest. "Don't even think about trying to sell them."

"No, sir."

"If anyone asks, you took me to Samovar, okay?"

"Yes, sir."

"Don't tell anyone about this place. Not even Kostya." He held the kid's gaze to make sure he understood how important it was that he keep this secret. "This apartment might be the only thing between you and a bloody fucking end someday. Okay?"

"Yes, sir."

"Change the locks tonight if you want to be safe."

"I will."

Certain he'd gotten through to Boychenko, he hooked his thumb toward the door. "Go on. Get out."

With a silent nod, Boychenko left the apartment. Nikolai followed him and locked the door. Alone in the apartment, he changed out of his suit and into the jeans and T-shirt hanging in the closet. He jammed his feet into the well-worn sneakers and ran his fingers through his hair before fitting a baseball cap into place. He was picking out a weapon when the burner cell started to ring.

"Hello?"

"You can retrieve your luggage at the following address."

Nikolai listened carefully as an automated computerized voice read off a number and street. The phone call ended, and he dismantled the phone. With both backpacks in hand, he left the apartment and used his key one final time. After he threw the backpacks onto the passenger seat, he flicked his apartment key into the garbage bin and started the old Corolla. He tried to remember to sneak away to drive it every month, but sometimes he forgot. It had been seven or eight weeks since the last time he'd started it up, but thankfully the engine turned over without a hiccup.

Paranoid that someone was following him, Nikolai made a series of unnecessary detours to reach the address that had been given to him. He threw pieces of the phone out the window as he drove. An hour later, he found himself pulling into an industrial sector near Jersey Village. The building at the address he had been given looked as if it might have once been used by an oilfield or natural gas company. The rolling gate was open wide enough to admit a vehicle and one garage door had been left open for him.

Hand on his weapon, Nikolai eased into the dark building. As his eyes adjusted to the single halogen light illuminating the large space, he spotted movement to his left. He turned quickly and breathed easier when he saw the familiar face of Zec. The Albanian reached for the long chain attached to the rollup door and gave it three sharp tugs. The metal clanged and clamored as it rolled closed.

Nikolai had met some hard bastards during his life as a street child and later during his prison stretches, but Zec was the hardest—and meanest—of them. He had been born in a Russian women's prison to an Albanian mother who had been brutally assaulted by the male warden. She had been allowed to keep and raise her baby there.

Whether that was a kindness the warden allowed because he felt guilty or a cruel and twisted punishment, Nikolai couldn't say. He leaned toward the latter. Despite the hell he had survived in the orphanage, Nikolai still would have chosen that over life in a prison. He could only imagine the horrible, viciously cruel things Zec must have seen as a child. It wasn't hard to understand why the man had his peculiar tastes.

Predictably, Zec had struggled to live on the outside after his mother had finally been freed. He had been in and out of prisons across Europe and Russia before finally settling into a career as a smuggler. Over the years, he had built up a massive empire that moved cargo, legal and illegal, around the globe.

"I hear you had a little problem at the airport," Zec said in that gravelly voice of his. A razor blade slashed across the throat had given him that rather charming trait.

There was no use in keeping anything from Zec. "I'm on the No Fly List."

"How?"

Nikolai shrugged and leaned against the door of the Corolla. The scent of industrial-strength cleaners and diesel saturated the air of the abandoned building so he tried not to breathe too deeply. "I suspect someone back home is trying to make trouble for me."

"Like Maksim?"

"Probably," Nikolai agreed. His father was the only person who could have gotten his hands on that information. Knowing Maksim, he had kept the originals for use in a situation just like this one.

"Because he found out that Tatiana Filipova is still alive?"

That had been Nikolai's first thought. The old man was probably furious that Nikolai had lied to him. He would want to make sure that Nikolai remembered who held the end of his leash. Eyes narrowed, he asked, "How long have you known?"

"About a year." Zec pulled a pack of cigarettes from the pocket of his lightweight jacket. "Would you like one?"

Yes. So fucking much. "No."

Zec lit up and exhaled a lungful of smoke. "I was doing a bit of work in Hong Kong, and I happened to see her across a restaurant. For a moment, I thought I was seeing things. It didn't take me long to piece together the clues." He took another drag. "It was smart to hide her right under Maksim's nose. She has a good life in Hong Kong. Why is she back?"

"Why do you think? You know everything. I'm sure you can fill in those blanks."

"Her brother just took a bullet to the back of the skull while on vacation in Istanbul, and her father had a heart attack last year while one of those young hookers he loved so much was riding him like a racehorse. There's no reason for her to hide anymore—if you've forgiven her."

"There was nothing to forgive."

"That's not the story I heard." Zec flicked his ash toward the concrete floor.

"My story is the only one that matters."

Zec shrugged. "Your city, your rules." He gestured to the black sedan with darkly tinted windows sitting on the far side of the empty building. "We need to go. You've got a long trip ahead of you."

Nikolai grabbed his backpacks from the car. "How are you going to get me to London?"

"We're driving across the border into Mexico. There's a private airfield near Tampico that I own. I have a shipment of a *sensitive* nature that has to get to Bogotá tonight."

"Colombia?" Nikolai already hated this plan.

"Surely that hot little wife of yours has taught you Spanish by now, *Papi.*" He emphasized the last word in a lewd way.

Nikolai shot Zec the finger, but the Albanian just laughed. "Get the door, Nikolai."

He pulled on the dirty chain to lift the rear door high enough for the car to exit and then slipped under it. He gave one of the metal handles a jerk and pulled the door the rest of the way down. After sliding into the passenger seat of the sedan, he asked, "And after Bogotá?"

"Lagos." Zec adjusted the air conditioning. "By the way, I hope you don't want that shitty car back. Ben's guys will collect it tonight and get rid of it."

"Consider it my down payment for this trip," Nikolai grumbled. "Why Lagos?"

"My client in Bogotá has a gift for a friend in Nigeria. We won't be there very long. They'll meet us at the airfield for the handoff while we're refueling and then we'll head to Tirana."

"Albania? I need to get to London."

"And you will," Zec promised, "but you can't fly into the country. If you're on the No Fly List here, you can be damned sure the Brits have you tagged, too. I'll have to get you into the country old school."

Nikolai really didn't like the sound of that. He envisioned a long, bumpy ride in the back of a freight truck and a stomach-churning boat ride across the North Sea. "Shit."

"Cheer up." Zec punched the gas while Nikolai fumbled with his seatbelt. "Luka has invited us over for a breakfast date."

"You mean he's going to hold me hostage over runny eggs and burnt toast until I agree to give Besian more territory or to increase the percentage of traffic that's thrown your way."

Zec laughed. "Runny eggs and burnt toast? No. For you? Luka will make sure there's a big steaming bowl of *paça* waiting."

"Lucky me," Nikolai dryly replied. Like a garlicky version of the *menudo* so popular among the Mexicans in Texas, the Albanian soup made from innards was one that he could hardly stand to smell let alone eat. He liked and respected the head of the Beciraj crime family, but he didn't think he could choke that soup down even for Luka.

Leaning back in his seat, Nikolai realized he had been wrong to think that his night in TSA and airport police custody was the worst. It seemed his bad luck was just beginning.

17   CHAPTER SEVENTEEN

Jet-lagged, exhausted and in need of a shower and clean clothing, Nikolai emerged from a car into the darkness of a very early Albanian morning. He scrubbed his hands over his tired face and felt three days' worth of stubble under his palms. It took him a moment to calculate the actual date. It was Wednesday morning.

"Nikolai! *Mirëmëngjes!*" Far too happy for this early of a morning, Luka Beciraj bounded down the front steps of his impressive mansion. "How was your trip?"

"*Mirëmëngjes.*" He returned the Albanian greeting and tried not to yawn. "It was long."

Luka shot a knowing look at Zec. "Yes, especially when your traveling companion is so talkative."

That brought a smile to Nikolai's face. Zec had kept to himself for most of the trip. He liked to read or watch the news and films. Nikolai suspected Zec's throat injury bothered him when he talked too much. That or he didn't care that he came across as boorish.

"English or Russian? I'm happy to indulge you either way." It was a not so subtle jab over the fact that Nikolai's Albanian wasn't as good as it should have been. Whenever he had needed to conduct business of that sort, he had always been able to rely on Ivan or Kostya. Both men were extraordinarily gifted with languages.

"It's your home." Nikolai deferred to his host.

"English then," Luka replied and motioned for Nikolai to walk with him. "I need to practice."

"Are you planning a trip my way?" He climbed the steps but let his gaze scan the area. There were armed guards fucking everywhere. Whether that was simply an abundance of caution or the evidence of real and present danger, Nikolai couldn't say. Surrounded by all those weapons and guards, he finally got a taste of what it was like for Vivian day in and day out at the house. Ten and the others never carried weapons in sight, and they gave her space—but my God. She must have felt surrounded and claustrophobic.

"It's almost time for me to take the final installment on the Dushku blood debt."

The mention of that bloody war between rival families was one that made Nikolai grimace. He had been an outsider watching that gruesome year unfold from afar. Sneaking a look at Luka, he was struck by how much the Albanian boss had changed in those twelve years. He had been just a boy of eighteen when his parents and sister were slaughtered by backstabbing rivals of his father's.

Rather than surrendering to the older, wiser and stronger Aleksander Dushku and Pali Gonaj, a teen-aged Luka had rallied the troops and fought tooth and nail to regain control. His tactics had been vicious and harsh, but he had won the war and put every single adult male member of the two families underground. There had been some in Luka's camp who had clamored for the women and children to join them, especially since so many innocents on their side had been badly injured or killed, but he had found a better way to end the bloodshed and to make peace.

Because blood ties were everything to Luka, he had decided that Dafina Dushku, the daughter of Aleksander and a granddaughter of Pali, was the answer. He invoked a *besa*, a sworn promise, from Dafina's mother that when the young girl finished college she would return to Luka's home and marry him. The families would be united that way and peace would be cemented for at least a generation.

To Nikolai, the arranged marriage seemed like such an archaic thing. Curious about the arrangement, he asked, "Have you ever met her?"

"Dafina?" Luka shook his head. "She's been living in Texas since before the war started. Her mother fled the country with her when she was three or four. She wasn't even here when the war began." He led Nikolai up a grand staircase. "Not that distance kept the blood from splattering her front door."

"So she has no idea that you intend to marry her?" Nikolai tried to wrap his head around it.

"I left the decision about what to tell her and when to her mother. Besian keeps an eye on her while she's at Rice University. I'm not concerned by the details."

You fucking should be, he thought incredulously. Did Luka really think it was going to be that easy to convince a young woman who had been raised with such freedom in the United States to just swan back over here as the wife of a mafia boss?

"This will be your room today." Luka showed him to a large suite. "I'll have a breakfast tray brought to you. The bathroom is through that door. I assumed you would want to shower and sleep. We can talk later."

"Thank you." Nikolai extended his hand and firmly grasped Luka's. "I owe you for this."

Luka laughed and clapped him on the back. "You can be sure I'll collect on this debt."

Nikolai smiled. "I have no doubt."

Left alone, Nikola stripped and showered but didn't bother shaving. When he left the steamy bathroom, he found a breakfast tray waiting on the upholstered bench at the end of the bed. He scarfed it down without tasting it and crawled between the sheets where he promptly passed out in a dreamless sleep.

A loud knock woke him sometime later. Confused and disoriented, he damned near jumped off the bed.

His fuzzy brain finally produced the right answer. He was sleeping in Luka Beciraj's mansion outside Tirana.

Rolling onto his side, he squinted at the door and cleared his throat. "Yes?"

The door opened and Luka poked his head through the small space. "You need to get up and get dressed. We have time for a quick meal before we hit the road."

He sat up and rubbed his face between his hands. "Where are we going?"

"Zagreb."

"Croatia? What the hell is in Croatia?" His patience was thin, and these endless side trips were getting on his last damned nerve.

"Your next ride," Luka said cryptically and shut the door.

Grumbling and sore from travel, Nikolai reluctantly left the warmth of the bed and stumbled into the bathroom. He took a longer shower this time, making use of the toiletries left for him, and shaved at the sink. The cheap disposable razor didn't give him the clean, smooth shave he preferred, but he wasn't about to complain.

He took a clean pair of jeans and a T-shirt from his backpack before slipping into the lightweight black hoodie he had packed. It was imperative that he keep his arms and neck covered while traveling. The tattoos that served as his calling card on the street garnered too much attention. He had to remember to keep his hands in his pockets whenever possible.

Nikolai moved some of his cash into the backpack with his clothing, weapons and burner phones. The rest he left as payment for Zec and Luka. With his bag slung over his shoulder, he exited the bedroom and wandered downstairs where he found Luka waiting for him. He was shown to a dining room and a hot meal was served. With so many eyes and ears around, they didn't talk business of any kind. It was the usual sort of empty conversation acquaintances shared when catching up.

After eating, he followed Luka outside to a convoy of black and silver Range Rovers. He joined Luka in the middle vehicle. The Albanian boss got behind the wheel and Nikolai settled in for yet another long fucking drive.

"I had wanted to put you on a train once we reached the border," Luka explained as they rolled out of the driveway. "Zec shot down that option. He worried that border crossings and the terminals might prove difficult. Government blacklists have a way of following you."

"Yes," he murmured unhappily.

"So we've arranged a series of pickups and drop-offs from Zagreb to Amsterdam," Luka said. "You're under my protection while you're traveling."

"Thank you, Luka." Knowing that his own father had probably leaked that incriminating information to teach him a lesson, Nikolai didn't trust his own network right now. "What happens in Amsterdam?"

"We have a shipment crossing tomorrow night. You're part of the cargo. You'll reach London early Friday morning. Transportation has been arranged. Our specialist will meet you in Amsterdam, at the safe house there, to fix your passport and travel record. Once you hit British soil, your papers will be fine."

"I left your payment in the room. If it's not enough—"

"I know where to find you," Luka replied with a cheeky grin. Sobering, he said, "Now, tell me what the fuck is going on with the cartel and your father-in-law."

He wasn't about to reveal the entire conversation he had shared with Romero before leaving Houston, but there were parts he could divulge. "Lorenzo Guzman is losing control of the paramilitary wing of his organization. They're led by Hector Salas. He's young, close to your age, and he's hungry. He's fucking smart, too. He likes things quiet. He has a plan that could potentially change the entire game in Mexico."

"And your father-in-law? How does he figure into all of this?"

"His last stretch in the pen disillusioned him. He came up through the ranks with Lorenzo. He killed Lorenzo's father to keep the cartel out of a war they couldn't win with the Colombians. Now he sees the same thing happening again with Lorenzo. I think, in his own twisted fucking way, he's looking for peace."

"By knocking off Lorenzo?"

"They'll try to isolate him. They'll try to force him into some sort of retirement."

"There is no such thing as retirement for men like us." Despite his young age, Luka seemed to have given that topic a fair bit of thought. "We don't walk away from this life. We live it until we die. God takes us or our enemies do. There is no other way."

"If Lorenzo is smart, he'll find one."

"And if he's not?"

"It's not my battle to fight." Nikolai adjusted the strap of the seat belt. "I only care about what happens in and around Houston. The drugs the cartel supplies aren't my main source of income. If Lorenzo falls, my only concern is keeping the streets of Houston safe."

"Let's talk about something that does concern you."

"What is that?"

"Guns."

"What about them?"

"Maksim is squeezing my connection. We aren't getting our usual shipments. They're delayed and the prices are sky fucking high."

"There's a war brewing with Kiev. That's a direct supply route for you."

"If I can't get my steel, I'll have to look elsewhere," Luka warned.

"If it comes to that, send Zec to Dublin. I'll put him in contact with a friend of mine."

"And cut out Maksim?" Luka seemed surprised by the offer.

After that little stunt Maksim had pulled with his Russian criminal record, Nikolai wasn't feeling particularly loyal. "It's business."

As they continued their drive through the Albanian countryside, Nikolai began to form a better picture of the way forward. The pieces were beginning to settle into place. It wasn't going to be easy, and there was a shit fucking ton of risk involved, but maybe, just maybe, he could put his crew in a better, safer position.

When they reached Zagreb, Nikolai left Luka's convoy for a single truck idling in a petrol station parking lot. Luka wished him luck. Nikolai had a feeling he was going to need it.

The rest of the day, all of the night and most of the next day was spent switching vehicles and drivers every few hours as they continued their northward trek. There were short stops to piss and eat and stretch but nothing else. His legs were cramping by the time they finally reached Amsterdam, and he had a headache from hell.

A beer, *broodje* and a couple of aspirin offered by the men at the safe house solved that problem. He squeezed in a short nap after the forgery expert handled all the paperwork and created a fake electronic travel trail. Nikolai got her information for the future. If nothing else, she would be a useful contact for Kostya.

Not long after nightfall, he was taken to the harbor where a boat loaded down with Afghan heroin waited for them. He tried not to dwell on how many years' worth of prison he would earn if they were caught with this cargo. He trusted the men who were sailing and guarding the shipment knew what they were doing. They didn't want to see the inside of one of Her Majesty's Prisons any more than he did.

As expected, the ride was nausea-inducing. He got another taste of what poor Vivian had been dealing with over the last few weeks. He craved one of those ginger candies she carried in her purse and kept around the house. The smell of cigarettes, a scent he had always associated with relaxation and fun, soured his stomach as the men on the ship burned through pack after pack in the small, cramped space.

When they finally reached shore around four in the morning, Nikolai left a few stacks of cash to pay for his fare and damned near jumped off the boat and onto solid land. He stumbled like a drunk down the pier and found a building to lean against while he dry heaved. *Never again,* he swore. He would never fucking again board a boat.

"Mr. Kalasnikov?" A posh British voice cut across the noise of the awakening shipyard.

Wiping at his mouth, Nikolai wished he had a bottle of water or a stick of gum in his backpack. He rose slowly and found a smartly dressed shorter man waiting for him. He looked completely out of place in that bespoke suit and spats. In fact, he looked like Hercule Poirot's doppelganger. "Yes?"

"Mr. Mikkelsen sends his regards." He held out a jet black business card.

Suspicious, Nikolai reached for the card. He could see the severe white lettering embossed on the black paper.

"With Mr. Mikkelsen's compliments," the man said and gestured to a gleaming black Phantom parked nearby. A driver in full regalia waited for them.

Nikolai glanced around the harbor, hoping to see a different driver waiting for him. Surely this wasn't the transportation Luka had arranged. His gaze returned

to the boat. It wasn't widely known outside of a handful of people, but Niels had gotten himself into a bit of
trouble as a young man—with Luka Beciraj's aunt. He
now owed a blood debt to the family that wasn't pay-
able with money but only with deeds.

Like this one?

Not wanting to stick around the harbor any longer
than necessary, Nikolai pocketed the card and walked
toward the idling luxury sedan. The driver opened the
door for him, and he settled onto the exquisite leather
seating. The Poirot lookalike slid into the space next
to him. He retrieved a bottle of water from a concealed
bar compartment and handed it over along with a discreetly palmed mint.

"Thank you." Nikolai didn't see any reason to be
rude just because he loathed the man's employer. He
drank some water and popped the mint into his
mouth. "You can take me to Yuri Novakovksy's penthouse in Knightsbridge."

The Poirot wannabe shot him a queer look. "I can
take you there, but you won't find your wife sleeping
under Mr. Novakovsky's roof."

Panic gripped him. "Where is my wife?"

"With Mr. Mikkelsen, of course." The man leaned
forward and tapped the glass partition between the
seats, and the driver sped off into the early morning
darkness.

Reeling from the discovery that Vivian was with
Niels, Nikolai clenched his fists at his sides. His eyes
closed briefly as he imagined the very worst. After
finding him with Tatiana, Vivian might have decided

that she wanted revenge. Perhaps she wanted to hurt him as much as he had hurt her.

She wouldn't do that. She has too much respect for herself. She's honorable and proud.

Nikolai would forgive her anything, absolutely anything, but he prayed she hadn't crossed that line.

18   CHAPTER EIGHTEEN

"I'm boring you, aren't I?"

I tore my gaze away from the strangely enthralling black square centered on the canvas in front of me to meet the intense stare of Niels Mikkelsen. His curiously colored eyes seemed to glitter as he studied me. A flush crept along my neck and into my face, but it wasn't the usual sort of blush that Nikolai's loving, heated gaze inspired. It was one born of discomfort and uncertainty. "No. I could never find you boring."

Niels chuckled and turned his attention back to the painting. "It's mystifying in its simplicity."

Inhaling a long breath, I titled my head and examined the piece by Malevich. "I keep looking at it, but I'm not sure why I can't stop."

"That's art for you, I suppose. Questions. Answers. More questions." Niels stepped away from the painting and moved to the next piece in the exhibit. He had used his connections to help us gain a very private, behind-the-scenes sneak peek of the Kazimir Malevich collection. The exhibit didn't open for two weeks so I considered myself extraordinarily lucky to have this chance.

I trailed him to the painting. It was one of Malevich's earliest works. "I don't like these as much. His abstract pieces speak to me much more clearly."

"That surprises me. I thought for sure you would like these more."

I flashed him a smile. "Well, you don't know me that well."

"It's not for lack of trying."

I rolled my eyes at his flirtatious grin and wiggled my right hand. "I'm married."

"A minor inconvenience," he teased.

His remark was playful, but it made me think of Nikolai and Tatiana and their secret assignation at the Four Seasons. "For some," I murmured sadly.

His smile faded. "I've overstepped the line. I'm sorry."

"You're forgiven." I moved to the next painting, and he followed me. Deciding that it was time to reinforce the line that he seemed to relish toeing right up against, I said, "Niels, I enjoy our time together, but we can only ever be friends."

"I know."

"But?"

"You are utter perfection." He dared to stroke my cheek and wrapped strands of my hair around his finger. He didn't allow his touch to linger. "There's something about you, Vivian. It's an alluring quality that I can't quite figure out." He lowered his hand and let my hair fall back. "But you've already been claimed."

I didn't step away from him. This close, I could easily read his face. He was interested in me. Maybe he was even a little infatuated. He wasn't going to make a move though. He would respect the line I had drawn.

"Come home with me."

Or maybe not.

"What?"

He laughed. "Not like that, *min lille en.* I want to cook you dinner and show you my private collection. Perhaps you'll allow me to photograph you."

"Photograph me?"

"It's one of my passions."

"I won't ask about the others," I said with a nervous smile.

"Come now, Vivian. You're a married woman. Surely my passions—of all flavors and intensities—are intriguing to you."

"Intriguing? Yes," I allowed. "But I don't think I'm brave enough to ask if the stories I've heard are true."

Niels leaned forward until his mouth nearly touched my ear. "They are."

I shivered and smacked at his chest. "You're impossible!"

"I'm complicated, but I think you like a complicated man."

"One of them, yes." Complicated was the easiest way to describe Nikolai. Complicated was the easiest way to describe our marriage. At least during the last week. I hadn't heard from him in days, but Kostya and Ten had both called. They had assured me Nikolai was coming to join me, but neither had been able to tell me why he hadn't simply flown over on a plane like a normal person. I had a terrible, stomach-twisting feeling about the whole mess.

Niels held out his arm. "Ready?"

Curious to see his private collection and ready to get off my feet, I took his arm and let him escort me out of the museum and into a waiting car.

"How are your friends enjoying the city?" Niels asked as we were driven through London.

"Erin and Ivan are like two kids in a candy store." My mouth lifted in the biggest smile. "You would never guess it by looking at him, but Ivan is, like, the biggest *Doctor Who* fan in the universe. They're doing a walking tour today."

"Really?" Niels seemed taken aback by that. "*Doctor Who*?"

"Apparently, watching bootlegged *Doctor Who* videotapes is one of the ways he taught himself English. *Star Wars*, *Star Trek*—he's huge into sci-fi and fantasy films and books."

"He was an orphan, yes?"

"Yes. Ivan, Dimitri, Yuri and Nikolai grew up in the same orphanage together. It wasn't a good experience."

"The understatement of the century, I'm sure," Niels murmured. "But loving fantastical fiction and films makes sense. I'm sure it was an escape for him." He stretched out his legs. "What about Bianca and Sergei?"

"They have family visiting them here. Sergei's mother and brother," I clarified. Thinking of the night I had gone to their hotel suite to support Bianca and meet Sergei's family, I added, "It's been, um, tense. His mother isn't exactly fond of her."

"Why? I've met Bianca. She's a wonderful young woman. She's tenacious, talented, hardworking—and my God! She's beautiful. Stunning, actually. That body? Those hips? I can think of a dozen Doms who would sell their souls for a submissive like her."

My jaw dropped at his description of Bianca and the mention of dominants and submissives in the same sentence with her.

"Why so scandalized?" he asked with an amused chuckle. "Surely, with your artistic eye, you can appreciate a luscious beauty like that." His eyes darkened and glittered, and I could tell he was thinking of something highly salacious. "That *zaftig* figure in a corset? I would pay a million pounds for the chance to photograph her for my collection."

"Well don't make that offer anywhere Sergei might overhear you," I warned. "He'll break you in half with one punch."

"I daresay he would do more than simply break me in half. Although my tastes run toward the more extreme ends of foreplay, I think allowing a Russian giant to beat me senseless might be a bit much, even for me."

I let loose a shocked laugh. "You are crazy."

"Like a fox," Niels countered with a grin.

Shaking my head at his strange sense of humor, I gazed out the window and enjoyed the London cityscape. His regal mansion sat on two acres of fenced land about twenty minutes outside the city. The gatehouse was manned by a guard, and the long, winding road toward the imposing manor that ended with a burbling fountain and circular drive was like something out of a romance novel.

Niels escorted me into his beautifully restored home. A short man with a flair for vintage style waited patiently near the doorway. His three piece suit and pocket watch plus the spiffy, bright white spats covering his black shoes made him look out of time.

"Vivian, this is René. He runs the household for me."

"It's a pleasure to meet you, Mrs. Kalasnikov." René bowed. "May I take your purse?"

"Oh, yes." I handed over my bag. "Please call me Vivian or Vivi."

"As you wish, ma'am."

"I'm taking Vivian to the gallery and then I'll be making dinner. You'll see to the rest of the household."

"Of course, sir."

Niels gestured for me to join him, and we crossed the grand foyer with its cream marble floors and vaulted ceiling adorned with twinkling chandeliers to the wide staircase. The rich, dark wood presented a stark contrast to the pale floors and bright ceilings.

"This is a beautiful balance," I commented as we climbed the stairs. "The brown and cream tones, I mean."

"The staircase is original to the home. The floors are new." Niels launched into a rundown of all the work he had undertaken during the restoration and renovation of the seventeen bedroom mansion. "I chose hardwood for the second floor. I wanted something that felt warmer than the marble downstairs."

"It's a nice contrast." Thinking of the massive size of the manor, I exclaimed, "You must have an army of housekeepers!"

"Not quite," he replied rather cryptically. "This way."

The house was shaped liked squared-off "C" with two distinct wings attached to a larger central structure. Niels had elegantly arranged his art collection on the walls. They were grouped by period and style. More than once, I stopped along the progression to simply stare and appreciate the brushstrokes and techniques.

"This is my pre-1900 collection," he explained as we examined a rather sinister and almost macabre El Greco painting. "My more modern pieces are in New York, Amsterdam and Copenhagen."

"They wouldn't look right in this house," I murmured, stepping closer to scrutinize the realistic shading to the fabric folds painted on the canvas. "It would be jarring to come across one of your Chegall's in this space."

Niels smiled at me. "You understand the dilemma perfectly."

Remembering the art theft at Yuri's mansion perpetrated by Lena's bumbling cousin, I asked, "How in the world do you keep all of these paintings safe? Aren't you worried about a burglary?"

"I don't think there are many art thieves stupid enough to steal from me. Where would they fence the paintings? I'm one of the top collectors in the world. If one of my pieces went missing, every black market dealer on the face of this planet would be looking for it and running right back to me for the reward money."

"I suppose you have a point there." I moved on to the next selection and shook my head in wonder and awe. "I can't imagine waking up every morning and strolling by these museum quality pieces in my jammies. What a trip that must be!"

Niels laughed and then tilted his head. I sensed the sadness radiating from him. "I forget sometimes how incredibly lucky I am. It's easy to become jaded and cynical when there's nothing you can't buy."

"There are plenty of things you can't buy, Niels." I crossed the hall to a religious piece that had caught my eye. One look at the painting, and I could tell it was Spanish and probably Baroque period. "Is this a Herrera?"

"The Elder," Niels confirmed with a nod. He joined me in front of the painting and rubbed the heavily gilded frame with his thumb. Glancing down at me, he asked, "What types of things can't be bought?"

I blinked and then frowned. "Love, obviously. Loyalty. Devotion. Honor. Respect. You can buy material things, but you can't buy the things that matter most, Niels."

His thumb moved along the frame, and he cast a knowing smile my way. "I've figured out why I like you so much."

"Oh?"

"You're good, through and through, Vivian. You're sweetness and light."

"You aren't the first man to tell me that."

"No?" He seemed almost disappointed to hear that.

"Nikolai calls me his sun."

"He must find the warmth of your light wholly intoxicating after so many years in the darkness."

He used to, I thought with a gut-wrenching pang of sadness. I turned away from Niels and walked to the next painting. We enjoyed the art in companionable silence for the next hour, moving from piece to piece until we reached the end of the east wing.

"Would you like to see my studio?"

"Of course!" I loved touring the working spaces of other artists so I happily trailed him to a room across the hall that faced out toward the gardens. What I discovered when I entered the studio surprised me.

Oversized windows allowed a great deal of natural light into the room. It seemed as if he had knocked down a wall or two to expand the space. Unlike the rest of the house, there were very few period details here. The ceiling was lined with professional grade lighting. One entire wall housed a fortune's worth of equipment.

A four poster bed with luxurious white sheets and a fluffy comforter sat along one wall. I noticed other props in the room that made me blush. I might not have ever played the types of games he liked, but I had read enough steamy novels to know what a spanking horse looked like. I didn't even want to think about what might be kept behind a door on the far end of the room.

"I suppose I don't have to ask what types of photos you're taking in here." I caressed the sheer white curtains and peered out the windows. My appreciative gaze landed on the garden blooming with flowers and herbs. The colors were simply amazing.

"I tend to prefer erotic photography, yes," Niels admitted as he moved around behind me, "but I also do shoots of a non-sexual nature. In fact, I'm hoping you'll agree to let me do one right now."

I glanced back with surprise. "Right now?"

"Yes." Niels sat on the edge of the bed and placed his hands on his thighs. Even sitting down, he seemed predatory and far too dangerous. Yet there I calmly stood, seriously considering his offer to photograph me. We were playing a strange game, one where he seemed determined to push against my boundaries merely for the pleasure of feeling me smack him back and shoo him away. Perverse, indeed.

"Let me see your portfolio. If I like what I see, I'll allow you to photograph me."

"Fair enough." He stood. "Have a seat, please."

I scanned the room for a spot that seemed safe and picked a run-of-the-mill leather club chair. Niels left and returned a short time later with a heavy garment bag slung over one shoulder and a photo album in the other. He placed the garment bag on the bed and brought the album to me.

After dragging over another chair, he sat next to me and opened the cover. "These are my private photographs. You won't see these in pose books or collections anywhere."

I had expected the photographs to only feature female subjects but was proven wrong on the first page. He had a remarkable gift for capturing his subjects with such emotionally vulnerable expressions. There was something so incredibly intriguing about the photos. I couldn't stop turning the pages. Even before I reached the end of the album, I had my answer.

I looked up from the album to catch Niels watching me with that intense and unnerving expression of his. He must have seen my answer on my face. "Say it," he commanded.

There was nothing gruff or intimidating about his direction. It was delivered calmly and without pressure. I gave my answer easily. "Yes."

With a pleased smile, he took the album. "I want you to wear what's in the garment bag. I'll step outside while you're getting ready."

"What's in the bag?" I rose from the chair and crossed to the bed.

"You'll see soon enough." He fixed me with a point-ed stare as he lingered in the doorway. "You'll wear *only* what's in the bag or I won't photograph you."

His condition pushed the strange game we were playing into dangerous territory. The idea of agreeing to something so scandalous both excited and terrified me. I experienced the briefest tremor of guilt but the still painful memories of discovering Nikolai with Tati-ana squashed it quickly. I was strong enough not to cross that line. This was artistic expression and noth-ing more.

I unzipped the bag and gawked at the luxurious white fur coat waiting for me. Never in my life had I worn fur. It simply wasn't practical in the Houston climate, even in the colder months. It was also beyond my price range and beyond my comfort level as far as animals were concerned. Petting the soft fur, I cringed to think about the foxes who had met their end simply to be turned into a garment.

I waffled back and forth before finally deciding to wear it. I soothed my conscience by focusing on the facts. I hadn't purchased or ordered the coat. If I did-n't wear it now, it would simply go back into storage. That was a waste in more ways than one.

I undressed slowly, toeing off my ballet flats and stripping out of my skirt, top and bra without too much hesitation. I couldn't bring myself to remove my panties though. Only one man had ever seen me with-out them. Only one man had been allowed to see or touch my naked body. That meant something to me.

I picked up the weighty coat and shook it free from the bag. I expected there to be an unpleasant scent associated with the fur but my nose detected nothing but a clean scent that had the faintest hint of lavender. I slid my arms into the silk-lined coat and closed the lapels around my almost naked body. The coat's hem kissed my knees and covered everything that needed to be covered.

"Vivian?" Niels knocked at the door. "Are you ready?"

No. "Yes."

He opened the door but didn't enter immediately. He stood there, staring at me as if he had never seen me before this moment. Somewhere along the way, he had lost his jacket. The white sleeves of his classic button-down shirt were rolled up to his elbows, revealing corded and muscular forearms. An unbidden image of those powerful arms swinging a flogger or striking a submissive lover with a riding crop entered my mind. I quickly batted away the image. *Don't go there.*

His keen gaze flitted to the bed, moving over my neatly folded clothing, and back to me. "You broke my rule." His gaze settled on my waist. "Open the coat."

"No."

"Yes."

"No."

"Vivian."

"I'm not yours to command."

A genuine smile brightened his handsome face. "No, you aren't." With an incline of his head, he stepped into the studio and shut the door. "There's no need for you to be skittish about removing your panties. I've already promised not to touch you, but if it makes you feel more comfortable, I'll allow the underwear."

I noticed he held my handbag in the grip of his left fingers. "Why do you have my purse?"

"I assumed you have your lipstick in here. I have makeup in that drawer, but I thought you would prefer your own."

"I would."

"There's a bathroom this way if you need a mirror."

Careful to keep the coat closed, I followed him to the room he had indicated. He put my purse on the long, deep counter and opened a series of drawers while I retrieved my tube of lipstick and twisted it to reveal the creamy red tip.

"What do they call that shade?" he asked as he moved to stand behind me.

I watched his movements in the mirror's reflection. "Russian Red."

He went still. "You're joking."

A grin teased my mouth. "No, it really is called that. Holly Phillips, my stylist, helped me choose it before my wedding. I've been wearing it ever since."

Niels laughed, the sound so rich and full that it inspired my own giggle. "What are the odds of that?"

"I thought Holly was kidding me when she read the box."

Still chuckling, Niels picked up a brush and began to comb my hair away from my face. I held perfectly still. I couldn't decide if I was uncomfortable or if this was entirely proper. It felt too familiar and almost intimate. Niels didn't touch anything but my hair. His strong fingers gathered the strands into a simple updo that he expertly secured with pins.

"What?" he asked as he added a few more pins to keep everything the way he wanted it.

"I had no idea you were so multi-talented."

"Oh, *min lille en*," he murmured so darkly, "you have no idea. Would that I had met you before the Russian! You might have learned to enjoy the full range of my talents."

His fingers flexed over my shoulder. He wanted to touch me. That much was evident from the smoldering intensity of his eyes. It was taking every ounce of his self-control not to break the trust between us. Clearing his throat, he stepped back. "Wait here."

When he was gone, I turned side to side to examine my reflection. The heavier application of my favorite red lipstick had a startling effect against the snowy whiteness of the fur. My black hair presented a similar contrast. I noticed that my tattoo was barely visible over the collar of the coat. Uncertain whether he would want me to conceal it, I adjusted the collar.

"Don't." Niels shook his head when he entered the bathroom to find me fluffing the collar. He held two emerald green jeweler's boxes embossed with a golden logo. "I want to see his mark on you."

The way he said it, the way his voice deepened and grew huskier, made every nerve-ending in my body buzz. Knowing what I did of his sexual tastes, I couldn't help myself. I had to ask. "Do your—"—I searched for the right word—"—paramours wear your mark?"

"Yes, but it's nothing so permanent." He placed the jewelry boxes on the counter. "I would never presume to mark one of my submissives in that way."

"Why not?"

"Because they don't belong to me," he answered matter-of-factly. "They place themselves in my care for a short while. I treasure their submission, and I reward them with pleasure and pain and my affection."

"But?" I asked breathlessly.

"But they aren't mine. They can never be mine."

"Why not?"

"It's very complicated, Vivian." He unlatched one of the jewelry boxes. "Much too complicated for us to discuss today." He presented me with a diamond and pearl necklace and matching earrings. They were ostentatious and decadent, and I gasped.

"I can't wear these, Niels."

"I insist."

"But—"

"I insist." His firm tone brooked no refusal. I could only nod, accept the pieces from him as he handed them over and put them on. "And now for the tiara."

He was dead serious. He produced a glittering diamond and pearl tiara from the bulkier jewelry box. "It's been in my family for generations. This all sat in a safe—until today."

"Why me?"

"If you have to ask..." Niels placed the tiara on my head and tucked it into place with a few pins. "There." He stepped back to admire his work. "Now you truly look like the Night Queen."

My head jerked toward his. "How did—?"

"I know everything, *min lille en*. There are no secrets from a man like me." He clasped my hand and
tugged me out of the bathroom. He motioned toward
the chair. "Sit."

I perched on the chair and gathered the coat
around my naked body while he moved equipment into
place and adjusted the gauzy curtains. Camera in
hand, he took a series of test shots and made more
adjustments to his lighting and the backdrop of the
window and the curtains.

When he was satisfied, he crossed the room to the
iPod docking station and picked up the small device.
He thumbed through his choices and settled on something that he liked. Moments later, the unmistakable
notes of *The Tsar's Bride* began to fill the air. The
famous voice of Anna Netrebko soon followed.

Niels shrugged and smiled mischievously. "It seems
appropriate. Now. Come here." He gestured to the
window. "Stand there."

I took the position he had indicated and waited for
more instruction. Niels snapped off a few more photos,
moving to different angles and crouching down to get
the shots he wanted. He checked the photos on the big
computer screen attached to his camera through a
curled cord. Whatever he saw didn't please him.

"What size shoe do you wear?"

"A seven. Why?"

Without answering me, he strode to one of the cab-
inets on the far side of the studio and opened a drawer. He produced a pair of impossibly tall stiletto heels

and brought them to me. He knelt at my feet. "Put your hands on my shoulders. It wouldn't do to have you falling in your delicate state."

Clutching the coat closed with one hand, I balanced precariously on one foot and relied on his shoulder as a brace. "How did—?"

"You make art with paints and pencils. My canvas is the female body." He slipped one heel and then then other onto my feet. While he fastened the straps, he confessed, "I've known you were pregnant since that evening in May when we had that video-call after your graduation."

"But how?"

"Your eyes, your face," he said as he straightened up and stood. "You looked vulnerable and hopeful, excited but scared. It's not the first time I've seen it."

My eyes widened. "Do you have children?"

He seemed taken aback by that question. "No. None."

"Oh. Sorry. I didn't mean to—"

"It's fine, Vivian." He gently clasped my shoulders and turned my body toward the window. "Look out across the garden. Yes. Just like that."

Niels retreated. He picked up his camera and began to snap photos. I kept my gaze fixed forward as instructed.

"When you reach seven or eight months, I'll come out to Houston to photograph you again. I've never had done a maternity shoot but something tells me yours will be extraordinary."

I didn't know about that. "I'll do it, but not in this fur."

"I hope to have convinced you to pose nude by then."

I made a small choking noise. "Fat chance."

"I'm a hopeless optimistic."

"Nikolai is going to snap when he sees these photographs, Niels. Let's not push it with nudes."

"I think that's exactly why you agreed to let me take these." Niels moved into a different crouched position. "I think you want to make him angry. You want him seething with jealousy and wondering just how much of that sweet, nubile body of yours I've seen and touched."

"Niels," I warned.

"You aren't the first woman to use me to hurt a husband or boyfriend, and you won't be the last."

I looked back at him. "That's not what this is."

"You can tell yourself that, but I know the truth."

Was he right? Had I agreed to do this because some part of me wanted to see how Nikolai would react? What kind of person did that make me? Petty? Smart? Mean? Vengeful?

"Tell me about your mother."

The question caught me off guard. I glanced back at him, but he scolded me rather sharply. "Turn around."

On reflex, I did as directed.

"Tell me about your mother."

"I..." What could I say about her? I had put the turbulent, violent memories of my troubled mother into a pretend box that I had stowed away in a corner of my mind I rarely visited. It was a Pandora's Box of pain I had no interest in opening—ever. "There's not much to say about her."

"That's not what I've heard. Turn your head to the left. Yes. Just like that. Hold."

The camera clicked four or five times.

"I heard that your mother tried to drown you in a filthy, roach-infested bathroom at some flophouse where she was hiding out from your father's enemies. I heard a young, skinny pimp called Nickel Jackson kicked down the door because he could hear you screaming. I heard your mother stabbed him and then ran off into the night, naked and bloodied and—"

"Stop," I whispered, my heart racing and my stomach trembling. "Just stop."

But he didn't. "Is that what scares you most, Vivian? Is it the fear that deep down inside that same monster that consumed her is waiting to claw its way out of you?"

"Please..."

"Look at me." The harsh, cold edge to his voice gripped me in its thrall. "Look at me!"

So I did. I looked back at him. A single tear dripped from the corner of my eye and rode the curve of my cheek. Niels snapped photo after photo while I held that pose.

When he had what he wanted, he set aside his camera and hurriedly crossed the distance between us. He wiped the wetness from my face and gazed down at

me as if he expected me to shatter into a million pieces.

"You're a bastard," I snarled and shoved at his
chest.

"Yes." He didn't even try to deny it. "I'm a sadist.
It's my nature to push and hurt and cause pain." He
tugged the bottom of his shirt from his trousers and
used the soft fabric to dab at my face. "It wasn't done
lightly. When you see the photo, you'll understand."

In some strange way, the idea that we had achieved
the perfect shot lessened my anger toward him. It
made the emotional turmoil he had forced upon me
seem somehow all right and worth it. A little pain for
a hauntingly beautiful moment forever encapsulated?
It was a small price to pay. For an artist, at least.

"Don't ever do that again, Niels." I held his gaze
and made sure he understood I was serious. "My mother, my father, my childhood—that's off-limits."

"Absolutely," he agreed without hesitation. "I will
never make you cry again."

"I won't give you the chance."

"No, I don't you think you will." He stepped back
and gestured toward the bed. "Now that the hard part
is finished, why don't we have a little fun?"

"Excuse me?" He wasn't asking for *that* was he?

He chuckled at my reaction. "I meant a boudoir
photo session. Classy with very little skin," he promised. "We'll aim for sensual—and jealousy-inducing. I
want Nikolai jumping over my desk and clawing at my
throat when he sees these photos."

The image was one that I shamefully found exhilarating. "You're playing with fire."

"I love the burn." He held out his hand. "Come, *min lille en*. Let me have my way with you."

Feeling mischievous, I placed my hand atop his. "I'm all yours."

19 CHAPTER NINETEEN

Still feeling off-kilter and slightly nauseated, Nikolai entered Niels Mikkelsen's grand country estate. The understated opulence was exactly what he would have expected from the billionaire descended from Danish nobility. Whatever his feelings toward the tycoon, Nikolai grudgingly conceded he wasn't a flashy bastard like some ultra-wealthy men.

"Mr. Mikkelsen is waiting for you in his study. If you'll follow me, sir."

Nikolai didn't move. "I didn't catch your name."

"René, sir. I serve as Mr. Mikkelsens's majordomo."

Majordomo? He fought the urge to roll his eyes. Only Niels would be so fucking pretentious as to call his personal assistant a majordomo.

"This way, sir."

Nikolai had no choice but to follow. As big as the house was, he would be searching rooms until sunrise to find Vivian. His gut churned at the image of his wife sprawled naked in another man's bed, her wild black hair splayed on the pillows and the silken sheets twisted around her thighs. How long since he had last been cushioned between those lush legs of hers? Too long. Too fucking long.

He ached for Vivian. It wasn't only a physical torment, a craving that couldn't be sated by anyone but her, but emotional and mental. His fragmented soul ached for her. It was her love and sweetness that fueled his desire to be good. Without her, he feared what he would become.

René stopped outside a pair of double doors and rapped his knuckles against the wood. "Mr. Mikkelsen, sir?"

"Send him in, René."

The majordomo opened the door, stepped aside and gestured for Nikolai to enter. He walked into the room, and the door was shut firmly behind him. Nikolai spotted a desk directly across from him but Niels wasn't there. The glow of computer monitors off to his right drew his attention. He glanced in that direction—and sucked in a choked, harsh breath.

Black and white photos of Vivian filled the six screens mounted on the wall. The photos of Vivian wearing a white fur and diamonds—and *only* a white fur and diamonds judging by the erotic glimpses of her supple skin—taunted him. Niels had captured her with

that aroused expression that—until today—had belonged to him and only him. The knowledge that Niels
had seen something that was his and his alone both
enraged and shattered him.

"She's lovely, isn't she?" Niels sat in a chair and
swirled a glass of liquor.

"She's my wife." Nikolai ground out the words
through a jaw clenched so tightly he was certain it
would break at any moment.

Niels set aside his glass and rose from his chair. He
leveled a hard stare. "I'm glad that you've finally remembered that fact."

"I never forgot."

"Does she know that?"

Nikolai glared at Niels. "Our marriage isn't any of
your fucking business."

"That's your opinion. Vivian is my friend. I care for
her. I want her to be happy and fulfilled. Until recently, you made her happy. Now I get the feeling that
you've become a source of pain and sadness."

It was a charge Nikolai couldn't deny. "We've hit a
rough patch."

"They happen not infrequently in all relationships."
Niels strode to the bar, uncorked a bottle of Armagnac
and splashed some into a glass. "Here. You look like
you could use this."

The twice-distilled brandy wasn't his favorite, but
he wasn't about to turn it down. Typically, he would
savor a fine XO bottling like this one, but after sitting
in a cramped boat and filling his nose with cigarette
smoke, it would be wasted on his ruined palate. He

smelled only the salty brine of the ocean and could taste only the strong bite of the mint that René had given him.

He sipped a small amount of the French brandy and let it roll around his mouth. The alcohol stripped his mouth of the mint flavor and cleared his nasal passages. Even so, the delicate notes of apricot and pepper that he would have expected in this brand evaded him tonight.

Not really caring about the experience, he knocked back the glass in one hard slug and inhaled a fiery breath as it burned his throat and blazed through his chest.

"That bad of a night, huh?" Niels carried over the short, fat bottle and splashed more into his glass. "Anders and Coos are two of the best captains for making that awful little trip, but sometimes the sea is against you."

Nikolai collapsed into the nearest chair and rubbed his haggard face. "You own the boats?"

Niels settled into the seat across from him. "Unfortunately, yes. That was the price I paid for a reckless youthful indiscretion and a mistake that can never be undone." He sipped his Armagnac, but his mind seemed to be following an old trail of memories. "I provide the boats, crews and bribes to make their drug trafficking possible. There are many, many, many layers between me and all of that mess, but someday, probably when I least expect it, the past will finally catch up to me."

"I know that feeling of dread." Nikolai drank his brandy a little slower this time.

"Let it go for now. You're safe here."

"In London?" he scoffed. "Hardly."

"In my home," Niels corrected. "No one and nothing can touch you or Vivian here."

Nikolai's hand stopped halfway to his mouth. He lowered his glass. "Is that why she's here? Do you know something?"

Niels drained his glass and set it aside. "When you didn't make your flight, I was mildly concerned, but Vivian was with Yuri so I felt she would be safe there. When I heard you might be coming across on one of my boats, I grew anxious and put a team of my security officers on her. She hasn't been out of my sight or beyond my reach since Monday evening. I knew that Yuri and Lena were planning on attending a gala tonight so I came up with as many reasons as possible to keep Vivian with me, just in case."

It would have been churlish to ask why Niels put so much thought into securing Vivian. Instead, Nikolai offered his gratitude. "Thank you."

"Someday I'm sure you'll return the favor. That's how this underworld of ours works, isn't it? Favors and debts, paid and unpaid." Niels rose from his chair and stretched his back. "I'm headed to bed. You'll find Vivian upstairs. Left at the top of the stairs. Fourth door on the right. I'll have René send for your things in the morning."

Nikolai moved to stand, but Niels waved his hand. "Don't rush on my account. Enjoy your drink. Have another if you would like. If there's anything that you need, dial '1' on any phone in the house. It will connect you straight to René."

Nikolai leaned back in the chair and watched his host disappear. Bewildered by the strange turn of events, he finished his glass of brandy and dug through his backpack to find his personal cell phone. He switched it on for the first time in days and sent messages to Ivan and Yuri. Kostya's contacts had probably already informed him of his arrival, but he called him just to be sure. Their conversation was short and to the point.

After zipping his backpack, Nikolai wandered over to the bank of computer screens. He found the mouse and clicked through the series of photographs. Others who saw the glossy boudoir shots might be drawn to the subtle hint of flesh beneath the fur or the curves of Vivian's body, but her eyes enthralled him. They were so damned expressive.

But when he reached the series of photos where Vivian stood in front of a window, he slowed his clicks. These were different than the more sensual photos he had just viewed. Draped in the coat and silhouetted against the window, Vivian presented an alluring image. He could see his tattoo on the back of her neck. A row of diamonds glittered beneath it. Her dark hair looked impossibly black against the snowy whiteness of the fur. The tear sliding down her cheek revealed a heart wrenching vulnerability.

It wasn't difficult to comprehend the message of the photo. The pure white fur represented the sweet

innocence of Vivian while the glimpse of flesh suggested a hidden eroticism and a coquettish quality. But
the tear dripping down her skin and the wounded,
haunted expression spoke of pain and heartache.

The image hit him right in gut. *Me. I did that. I'm
the one who hurt her.*

The earlier flare of jealousy that had burned
through him upon finding Niels with these photographs morphed into a low, thrumming ache of desire.
He realized there was no reason to be jealous of anyone
who saw these. They could only see a moment Niels
had captured, but he could touch and caress and kiss
and love her.

If she still wants me...

Needing that answer, Nikolai followed Niels' direction to the guest suite. He entered quietly. He wasn't
surprised that the bathroom light had been left on and
the door remained slightly ajar. Not long after they
had married, he had come home one evening to find a
night light in one corner of their bedroom. After what
she had survived as a child, her need for light to sleep
well made sense.

He leaned against the closed door for a long time
and simply watched her sleep. She had taken the right
side of the bed, the same side that she slept on at
home, the side farthest from the door. She had
wrapped her arms around a pillow. *A makeshift me.*

A simple black nightgown covered her naked body.
The lace trim flattered her cleavage. He tried not to
think about Niels giving her that flimsy bit of lingerie
for the night. A man like Niels probably had a de-

partment store's worth of women's underthings for his lovers.

Though he wanted nothing more than to crawl into bed with Vivian, to embrace her and beg her for-giveness and a chance to start over, he ducked into the bathroom instead. Filthy from a night on the sea, he needed a good scrub. The cabinet under the sink held a selection of toiletries for overnight guests. He smirked at the boxes of condoms, dental dams and lubricants. Niels clearly believed in seeing to every need that might arise for his guests.

After a long, hot shower, he emerged from the bathroom with only a towel tied around his waist. The light from the bathroom illuminated the space, and he spotted Vivian sitting on the edge of the tall bed. Her bare legs dangled over the side, and the short negligee had bunched around the tops of her thighs.

As if nervous, she combed her fingers through her hair to tame it. She didn't need to bother with such things. Messy hair, perfect hair—he didn't care. She was always beautiful.

Vivian bit her lower lip and stared at him. There was no mistaking the glimmer of fear in her eyes or the concern drawing her mouth tight. Loathing himself for causing her so much stress, he crossed the distance between them with slow, deliberate steps. She gazed up at him, her confused expression a mirror of her emotions.

Nikolai was suddenly thrown back to the night they had gotten their matching tattoos. It was the night he had confessed that she was the only person in the world who could bring him to his knees. Wanting her to remember that, wanting to rewind the clock and return to the moment when everything was good and wonderful and beautiful between them, he dropped down in front of her.

Heart pounding and mouth dry, he didn't know what to say. There were so many words, but none of them came close to describing his love for her. Feeling vulnerable and exposed but trusting that she wouldn't spurn or hurt him, Nikolai slid his arms around her waist and rested his cheek on her thighs. "I'm sorry. It's not enough, I know, but I'm sorry. For everything." Eyes closed, he said, "*Ya tebya lyublyu.*"

I love you.

He pressed a tender kiss to the soft skin of her leg. "*Ya lyublyu tebya vsey dushoy.*"

I love you with all of my soul.

He pressed a loving kiss to the rounded curve of her pregnant belly. "*Ya ne mogu zhit' bez tebya.*"

I can't live without you.

He dropped his head into her lap. "*Ty nuzhna myne.*"

I need you.

Vivian's gentle hands stroked his head. She rubbed between his shoulder blades and dragged her fingers through his hair. "*Ty nuzhen mne.*"

I need you.

She tugged on a handful of his hair, not painfully but with enough pressure that he looked up at her. "*Ya lyublyu tebya vsem serdtsem.*"

I love you with all of my heart.

"But you have to be honest with me, Nikolai." Her eyes glittered with unshed tears. "No more lies. We start over right now with the truth—or else."

Her unspoken threat rattled him to the core. "No more lies, Vee."

"I mean it, Nikolai. Everything has to be out on the table."

He nuzzled her belly. "I'll tell you anything you want to know."

She clutched his face between her small hands and lifted his head. The tears glimmering in her eyes began to spill down her cheeks. "Is Tatiana your mistress?"

He sagged back on his heels. "No!"

"Do you have a child with her?"

"What?" He went ramrod straight. "Why would you ask—?"

"I heard you. At Quattro. I heard everything."

Yes, it was clear that she had heard more than he had ever intended—but completely out of context.

Vivian sobbed now. "Do you love her?"

"Oh, baby." He whispered the words on an anguished breath and gathered her in his arms. "No. Never. Never like that."

"Swear it."

"I swear." He put a knee on the bed and dragged her up against the pillows before dropping down beside her. Locking a leg over hers, he pulled her in tight and gazed down at his wife. *Mine. Always.*

He sifted his fingers through her hair and traced her pouty lips with his thumb. "I've never even kissed Tatiana."

To prove his point, he lowered his hand to the swell of her stomach. It amazed him to think his child was growing in there. "This is the only child I have ever made. You," he kissed her lovingly, "are the only woman I have ever shared this with. You're the only one I trust with something so precious."

Nikolai took his time loving her mouth. He relished the sweet softness of her lips and kissed away the tears clinging to her skin. When she had quieted and seemed calm, he stroked her face. "It's time for me to tell you a story."

"About?"

"About a boy and a girl," he said with a teasing smile. "That's how they usually start anyway."

She narrowed her eyes at him. "Which boy and girl?"

"Tatiana Filipova."

"And?"

Nikolai steeled himself for her reaction. "Eric Santos."

Vivian stiffened and bolted upright. Her hair fell around her face as she gawked down at him, and she roughly shoved it behind her ear. "Bullshit!"

He shook his head. "Not bullshit. It's the truth."

"But—"

"Haven't you ever wondered why Eric hates me so much?"

"I just assumed it was because of your connection to the mob and to me."

"That's a large part of it, yes, but my history with Eric goes back a decade."

Vivian slumped against the pillows and rolled onto her side. "Tell me all of it."

"I first met Eric when he was just a beat cop. It wasn't long after the night I—"

"Shot me?" she filled in with a sad voice.

He grimaced and hugged her even closer. "Yes. It might have been late May of that year. I think he suspected I had more to do with the shooting than was publicly known. He pulled me over and did the usual frisk and search. When he didn't find anything, he warned me to stay away from your grandparents and you. I didn't know who the hell he was until later that night when Kostya filled in the blanks for me." Nikolai brushed hair back from her face. "Even back then, Eric was looking out for you."

"I didn't know that. We didn't get close until I was starting high school."

"He wanted to protect you. Whatever my disagreements with Eric, I've always admired and respected him for that."

"Maybe you should tell him that."

He snorted. "Not a chance in hell."

"Nikolai!" She swatted at him, but he captured her hand and brought it to his mouth where he proceeded to kiss the fingertips that held paintbrushes and created such exquisite art.

"Tatiana joined me in Houston not long after that. She had been accepted into an MBA program, and our fathers thought it was time for us to get close. We hated each other at first. She thought I was a bastard and worse than the shit scraped off the bottom of a boot, and I thought she was a spoiled, rich bitch."

"Ouch."

"Yes," he murmured, thinking of their spectacular fights. Looking back, he realized they fought more like siblings than lovers. "Eventually, we realized we were better off as friends than enemies. Neither of us wanted to get married. That was an unholy alliance that we couldn't stomach. I turned a blind eye to her going to clubs and parties, and she left me alone when it came to my business. When she finished her MBA, I made sure that she got a good job with one of the energy trading firms. She taught me everything she could about running a business, accounting and tax laws."

Nikolai paused and gathered his thoughts. "I knew that she was seeing someone, and I knew that it was getting serious, but she wouldn't tell me his name. I had Kostya follow her a few times, just to be sure that she was safe, but she gave him the slip. She was good. So fucking good," he said with a laugh. "If she had been a freelancer, I would have snapped her right up and put her on my payroll. She's a natural when it comes to tradecraft."

He wiped a hand down his face. Next to him, Vivian patiently waited for him to continue his tale. "Tatiana's father started to get impatient when we still hadn't set a date. I was finding it hard to come up with believable reasons to put him off, and Maksim was starting to ride my ass about getting it done. Tatiana's father was holding a hard line on negotiations and making his life miserable."

He expelled a slow breath. "So Tatiana and I sat down and decided that we would go through with it. We would get married and share the same home—but live separate lives."

Vivian made a noise of disbelief. "I find that hard to believe."

He tried to see things from her point of view. She had only ever known him to be a protective, possessive and alpha husband. "The way I am with you is different, Vee. The three weeks you were in my home before I married you were the hardest, longest weeks of my life." He decided not to admit that doing a bid in solitary was easier than keeping his hands off of her. "Tatiana and I would have kept separate rooms. There would have been no intimacy between us."

"So what went wrong?"

"On the night of our engagement party, she went missing before I gave my toast. I sent Artyom and Ten to find her."

"And?"

"And they found Tatiana and Eric in an alley."

"And?"

He avoided her questioning stare. He didn't imagine she wanted to hear that her cousin had been discovered balls deep and pumping into Tatiana as he fucked her against a wall. "They were in a rather precarious position."

"No!"

"Yes," he grimly confirmed.

"What happened?"

"What do you think? Ten lost his fucking shit, and Artyom had to run inside to grab Vanya. Once I spotted Vanya rushing out of the party, I hauled ass because I was sure we were being attacked or worse. When I got out there, Vanya, Ten and Eric were brawling in the alley. Artyom was holding Tatiana to keep her from getting hurt. I stepped in front of Eric and shoved him out of the way—and Ten hit me so hard I was knocked off my feet."

"Looks like we have something new in common," she remarked.

"How so?"

"I stepped in between Eric and Ten when they were fighting at our house. Eric threw me out of the way, and Ten punched a lamp instead."

"He did *what*?" Anger burned through him. What the fuck was Ten thinking picking a fight in his home? With his pregnant wife standing right there? "When I get back to Houston, I'm going to break his fucking kneecaps."

"No, you aren't." Vivian petted his chest. "I need him."

He turned his head. "That's a different tune from you."

"He's been good to me. In his own way," she amended. "When I opened my luggage, I found a bag of burner phones programmed with emergency contacts and the address of a safe house. Ten has checked in on me every day."

Nikolai shouldn't have been surprised by Ten's behavior. The man had a list of faults a mile long, but he always completed the jobs assigned to him. He was utterly devoted and loyal. Nikolai breathed easier knowing that Ten's loyalty had shifted to Vivian. She and the baby were in good hands.

Curious, he asked, "Where is the safe house?" Vivian recited the address, and he went rigid. Very carefully, he inquired, "Did Ten tell you anything about that place?"

"He just told me not to sit on the bed if they gave me a room. Bed bugs, I guess."

Nikolai guffawed and rubbed his eyes. "*Kotonok*, he gave you the address of an infamous whorehouse that an acquaintance of ours owns."

"What?" she indignantly cried. "He wanted me to seek refuge in a—a—brothel?"

"You would have been safe there."

"I would have been mortified."

"But alive," Nikolai countered. "That's all matters in the end." He shifted his position so he could caress her side while he finished his story. His hand moved from her breast to her hip and back up again in slow, easy strokes. "After I got them all separated, I had Artyom take Eric home. I trusted him not to do anything stupid. Ivan was the only one who could handle Ten so I sent them away together. I took Tatiana back inside the restaurant. We cleaned up as best we could, skipped the toast and made it look as if we couldn't wait to get home."

"And then what happened?"

"Tatiana told me everything. She had met Eric through a college friend. There was an instant attraction, and before she could stop it, they were madly in love. They carried on in secret, but Eric wanted to go public. He wanted to marry her. He wanted to take her away."

"So why didn't he?"

"Maksim and Tatiana's father never would have allowed it. They would have killed him if they had known about him."

"How is he still alive?" She sounded worried and nervous.

"A few days after the brawl, the word got out that Tatiana had a lover. Someone at the party must have seen something. Artyom, Ten, Vanya—they would never have breathed a word of it. It had to have been a member of the catering staff or a guest. Maksim and Mikhail—Tatiana's father—were furious. I had hoped to use her indiscretion as a way to quietly end the arrangement—but they wanted blood."

"Her own father wanted her dead?"

"She had brought shame to their family. She had embarrassed him. She put him in an impossible position with Maksim." Nikolai scratched the top of his head. "I knew exactly how it would end. *Mokroye delo*." He grimaced. "A total fucking wet job."

Vivian shuddered next to him. She wouldn't have to think hard to fill in those blanks.

"I grabbed her in the middle of the night, threw together one suitcase and put her in a stolen car. I took her to one of Kostya's bolt-holes to hide out while I figured out what the hell to do with her—and that's when she told me that she was pregnant."

Vivian gasped. "She was pregnant? With Eric's baby?"

"Yes." Now familiar with the overwhelming need to protect his own baby, Nikolai better understood Tatiana's desperate desire to save hers. "I had to do something. Kostya made the arrangements while I sniffed around to make sure no one had seen her with Eric. We got lucky. Neither Maksim nor her father knew she had been fucking around with a Mexican cop." He blew out a strangled breath. "They would have gone ballistic if they had connected the dots back to your father." Then, with a harsh laugh, he added, "Of course, I went right ahead and drew a straight line to Romero eight years later."

Vivian seemed to mull over his statement. "Do you regret it?"

"What? Helping Tatiana disappear?"

"No. Drawing that straight line. Marrying me."

His gaze snapped to her face. "Never. I've said it before, and I'll say it again and again and again. You are the best thing that's ever happened to me." He cupped her pregnant belly. "The family we're building is the greatest achievement in my life. You and this baby are my reason for living."

Satisfied with his response, Vivian nestled into his embrace. "How did you help Tatiana disappear?"

Nikolai didn't want to burden her with too many of the gruesome details, but he had promised to tell her the truth about everything. "Kostya bruised her up, wrecked a car and stuck her in it. He covered her in blood and glass. We made sure Ten was with me when

Kostya called to tell me that he had been chasing her, and it had gone wrong. We needed a witness. Ten and I found the scene Kostya had staged."

"And then?"

"Ten was tasked with getting rid of the car. Kostya wrapped Tatiana's sedated body in a tarp and put her in the back of his SUV. I went with him to his workshop where the rest of it was done."

"What do you mean?"

"Kostya got ahold of a fresh male body. He figured that a Latino guy would be the best cover, especially if someone had gotten a glimpse of Eric. We needed to make sure the bosses over in the old country had no reason to come over here to sniff around and ask questions. Kostya ruined the dead man's face to make sure that no one would be able to tell if it was Eric or not."

"Where did he get a body?"

"*Sladest.*" He kissed her forehead. "We don't ask questions like that of Kostya."

"Never?"

He shook his head. "There are things that even I don't want to know."

"So what happened next?"

"We took photographs—and fingers."

Vivian sucked in a horrified breath. "You cut off her finger!"

Nikolai cringed. "It was distasteful in the extreme, but it had to be done. Kostya made sure the procedure was as painless as possible and as safe for the baby as he could make it. He took the pinkie off her right hand. It was sent back to Russia with the man's finger. Maksim and Mikhail accepted the proof—and that was that."

"But Ten must have seen Eric later. And Arty and Ivan," she added. "What did they think?"

"They didn't need to think anything. Tatiana was dead. The big bosses were happy. That's all that mattered. If they did think anything, it was that Kostya had accidentally clipped the wrong man. But it was done. Finished. There was no point in talking about it or asking questions."

"Why did you send her to Hong Kong?"

"We didn't. Not at first. She went to Sydney to lay low until the baby was born." He didn't want to tell her this part of the story, but there was no stopping now. "She lost the baby around twenty weeks. There was some sort of birth defect. Bad chromosomes." He swallowed hard at the fear of something so terrible happening to his own child. "It was a girl."

"Does Eric know?"

"No."

"Why not?" Anger filled her voice. "He was that baby's father. He has a right to know!"

"Tatiana didn't want him to come looking for her. It wasn't safe. I agreed with that. We planned to tell him when the time was right...but then she lost the baby and she decided that it was better to let him go."

"What about Eric? What about what he wanted?"

"That wasn't my problem or my concern." Vivian clicked her teeth, and he cast a glance her way. "I know how cold that sounds, but it's the truth. Tatiana was my friend. Eric wasn't. I protected her and him at great cost to myself."

She digested that statement before asking, "Didn't Eric dig around and look for her?"

"He did. He only came up against dead ends. You know what Kostya is like. He's frighteningly thorough. We made it look as if she had packed up and run in the middle of the night. There was no trace of the car wreck we had staged for Maksim and her father."

Nikolai hesitated before admitting, "Eric came to see me one night, in the alley behind Samovar. He was drunk and angry. He tried to force me to confess to hurting her, but I wouldn't. He attacked me. We fought. It was bloody and violent. The little bastard cut me with a beer bottle he scrounged out of the garbage, and I knocked him out with a knee to the head."

"That's awful!"

"It was."

Vivian's finger traced the thick, knotted scar that arced across his chest. "Here?"

Nikolai nodded. "We've been enemies ever since. Everyone in the underworld assumed I had had Tatiana and her boyfriend killed. I was happy to let them all think that, including Eric."

"Nikolai," she said sadly.

He patted her hand. "It was the right thing to do. People think the worst of me anyway. Better to let them think I had clipped my fiancée and the man she cuckolded me with than to have them questioning my authority or resolve."

"I still don't like it."

"I know you don't. I did it to protect both of them. It was the only way."

Vivian sighed. "If you went to all of this trouble to help her disappear and to build a new life as Tatiana Melnikova, why in the world is she back now? Why is she risking everything?"

"Her father is dead. Her brother is dead. She has no blood family left. Her father's crime family has fallen to pieces. Most of it was absorbed into Maksim's organization. There is no threat to her life or Eric's now." He paused to re-evaluate his words. "Well— there shouldn't be, but I think Maksim is unhappy that she's still alive."

"Because you lied to him?"

"That's part of it, yes." He trailed his finger down her cheek and along her jaw. "She found something during an audit this spring. There's a series of payments twice every year that go from a Moscow bank account to various accounts from Hong Kong to San Francisco to Houston. She tracked the funds back to one of Maksim's shell corporations. She assumed I was on the other end of that transaction, but I'm not. We don't know who he is paying, but it's a lot of money. It goes back twenty years."

"Twenty!"

"Curious, huh?"

"Very."

"But the main reason Tatiana wanted to see me is that she's been offered an amazing new job. Evgeni Zhukov has been trying to headhunt her to join his firm. If she makes the jump, she might have business that would bring her to Houston. She didn't want to cause problems for me."

"But she did cause problems for you," Vivian insisted.

"Yes, she did." He brushed his knuckles along her face. "But most of that trouble was of my own making. I should have been straight with you about Tatiana and Eric. I should have told you she was back in town. I should have told you that we were going to have a private meeting."

"But you didn't," Vivian whispered.

Shame gutted him. "I didn't."

"Why?"

"I don't know." He shook his head. "I never wanted any of that to touch you. I didn't want to put you in a position where you had to keep a secret from Eric. I didn't want you to worry about this woman coming back into my life." He touched his forehead to hers. "It was stupid. I made it worse by trying to shield you." He gulped anxiously. "Can you ever forgive me?"

"Yes." She gave her answer freely and without reluctance or hesitation.

"I don't deserve it."

"I love you. I want to make our marriage work— but you have to work with me."

"I understand that now. Lately, I've done everything wrong. I've hurt you and made you cry. I'm a miserable fucking bastard for that. I'll try harder, Vivian." He held her gaze and swore his vow. "I'll try so fucking hard to be good and to make you proud. I'll do anything, Vivian. I'll do anything you want."

Her elegantly shaped brows arched. "Anything?"

"Anything."

She pushed up onto one palm and gazed down at him. For a long, unnerving stretch of seconds, she studied him. He couldn't read her face. The shadows in their dark bedroom hid her expressive eyes. The corners of her mouth twitched. He spotted her soft pink tongue flick out against her lower lip. It was a sight that aroused him as he thought of all the other ways he would enjoy seeing that pink of tongue of hers.

"Vee?"

As if gathering her courage, she breathed in deeply. "I want you flat on your back. Put your hands behind your head and keep them there."

"What?" He blinked with surprise at her order. When had she grown so empowered? Why did he find the thought of his sweet, innocent Vee taking charge so damned exhilarating?

"You heard me." She traced the tattoo of Orthodox wedding crowns with their names and wedding date inscribed underneath. "You said you would do anything for me. I want this." She circled his nipple and then pinched it with enough of a bite that he hissed. "On your back. Hands behind your head."

God help him, but his cock went rock-hard. The stiff length of it tented the towel still twisted around his waist. Vivian moved into a kneeling position next to his hips. She waited for him to comply with her instruction. He didn't move immediately. "Where did you learn this?"

"I spent a very illuminating afternoon and evening with Niels."

Remembering those sensual photos, Nikolai burned with jealousy. What had Niels taught her and how? "If he touched you—"

"I know, I know," Vivian said with a dramatic huff and a roll of her eyes. "You'll cut off his fingers and break his legs." With a sinful smile that promised a romp he would never forget, Vivian gave his shoulder a hard push that forced him onto his back. "But later." She lifted one leg at a decadently slow pace and straddled his upper thighs. "Right now, it's my turn to play."

His breathing turned hard and fast. "*Solnyshka.*"

Grasping his hands, she interlaced their fingers and brought his arms up and over his head. She pinned him to the mattress and teased her mouth against his. He tried to kiss her, but she denied him. "No."

A pounding thrum of need pulsed through his body. Astounded by this change in his wife, he asked, "What happened to you while I was away?"

She leaned down and nipped his lower lip. The sting of it sent a shockwave through his chest and stomach. "I've finally learned my place."

Nikolai had feared those words would come back to haunt him. He had a sneaking suspicion he was about to do his full penance.

20 CHAPTER TWENTY

You can do this.

Still awash in the exalted relief of seeing Nikolai in the flesh and unharmed, I straddled his upper thighs and held him in place by trapping his hands overhead. I looked him over for signs of fresh wounds or scars but found none. I still hadn't asked him where he had been for the last five days.

Over dinner, Niels had finally let slip that he had been tracking Nikolai's movements across Europe. The sneaky Dane wouldn't tell me why all this cloak-and-dagger nonsense had been necessary, but he had promised that Nikolai would be returned to me before sunrise, whole and unharmed.

And now here he was, flat on his back beneath me and staring up at me with bewilderment.

I witnessed the briefest flash of panic in his pale eyes, and I smiled encouragingly. After the horrible abuse he had survived as a child, I had to be extremely careful with him. There was a reason he always liked to be in control—in the bedroom and outside of it. It was a defense mechanism for him and a way to ensure that he would never be harmed again.

Nuzzling our noses together, I whispered, "I won't hurt you."

Nikolai's jaw tensed. He swallowed. "I know."

"I just want to make you feel good." I kissed his left cheek and then the right. "I want to make you remember all the reasons you love me." I tenderly claimed his mouth. "And all the reasons you want me."

"I don't need a reminder. I've never forgotten." Nikolai bucked beneath me, forcing the hard length of his erection between my thighs. The plush softness of the towel rubbed against my inner legs. The head of his cock escaped the towel and prodded the bare lips of my sex. He growled at the contact. "Let me have you, Vee. I need to be inside you."

I squeezed my knees on either side of his body, halting his attempts to fuck up into me, and wagged my head. "No."

"Vee." He groaned with need and tried to lift up to kiss me. "Yes."

"No." I evaded his searching mouth. "There are three rules to this game. You keep your hands up here. You hold still. You don't touch me."

"Vivian," he breathed my name on a loud huff. "I can't. It's been too long."

"You can." I flicked my tongue against his lips. "You will."

"If I don't?"

"I go to the guest room next door and lock myself inside." I remembered the advice Niels had given me after dinner while we shared a rather interesting discussion about men and sex. "Tonight, we start this game all over again."

His eyes narrowed. "Was this Niels' idea?"

"Actually," I dotted kisses along his jaw, "this started off as Yuri's idea."

"Yuri?" He seemed shock. "Why?"

"He heard about our blowup in the kitchen. He told me that I should help you remember your place." I pressed my lips to the dagger tattooed on the side of his neck. "He said you should come home every night, drop to your knees and kiss my feet in gratitude."

My amused smile died when I met Nikolai's dark and serious gaze. His impassive, unreadable face worried me. *Have I gone too far?*

"He's right." Nikolai relaxed his tense body. "I'm the luckiest fucking man on the planet that a girl like you would ever agree to tie herself to me." He gulped, looking suddenly anxious, and confessed, "I think I take you for granted sometimes. I shouldn't do that." He closed his eyes. "It's hard for me, *solnyshka*. I don't know what *normal* looks like. I don't have married parents to emulate. I'm stumbling around in the dark."

The last of that cold, icy wall that I had erected in bitterness and anger melted. "I feel the same way. I look at Dimitri and Benny for guidance. They seem to have it together."

"Yes. Dimitri is a good husband and a wonderful father." Nikolai complimented his friend in a glum tone. "He's always been better at that sort of thing. Ivan, too," he added. "I see the way he is with Erin. It's easy between them."

"I think they work really hard to make it look that easy. Please don't feel badly about that, Kolya. You and me? God, we're all sorts of twisted and broken." I leaned down and kissed him, long and deep and loving. "We just have to keep trying."

"I'll try," he promised. "I'll try so fucking hard for you."

"Right now, I want you to try to hold still and keep your hands to yourself."

He swallowed and nodded. "I'll try."

I grasped his wrists and tucked his hands behind his head. Once they were secured and out of the way, I started at the very top of his forehead and began peppering kisses down his body. Nikolai shuddered beneath me. I let my lips hover on more erogenous zones and skimmed them lightly over the areas that weren't as sensitive.

When I got to his navel, I dragged my tongue straight down to the thatch of curls that crowned his cock but no farther. I deliberately avoided going anywhere near his erection and kissed his thighs instead. I even dotted kisses on the stars adorning his knees and the tops of his feet.

"Vee," he said with a guttural groan. "Let me touch you."

"Not yet." I smiled impishly while I kneaded the tight muscles in his thighs. I grabbed the towel and applied pressure to his hip so that he would lift his backside. I tugged free the towel and tossed it onto the floor. "It's still my turn to have fun."

"I can make this fun for you."

I put a finger against his lips. "Sh. Patience."

Wanting to really drive him crazy, I turned toward his feet and straddled his chest. I spread my thighs wide open so he could see all of me and then licked his cock from the thick base to the throbbing tip.

"Fuck, Vee!" He inhaled a shaky breath. "You're killing me."

Deciding I liked the sound of him groaning for me, I continued to swipe the rigid length of him with my tongue. I swirled it around the blunt crown and slowly sucked him between my lips. Nikolai's legs tensed as I teased my mouth down his shaft. He was so excited that he was already leaking pre-cum. I lapped at the slick sweetness and sucked him harder.

When I cupped his sac and worked my mouth up and down his cock, Nikolai pumped his hips. I planted both hands on them and pushed them back down. I didn't take my mouth off him. I wasn't *that* mean. Bobbing up and down, moving fast then slow, shallow then deep, I tormented him with my mouth. His toes curled, and his body strained beneath me. He wanted to come—but I wasn't ready.

I climbed off him and kissed his chest and neck. Lifting his head, he sought a kiss that I let him have. He plundered my mouth, stabbing his tongue between my lips and even sucking on the tip of it. Nikolai's erotic kisses made my belly tremble and my thighs quiver.

Straddling his thighs and facing him, I kept his cock trapped between my legs. His burning gaze roamed my body as I pulled off the negligee and dropped it on the floor. He zeroed in on my heavier, fuller breasts. I cupped them and started to play with my nipples the same way he liked to toy with them. I pinched and rubbed them until the peaks were bright red and stiff.

My clitoris throbbed now. Feeling more emboldened, I placed two fingers against his mouth. "Lick them."

He obliged, flicking his tongue over my skin and sucking my digits between his lips. I dragged my fingers away from his mouth and slid them between my thighs. I leaned back on my heels, opening my legs wider and showing him my pussy. I wanted him to see everything.

"Vivian." He breathed my name as I swirled my wet fingertips around my clitoris and then dipped them into my entrance. Slick and creamy, my channel was dripping for his cock and aching with emptiness. His hard shaft jutted against my bottom, and I rocked back against it, giving him just enough stimulation to make him hiss. I fingered myself slowly. This wasn't about getting off. This was about driving Nikolai crazy. This was about showing him what he had missed.

"Come up here," he urged in a silken voice. "You said I can't touch you with my hands, but you didn't say my tongue was off limits."

I blinked with shock. "You want me to...?"

"Yes. I want you to get up here right now. I'll play your game, but I want a taste of your sweet cunt in return for my cooperation."

Heat streaked through my belly. My pussy pulsed around my fingers. It was an illicit request, but I couldn't find a reason to say no. Very carefully, I inched my way up the bed until I had my knees planted on either side of his head. I didn't say a word when he moved his arms out of the way and offered his hands to me.

Grasping them, I interlaced our fingers and leaned forward. I had never felt so open and exposed to him. Nikolai's tongue swiped my slit, starting right down at my opening and not stopping until he touched my clitoris. He lapped at the little bundle of nerves and suckled it with leisurely tugs. I didn't know if it was because we had been separated for so long or if it was simply the new and scandalous position, but I was already hovering on the edge of a release. Every flick of his tongue sent pleasurable shocks from my belly to my chest. I panted and shuddered and tried to hold off on coming.

But it was a futile attempt. Nikolai's tongue fluttered over that little pearl, and I lost it. I came hard, grinding against his mouth and crying out his name as the bursts of ecstasy lit up my belly and burned through my chest.

Shaking with aftershocks, I crawled off of him. He wiped his mouth with the back of his hand and dared me to tell him not to move. He must have known that part of our game was over. Whatever lesson I had been trying to teach him no longer mattered. I wanted him. I wanted him inside me so badly I hurt.

He grabbed me and hauled me on top of him. He was a bit rough and impatient as he pushed me down toward his cock. Gripping my bottom in his hands, he lifted me into the right position and thrust up into my slick heat. He eased into my pussy with those first few strokes and gave me a chance to acclimate to having his shaft stretching and filling me.

Tangling his hand in my hair, he sat up and crushed our mouths together. The erotic musk of my scent invaded my senses. Nikolai did the same wicked things with his tongue that he had just done between my thighs. "*Solnyshka.*"

He fell back against the pillows, and I took control of our coupling and started swiveling my hips. He caressed my body, his hot palms gliding along my ribs and backside before curving back up to my breasts. He treated them gently and used his thumbs to stimulate my nipples.

Every graze of his thumb sent a frisson of sheer delight straight down to my clitoris. The connection between the two erogenous zones seemed to grow stronger as my pregnancy progressed. I shuddered to think what he would be able to do to me with his fingers and mouth in a few months.

Hands planted on the stars that adorned his chest, I rode him harder and faster. Soon we were both covered in a light sheen of sweat. Nikolai's finely honed abdomen rippled. He gazed up at me adoringly. His hands worshipped me. How I had ever doubted that this man loved me and only me I would never understand.

That familiar tightness started to coil in my belly like a taut wire. I shifted forward a little, making sure my clitoris rubbed against his body with every stroke. He grasped my bottom in both hands now and thrust up into me. "Come on, baby. That's it," he urged. "Let me feel you come."

One of his hands moved to my chest as I rocked faster. His fingers glided toward my neck, and he pushed my head back, baring my throat. I couldn't help it. The feel of his hand on my neck drove me crazy. I cried out with wild abandon as the first fluttering pulses took my breath away. "Oh! *Ah*!"

With one hand on my neck and the other gripping my bottom, he thrust up into me at such a fast pace that the bed started to shake. I thought he would come with me, but Nikolai marshaled his control and clamped down on his orgasm. When I sagged forward and collapsed on top of him, he embraced me lovingly and kissed my cheek and temple. "Oh, God," I panted. "That was intense."

He laughed darkly and carefully shifted me off of him. "We're just getting started."

Flat on my back, I didn't have to wonder what he had in mind for very long. He dropped down on his stomach, grabbed the backs of my thighs and shoved my knees toward my chest. A second later, he buried his face between my legs. "Kolya!"

He hummed hungrily and feasted on my sensitive flesh. I clawed at the bedding and pillows, desperate for something to hold onto as he attacked my still throbbing clitoris. It felt so good I thought I might die from the sheer pleasure of it.

Just when I started to climb toward another climax, he dragged his mouth away from me and moved to a kneeling position. He plunged into me on one thrust, burying his cock right up to his balls, and held still. He exhaled roughly and then started to move slowly, deeply. His carefully timed thrusts were designed to keep us both on edge for as long as possible. He was drawing this out, torturing us with the sensual wonder of it, and teasing us both with the promise of orgasms that would leave us trembling and limp.

He claimed my mouth with erotically charged kisses, and I wound my arms around his shoulders, pulling him in tight and holding him close. I couldn't get enough of him. I wanted to feel his heat radiating through me. I wanted to get drunk off his smell and taste. I never wanted him out of my sight again.

Nikolai lifted my right leg until my calf rested on his shoulder. The new angle of penetration made us both gasp and groan. He kissed my leg before leaning down to capture my mouth. His lips moved to my neck. He nipped playfully at my skin, then took both of my hands and trapped them overhead.

"I love you, Vivian." He thrust into me with more force. "I love you." He thrust into me again. "I love you."

Lost in his smoldering gaze, I surrendered to the building inferno between us. He punctuated every thrust with those three words. It was as if he were weaving some sort of spell, using his declaration of love and the powerful, sensual energy of our lovemaking to bind us together for eternity. We came together with that promise between us. Eyes locked, mouths mating, we clutched and rocked until the last waves of pleasure faded.

Nikolai dropped onto his back and draped his arm across his eyes. I slipped out of bed and ducked into the bathroom. Upon returning, I rolled onto my side, and he spooned up against me. He whispered sweetly into my ear before lovingly kissing my cheek. I held tight to the arms wrapped around me and smiled. We had a lot of work ahead of us, but I wasn't afraid to tackle it. Neither was he.

"It feels good to be home," he murmured tenderly.

Home? Me. I was his home. I was his sanctuary.

Closing my eyes, I melted into his loving embrace. "Yes, it does."

21 Chapter Twenty-One

"*Milaya moya ty samaya krasivaya zheshina v mire.*"

I lowered the mascara wand I had been using to dab at my eyelashes and smiled at Nikolai's reflection in the bathroom mirror. He leaned against the frame of the door and watched me with eyes aflame with love and desire. We had spent the entire day hiding out in the guest suite at Niels' eetostate, but now it was time to go out and face the world—together. "Thank you."

"I have a gift for you." He pushed off the door frame and sauntered toward me.

I instantly recognized the colors and logo of the bag he placed on the counter. It belonged to the jewelry store owned by Kazimir Abramov. His daughter Zoya was the finest jewelry designer in Houston.

"Go head." He gestured to the bag. "Open it."

I set aside my mascara and plucked the golden tissue paper from the Prussian blue bag. I reached in and withdrew the jewelry boxes. Heart racing with excitement, I opened the long, thin box and gasped. "Kolya!"

"I wanted you to have something special for tonight. Zoya amazed me with this one."

I touched the delicate, glittering gold and diamonds. She had incorporated Nikolai's nickname for me into the design of sunbursts. It was luxurious and elegant and a true statement piece.

"Let me." Nikolai took it from the box and draped it around my neck. He swept aside my hair and fasted the clasp. He kissed the back of my neck. His lips lingered there, and I reveled in the sensual touch.

Piece by piece, he helped me put on the rest of the jewelry. It looked stunning with my black dress. Hands on my shoulders, Nikolai pressed a sweet kiss to the top of my head. "I'm so proud of you, Vee. I hope tonight is everything you want it to be."

I leaned back against him and welcomed the arms that wrapped around me. I placed my hands on the sleeves of his suit jacket and held his gaze in the mirror. "I'm so glad you're here with me." I clasped his fingers and brought them down to my ever-growing stomach. He rubbed the small bump there, and I amended, "I'm glad you're here with us."

"There are a dozen men we owe thanks to for that." Over a late breakfast, he had told me the entire crazy tale of his global trek. I sensed he didn't want me to worry about the No Fly List, but I had a bad feeling that it was a shot across the bow from Maksim. It was his way of sending a message. *Get in line—or I'll bury you.*

"I would suggest we send fruit baskets or a nice bottle of wine as a thank you, but..."

Nikolai laughed. "I'll think of something more appropriate for them." He placed a noisy kiss on the curve of my throat. "Are you ready?"

"Almost." I untangled myself from his arms and finished primping in the mirror. After packing my clutch with necessities, I left the bathroom and found Nikolai waiting patiently near the window overlooking the gardens. "We'll have to explore them tomorrow morning. I know you're just champing at the bit to get down there to investigate and compare."

"There's no comparison. I tend our garden with my own hands. I saw his landscapers out there this morning." Sounding wistful, he said, "I left Ten and Boy in charge of my trees and plants. God only knows what we'll find when we get home."

Only too aware of his love for the garden and small orchard that he had painstakingly nurtured since buying and renovating the home we shared, I reassuringly patted his chest. "I'm sure they'll take good care of your tomatoes and peaches."

"They had better," he grumbled before taking my hand. "We should go. We'll want to get there early."

Hand in hand, we ventured downstairs. René seemed to appear from nowhere to inform us a car was waiting outside. We slipped into the backseat, and

Nikolai reached for my hand. "We should have made time for dinner reservations before the show."

"Actually, we have plans for after the show." I couldn't believe I had forgotten about Sergei's request!

"We do?"

"Yeah. I sort of forgot." Heat flooded my cheeks. "We were a little busy, after all."

"A little?" He chuckled deeply. "*Sladest.*" He pecked my temple. "I don't think we've spent that much time in bed since you were on Spring Break."

His comment inspired memories of those lust-filled mornings and afternoons and even wilder nights. My skin flushed, and I squeezed my thighs together. "I think you're right."

He smirked in the most annoyingly handsome way. "So, what do you have planned for after the show?"

"It's not me. It's Sergei."

That perked him right up. "Sergei?" His mouth settled into a worried line. "How did Galina react to Bianca?"

"Better than I expected," I admitted. The dinner I had attended at their hotel suite the evening Sergei's mother and brother had arrived in London had been an interesting affair. "I tried to act as the buffer between the two of them. The conversation and dinner went fine."

"But?" He seemed to sense there was more coming.

"Ivan called me the next morning. He told me that he had run into Bianca in the hallway of the hotel. He could hear Sergei and Galina arguing in their room. It wasn't good."

"Shit."

"Right? You know what a softie Ivan is when it comes to women. He told her a little of what he had overheard and then invited her back to their room to see Erin. Bianca stayed there until Sergei came to get her."

"Have you spoken to Sergei or Bianca?"

"Yes. Both."

"And?"

"Sergei thinks it will get better with time. Bianca is pretty much convinced that Galina is going to hate her until the end of time."

"She won't. She'll come around."

"How can you be sure? Look at my family, Kolya. My grandparents hated my father until they died. My father's family won't even meet or see me. Only Eric is brave enough to do that."

"Bianca is a wonderful person. She's smart. She's beautiful. She's tough. She operates a highly successful business."

"That's not what Sergei's mother dislikes and you know it."

Nikolai exhaled roughly. "I know. It's stupid." He shook his head. "The color of Bianca's skin has nothing to do with her worth as a person." He gave my hand a reassuring squeeze. "I'll take care of it."

I wasn't sure how he was going to convince Galina to abandon a lifetime of prejudice and overcome in-grained social mores, but I trusted he would find a way.

"What does Sergei have planned for this evening?"

I nearly bounced in my seat as I said, "He's going to propose to Bianca tonight."

"Tonight?"

"Yes." I studied him with surprise. "You don't seem as shocked as I had expected by that news."

"I saw Sergei at Abramov's. I helped him pick out the ring."

I could just imagine the pair of them, shoulder to shoulder over a jewelry case trying to pick a princess or round cut. "Is it pretty?"

"It's perfect for Bianca. She's going to love it." He smoothed his hand down his tie. "Where is he proposing?"

"On the rooftop of the gallery," I said with an excited smile. "They rent it out for small parties and other functions. Niels helped him secure it for the night. He's going to propose during the show. We have reservations to celebrate at a restaurant Yuri recommended. It should be nice."

"We should pick up the tab."

"You already have," I admitted nervously. "I used our card for the reservation."

Nikolai just laughed. "I take it you've gotten comfortable spending *our* money now."

"Well, I was still pretty pissed off with you when I made the reservation for their best tables. I may have, um, possibly ordered an obscene amount of champagne and wine."

"That you can't even drink?" He seemed amused by that. Sifting his fingers through my hair, he smiled. "It's fine. I'm actually thrilled you didn't hesitate to spend the money." He stroked my bare shoulder. "I hate to ask you this, but can we hold off a little while longer before we announce your pregnancy? I know it will be difficult to keep this secret tonight, especially with everyone celebrating, but we are in a precarious position here. We need to be on our home turf before dropping that news."

"Because of Maksim?"

Nikolai seemed to carefully consider his words. "I think we should be cautious."

"I won't say anything but this," I took his hand and placed his palm against my stomach, "is getting hard to hide. I'll have to start shopping the maternity section when we get home."

A warm look crossed his face. He lovingly caressed me. "It's happening so fast. I feel like it was just yesterday morning that I was pushing you into the bathroom with the test." He nuzzled my neck and turned my face so he could capture my mouth in a sweet, tender kiss. "I need to slow down and spend more time with you. I don't want to miss anything."

I covered his hand with mine. "As quickly as we made this one, I'm sure there will be other chances in the future for you to catch anything you miss with this baby."

He glanced away briefly, but I still noticed the pleased, hopeful expression that danced across his handsome face. When he looked back at me, his usually controlled expression in place, he said, "I hope we get the chance to do this many more times."

I rested my head against his arm and enjoyed the remainder of the drive comforted by his familiar heat and scent. Things felt right between us again. It was strange, but the arguing and the forced separation and Nikolai's willingness to cross half the world in the belly of a cargo plane, the front seat of old cars and the cabin of a rickety boat seemed to have reminded us of what was truly important. Nothing else—*nothing* else—mattered except for the two of us and our baby.

When we arrived at the gallery, Nikolai cupped my face and grazed his thumb along my cheek. His genuine happiness and the love burning so brightly in his eyes warmed me right through, left me feeling relaxed and able to conquer anything. "It's your time to shine, *solynshka.*"

Yes, it was.

Nikolai shook his head at a waiter offering him a glass of champagne and continued weaving in and out of the invitation-only crowd. He had lost sight of Vivian while talking to Sergei's mother and brother. He had made a point of warmly welcoming Bianca and speaking highly of her to Galina. He hoped his good opinion of Bianca would go far in helping Galina warm up to the woman who would soon be her daughter-in-law.

When he spotted Vivian with Niels and a couple he didn't recognize, he slowed his steps. He scanned the room, his gaze lingering on familiar faces, before flicking to the next ones. Judging by the response to his wife's paintings, the show was a smashing success. Not that he had ever doubted otherwise.

He had already seen most of the pieces she was exhibiting and offering for sale, but they looked different on the walls of the gallery. The mix of recessed and spot lights and smoky gray walls perfectly highlighted the colors and textures of each piece. He started to form an idea of what he might give Vivian for Christmas. After everything he had put her through in the last two weeks, she deserved a grand romantic gesture. He wanted to give her something that made her weak in the knees.

Already making plans for the gift, he enjoyed the sight of the guests, most of them journalists and collectors, standing in front of the paintings and animatedly talking about them. A few made critical remarks. He memorized their faces before making damned sure they saw his. He didn't often take pleasure in scaring the shit out of people, but he couldn't hide the triumphant smirk when the critics scurried away from his path.

"Kolya." Ivan stepped in front of him, but he wasn't smiling as he had been when they had spoken earlier in the night. "We need to talk."

"Now?" Nikolai glanced around the gallery. "Can it wait until dinner?'

"No." Shoulders squared and his stance shifted slightly forward, Ivan looked as if he wanted a fight.

"Fine. Let's talk."

He steeled himself for an onslaught about his recent problems with Vivian. Ivan was intensely protective of Erin and the people she loved. He had always been fond of Vivian and would take it personally if she were unhappy.

"Whatever the hell you've been doing to make Vivian so sad has to stop." Ivan kept his voice low so no one around them would overhear. He had relaxed his stance so it simply looked as if two old friends were having a chat. "I'm not going to stand by and watch you ruin the best thing that ever happened to you."

"I've learned my lesson. It won't happen again." There were few men brave enough to tell him what he needed to hear, and he was lucky Ivan was one of them. He put a hand on his dear friend's shoulder. "Vanya, thank you for looking out for me."

"I may not be in your family anymore, but I'm still your family."

"You're a good little brother."

"This little brother will kick your ass if he finds out that one of his best fighters is moonlighting as a guard for you anymore." Ivan whacked his back with an exaggerated force to prove a point. "I mean it, Kolya. I want Kir off your payroll. He's a good kid. He's got talent. He's going places."

"I didn't seek him out. He came to me and asked for a job. He's only there at night."

"Which is the most likely time shit will go bad," Ivan insisted. "You've got plenty of muscle on your payroll already. Kir is mine."

It wasn't worth bad blood and fighting between them so he nodded. "You're right. He's yours. When I get back, I'll let him go. But," Nikolai held his gaze, "you need to keep an eye on him. He needed money badly enough to come to me."

"It's his ex-wife." Ivan tapped the crook of his elbow in a gesture that Nikolai understood only too well. *Heroin*. "She got herself into some trouble. I've taken care of it."

He could tell Ivan was frustrated that Kir hadn't come to him first, but Nikolai understood why Kir had looked for help from others. These men who climbed into the ring were a prideful bunch. For Kir to go to his mentor and ask for money? Impossible.

Their business conducted, they parted with smiles and promises to find each other later. Nikolai finally joined Vivian and was introduced to Alastor and Henriette, the aristocratic couple fawning over her latest works. As he spoke to the husband and wife, he noticed they seemed strangely close to Niels. They hung on his every word and gazed at him with something very similar to adoration.

It wasn't hard for him to add up the clues and arrive at an answer that he found oddly amusing. Apparently Niels didn't confine himself to sexual escapades with only women. Nikolai tried not to imagine the glitzy middle-aged couple trussed up with rope and leather or kneeling at the Dane's feet. He concen-

trated instead on the discussion about a pair of paintings they wanted to buy. Vivian deftly handled the
proposed transaction by mentioning the gallery agent,
and Niels stepped away to speak to a man who had
caught his eye. Then the conversation took a decidedly
strange turn.

"So, are you two lovebirds enjoying the city?" Alastor asked in between sips of champagne.

There was something in the man's tone that set off
Nikolai's radar. He slid an arm around Vivian's waist
and pulled her a little closer. "I've only just arrived
this morning. Business kept me in Houston longer than
I had expected," he explained. "I'm sure we'll explore
all London has to offer over the weekend."

"That sounds lovely," Henriette remarked with a
smile. She eyed Vivian with obvious interest, but his
wife seemed totally oblivious to the lusty glint in the
other woman's eyes. "We're having a bit of a small
get-together tomorrow night. We would love for the
two of you to join us." She took a flirtatious step toward Vivian. "Friends of Niels are always welcome at
these little parties of ours."

Vivian's smile faltered, and Nikolai couldn't decide
if he was annoyed or entertained by the subtle invitation to a wild sexy party with a crowd that promised
to include London's poshest set. Giving Vivian's waist
a gentle squeeze, he said, "We're flattered, but we have
plans."

"Maybe some other time," Henriette replied, not the
least bit daunted.

"Maybe some other time for what?" Niels wondered as he returned to the conversation.

"Oh, just one of our get-togethers," Henriette said with a swirl of her champagne glass. "We thought you would enjoy having them join us."

The Dane's eyes widened fractionally. The corners of his mouth twitched. "I would very much enjoy *having* them."

Nikolai managed not to openly glower at Niels. They shared an intense look, but the tycoon wasn't the least bit affected. If anything, he seemed highly amused by his little joke. Vivian's small hand rubbed his lower back so he made nice. "Some other time."

The talk turned to networking as Alastor pointed out faces among the crowd that Vivian absolutely had to meet. Nikolai's attention wavered when he noticed Erin speaking with a man who seemed too familiar and close. The unknown man had the look of an attorney about him, slick and dressed to impress. Erin seemed comfortable with him, maybe too comfortable.

He scanned the room for Ivan and found his friend crossing the room with purposeful strides. At the same time, he noticed Sergei taking a step in Erin's direction. The fighter was so tall that he had a better vantage point of the room. Nikolai trusted that Ivan wouldn't make a scene, but the other man was being deliberately provocative in the way he touched Erin's arm.

Ivan finally reached Erin. He extended a hand to her friend, but the man ignored it. The stranger leaned forward and kissed Erin's cheek while passing her a card. Now Nikolai worried. Ivan wasn't the type of man to allow such outrageous disrespect. He glanced at Sergei who looked ready to pounce if it went south.

Erin handled Ivan beautifully. She tore up the card and stuffed it into her champagne flute. She caressed the back of his neck and lifted on tiptoes for a kiss. Ivan pressed his forehead to hers, and Nikolai looked away, leaving the pair to their tender moment.

Despite everything he had accomplished in life, Ivan's self-confidence where Erin was concerned was easily shaken. He loved that woman so much. He fucking lived for her. But Nikolai could see that Ivan remained uncertain about his ability to keep her. It was a foolish thing to worry about in his opinion. Erin adored Ivan and had eyes only for him.

Out of the corner of his eye, he caught a flash of blonde hair. His searching gaze flicked back to it, but he found only Lena. Their eyes met across the gallery, and she scowled at him. *What the hell?* She spun on her heel, her dark hair whipping dramatically, and disappeared from his view.

He watched Sergei and Bianca sneaking out of a rear exit. He didn't think Sergei would have any trouble with his proposal, but he silently wished his former enforcer the best of luck. He had his own suspicion about why the couple were hurrying to get married but kept it to himself.

"Who are you staring at?" Vivian's hand had slipped under his jacket and glided along his chest.

Nikolai realized they were alone. He brushed his lips against her temple. "Ivan and Erin. Sergei and Bianca."

"Did Sergei take her up to the roof?" Interest brightened her voice.

"I think so." His eyelids drifted together as her perfume teased his nose. God, he had missed her scent so much. The urge to swing Vivian up in his arms and runaway with her hit him hard. He wanted to hide her away in some secret, quiet place where he could slide between her thighs and stay there as long as he liked. He wanted to worship her growing curves with his hands and mouth. He wanted to feel her shuddery breaths against his ear as he pushed her over the edge.

"Let's runaway together." He couldn't believe he had said it aloud. Judging by Vivian's stunned reaction, she hadn't expected it either.

A bemused smile played upon her face. "What?"

He grasped her hand and held it against his chest, right over his heart. "When everyone heads back to Houston, let's stay."

"Stay here? In London?"

"If you'd like," he said with a generous shrug. "Or we can go somewhere else. We'll go anywhere you would like."

"What about your travel problems?"

"Let me worry about that, *solnyshka*. I owe you a honeymoon. A proper one," he murmured, thinking of all the things she had given up for him. "Let me do this for you."

She bit her lower lip and seemed to be thinking of a million reasons why they couldn't go away. "Your business—"

"You come first."

Vivian grazed her fingers down his cheek. "Then take me away, Kolya."

So he did.

22 CHAPTER TWENTY-TWO

With a long, slow inhale, I filled my lungs with the scent of the Adriatic Sea. I leaned against the balcony overlooking the private strip of Croatian beach and watched the moon's reflection glittering on the dark water. The sun would be rising soon and a new and beautiful day would dawn.

Our whirlwind belated honeymoon had been like something out of a fantasy. We hadn't left London until the evening after our friends had departed for Houston. The night before everyone left, Bianca and Sergei had experienced a medical scare. We had been floored to learn they were pregnant—and expecting twins! Their hasty engagement suddenly made sense, but more than anything, I prayed the news would soften Galina's feelings toward her future daughter-in-law.

"Are you all right?" Nikolai slipped out of our suite and onto the terrace.

"I'm fine." I glanced back at him and felt a flutter of desire at the sight of his lean, tattooed body striding toward me. He wore only his usual black boxers and prowled like a jungle cat tracking its prey through the shadows of night. "I woke up and couldn't fall back to sleep."

"I have a prescription for that." He embraced me from behind and dotted a line of meandering kisses from the crown of my head to the side of my throat.

I giggled softly and then moaned when he sucked hard on the curve of my neck. "Kolya."

"Vee." He nipped lightly at my skin.

"We're outside," I reminded him breathlessly.

"It's dark. This beach is private." He pushed aside the thin silk robe guarding my shoulders and planted ticklish kisses on my skin. His strong hands glided from my breasts to the swell of my stomach and then settled on my hips. His lips brushed my ear. "I want you."

"Again?"

"Yes." Nikolai surged against me, pressing his erection against my bottom, and I gasped.

He had been utterly insatiable lately. Luckily, my first trimester woes had faded into the background. My craving for sex rivaled his. I might have been imagining it, but I swore every orgasm felt better and stronger than the last. I had mistakenly admitted that to

Nikolai a few mornings earlier as we lounged in bed. Now he seemed intent on seeing just how good they could get.

"Lean forward," he urged with a gentle hand on my upper back. He peeled off my robe and tossed it somewhere behind us. Grasping the bottom of my nightgown, he rucked it up around my hips before sliding to his knees. He shocked me by nibbling my plump backside and the tops of my thighs. I cried out, but he just laughed and kept tormenting me.

With a bit of a rough shove, he flipped me around and buried his face between my thighs. I braced my elbows on the balcony ledge and prayed my knees wouldn't give out as Nikolai swiped my slit. As if he needed to get deeper, he lifted my left leg and draped my knee over his shoulder. His tongue fluttered around my clitoris before stabbing into my opening.

"Kolya!" I gripped his hair and pressed my hips against his wonderful mouth. He groaned against my hot flesh and flicked faster against my swollen nub. My breaths were coming fast now, and I felt that clenching tightness in my core. "Oh, please. *Oh!* I'm close."

He slid two fingers into me, curling them just right, and pumped them quickly. My legs trembled, and I gasped for air. His tongue did wicked things while his fingers drove me right over the edge. I bit my lower lip to stifle a scream. We were hidden in the shadows, but a cry of pleasure would draw the wrong sort of attention.

He tore his mouth away from me and kissed his way back up my body. Standing up suddenly, he lifted me in his arms. He carried me into the bedroom and placed me on the bed. We met in a clash of tongues and teeth and ripped at each other's clothing.

Nikolai roughly kissed me before shoving my thighs apart and thrusting into me without warning. I cried out in surprise, but he misread it as a cry of pain. He went still above me and between my legs. "Baby." His voice was gruff but concerned. "Did I hurt you?"

"No." I hooked my ankles behind his back and lifted my hips. "Don't stop." I rocked against him. "Please don't stop."

With a needful groan, he obliged me. His thrusts started off slow and easy, but they grew faster and deeper. His mouth was all over me, marking my cheeks, my neck, my breasts. He took me with an unhurried and leisurely pace all while murmuring the things I loved to hear.

I clutched at his sides and then his shoulders, burying my face in the crook of his neck and enjoying every single thrust into my slick heat. His hand moved between my thighs, and he shifted the angle of his thrusts. As his fingers strummed my clitoris, I clawed at his shoulders and scratched at his scalp. "Kolya. *Please.*"

He kissed me hard, his tongue stabbing against mine, and then started whispering dirty things to me in Russian. He knew what that did to me. He could feel it for himself.

"Fuck, Vee." His cheek brushed mine, and his shuddery breaths rippled across my skin. "Your pussy drives me crazy. Wet." He punctuated the word with a thrust. "Tight." Another thrust. "Hot."

I came so hard I couldn't breathe. The pleasurable explosion knocked the air from my lungs. My mouth gaped, and he took advantage of it. He plundered my mouth and continued thrusting into me while I rode those intensely erotic waves.

I thought he would follow me with a shared release, but he pulled out of me and turned me onto my stomach. He grasped my thighs and hauled me up onto my knees before entering me from behind. Sweeping aside my hair, he kissed my neck and upper back and started to pump his hips.

I gripped a pillow in one hand and the sheet in the other. My endless cries echoed off the walls and ceiling. Too late, I remembered the doors leading out to the balcony were still wide open, but suddenly I didn't care. We were doing what we loved doing the most, and it was passionate and perfect.

I couldn't come again, not after two intense back-to-back orgasms, but I enjoyed every second of our coupling. His fingers gripped my hips with enough force that I was certain there were would be small bruises there by sunrise. He restrained the power behind his thrusts though, always mindful of hurting me or the baby.

"Vee." My name left his lips on a long, drawn out groan.

We collapsed onto the bed. Nikolai rolled onto his side and dragged me back against him like a caveman claiming his mate. He draped his leg over both of mine and engulfed me with a warm embrace. His lips danced along the shell of my ear, and I dozed off to Nikolai telling me how much he loved me.

Sometime later, I woke to the sound of a cell phone ringing. I glanced behind me to find Nikolai fast asleep. He seemed to be sleeping much better since leaving London, and I didn't want to wake him unless it was important. I slipped out of bed and back into the nightgown that had been tossed to the floor a few hours earlier.

Early morning sun filled the suite. It took me a moment to realize the ringing wasn't coming from our two phones plugged into their chargers across the bedroom. I followed the ringtone into the living area and over to my purse. The sound perplexed me until I remembered Ten's emergency package.

The burner phones!

I dug through my purse until I found the pair I had tucked away in a pocket. Only one had been powered up and activated, just in case. I retrieved the ringing, vibrating phone and hurried to answer it. "Hello?"

"Vivian, it's Kostya. I need to speak with Nikolai. *Now.*"

The tension in his voice scared me. Kostya had a gift for remaining calm even in the worst situations. If he was this anxious, it wasn't good. "Hang on."

I ran back into the bedroom, put my hand on Nikolai's arm and gave him a shake. "Kolya! Wake up."

Making a low, humming noise, he stretched his arms over head and rolled onto his back. He must have seen the look on my face because he quickly sat up and grabbed my hand. "What's wrong?"

"It's Kostya." I thrust the cell phone at him.

"On a burner phone?" He snatched it away from me. "Kostya?"

I left the bed and ventured onto the terrace to grab my robe. From the snatches of conversation I overheard, I could tell it wasn't good. I headed into the living area and dialed up room service for a breakfast order and then inquired about the flight schedule to Tirana. I was making notes when Nikolai came into the living room while shrugging into a shirt.

He blew out a noisy breath and raked his fingers through his hair. "I'm sorry, Vee, but we have to leave."

"What's happened?"

"Besian Beciraj has been shot."

I didn't know what to say. Who would be crazy enough to shoot a mob boss? "Is he alive?"

"Yes. Barely."

"Who shot him?"

Nikolai wiped a hand down his face. "The hit man Julio Jimenez hired to kill Mando Fernandez. It seems there was a tape of the hit. The tape was still on a camera that ended up at Kirkwood's."

"Abby Kirkwood's pawn shop?"

He seemed surprised by my interruption. "You know Abby?"

"I know her through her brother, Mattie. He attends the classes at Hadley's arts center where I volunteer a few times a month."

His expression turned grim. "Before the meeting where Besian was nearly killed, the hit man took shots at Abby and her brother at the arts center. Finn Connolly saved Hadley when she was caught in the crossfire."

"Oh my God." I put a hand to my mouth but dropped it fast. "Eddie Rivera is going to be furious."

"He's going to be trouble," Nikolai agreed. "A man with that much money and the political connections he has? It could get very messy." He laughed harshly. "Messier," he corrected. "Besian is in the hospital. Julio is dead. Lorenzo ran back to his cartel stronghold. The Albanians will want to declare war on the cartel now. Of course, they'll have to get in line behind Romero and Hector Salas."

During the time spent together on our getaway, Nikolai had slowly filled me in the friction between the various underworld parties. If Julio was dead, the cartel's Houston dealers would start jockeying for his old position. Knowing my father, he would find a way to exploit Julio's death to his own advantage.

I glanced at Nikolai with apprehension. "My dad? Was he there?"

"He's alive." Nikolai scratched his fingers through his sandy-colored hair. "I need to get back before the whole fucking city catches fire."

"Of course." Though I was saddened our honeymoon had to be ended so abruptly, I understood the stakes were high. "I've ordered breakfast. There is a flight to Tirana leaving in three hours. I assumed that since you came into Europe through Albania, you would want to go back the same way."

"I'll have to, just to be on the safe side. We'll fly straight to Tirana. You'll go back first class on a commercial flight to Houston. I'll make sure one of Luka's men, someone with clean papers, flies with you. I'll be heading back with Zec. I'll be a few hours longer than you because I'll have to land in Mexico and drive up to Houston. Ten, Danny, Boy and Ilya will be waiting for you at the airport."

I didn't like the idea of being separated but knew it was for the best. "Okay."

A flash of guilt crossed his face. He came toward me and cupped my face. "I'm sorry, *solnyshka*."

I placed my hand atop his. "I'm sorry that we have to leave, but I'm glad that we were able to get away, even if it was just for a little while."

"We'll do it again." He embraced me, hauling me in close and burying his face in the curve of my neck. "It's going to be dangerous in Houston, Vee. The next few months will be difficult, but I need you to trust me."

"I do." I wound my arms around him and kissed his temple. "We'll figure a way through this."

"Together," he said firmly. "We'll do it together."

Clinging to him, I pushed aside the fear that made my knees weak. Even though I wished we could stay here and pretend the real world didn't exist, I accepted that was impossible. We had to go back. It was time for Nikolai to make his stand—and I would be right there beside him, holding his hand the entire way.

23 CHAPTER TWENTY-THREE

"You look like shit." Romero gruffly and rudely greeted Nikolai when he stepped off of one of Zec's private jets nearly twenty-four hours later.

Nikolai coolly appraised his father-in-law. He had bags under his eyes and an arm in a sling. There were cuts and scrapes on his neck and wrist, probably from flying shards of window glass shattered by bullets. "Have you looked in a mirror lately?"

"It's been a long couple of days." Romero's hard gaze softened fractionally. "Vivian made it home safely."

The tightness in his chest eased some. Vivian and the baby were safe. Now he just had to figure out a way to fix this awful fucking mess so he could put himself in a stronger position to keep it that way.

"That was an interesting choice of escort you arranged for her."

Nikolai shrugged. "Luka insisted. It was the best option."

Although Luka had personally volunteered to see her safely home, the boss had ultimately bowed to the concerns of his top men. He had assigned his cousin and uncle to watch over Vivian. Both were battle-hardened men who could be trusted to get her on the ground and into Ten's custody.

Romero glanced at Zec as he descended the plane's stairs. He nodded in the other man's direction, but Zec paid him little attention.

"I'm leaving," the Albanian announced. "I trust you'll be fine on your own."

"This *güero* is family. That means he's safe with me." Romero's dark eyes locked on with Zec's equally black irises. "I would offer you my protection, but I don't think you're going to need it."

"You might need it from me." Zec turned away from Romero and offered his hand. "Good luck."

Nikolai firmly grasped it. "Thank you, and good luck to you, too."

He had a bad feeling about what Zec might get up to if left alone to roam the Mexican countryside, but the Albanian wasn't his problem. If he wanted to get revenge on the cartel for hurting his best friend, so be it. The less of them that were fit for fighting when the time came, the better.

Alone with his father-in-law, Nikolai trailed him to a waiting truck. Despite the setting sun, it was still miserably hot. The ice cold interior felt good, and it perked up his weary bones. He leaned heavily against the seat and reached for his seat belt as Romero slid behind the wheel.

"This is a hell of a family reunion," Romero remarked as he punched the gas. A column of motorcycles and SUVs trailed them off the private airstrip. Six of the bikers revved their bikes and sped by to take the lead. Nikolai caught the sunlight glinting off the steel strapped to their leather clad bodies. They were armed for war.

Irritated by the situation, he snapped, "I fucking told you to give Mando to Julio. I warned you something like this would happen. Besian's been shot. Your VP's daughter was nearly killed."

"Stepdaughter," Romero corrected. "Marley is Spider's old lady's kid."

"I've seen Spider around town with Marley. He doesn't seem to make the distinction between blood and not blood. That's his daughter." Nikolai couldn't believe Romero would even pull that line. "You're just damned lucky that Vivian was in London. Julio's hit man would have gone after her next."

Romero's jaw clenched. "I can't change the past. She's safe and that's all that matters."

"She's safe for now." Nikolai's stomach twisted. "Until this shit with the cartel is put to bed, she'll never be safe."

"There's only one way to put this to bed." Romero glanced away from the windshield to Nikolai's face and then back again. "Are you ready to make that call?"

Before Vivian, he wouldn't have hesitated to say yes. His life seemed to be divided into two distinct halves. The life he had led before crossing paths with her had been so violent and brutal. His soul had been forever blackened by the dark deeds he had performed to help Maksim gain more territory back in Moscow. He had come to Houston fully intent on using the same tactics.

Until the night those violent, brutal tactics had nearly cost one innocent little girl her life.

Lorenzo Guzman was becoming a problem. He sat at the top of a pyramid of drugs and money and greed that required a strong hand. His men had to believe that he had everything under control, but this thing with Julio had proved that he didn't. He was slipping and the way down would be fast and furious.

Lorenzo had to go, but there had to be someone waiting in the shadows to step up and take control. Hector Salas was young, but he was hungry and fucking brilliant. He had made a miscalculation with Bobby Pham, but Nikolai believed that if the girlfriend hadn't been part of the equation, it would have worked. Bobby would have been the perfect shipping conduit for Hector's newer, leaner vision of the cartel.

But that vision was dead. Hector needed a new plan. Romero had already thrown his weight behind Hector and had promised to back him. With the guns Maksim funneled through Romero and into Central America, Vivian's father was in a prime position to be a huge player.

But they couldn't jump the gun. If they pulled the trigger too soon, Hector's coup would fail—and then what? Who would take control? Would there be a civil war? Would two or three cartels fight for the Guzman slice of the pie?

Lorenzo had to go, but Nikolai had to give that order at the perfect moment. He fucking cringed to think of Vivian's crestfallen expression when she learned he had given an order like the one her father wanted. She believed in him. She believed he could be a better man—but fuck. It was getting harder and harder to walk that line.

"Lorenzo didn't hire that hit man. He didn't send a killer to my city. That was Julio's fault—and yours." He made sure that Romero wouldn't escape any blame in this situation. "You knew that Julio was cracking up after his kid was killed. You knew that Mando had slammed into that little boy and ripped him to pieces with his bike. You covered it up and helped him run so Julio did the only thing he could to get justice for his son."

Nikolai stretched out his legs and sighed. "Now Besian is in the hospital, and Lorenzo is watching his power base crumble." He shook his head. "And you and Hector aren't ready yet. The plan you told me about before I left for London isn't even close to completion. You need more time. If this is going to work, you must be patient."

Romero didn't say anything. He clutched the wheel even tighter with his tattooed fingers and drove in silence. He waited so long to say anything that Nikolai doubted he would receive a reply at all. "My last stretch was ten long years of waiting. I can be patient for a few more months."

Nikolai figured that was the best he was going to get from Romero.

"It's strange, huh?" Romero asked a long while later as they barreled down a dusty road. "You and me? Working together?"

"Strange isn't quite strong enough." Nikolai frowned at the man seated next to him. "You did try to kill me once."

"And you tried to kill my daughter."

"That was an accident! You were going to take me out on a hit contract."

"I saved your life a few months ago. I let you marry my daughter."

"Let?" Nikolai guffawed. "The day Vivian needs you to *let* her do anything is the day pigs fly."

Romero cracked a smile at that. "She's strong. I wasn't sure when I went inside that last time what sort of woman she would become."

"She's perfect."

Romero cast a sidelong glance his way. "It's good that you think that. She needs someone who believes in her completely." He cleared his throat. "How was the show?"

"It was a success." Nikolai wasn't sure that did her justice. "The write-ups in the art media were very good. She sold every single piece and has quite a few commissions to tackle."

Romero hesitated. "And the baby?"

"Everything seems fine. She's due for another checkup next week."

"Good. That's…good."

They lapsed into silence as they continued their drive to the compound where Romero headquartered his outfit. The Calaveras motorcycle club had continued to grow while Romero had been on the inside. As vice president of the original chapter, Spider had beaten the recruitment drum hard and often. They had chapters across Texas, New Mexico, Arizona, California and Louisiana now. A sizeable number of their nomad members were in Mexico living at the compound Romero had overtaken.

Since their inception, they had run protection and drugs for the cartel, but now that Romero was on the outside, they were branching out and funneling weapons into the country for Maksim. Nikolai managed not to show his shock at the size of Romero's operation. He had known that Vivian's father had been busy, but Jesus Christ!

Nikolai was glad to see a familiar face as he exited the truck. Artyom leaned against a silver Tahoe and sipped from a water bottle. Haggard and tense, he still flashed a smile as Nikolai drew near. They shook hands and whacked each other on the back.

"The tan looks good on you, boss."

Nikolai needed a good laugh so he let one escape. "Thanks."

"It's good to have you back, but I wish the circumstances were different."

"So do I."

"And Vivian? Is she well?"

Nikolai understood what Artyom was asking. He nodded. "She's wonderful."

Artyom smiled, relieved. "Good. I'm glad."

Sensing Romero's stare, he sighed. He wanted nothing more than to get into that Tahoe and race back to Houston, but this had to be handled first. "Let's this over with so we can get the hell out of here."

Nikolai rubbed his tired eyes. Nearly thirty-seven hours of traveling by plane and car had taken their toll. Only the knowledge that Vivian and the baby were under guard and waiting for him in Houston kept him going.

He glanced at Artyom who mashed gum between his teeth and concentrated on the dark stretch of highway in front of them. Two members of his street crew manned the SUV in front of them. Six of

Romero's most trusted Calaveras MC brothers had ridden escort from south of the border.

"When we hit the city limits, we're going to lose the bikes." Nikolai stared at the reflection of the motorcycle headlights in the mirror. "They're too damned noisy and attract too much attention."

"Sure, but they're crazy fucking bastards who aren't afraid to fight." Artyom seemed to be warming toward the rough, leathered up bikers flanking the Tahoe. "If the shit with the cartel goes bad, I wouldn't mind having them on our side."

"There is no *if*, Artyom." Nikolai had been thinking long and hard about the cartel situation on the transatlantic flight. "Julio's stunt just revealed all of Lorenzo's weaknesses. Now we all know that he's lost control. He's weak and vulnerable."

"Who will strike first?"

"Not us," Nikolai replied firmly. "The first one through the door gets it in the neck. We'll let someone else have that honor."

Artyom didn't ask who that someone else might be. He was probably assuming it would be Romero, but Nikolai had his money on Hector Salas and the tight band of enforcers and street soldiers he had been quietly gathering to support him. Lorenzo tucking tail and running back to Mexico with egg on his face had given Hector and his little army one hell of an opening. Would they use it wisely? Only time would tell.

When they reached the city, the bikers blew by them and disappeared from the highway. Nikolai and his men drove to an arranged meeting spot where Kos-

tya waited with the man everyone called Devil. Besian's scar-faced street captain nodded in respect and
slid into the backseat of the Tahoe along with Kostya.
Soon, they were on their way to the Houston hospital
where Besian remained in the ICU.

"How bad is it?" Nikolai twisted in his seat to better see Kostya and the Albanian giant who rivaled Ten
and Sergei in size and ferocity.

"He's a lucky fucking bastard." Kostya shook his
head in awe. "The bullet missed his heart by this
much." He held up two fingers separated by only a few
millimeters of space. "One of his lungs collapsed, but
he's a fighter. The surgeons told Ben that he'll be
moved to a step-down unit this afternoon if he continues to improve."

"That's good." He and Besian hadn't always seen to
eye-to-eye, but they had developed a friendship during
their many years working in the same underworld
space. He would never be as close to Besian as he was
to Ivan or Yuri or Dimitri, but he didn't want to see
the Albanian loan shark and boss killed.

"What happened to Zec?" Devil asked. "I thought
he was coming with you."

Nikolai shook his head. "He decided to stay in Mexico."

Devil swore in Albanian and nervously tapped his
hand on his knee. "I should get down there. He's going
to need someone to rein his ass back in when he goes
to far."

When, Nikolai noticed, not *if*. Devil obviously knew Zec's penchant for mayhem. "You're going to be needed here."

The side of Devil's badly scarred face twisted with a scowl. "You're not my boss."

"No, I'm not. Your boss is fighting for his life in a hospital bed downtown. If someone wants to get to him, they'll try right now. You and Ben and the other *miks* should be there at the hospital or out on the street holding your territory. You think Nicky Jackson is just going to sit around with his thumb up his ass while Besian recovers? No. He's going to make a play for that territory the skinheads are holding—and then he's going to try to cut into yours."

Devil glared out the window but gave a stern nod. Nikolai let the issue drop. He could give advice, but he couldn't make Besian's men take it. If they wanted to go running south to pick fights with the cartel, he couldn't stop them. But if they tried to bring any of that bullshit back into the city, he would make them hurt.

This early in the morning, the hospital parking garages were nearly empty. They would have to wait another hour or so before visitation hours opened. Nikolai couldn't stand the idea of waiting in the Tahoe. "I need to get out and walk. I need coffee."

Artyom checked his watch. "There's a Starbucks on the first floor. It's open now."

Nikolai wasn't a fan, but Vivian absolutely adored their iced coffees and teas. Thinking of her, he decided it was safe to call her. He didn't like the idea of waking her up, but she would want to hear from him.

As their small group made their way into the hospital, Nikolai slowed his pace so he would have some privacy to make his call. The phone rang four times before she answered in a sleepy voice. "Hello?"

"Vee."

"Kolya! Are you okay? Where are you? When are you coming home?"

"Vee," he said with a laugh. "Calm down. I'm fine. I'm in Houston at the hospital. I'll be home as soon as I've seen Besian."

She sighed softly. "I miss you."

"I've missed you so much." He didn't care if the others overheard him sharing a tender moment with his wife. "I love you."

"I love you. Come home soon."

"I will."

He ended the call and tucked away his phone. The Starbucks was as busy as he had expected, even this early in the morning. The crush of physicians, nurses and medical technicians about to start their shifts made it impossible to reach the counter at first. Only his dire need for caffeine kept him in the long, bustling queue.

Hot coffee in hand and flanked by his men and Devil, Nikolai headed toward the elevators. It was the same story there. Too many bodies and not enough space. He sipped his coffee and scanned the faces in the crowd for any signs of malice. It would be so easy for someone who wanted to hurt Besian to infiltrate the hospital. No one paid much attention to anyone wearing scrubs. With the properly faked credentials, a person could gain access to any area in the hospital, even the ICU.

Upstairs in the ICU waiting area, they found Ben Beciraj slumped in a chair. He awakened immediately at the sound of footsteps and sprang from his chair. Nikolai put a calming hand on the street captain's shoulder. "Hey. Easy."

"Sorry." Ben blew out a breath and rubbed the back of his neck. "It's been a long couple of days."

"I know." Nikolai clapped him on the back. "How is he?"

Ben gestured to an empty chair and Nikolai sat. "He's doing well. It's a good thing he's so damned stubborn. Anyone else would have died after a sniper's bullet blew a hole through their chest."

Nikolai couldn't argue with that. "Will he get out of here soon?"

"Today," Ben said. "They'll move him to a step-down unit for a day or two and then down to a regular room. He's got a long road of recovery ahead of him." The young *mik* lowered his voice and dipped his head. "Besian wants to speak with you as soon as possible. He told me to tell you that we stand with you."

"I've never doubted that." Nikolai clapped Ben's back again. "If you don't mind, I'll go in to see him first. You should go get some breakfast or go home and rest. Devil is here. I'm sure he would be happy to sit with Besian."

Ben's reluctance to leave his adopted uncle was clear, but eventually he yielded. "Yeah. Okay."

Nikolai rose from the uncomfortable waiting room chair and made his way to the room number Ben had given him. There were two nurses and a pair of doctors in the room so he waited in the hallway until they were done. He entered quietly and closed the door. Noisy machines beeped. There were wires and tubes everywhere.

Propped up in the bed, Besian looked fucking miserable. He had a sheet covering his legs. His hospital gown was open and had fallen to his waist to reveal a long strip of blood-stained gauze covering a gnarly incision straight down his sternum where his chest had been cracked. Eyes closed, he seemed to be making every effort not to move or breathe too deeply.

"It's not contagious," Besian croaked in a low voice. "You can come closer."

Nikolai's mouth slanted with amusement. He moved to the chair at the bedside and sat on the edge of the seat. "I won't ask how you're feeling."

"High as a fucking kite," Besian said with a smile. He lifted the small controller that gave him a quick dose of morphine when he needed it. "I need one of these for the house."

"I'm sure Kostya can find one that's fallen off the back of a truck." He reached into his pocket and withdrew the handful of jaw breakers he had picked up at a convenience store in Harlingen. He placed them on the rolling table next to Besian's bed.

Besian smiled but warned, "Don't be funny, Kolya. Only a bastard would try to make me laugh right now." Then, with a great deal of effort, Besian raised a finger to his mouth. He barely had the strength to touch his lips but Nikolai got the message. Besian feared the room was bugged.

Nikolai glanced around the room, his gaze landing on the various pieces of equipment and furniture where a bug might be placed. He decided all the questions he had for Besian would have to wait. The Albanian looked dreadfully tired and pale, much too exhausted to talk anyway.

He placed his hand on Besian's arm. The other man's eyes flashed open and locked onto his face. "Get some rest. I'll look after your house for you."

Besian understood what Nikolai was saying and nodded slowly. "Don't let my dogs off their leashes. They're too young and not very well trained."

Nikolai thought of Ben and Devil. They were hot-headed pricks. "I'll keep an eye on them." He stood up and backed away from the bed. "Get some sleep."

Besian waved the fingers on his left hand before closing his eyes.

Out in the waiting room, Nikolai spotted a young woman sitting alone. There was something familiar about the auburn-hued ponytail. She had a shell-shocked look about her and anxiously chewed her thumb. When she caught him staring at her, she nervously dropped her hand and tugged at the sleeves of her oversized plaid shirt. She wasn't fast enough. He still managed to see the dark bruises on her wrists.

His tired brain finally put together the pieces. A memory of Spider with a younger version of this woman at a steakhouse that Nikolai frequented moved to the forefront of his mind. This was Marley. This was the young woman that Besian had nearly given his life to save.

An idea began to take shape in the back of his mind. He remembered the way Besian had lamented there were no other women like Vivian out there. The Albanian boss couldn't have been more wrong. Marley had a sweet, gentle air about her, and those big, blue eyes and reddish-brown hair set her apart in a sea of brunettes and blondes.

Devil stood up to take Nikolai's place at Besian's bedside, but he held up a hand to stop him. He crossed the waiting room to stand in front of her. "You're Marley."

She swallowed and glanced around the room. "Yes."

"Do you know who I am?"

"Of course." A hint of a smile brightened her face. "Everyone knows who you are."

"Are you here to see Besian?"

"Yes." Her answer came quietly. "I just—I wanted to say thank you. He doesn't even know me, but he saved me."

Nikolai had his suspicions as to why Besian had run into the line of fire for this woman, but he kept them to himself. "You can go in and see him. If the staff asks, tell them you're his little sister."

"His sister?" she repeated skeptically.

"A little white lie here and there?" He shrugged. "If you don't want to see him—"

"I do." She was on her feet in an instant.

Nikolai stepped closer and lowered his voice. "I'm sure I don't need to tell you this, but be careful about what you say in that room and to anyone else."

Marley nodded gravely. "I understand."

He was certain that she did. A girl didn't grow up around an outlaw motorcycle club like the Calaveras without picking up some useful underworld survival skills.

Nikolai watched her disappear around the corner and into the ICU ward before joining Devil. "Make sure that she gets home safely. I'm sure Spider has a tail on her, but add one of your own. Your boss took one to the chest to protect her. Let's try to make sure she's still alive for him to chase when he gets out of here."

The smile that contorted Devil's badly scarred face seemed more sinister than amused. "I'll keep an eye on her."

Satisfied that he had done his duty to Besian, Nikolai left the hospital with Artyom and Kostya. His legs grew heavier with every step. By the time he reached the Tahoe, he felt as if he were dragging around cinderblocks. He sagged against the seat and mustered what was left of his energy so he could finish what needed to be finished before going home to Vivian. "Tell me about the shooting."

Kostya leaned forward from the rear seat. "There's not much to tell. We went to the meeting to exchange the tape Abby Kirkwood had in her hands for Lorenzo Guzman's promise that he would extend his protection to her and her brother. Julio crashed the meeting by driving a van right into the middle of it. A standoff happened. He held Marley like a shield, kept a gun to her head, and went bat-shit fucking crazy. Romero taunted him. Lorenzo begged him to stop. Besian was the only one who tried to negotiate with him."

Nikolai imagined the chaotic scene. "And then what happened?"

"I saw Julio's head explode." Kostya tapped his temple. "Blood and bone and brain went fucking everywhere. The girl screamed before I even heard the shot's report. She was blindfolded and tied up. She couldn't move or see. The bullets started flying. I went for cover. There was glass blowing all over the place. I couldn't find the shooter. The echo was so bad down there."

"Besian?"

"The girl fell, and he ran out after her. It was brave but stupid. He scooped her up and ran, but the sniper was fast. Besian got hit, and he threw the girl at Jack Connolly. Jack was a Marine. He didn't panic like the others. The second those bullets started snapping, he picked up his woman and tossed her behind the closest engine block. When Besian threw Marley at him, he caught her and stowed her away with Abby. I couldn't believe my fucking eyes when Jack saved Besian."

"Jack Connolly?" Nikolai blinked. "Jack saved the man who nearly got his little brother killed in those fights? The man who threatened to take away his gym because of their father's bad debt?"

"Those Connolly guys are a different breed. It's that Marine training. It changes a man. I've never met one who went bad after leaving the military. That honor and loyalty gets into their bones." He reached into his pocket and retrieved a small plastic bag that he handed forward. "Speaking of the Connollys..."

"What is this?" Nikolai took the bag from Kostya and held it up to examine it. He found himself staring at a bloodied bullet. "Is this—?"

"From the Ghost," Kostya confirmed. "I dug it out of the wall before I took the corpse and put it on ice."

"Where is he?"

"In one of my facilities."

"Finn Connolly shot him?" Nikolai rolled the bullet around between the plastic.

"One shot. Perfectly placed between the eyes," Kostya stated. "He's one hell of a sniper. It's too bad he doesn't freelance. We could use him."

"There are other ways to get him to work for us." Nikolai handed back the bullet. "Keep that safe. The body too."

"*Da.*"

"Do you know what he did with the rifle?"

"Finn?" Kostya shrugged. "I would assume he put it right back into storage. I can find out."

"Find the gun. We might need it."

Neither Artyom nor Kostya asked why. They both knew what he was planning. Nikolai didn't relish the idea of blackmailing and extorting a man like Finn

Connolly, but his endgame was clear and hard choices had to be made.

When they reached the house, Artyom dropped him off at the back gate. He felt his burden lightening as he walked onto his property. He zeroed in on Ten sitting on the back steps. He scowled like a misbehaving puppy that had been banished outside.

With a sigh, Nikolai meandered over to check the garden beds. He didn't spot any weeds or wilting. So far so good. He walked toward the pergola and noticed too many dead and dying center roses on the clusters. He didn't often dead-head these in the summer, but Vivian spent so much time out here. He wanted her to have a beautiful place to sit and enjoy her mornings and evenings.

As Nikolai picked up the pail and pruning shears he kept near the pergola, Ten lumbered over and watched him snip away the center roses and trace canes to healthier shoots for pruning when necessary. He glanced at Ten and asked, "What did you do to piss her off this early in the morning?"

"The detective is here. She sent me outside before he arrived."

Nikolai lowered the shears. "Eric is here?"

Ten nodded. "He's in the kitchen."

Nikolai dropped the shears into the pail and pushed it into Ten's hands. "Dump these in the compost."

With powerful, long strides, he crossed the yard and took the steps two at a time. He entered the sunroom through the French doors there and immediately heard the loud voices coming from inside the house. *Shit.*

So much for his quiet morning catching up on sleep and enjoying Vivian.

24 CHAPTER TWENTY-FOUR

"Miss Vivian?" Boychenko poked his head into the kitchen where I sat at the breakfast table enjoying a cup of tea and some peanut butter toast. Ten sat across from me and shoveled a shocking amount of bacon and eggs into his mouth. His appetite trounced Sergei's. If he ever cut back on his workouts, Ten was going to get flabby fast.

Tearing my gaze away from Ten's plate, I asked, "What is it, Boy?"

"The detective just pulled up out front."

"Oh." I glanced at Ten who had stopped chewing. "You need to go outside and stay there until Eric leaves."

He swallowed. "I'm eating."

"There's a bench in the pergola."

Ten started to argue but didn't. He used his fork to push the last of his eggs and bacon onto a slice of toast. He smashed the hastily arranged sandwich between another thick toast slice, picked up his glass of orange juice and left the kitchen. I rolled my eyes at his broad back but couldn't help the little smile that tugged at the corners of my mouth.

The doorbell rang, and Boychenko waited for my instruction. "Let Eric inside, please. Ask him to come back to the kitchen."

"Yes, ma'am."

I finished my toast and tidied up the table. Eric walked into the kitchen as I was wiping crumbs off the counter. He stalked across the room, wrapped his arms around me and lifted me up in a bone-crushing hug. "God, I'm so glad you're all right."

"Eric," I said with a laugh. "I'm fine. Um—maybe you could loosen up a bit?"

"Sorry." He put me down and let go of me. His hand settled on my shoulder as he looked me over. "You're sure you're okay?"

"I'm perfectly fine."

Eric's face suddenly slackened as he got a good look at me. His brown eyes glinted with panic. "You're pregnant."

My hands moved to the noticeable curve to my once-flat stomach. The yoga pants and tank top were too slim-fitting to hide anything. "Yes."

"No." Eric slashed his hand through the air. "You can't be pregnant."

"Eric," I huffed with laughter, "I absolutely can be. That's sort of what happens when people get married."

As if on the verge of a full-blown anxiety attack, he gripped both my hands and gave them a shake. "But he'll never let you go now. He'll own you. He'll own this baby. Jesus, Vivian! What were you thinking?"

"Eric." I shouted his name in the hopes of breaking through his frenzied state. "Calm down!"

"Calm down?" He let go of my hands and cupped my face. "Vivian, open your fucking eyes. Do you see what's happening? The cartel war is *here*. You aren't safe anymore. Your father is poking his finger in Lorenzo Guzman's face and daring him to attack. You'll be at the top of his list of targets."

He wasn't telling me anything I hadn't already worked out for myself. "Nikolai will keep me safe."

"Nikolai is the biggest danger to you and this baby." One of his hands moved down to cup my bump. His eyes flashed with such pain and anguish. "He'll kill you just like he killed her. Only this time? It won't be his hands that do the dirty work. It will be some *sicaria* who gets close enough to you to jab her blade between your ribs."

Jerking on my hands, he tugged me forward. "No. I'm not letting him kill someone else I love. You're coming with me. I know people who can hide you."

"Eric!" I tried to pull free but his grip was too tight. "Stop! Let me go!"

"You can kick and scream all you like, but you're coming with me."

Why hadn't Boy come to my aid? Surely he could hear us arguing.

"That kid isn't coming to help you," Eric said as if reading my mind. "He's passed out and tied up in the entryway."

"Eric! Are you insane? You can't do this!"

"I'd like to see someone stop me. I have a badge and a gun." He tugged hard and pulled me out of the kitchen. "I should have done this last December. I should have made you come with me then. None of this would have happened. You never would have been kidnapped. You wouldn't have married Nikolai. You wouldn't be pregnant with his baby."

"Eric!" I smacked his arm and back. "Let me go! I'm serious! Stop!"

"No. I'm doing this for your own good. I'm doing this to save your life."

This was what Nikolai and Tatiana's lies had done to Eric. They had reduced him to this panicked, paranoid man who was trying to kidnap me. It was time for me to tell the truth and shame the devil.

I planted my feet against the wood floors of the dining room and dug in my heels. "Tatiana isn't dead. She's alive."

Eric stopped cold. He spun toward me. His eyes narrowed with suspicion. "Who told you that?"

"Nikolai."

"He's a liar."

"Sometimes," I agreed, "but he's not lying about this. I saw her."

"That's impossible. She's dead. I saw the photos of the car wreck."

"You saw the photos?" But Nikolai had said that only Maksim and Tatiana's father had been sent the photos. "How?"

Eric ignored my question. "Whatever you think you know about Tatiana is wrong. Nikolai killed her because of me."

"No, Eric." I tried to be gentle. "Everything you know is wrong. He didn't kill her. He saved her—and you. He had Kostya fake a car wreck. They made it look real. They sent photos to Maksim and to her father. She let Kostya take her finger as proof."

I hesitated and decided not to tell him about the pregnancy. Not yet.

"Kostya and Nikolai got her out of the country. They smuggled her into Australia. She stayed there for a while before moving to Hong Kong and starting a new life as Tatiana Melnikova. She built a new identity around her old one. She's alive, Eric."

His fingers loosened their grip. My hands dropped to my sides. He swallowed once, then twice, and turned his back on me. For a moment, I thought he was going to be sick. I placed my hand on his shoulder, but he roughly shoved it off. "Don't."

"Eric..."

"Don't." He whirled on me with fiercely angry eyes. "How long have you known?"

"I found out the morning of my show." That seemed to lessen his intense feelings of betrayal. "I've only been home for a day, Eric. I'm telling you now because you have a right to know."

"A right to know?" he ground out furiously. "I had a right to know before she left!" Eric blew up suddenly and swept his arms across the top of the sideboard. Dishes and dining accessories went flying everywhere. Serving bowls and platters crashed onto the floor. Napkin rings bounced and rolled with a clatter. Candles hit with a thud. I took a quick step back and hugged the wall.

"Eight fucking years! Eight motherfucking years!"

My jaw dropped. I had never seen Eric this angry. I had never heard him talk like that either. He was enraged to a point where he wasn't thinking straight.

"What the hell is going on in here?" Nikolai ran into the dining room and stepped in front of me. He reached back with one hand, searching for me, and touched my hip. I rested my hand on his lower back. "Santos, why are you tearing up my dining room?"

"Tatiana's alive!" He said it as if daring Nikolai to deny it.

My husband glanced back at me. His taut expression told me he wasn't thrilled I had told Eric the truth. Looking back at Eric, he nodded. "Yes, she is. She was in Houston a few weeks ago. She's back in Hong Kong now."

"Houston? She was here?"

"Yes. We met at the Four Seasons."

"She saw *you*. Eight fucking years—and she goes to *you*?" A sound that reminded me of a wolf's lonesome howl escaped Eric's throat. He picked up the vase of flowers from the center of the table and tossed it against the wall.

Nikolai jumped back and used his body to cover mine. I clung to his back and squeaked as the crystal shattered and rained down on the floor with the flowers and water.

"Eight years I grieved for that woman!" Eric jerked the antique lace tablecloth like a magician, but his trick wasn't well practiced. Votives in crystal cups flew through the air. "Eight years I let the guilt eat me."

"Eric!" Nikolai walked toward my cousin. "Stop."

"Stop? Stop what?" Eric let loose a strangled laugh. "Stop hating myself for being the reason the woman I loved was killed? Stop hating you for taking her from me? Stop spending night after night dreaming of all the ways I could kill you without getting caught?"

Nikolai didn't miss a beat. "One thing at a time, Eric. You don't want to cross all your favorite hobbies off your list at once."

"You bastard! You think this is funny?" Eric charged Nikolai for making that joke, but Nikolai was ready for him. He stepped just to the left before Eric made contact, wrapped his arms around Eric's shoulders and neck and swept my cousin's legs. Eric went down to his knees, and Nikolai slipped behind him, squeezing his arms around Eric's neck and shoulders with enough force to make him stop fighting.

"Enough, Eric." Nikolai held tight, but he wasn't trying to hurt him. "That's enough."

Eric raged for almost a minute and then surrendered with a sag of defeat. A ragged sob tore from his throat. "I fucking loved her so much. She was the only one. The only one."

"I know." Nikolai's grip loosened and changed to one of comfort. "I am sorry, Eric."

I watched the sworn enemies with a mix of shock and bewilderment. The tepid peace between them didn't last long. Eric threw his elbows back, slamming them into Nikolai's ribs in a cheap shot that sent him staggering backward. He clambered to his feet and leveled a dead-eyed but still wet stare toward Nikolai. "If you expect a thank you—"

"I don't expect shit from you, Santos." Nikolai winced as he touched his bruised side. "What I did wasn't for you. It was for her. She deserved a chance to live. She got it."

"This doesn't change things between us."

"Of course it doesn't."

Eric stormed out of the dining room, but I raced after him. Glass shards crunched beneath the white soles of my slip-on walking shoes. "Eric! Wait!" I caught up with him in the entryway, but I had to hop over a bound and unconscious Boy to reach him. "Please!"

He whirled around on me. "What?"

"Eric, I'm sorry." I blinked rapidly and hot tears spilled onto my cheeks. "I'm so sorry it came out like that. I never wanted you to find out like this."

"Why the hell are you apologizing to me for something you didn't do?"

"You just destroyed my dining room. You tried to kidnap me. I'm a little on edge, Eric! Apologizing for breaking your heart all over again seemed like the right thing to do."

Eric exhaled roughly and wiped at his own wet face with the back of his hand. "I'm sorry. I'll replace all of that stuff I broke. Just send me the bill."

"Are you kidding me? It's just stuff. It doesn't matter." I clasped his hand. "You're my family." I touched the baby with both of our hands. "You're this baby's family."

"God," he said on an anguished sigh. "Are we the most fucked up family or what?"

"I don't know. We are what we are. This is it." I gestured between us. "I want you in my life, Eric. You're important to me. But..."

"But?"

"I know how hard it is for you to see Nikolai. Especially now," I added, thinking of the lies that had just been blown open in our dining room. "If you need to cut me out of your life for your own sanity—"

"Stop," he said gruffly. "I'm not cutting you or the baby out of my life." His fingertips grazed my stomach. "We'll figure it out. Somehow."

"Okay."

He drew back his hand. "I need to go, Vivian."

"I understand."

He reached for the door and left the house. He was almost to the steps when he turned back around and crossed the porch, not stopping until he was standing so close to me I could count each and every one of his eyelashes. "Seven years ago, a woman contacted me after Tatiana went missing."

"What woman?"

"I don't know. I only met her once. I got into my Explorer at the end of my shift, and she was in the backseat. I damned near had a heart attack!" He shook his head. "She knew a lot about me. She knew even more about Tatiana. I wanted her to tell me more, but she got out of my SUV and disappeared like a fucking ghost. She left behind a dossier."

"Come on, Eric! This sounds like something from a spy movie!"

"That's what I'm trying to tell you, Vivi!" His harsh whisper made that point. "I think she was a spy. Not for us, though. For *them*."

"Them? Wait. You mean Russia?"

"Yes."

"You think she was...what? KGB? FSB?"

"I don't know. She was older. So probably KGB."

"Eric," I said with a disbelieving laugh. "That's crazy."

"Is it?" He stepped even closer. "Who else but a fucking spy would know that Maksim Prokhorov is Nikolai's biological father?"

My heart fluttered in my chest. "Eric, please tell me that you haven't repeated that to anyone."

"I'm still alive. Obviously not."

Trying to wrap my head around the idea that a Russian spy had been feeding Eric information, I asked, "Has she contacted you since then?"

"No. I think she was disappointed that I took so long to act on the information."

My belly flip-flopped with nervousness. I tried not to freak out. "What do you mean? How did you act on it?"

Eric's gaze dropped to his shoes. It took him a long time to admit, "I'm the one who got Nikolai put on the No Fly List."

"What! Why would you do that?" Before he could answer, I snarled, "Do you have any idea what that was like for me? Do you have any idea how dangerous it was for Nikolai to get to me in London?"

"Give me a break, Vivian! He wouldn't be on that list if he didn't have a past that had earned him a spot."

"He's not a terrorist!"

"No, he's a fucking gangster who belongs to an organization that sells arms to some of the worst people on this planet! He deserves to be on that list, and I'm sorry if it inconveniences your vacation plans."

"Are you finished?" I crossed my arms and refused to take the bait. I wasn't going to get into an argument with Eric over this. I had made my choice to be with Nikolai with eyes wide open. There was nothing Eric could say right now that would change that.

"Yes." His shoulders deflated from their high, tense positioning once he realized I wasn't going to fight with him.

"Do you still have the dossier?"

"Yes."

"I want it."

"Excuse me?"

"I want the dossier, Eric."

"No."

"That wasn't a request. I'm telling you that you're going to give me the entire dossier."

"Or what?"

"Or I'll call Kostya," I threatened. "When he's finished, I'll call my dad. If that doesn't work, I'll send Ten to visit you."

Shock filtered across Eric's face. "You're serious."

"I'm protecting my family." I touched his arm. "You included."

"Me? How is threatening me to get that dossier protecting me?"

"Did you ever stop to wonder why this ex-spy chose you? Did you even consider for one second how much trouble you are in now? Those documents that you used to get Nikolai on that list? They were all destroyed under Maksim's orders. He wanted them gone for a reason. Now you've dragged copies that shouldn't exist back out into the light of day, Eric."

My heart raced as I considered the lengths Nikolai's father would go to in order to preserve his standing and Nikolai's. "You have to let me protect you, Eric. Let me see what's in that dossier."

Eric looked at me as if he didn't recognize me. "You've changed. You're...hard."

The reason for that change came to me swiftly. I cover my small baby bump with my hands. "I'm going to be a mother soon. I don't have the luxury of being soft anymore."

Eric glanced away from me. He stared at the hanging pots of brightly colored calibrachoa decorating the porch. "You can call off your dogs. I'll get the dossier and bring it to you tonight."

"Thank you."

He nodded and stepped back. His gaze landed on Boychenko who was beginning to wake up behind me. "Tell the kid I'm sorry about that. If he ever needs to get out of a ticket or something, tell him to call me. I'll take care of it."

Knowing Boy, he would consider a throbbing head a fair trade for the chance to get out of a future scrape with Houston PD. Eric left without another word, and I closed the door. When I turned around, Nikolai knelt next to a moaning Boy and whipped out the knife he kept in his boot. He quickly cut the zip ties binding Boy's wrists and ankles. Without warning, he ripped the strip of duct tape off his street soldier's mouth. Boy cried out in pain and slapped a hand to his red lips.

"Sorry." Nikolai patted Boy's chest. "It's better to just get it over with, Roman. Can you sit up?"

"Yes." He grasped Nikolai's hand and groaned when he was upright again.

"Vee, get Ten."

"Okay." I scurried out of the entryway and across the house. I opened the French doors in my studio and called out for him. "Ten?"

"Yeah?" He emerged from the small potting shed where Nikolai kept most of his garden tools.

"Come inside."

He must have heard something in my voice because he jogged across the yard. "What's wrong?"

"I think Boy may need to be taken to the emergency room."

"What?" He stayed a step behind me on the trek back to the front of the house.

We found Boychenko sitting on a chair in the living room. Nikolai crouched down in front of him. He didn't look happy. He barked a set of orders at Ten in rapid-fire Russian. Ten helped Boy off the chair, and Nikolai followed them out of the house.

I made my way to the dining room where I surveyed the damage. With a heavy sigh, I started picking up unbroken dishes and tableware.

"Leave it," Nikolai ordered gently. He stood in the doorway between the kitchen and dining rooms looking a disheveled, exhausted mess.

"But—"

"Leave it," he said more firmly.

I put the serving platter in my hands back on the sideboard. Holding his gaze, I asked, "Did you hear everything Eric said?"

Nikolai nodded stiffly.

Wringing my hands, I asked, "What are we going to do, Kolya?"

"We do nothing." His answer surprised me. "Right now, I'm tired. I need a shower—and I need you." He closed the distance between us, cupped the back of my neck and tilted my head back before crashing our mouths together. The intensity of his kiss made my knees weak. I clutched at the lapels of his wrinkled suit jacket and held on for dear life as he kissed me as if it

might be the last time he ever tasted my mouth. "I
need you."

"I'm yours." I lifted up on my toes to return his kiss
with the same ferocity. "I'm yours right now."

Nikolai locked lips with me again and walked me
back toward the dining room table. He grasped my
bottom in both hands, kneading and squeezing my
plump flesh. I pushed his jacket off his shoulders and
jerked on his belt buckle. This wasn't about sensual
lovemaking. This was about the two of us reconnecting
in a burst of heat and passion.

I moaned as his wicked mouth dotted kisses along
my throat. Shivering, I gasped when he jerked down
the front of my tank top to gain better access to my
breasts. He kissed the swell of each one but couldn't
get what he really wanted. Grasping my shirt in both
hands, he jerked it up and over my head. I hadn't
worn a bra this morning because my breasts were so
sensitive, and none of them fit well anymore.

He cupped them gently. I marveled at the way they
filled his hands now. He brushed his thumbs across my
nipples and swirled them in a circle to tease my flesh
to stiff peaks. His head dipped, and I cried out when
he suckled me. A rush of wet heat went straight to my
core.

While his mouth tormented me, his hand rode the
curve of my belly to the juncture between my thighs.
His palm settled there, and I rocked against it, desperate to get some stimulation where I wanted it most.
My wanton movement broke his control.

Without warning, Nikolai spun me around. A hand between my shoulders pushed me down toward the table. I trembled with need as I leaned forward on my arms. Nikolai gripped the waistband of my yoga pants and panties in both hands and jerked them down my hips and thighs. He ripped off my shoes and then grasped my left ankle and then my right, lifting them so he could pull my clothes off my body.

"Don't move." He gave the order gruffly. "There's fucking glass everywhere. Hold still or you'll get cut."

I couldn't explain it, but the risk of getting hurt while Nikolai ravished me made my clit throb. There was something outrageously wrong with that response, but I couldn't help it. In the back of my mind, I knew that a member of his crew could show up at any moment. It would be so easy to discover us here in the dining room. The danger of it all excited me so much I could feel the slick wetness spreading on my inner thighs.

"I've been thinking about this since I watched you board that plane in Tirana." Nikolai nipped at my shoulder and swatted my bottom twice. "Did you think about me? Did you dream about this last night?"

His hand sneaked between my thighs. His fingers traced the seam of my sex. His deep breaths buffeted my ear as he began to say filthy things to me in Russian. "You're soaking my hand." He bit my earlobe and thrust a finger inside me. "Do you want me to pound your tight cunt until you scream?"

I pressed back against his invading finger. "Yes."

"Say it." He sucked hard on the curve of my throat. It would leave a mark that he would idly trace later.

"Make me scream."

Nikolai gripped my hips and tilted them up. He pushed my knees wider apart with his leg while unbuckling his belt and lowering his zipper. I blushed hotly when I felt his hands pulling apart my backside so he could get a better look at my pussy. His finger slid between my cheeks. I gasped when he pressed his thumb against the pucker hidden there. We had never done *that* but I sensed he wanted it on the table as a possibility.

"After the baby comes," he said, as if reading my mind.

I didn't have to ask why he wanted to wait to try something so naughty. He was old school through and through and so outrageously overprotective. The slightest hint of discomfort or the tiniest chance of causing harm was too much for him to accept when it came to me, especially while I was pregnant.

The head of his cock nudged my slick folds. He adjusted the angle of his probing and slid home, filling me up with his hard shaft and making me arch up onto my tiptoes. He retreated slowly, leaving just the crown of his cock inside my wet channel, and then thrust forward again.

After a few teasing moves like that, Nikolai held onto my waist with one hand and clamped the other on my shoulder. He held me right where he wanted me as he did exactly as promised. He pounded into me from behind. The table shuddered beneath me. My fingertips squealed against the polished wood. Mouth agape, I cried out again and again. "Ah! Ah! Ah!"

The hand that had been on my waist snaked around to my front. Nikolai clutched my thigh and forcefully lifted my leg. He placed my left knee on the table, opening me even more and making it possible for him to thrust deeper and harder. My stomach wobbled with the intensity of it. The sounds of our bodies slapping together and our panicked, hard breaths filled the house.

Flushed and trembling, I wanted to come so badly. I could feel the tell-tale stirrings in my core. Nikolai could read me like a book. His hand moved to my clit. He framed that swollen little pearl between two fingers and rubbed tight, fast circles. I clawed at the table and panted for air. "So close. So close."

He knew. He didn't need me to tell him. Grasping my hair, he shoved it aside and bared my neck. While his fingers strummed my clit, he leaned down and bit the back of my nape. I exploded with a wild scream. My pussy fluttered around his cock, and I prayed that I wouldn't pass out as the incredibly powerful ripples of pure bliss overwhelmed me.

"*Solnyshka!*" Nikolai gripped my shoulder again as he rocked against me with jerky thrusts and filled me with a spreading heat. He stayed buried inside me for a long time. My eyes closed as he peppered light kisses up and down my back and across my shoulders. He eased out of me and tucked himself away before kicking aside a dining room chair and dropping onto it like a falling tree.

"Come here." He wound his arms around my waist and dragged me down onto his lap so that my legs were draped across his thighs. He nuzzled my throat and kissed my cheek. Sated and content, I placed my head against his shoulder and enjoyed the soft caress of his warm hands.

"That dossier changes everything." Nikolai's voice was rough and unsteady, his breaths still coming in small pants after all that exertion. "I shouldn't be surprised that someone from the old country has me in their crosshairs."

"What are we going to do?" I played with the top button of his shirt. "What *can* we do?"

Nikolai's lips brushed my forehead. "I'll do whatever it takes to keep you and the baby safe." He lowered his head and claimed my mouth in a promising kiss. "Whatever it takes."

And that was what scared me the most.

25 CHAPTER TWENTY-FIVE

Later that night, I was catching up on recorded television episodes from my favorite summer shows when the doorbell rang. Ten set aside the Sudoku puzzle he had been working on and hefted himself off the couch. He had returned after taking Boychenko home to help me clean up the dining room while Nikolai crashed out upstairs. Ilya had come to the house to take Boy's place, but I hadn't seen much of him. He liked to spend more time outside, smoking and talking on his phone.

Ten wasn't gone long. He returned faster than I had expected with an oversized gift bag that he placed on the coffee table with a loud *thunk*. "From Eric."

Curious, I tossed aside the remote control and leaned forward to investigate the bag. Inside I found a crystal vase nearly identical to the one he had destroyed and a thick but well-worn oversized envelope. The brads no longer worked so three big binder clips and a rubber band kept the files safe inside.

"That's an interesting gift." Ten had settled back onto the couch but hadn't picked up his puzzle.

"Yes, it is." Envelope in hand, I headed for the door. "I'll be in Nikolai's office."

"And I'll be here, watching housewives catfight," he grumbled before kicking back on the couch and grabbing his puzzle booklet.

I smiled at that. Ten liked to pretend that he couldn't stand my guilty pleasure televisions choices, but he sure liked to discuss the episodes when we were done.

The door to Nikolai's office was shut. I leaned in and heard him talking to someone. He spoke Russian but I couldn't make out much of the conversation. Not wanting to eavesdrop, I knocked on the door and stepped back. He continued talking as he strode toward the door and opened it. The smile inspired by finding me in the hallway disappeared when he saw what I was holding.

Still talking, he reached for my hand, entwined our fingers and tugged me inside his office. He led me over to one of the chairs surrounding his chess board, and I took a seat. Nikolai returned to his desk and grabbed a notepad so he could jot down something as he finished his phone call.

"That was a contact of Yuri's who works in the immigration office," he explained as he scribbled something on his notepad. "I was going through my closet after my shower, and I came across my tuxedo. It made me think about Sergei and Bianca's wedding. I thought we might do something special for their wedding gift."

"Like?"

"I want to see if we can get Vladimir and Galina here."

"Is that even possible? I mean, the immigration process is really slow, right? I'm sure that Bianca and Sergei are going to rush their wedding because of the baby."

"I think I can swing it, but let's not say anything, okay? I don't want to disappoint them if it can't be done."

"I totally understand. I'll pick up something ridiculously expensive from their wedding registry, just in case."

Nikolai laughed and dropped his pen onto the desk. He went to his office door first and turned the lock before walking over to the chess board. He lowered himself onto the chair directly opposite me and held out his hand. "May I?"

"Yes." I gave him the dossier. "I didn't get a chance to look at it yet."

"Clear the board. We'll go through it together."

I picked up the chess pieces and dropped them into the basket that fit underneath the table. Nikolai retrieved the stacks of papers and folders from the envelope and placed them on the chessboard. There were a few pages of notes from Eric where he had tried to translate the information by himself. Apparently he had been smart enough not to let anyone else see any of this.

"I'm surprised he didn't come to you," Nikolai admitted as he picked up a folder and began scanning the contents. "I would have put money on Eric dragging you into this in the hopes it would drive a wedge between us in the early days of our friendship."

"Maybe he worried it would put me in danger." I chose my own folder and began reading. "Or maybe he knew even back then that I was too connected to you to be convinced to let you go."

"It's selfish of me, but I'm glad you're so stubborn." Nikolai watched me over the top of the folder. "I feel so guilty some days about the life I've pulled you into, but then I think of how happy I am with you and how much I already love the baby. I would do it all over again. I would fall in love with you and marry you again and again and again."

"*I* chose *you*. Don't ever feel guilty for loving me and building a family with me."

Nikolai glanced down at the papers in his hands. He seemed unable to look into my eyes as he confessed, "I never thought I would be this happy. I never thought I would earn the love of a woman like you. I was so jealous when Dimitri announced that Benny was pregnant. I didn't see how any woman would ever agree to give me the chance to be a father."

"But I did," I said quietly.

He lifted his head, his eyes glittering, and swallowed. "But you did, *solnyshka*. You've given me the chance to *live*. To really and truly *live*. I will never be able to thank you enough for that." He cleared his throat and dropped his gaze. "But I'll spend the rest of my fucking life trying."

I didn't know what to say after that so I said nothing. I sensed that Nikolai didn't need me to say a word.

We sifted through the pile of information for hours. I moved from the chair by the chessboard to the small couch and then stood at his desk while reading to keep my legs from cramping. He left the room and returned with a light snack of fruit, crackers and cheese and ordered me to eat. I wasn't hungry, but I humored him and nibbled on some grapes and cheese cubes while trying to make sense of a hand-drawn web of underworld ties in the Eastern bloc.

"This is making my head hurt." I tossed down the papers and grabbed a handful of grapes. "Is there anything in this dossier that's, like, a bombshell to you? Is there anything that we should worry about?"

"There are some interesting connections here with the Middle East that I knew nothing about," he said. "It's helped make sense of some strange dealings that I witnessed as a kid working the streets for Maksim."

"Is there anything in here that can hurt us?"

"These photos of Tatiana's faked death could be a problem." He touched the folder he wouldn't let me see. Even though the photos were fake, he didn't want me to put those images in my head.

"This stack is troublesome." His fingertips brushed a thin stack of papers. "There are some crimes in here that I was never arrested or prosecuted for when I was a teenager and in my early twenties. I doubt anything will ever come from them, but it's probably a good idea for us to never set foot on Russian soil."

"Was that ever even a possibility?"

"No. When I left, I cut ties for good." He shot me a strange look. "Why? Did you want to go?"

"There was a time when I wanted to visit Russia. I wanted to see where my mother was born and where my grandparents grew up."

"You wouldn't like any of those places."

"Probably not," I agreed, "but it would have been nice to know where I came from."

"If it's that important to you, I can get pictures or video."

"It wouldn't be the same."

He sat back in his chair. "I'm sorry."

"Don't be." I moved to the seat across from him. "That's just life." I popped a couple of the sweet, firm grapes into my mouth and enjoyed the flavor that burst onto my tongue.

"I'm not concerned so much about what's in this dossier. I'm more concerned about the fact that it exists." Nikolai began stacking up the folders and papers on the chessboard into one neat pile. "The person who put this together wants to hurt Maksim."

"You know what they say." I handed him the battered envelope. "Hell hath no fury like a woman scorned."

Nikolai glanced at me in surprise. "You think this is romantically motivated?"

"Eric said a woman brought it to him. He said she was an older woman, right? So what if Maksim did some KGB lady dirty and this is her way of giving him the middle finger?" I gestured to the files I had been reading. "The woman that compiled this spent a lot of time keeping track of all the different ladies Maksim dated and, um, visited."

One side of his mouth lifted at the way I had carefully glossed over his father's penchant for high-end prostitutes. I had been terrified that I would find Nikolai's mother's name among the list of sex workers, but if her file was to be believed, she had been a young schoolgirl his father had seduced and cast aside. Of course, that bit of truth wasn't exactly a good thing to discover.

"The money," he said cryptically.

"What money?"

"The payments Tatiana uncovered," he reminded me. "She said they've been coming from Moscow to Houston for twenty years. What if those were payments to this woman?"

"So what? Something happened seven years ago that set her off? The money is still coming, right? Wouldn't he have stopped sending it once he found out she had betrayed him with this?"

"But nothing happened," Nikolai insisted. "Eric didn't use the file to come after me. Maksim wasn't implicated in anything. As far as he knows, this doesn't exist."

I blanched. "What happens when he finds out?"

"This woman had better hope she's still skilled at her tradecraft," he murmured darkly. "As for me? I'm just a pawn," Nikolai said. "She wants Maksim. I'm just a piece she wants to push around the chessboard to exert pressure on him, but it didn't work because Eric didn't take the bait until it was too late. Most of the people in these files are dead or in prison. There are details in here that I would prefer not to have widely known—"

"Like the fact that Maksim is your father?"

"Like that," he agreed. "But I'm not as concerned as I was before Eric gave this to you. We can manage this."

I started to ask him how but stopped the thought before it ever made it out of my mouth. Even though we had an open policy between us, there really were some things I didn't want to know. I had a feeling this was one of them.

Nikolai placed the stack of files aside and leaned down to grab the basket holding the chess pieces. I made a face. "Kolya, I'm really not in the mood for a game of chess. I'm so sucky at it."

He frowned. "You're not sucky."

"I've never won a single game. Not one. Ever. My grandfather, you, Lena—you've all throttled me."

"You need to practice more."

"I need to stick to checkers."

He laughed and started placing the pieces on the board. "We aren't playing chess tonight."

"Then what are we doing?"

"I'm educating you."

"On?"

"My world."

"Oh."

Nikolai grouped pieces together on separate corners of the board. He started touching the pieces and giving them names. "Besian and his Albanians; the cartel; Lalo Contreras, Diego and the Hermanos; Nicky Jackson; the Red Baron and his skinheads; Mr. Lu and the Asian syndicate; Romero and the Calaveras." He touched a black king and a white queen. "Us."

"Lorenzo Guzman," he picked up the white king and gave it a shake, "won't be around much longer. One way or another, he's going to be replaced. If he's smart, he'll step down when he pressure gets too high. He'll take the money and run." Nikolai knocked the drug lord's piece off the table and onto the floor. He pushed two white nights forward. "Hector Salas and Lalo Contreras will step into his place."

"Is that a good thing or a bad thing?"

"It could go either way. It depends on the alliances they make. Your father and his motorcycle crew have aligned themselves with Hector and Lalo. It's a perfect match. They all want the same thing."

"Money?" I guessed.

"Money," he confirmed. "Your father wants to control all the steel—the guns—south of the border and into Central America. Maksim wants Romero to succeed. He has more weapons than he can unload, but he needs higher bidders. Romero is the key to that. And

Hector? Hector has big dreams. He wants to get product into far flung corners of the world."

"But he needs a way to move it," I said, as everything started to make sense. I picked up the piece he had designated as Mr. Lu. "When I was at that house with the judge, I thought it was strange that Bobby Pham had his hands on all of that *llelo*."

Nikolai smiled at my choice of word. "Hector and Lalo thought Bobby was the perfect answer. He handled all the counterfeit imports so he would have had very little trouble moving product *out* of Mexico and into Southeast Asia."

"But now he's dead. Who will they use now?"

"Zec," he said moving a white bishop onto the board. "Luka will jump at the chance to get at discounted cocaine and guns."

A sour feeling made my stomach ache. "Doesn't it ever bother you? Do you ever sit back and think about all the people who get hurt because of those guns? Or the people like Ruby or the judge's daughter who get hooked on these drugs and ruin their lives?"

"I did. Once," Nikolai admitted. "The days of feeling guilty are long gone for me, *sladest*. I am what I am. I accepted that long ago." He started rearranging pieces on the board. "I've pulled as far away from this world as I can, but I won't ever be able to get both feet out of it. Frankly, it's too dangerous for me to even try to get out. To keep my family safe? I have to be in it. I have to have both feet planted on the dirty side of the line." He hesitated. "Does that answer disappoint you?"

"Honestly?"

He nodded.

"A little," I admitted. "I don't like thinking that we live in this beautiful home and have this luxurious life because of guns and drugs and God only knows what else."

"This house and the life you enjoy is paid for by legitimate money, Vee. The dirty money? It goes someplace else."

"Where?"

"Evgeni."

"I don't understand."

"He's very good at taking dirty money and making it clean."

"How?"

"Financial alchemy." Nikolai shrugged. "I don't ask those sorts of questions. I just make sure the money gets into his hands. He washes it a few times, and it comes back to me all neat and clean."

"Just like that?"

"Just like that." He bent down to pick up Lorenzo's king. Gesturing to the chessboard, he explained, "The problem I face right now is where to stand while this shit goes down."

He moved his piece in front of mine and backed it into a corner. "Lorenzo isn't stupid. He knows that there's a coup in the works. He knows his days are numbered. He's going to grow paranoid. He'll do something stupid."

"Like?"

"Strike out at Hector and Lalo here in Houston." He knocked over their pieces with the white king. "To stay in power, he'll have to cull the cartel of anyone with enough strength or power to rival him. He'll cripple his organization doing it, and he'll upset the power balance south of the border. It will be an unholy mess."

"But he won't stop there," Nikolai warned. "He'll strike out at your father." He knocked over my father's piece with Lorenzo's. "Romero has been poking his finger in Lorenzo's eye since the morning he was popped from prison. Lorenzo hasn't done anything to rein him in yet. He's turned a blind eye to your father building up his little army, but he can't afford to play nice any longer. After this bullshit with Julio, he'll have to show that he has the balls to lead the cartel."

"And when he's done going after those three, he'll come for us." He knocked over his black king but left my white queen standing. With great care, he picked up my piece and held it tightly in his hand. "Do you remember that morning in the apartment you shared with Lena when I told you that love is a weakness?"

I swallowed hard at that memory. "Yes."

"Lorenzo knows that I fucking adore you. He knows that I'll die before I let anyone touch you. When he finds out about the baby, he'll know exactly how to hurt me."

My hands moved to my stomach and covered my bump. "I won't let him hurt our baby."

"No, you won't." Nikolai placed my piece on the far side of the board, away from all the conflict. "You and the baby will be safe because you're going to run at the first sign of trouble."

"What?" I couldn't believe what I was hearing. "I'm not leaving you behind!"

"Yes, you will," he stated calmly but firmly. "You have to think of our baby. I love you, and I love the baby, and I want you to live."

"Kolya..."

"No." He shook his head. "This isn't up for discussion. Over the next few days, I'm going to teach you how to disappear. I'll teach you how to get a clean name and how to build a new life. I'm going to show you where I keep our money. The cash and the diamonds," he clarified.

I blinked with confusion. "Diamonds?"

"They're light. They're easy to carry. They're untraceable. You can sell them anywhere. You'll need them when you run to one of the safe houses I own. I'll make sure you get more target practice at the range. I have to know you can defend yourself."

"Kolya..."

"Vee, you have to understand that you can trust no one. Not your friends, not my men, not your father—you will be on your own if something happens to me." His jaw tensed, and I could tell it killed him to tell me that. "Everyone has a price. Everyone has a weakness. If someone wants to get to us, they'll go through our friends. They'll kidnap one of them and hold them hostage until we're lured to a meeting where they'll kill us."

He must have seen how shaken I was by the dark turn of our discussion because he got out of his chair and knelt in front of me. He took my hands in his and kissed my fingers. "The only true allies we have are each other."

Terrified by the stark picture he had painted, I asked, "Will this ever stop?"

"Soon," he promised. "Very soon."

"What are we supposed to do until then?"

Nikolai cupped my face in one hand and caressed my jaw. "We wait."

26 Chapter Twenty-Six

The weeks crawled by slowly for Nikolai. Too slowly. The ball of tension in his gut expanded with every passing day. Constantly on edge, he developed a need for antacids that rivaled Vivian's. The only thing that lowered his blood pressure and eased the throbbing in his stomach was coming home to his wife.

He couldn't get her into bed fast enough most nights. There were evenings when he simply ambushed her in her home studio or in the kitchen. She obliged his increased desires without complaint and began to encourage them by sending racy texts throughout the day. The first one had been so unexpected and so arousing that he had cut out of Samovar during the lunch rush so he could race home and have her.

Needless to say, Ten and Boychenko quickly learned to make themselves scarce once he hit the backdoor. Ten and Vivian seemed to have finally settled into a routine that worked. Though he had never expected a friendship to blossom between the pair, he was glad to see one forming.

While he spent his nights at home enjoying his wife, he spent his days at Samovar or bouncing around Houston job sites to monitor his legitimate business interests. He kept an eye on the continuing escalation south of the border and quietly got his men ready for the inevitable showdown.

One by one, his underworld counterparts approached him to make deals and strengthen alliances. Most of them wanted something small in return for protection or assurances that the cartel wouldn't bring their brand of violence to the city. Besian was the only who asked for something very specific—revenge—but it was An who surprised him the most when she came asking for a meeting to be arranged with Hector Salas. He made that get-together happen but stayed far away from it. He didn't want any part of that arrangement. It was much too high profile and risky.

Before he knew it, August was drawing to an end. Sergei and Bianca would marry in a few days. Galina and Vladimir's entrance to the country had been quietly and secretly arranged. Yuri would be handling all of their travel arrangements to ensure they reached the church on time.

On a scorching hot August afternoon, Nikolai sat on a rolling stool next to Vivian as she reclined on an exam table in a cool room with very dim lighting. He hadn't missed a single one of her appointments since that first one. He had even been reading all the books she had purchased about pregnancy and raising children.

She had been talking about a natural birth, and he had to bite his tongue so he wouldn't beg her to take the drugs. The thought of Vivian suffering through agonizing pain for hours on end made him sweat and feel sick. He didn't know how the hell he was going to make it through her labor and delivery.

Nikolai reached out to sweep a lock of hair away from her cheek. He tucked it behind her ear and adjusted the long, jingling necklace that she had chosen to wear with her simple top. The silver baubles and teal feather now nestled enticingly in her cleavage. If there hadn't been an ultrasound technician in the room with them, he would have surrendered to the urge to bend down and nuzzle the creamy swell of soft flesh.

The technician had readied all of her equipment and waited for Vivian to pull up her shirt and bare her swollen belly. At five months pregnant, her baby bump had grown impossible to conceal. They had announced the pregnancy to friends not long after returning from Europe at a small, intimate dinner at the house. A few days later, Vivian had attended church and then Sunday dinner at Samovar wearing a dress that highlighted her new curves. The congratulations had poured in for two weeks. His office at Samovar and the living room of their home had been overflowing with flowers and gift baskets.

The most ostentatious display had been sent by Lorenzo. Nikolai had taken the message exactly as intended. Lorenzo was letting him know that Vivian and the baby were on his radar. At the first hint that Nikolai supported the coup that threatened to topple him, Lorenzo would strike out at her.

But not if I hit you first.

"This gel tends to get everywhere." The technician tucked a few paper towels into the waistband of his wife's skirt and under the neat folds of her shirt. "I try to be as neat as possible, but just in case."

"Thanks." Vivian did that nervous thing where she rolled her lips under her teeth. He dragged his thumb across her mouth in a soothing gesture and coaxed her to stop. He clasped her hand between both of his. There was nothing to be nervous about, but she worried so much about the baby. She flashed him a grateful smile before turning her attention to the ultrasound screen.

After squirting an obscene amount of the gel onto Vivian's stomach, the technician picked up her wand and began to swirl it in slow circles. The image of his baby coming to life on the screen knocked the air out of his lungs. *I made that.*

It was the first purely good thing he had ever done in his life. This sweet, innocent baby—*my baby*—had been created in love. A powerful need to protect this precious life he had made with Vivian gripped his stomach. *I'll do anything. Whatever it takes, I'll keep them safe.*

His chest felt unnaturally tight. A ball of emotion clogged his throat. Nikolai tried to swallow around it. Vivian turned her hand and gripped his fingers. She turned her head to smile at him. He gazed at her with love and wonder. Everything that was beautiful and good in his life he had because of her.

Not caring about the technician seeing him, Nikolai leaned forward and kissed Vivian's forehead. She caressed his jaw and smiled shyly. After sharing their tender moment, they focused on the screen where their surprisingly active baby waved its arms and kicked its legs. Nikolai couldn't even imagine what that felt like for Vivian.

In the last three weeks, he had been lucky enough to catch the baby kicking and moving more frequently. He liked to keep his hand on Vivian's stomach while she slept. He tried to stay awake as long as possible so he could enjoy those private, touching moments with the baby.

The technician narrated her exam in a way that kept him interested. She estimated the baby's size and measured its head before checking its legs and arms. She spent more time on the baby's heart and stomach to get the right angles and images. Fascinated by the whole process, Nikolai sat quietly holding Vivian's hand.

"Do you want to know the gender?" The technician tapped away at her keyboard. "Some parents do, but some don't. I can finish the last of the exam without telling you."

"We want to know." Vivian looked giddy with excitement at the prospect of finding out whether she carried a boy or girl. She had held off on buying anything for the nursery until she knew the baby's sex. Now she was finally going to get her chance.

"I can tell you without looking again," the technician said. "I got a clear shot when I was measuring his legs."

"His?" Nikolai seized on the word. "We're having a boy?"

The technician smiled at them. "Yes, you are." She moved the wand low on the curve of Vivian's stomach and then pointed at the screen with her free hand. "There you go. That makes it a boy."

A son. I'm having a son. Flashes of an imagined future appeared before him. A little boy taking his first unsteady steps in the library. A little boy chasing after dragonflies in the garden. A little boy learning to catch a baseball at the park. A little boy sitting on the corner of his desk at Samovar. A little boy with paint-covered fingers smearing color on a canvas.

He glanced at Vivian who grinned. She looked at him with teary eyes and blinked rapidly. "A boy."

"A boy." He kissed her sweetly. "Thank you."

The rest of the appointment was a blur for Nikolai. They left the hospital and made their way to the parking garage where Ten waited. They got into the backseat of the Land Rover. The enforcer twisted in his seat to speak with Vivian. "The baby is okay?"

"Yes," Vivian said with a bright smile. "*He* is doing great."

"He?" Ten's mouth lifted in a grin. "It's a boy? Congratulations, boss."

"Thank you."

"Hey!" Vivian leaned forward and punched Ten's arm. "I'm the one doing all the work. You should be congratulating me."

"Congratulations, Mrs. Boss."

She rolled her eyes. "You've been talking to Sergei again. Now you're even using his nicknames."

Ten laughed and put the SUV in reverse. "It's a good one." When he was out of the parking spot, he asked, "Where to now?"

"Lunch," Vivian said, rubbing her stomach. "I'm starving."

Nikolai decided not to remind her about the snack of almonds and dried apricots she had devoured in the waiting room. He had never seen one tiny woman eat so much food. He would have expected her to gain more weight than she had, but he suspected her mornings runs, though shorter and only three times a week, and the baby yoga she had started doing every afternoon helped her burn most of those extra calories.

Not that he minded a little extra weight on her. The soft, lush curves of her body drove him fucking crazy. Even now, he couldn't stop thinking about dragging her into his office at Samovar, lifting her onto his desk and sinking down to his knees to feast between her thighs. Then, maybe, he would tug her over to the chair he kept in front of his desk. The one that didn't have any arms on it. It was the perfect height for her to ride him. Her fuller, heavier breasts would be easy to enjoy that way. She loved having them—

"Kolya?" Vivian lightly pinched his leg. "Are you listening?"

"Sorry." He mentally batted away the tantalizing image of Vivian on her knees, licking him clean and humming enthusiastically. "What were you saying?"

"I asked if you had a preference for lunch."

"No." He brushed his knuckles down her arm. "We can go anywhere you would like."

She chose a steakhouse and insisted that Ten join them. He seemed reluctant to intrude, but Nikolai enjoyed his company. Halfway through their meal, his cell phone vibrated. Nikolai glanced at the text message from Kostya.

Bathroom. Now.

Phone in hand, he excused himself from the table. When he reached the restroom, he found Kostya waiting for him. The cleaner locked the door and leaned against it. "I've cleared the stalls. We're good."

"What is it?" Nikolai pocketed his phone. If Kostya had gone to these lengths to meet, it was serious and couldn't wait.

"I had a call from the Liquidator."

Nikolai's insides went cold. Earlier in the summer, he had instructed Kostya to contact the team of brothers known as the Professionals to take out a protection contract against Vivian's life. Now that Julio was gone, he hadn't expected to ever hear from them again. "What did he say?"

"He said that Lorenzo Guzman sent one of his cartel cronies for a meet-up. They asked about taking out a contract on a woman."

"Which woman?" His heart pounded against his chest now. He could hardly drag a breath into his lungs.

"The cartel guy didn't give a target to the Liquidator. I asked Hector if he had any information. He knew three things." Kostya held up his fingers and ticked off the details. "It's going to happen soon. The cartel is going to use Finn Connolly since no hit man will come close to Houston after the botched attack that nearly killed Besian." Kostya touched a third finger. "And the target is a daughter."

"A daughter? Whose daughter?" His heart fluttered in a wild panic. "Is it Vivian? She's Romero's daughter. That's a hell of a message for Lorenzo to send."

"It's probably Vivian." Kostya didn't even try to lie or soften the blow. "It could be Hector's little girl."

Nikolai's eyes widened. "Hector has a daughter?"

Kostya nodded. "There aren't many people who know about her. He's not married to her mother. From what I can tell, it may have been a one night stand with lifelong consequences. She's not quite two."

"She's a baby! A two-year-old girl? *Blyat sovsem ahuyeli!*"

"*Da*," Kotya solemnly agreed. "This is fucked up beyond belief."

Nikolai turned his back on his friend and walked to the sink. He placed both hands on the porcelain and leaned forward. His mind raced with possibilities. Fi-

nally, he made a decision. "Pick up Finn Connolly tonight. Take him to the barn. It's time for him to pay
back a debt his little brother owes me."

Kostya unlocked the door and left without another
word. Nikolai took a moment to compose himself. This
was a piece of information he had to keep to himself.
The stress of hearing that there might be a hit contract out on her life would be too much for Vivian. He
couldn't risk her health or the baby's.

No, this was a burden he had to bear alone.

Composed and acting as if he hadn't just heard
that someone wanted to kill his wife and baby, Nikolai
emerged from the restroom and returned to the table.
Ten and Vivian were laughing about something as he
joined them. She turned toward him and placed her
small hand on top of his. He fought the urge to gather
her into his arms and run out of the restaurant with
her. He thought of a dozen places where he could hide
her, places where no one would ever find her again.

Places where she would wither like a flower at the
end of its bloom.

"Is everything okay?"

He squeezed her hand and lied through his fucking
teeth. "Everything is fine."

Finn Connolly wasn't nearly as big or tall as Nikolai had expected. He watched the middle Connolly brother cautiously enter the barn where he sometimes conducted business of a sensitive nature. The man had been out of the Marine Corps for years, but those skills that had kept him alive during countless battles had never left him. He scanned the building with a practiced eye, his gaze lingering on possible weapons, exits and threats.

Nikolai didn't want to be rude so he tried to conceal his interest in Finn's smooth movements. The former sniper's leg had been blown off by an IED, but he had only the slightest hint of a limp as he walked. It was clear Finn had put a great deal of effort into his recovery. Kostya had also told him that Finn was an alcoholic. He had been sober for nearly three years. He didn't know the man, but Nikolai found that admirable.

Wanting to keep Finn on edge, Nikolai tossed his lucky lighter between his palms and glared at him. "You're late."

"Blame it on the invitation I never received." Finn's gaze shifted to the table at Nikolai's side. No doubt, the Marine had deduced what was under the blue tarp. Nonetheless, he asked, "What the fuck is that?"

Nikolai ignored the question and exchanged the lighter in his hand for a jar containing the crunched round that had been pulled from the wall the night of the shooting. "Do you know what this is?"

Finn's expression hardened. "It's the bullet I put between the eyes of the cartel bastard who tried to shoot my brother and his girlfriend." He glared at Kostya. "The one your man there promised Jack he would dig out of the wall and toss."

"To be fair," Kostya said, "I said I would take care of it. I didn't say I would destroy it."

Nikolai moved to the table and yanked back the tarp covering the body-shaped lump. Finn's expression turned to one of disgust as he took in the sight of the frozen corpse. Was he wondering why the body hadn't been destroyed or dumped in the ocean? Was he wondering where Kostya kept his freezers?

"The Ghost." Nikolai named the body. "He's not nearly as terrifying as I had expected." The man's ruthless reputation had created an image of someone who resembled Romero, not this slightly paunchy, overly tanned and freckled middle-aged nobody. "His name was Erwin Goode, in case you care. He was forty-four and lived in Mesa, Arizona when he wasn't killing people for the cartel."

"Is there a point to this?"

Nikolai liked Finn already. He was a straight-shooter—in more ways than one.

"Just one more thing." Nikolai motioned for Boychenko to bring him the rifle. Boy held up the weapon in hands clad with black leather gloves.

The effect on Finn was instantaneous. "You broke into my storage locker to steal my rifle?"

Nikolai waved his hand and Boychenko put the rifle back on the worktable. "I needed you to know the score, Finn. You need to understand your position."

"And what position is that?"

"You're going to be contacted by a representative of the Guzman cartel. He's going to offer you a job as a way of repaying your debt for killing their man here." He tugged the tarp back over the corpse and tucked the bullet back into his pocket. "You're going to take that job."

"Like. Fucking. Hell. I'm not some puppet on strings you can yank whenever you feel like it."

Silently, Nikolai advanced on Finn with deliberate, slow steps. He noticed Finn's gaze flicking from visible tattoo to visible tattoo. He saw the realization dawn on Finn's face. This was a battle the Marine couldn't win.

Hands clasped behind his back, Nikolai asked, "Do you love your family?"

Anger flared in Finn's eyes. "I will tell you this once and only once. Don't threaten my family."

Behind him, Ilya and Boychenko stepped forward, but Nikolai flicked his fingers, wordlessly telling them to stop.

"You might scare the piss out of everyone else, but I spit in Death's face when a bunch of coward terrorists blew me up on the side of some shithole road outside Gardez. Don't think for one fucking second that I'll hesitate to spit in yours."

Nikolai didn't take that as an insult or a threat. He took it as it was meant to be. This was Finn stating the facts.

"You say you've seen war. Well there's a war coming to Houston. Unless you want to see it rage on the streets of this city where your family and mine live, I need your help."

Finn's taut body relaxed. "What kind of help?"

"The cartel is fractured. Lorenzo Guzman is scrambling to stay in power. There's word that he's going to order a hit on someone important in the city. I need to know who that person is."

"So you can save them?"

Nikolai wasn't going to tip his hand. He decided to act nonchalant. He couldn't let on his greatest fear. He couldn't give Finn even the slightest clue that the target was more important to him than anything in this world. "If saving their life furthers my position and keeps the city quiet? Yes."

"So you want me to betray a fucking cartel?"

"I want you to survive, Mr. Connolly. If you tell the cartel no, they'll kill you, your brothers, their girlfriends, their girlfriends' families and everyone who ever made you happy. If you say yes, you feed the information to me, and I'll protect you and the people you love."

His offer made, Nikolai left the barn without another word. Ilya and Boychenko followed with the body and the rifle. Both were placed in the produce van waiting outside. Kostya stayed inside to give Finn his instructions. When he exited a short time later,

Kostya's expression was unreadable. Kostya waited until they were driving away from the barn to say, "I don't know if we can count on him to do it."

"Where was he tonight?"

Kostya glanced at him and then back at the road. "He was with Hadley Rivera."

"No shit? He was with Eddie Rivera's daughter? The one with...?" He touched his chest, right near his heart, and Kostya nodded. "Is it serious?"

Kostya shrugged. "I tried asking him about her, but he shut me down."

Nikolai hated himself for even thinking it, but he said, "She could be useful."

"I know," Kostya confirmed in an equally loathsome voice. "She's Hector's cousin. She's sleeping with Finn. She's the perfect hostage."

"If it comes to that," Nikolai said, his voice tight and his stomach clenching with unease. He didn't want to kidnap some innocent girl to force Finn to do his bidding, but he would if it came to that. He would cross any fucking line to protect Vivian.

"I heard the baby is a boy." Kostya offered a genuine smile. "Congratulations."

"I would have been just as happy with a girl." He didn't understand why everyone who had congratulated him today seemed to think having a son was something worthy of such adulation.

"Not me," Kostya grumbled. "They're trouble, and the boys they want to date are trouble."

Nikolai couldn't even imagine his son dating. "I think they're all trouble at that age." He chuckled at the memories of his own teenaged romantic escapades. "If he's anything like me, he's going to be a handful."

"Maybe you'll be lucky, and he'll inherit all of Vivian's sweetness."

"God willing." Nikolai tapped his fingers against the warm window glass. "I need to see Ben tomorrow."

"Ben Beciraj? At Merkurie Motors?"

"Yes. I want him to customize a vehicle for Vivian and my son." *My son.* Would he ever get used to saying that? "It needs to be bullet-proofed. I want it done right. Ben is the only one I trust."

"I can get a meeting in the morning, if you'd like."

"Fine. The sooner, the better," he added. "Vivian is five months pregnant. It's going so fast. The baby will be here soon."

Too soon, he thought in a panic. Things weren't settled with the cartel yet.

But the pieces were in motion now. It was only a matter of time until all hell broke loose.

27 CHAPTER TWENTY-SEVEN

Two Weeks Later

"Kolya."

Nikolai grumbled and lightly swatted at the finger poking him in the ribs. Only one person in the world would dare to poke at him like that when he was trying to sleep. Face still buried in his pillow, he grumbled, "What, Vee?"

"Are you going to get up? It's almost noon! I've already been to church. I thought for sure you would be awake by now."

Noon? His fuzzy brain couldn't tell him why he was so tired.

"Come on! You need to get up. Galina and Vladimir are waiting. We promised Sergei and Bianca we would look after them until they meet us tonight for dinner at Samovar."

Bianca and Sergei? His brain finally sputtered and produced an answer.

The wedding. The vodka. The dancing. *The vodka.*

"Kolya." The bed shifted as she bounced onto it like an overeager puppy.

The movement drew his attention to his throbbing head. He groaned and reached for her, his hands landing on her hips. "Christ, stop moving. My head is killing me."

"I'm not surprised." Amusement filled her voice, but she tenderly stroked his jaw and temples. "I left some aspirin and a glass of water in the bathroom for you." She kissed his cheek. "You'll feel better—and smell better—after a shower."

Nikolai cracked one eye. She wrinkled her dainty little nose. He inhaled deeply and grimaced. She was right. He smelled like sweat and alcohol—and sex. "I'm sorry," he croaked. "I shouldn't have had so much to drink."

"It's all Yuri's fault," she assured him. "After Sergei and Bianca left, I went to chat with Lena. The next thing I knew you were on the dance floor with Yuri and some of Bianca's cousins. It, um, got a bit rowdy after that."

Nikolai paled. "Please tell me I didn't dance on a table."

"Well..."

"Shit." He wiped his hand down his face. "I'm sure everyone is talking about that today."

"So?" She rubbed his chest. "You're a grown man. The baby isn't here yet. It's okay for you to let loose a little." She traced a tattoo on his skin. "It's better to get all of that out of your system now. Once January comes and the baby is here? You're on diaper duty."

"Gladly," he said, picking up her hand and kissing her palm. She smelled so good, like lavender and vanilla. With both eyes open and his vision no longer blurry, he raked his gaze over her body. She wore a simple little dress in a bright pink color. It highlighted all the lush roundness of her pregnant body. "You look beautiful."

"Mmmhmm," she hummed. "You tried that with me last night."

He didn't like the sound of that. "How did we get home?"

"Vladimir drove, but Ilya and Artyom followed us. We were safe."

"I shouldn't have put you at risk, not now. It was reckless and stupid of me." He couldn't believe he had been so careless. *What the hell was I thinking?* "How did you get me upstairs?"

"Vladimir helped. He thought it was funny."

"And you?" He was almost afraid to ask.

"I'd rather we not have a replay of last night's stumbling and singing," she said with a frown, "but

I've never seen you like that before so I'm giving you a pass."

"It won't happen again." He kissed both of her hands. "I promise."

"I'm holding you to that." She leaned down and kissed the tip of his nose.

The front of her dress gaped and gave him a tantalizing view of her breasts. A dark purple mark on the left one concerned him. He ran his thumb across the small bruise. "Did I do this?"

She flushed scarlet and sat up quickly, tugging her dress back up to cover the mark. "Things got a little wild last night."

"How wild?" Nikolai could only remember snatches of their night. Memories flashed before his eyes. Undressing Vivian. Squeezing her breasts and lavishing them with attention. Sucking on those perfect little nipples of hers. Burying his face between her thighs and lapping at that sweet honey and her pink clit until she was crawling up the bed and slapping at the headboard. Dragging her on top of him and reveling in the sight of her bouncing wantonly on his cock. Flipping her onto her hands and knees and driving into her wet, tight pussy until she came hard on his cock. Flipping her back over and licking her juicy slit until she came and begged him to stop, her small hands shoving at his head and her thighs quivering. Coming in her mouth, his cock sliding between those pouty lips of hers while her tongue did things to him that made his knees buckle.

Curious about his memories, he lifted her skirt and pushed her legs apart. Vivian swallowed nervously but let him look. Sure enough, he found even more love bites on her inner thighs. He shoved her dress up around her breasts and found a few more on her belly.

"I'm sorry, Vee." Shame gripped him. "I shouldn't have been so rough with you."

"I'm not complaining, Kolya." Her blush deepened as she lowered her dress and smoothed her hands down the fabric. "Actually, if we could do that again, without the alcohol, that would be nice."

"Nice?" He looked at her love-ravaged body and thought of the way he had fucked and feasted on her last night. "I'm not sure nice is the word I would use."

"It was some of the best sex we've ever had. I liked it. A lot," she added bravely.

"Well," he sat up slowly and slid his arms around her waist. "In that case, we'll have to see if we can replicate last night."

Vivian kissed his cheek. "I'm not sure if we can replicate perfection." Her sensual mouth curved with a mischievous smile. "But I'd damned sure like to try."

Nikolai laughed and noisily kissed her neck. "Go downstairs and entertain Sergei's family. If you stay up here much longer, I'll give into the temptation to try right now."

Vivian crawled off the bed and left the room with a backward glance. He inhaled a long, deep breath and threw his legs over the side of the bed. Not used to drinking like that anymore, he was feeling every shot of that top-shelf liquor. He found his cell phone in the organizer atop the dresser. She had neatly arranged his wallet, keys and phone for him. He could just imagine her walking around their bedroom, stark naked and bearing the red marks from his overanxious mouth all over her body, as she picked up the mess he had made in his drunken state.

He picked up his phone and checked for missed calls or texts. There were two text messages from Yuri that he opened. It made him smile.

Y: Lena says I need to apologize. Sorry.

Y: My head is fucking killing me. We're getting too old for this shit.

Smirking, Nikolai set aside his phone and walked into the bathroom. After knocking back the pain relievers, he took the longest piss of his life. He noticed the red smudges on his cock and grinned lasciviously. That was a shade of lipstick he would recognize anywhere. Russian Red. Vivian's favorite.

Thoughts of his little temptress wife had him half-hard before he stepped into the shower. He took his time lathering up and scrubbing his hair. There was something important he had promised to do last night, but he couldn't for the life of him remember what it was. It was a favor. A big favor.

Who asked for my help last night?

At a big party like a wedding reception, he had people constantly coming up to him. Faces flooded his mind. Snippets of conversation raced through his head. He had made a lot of promises last night.

Yes, I'll talk to your landlord.

Yes, I'll see what I can do about your daughter's loser boyfriend.

Sure, I'll come take a look at the house you're having trouble selling.

Yes, I'll see if I can get Besian to give your husband a few more weeks to pay back that loan.

Yes, I'll get your wife and mother-in-law safe passage into that prison.

Nikolai yanked his head out of the shower spray. His conversation with Sergei barreled to the front of his mind. Sergei had told him that Bianca and her mother planned to visit Adam Blake, the man who had killed her brother and beaten her during a hate-motivated convenience store robbery, in the prison where he was recuperating after being attacked in the yard.

It was a bad idea. The worst idea, really. Prisons were notoriously dangerous places for a reason. Like any good mob boss, Nikolai owned a number of prison guards. It wasn't that hard or expensive to buy them. Unfortunately, there was always someone willing to pay a higher price for them. To secure safe passage for Bianca and her mother, he would have to shell out huge amounts of cash.

But money wasn't the real issue. The real issue was what Adam Blake would say during his meeting with Bianca and her mother. Adam had to know about his older brother's death. His older brother and two of his skinhead goons had attacked Bianca in her bridal boutique. Needless to say, the trio hadn't survived the night.

Would Adam ask Bianca about the deaths? Would he try to get her to implicate herself or Sergei or Kostya? It was a headache he didn't need right now.

But he had made his promise, and he wouldn't take it back. Somehow he would get Bianca and her mother into and out of that prison untouched.

Nikolai dressed in jeans and a long-sleeved shirt and his favorite brown leather boots before heading downstairs. He found Vladimir and Galina in the living room. He made sure to apologize for his behavior, but Galina just patted his cheek. The motherly touch set off a pang of longing within him that he had thought long buried. As he left the living room to find Vivian, he glanced back at Galina and Vladimir. He prayed his son would know the love and affection and support that Sergei and Vladimir had known from their family.

When he entered the kitchen, Vivian was finishing up a phone call. From the sound of it, something bad had happened. He poured a glass of orange juice and leaned back against the counter to drink it. She put down her phone, and he asked, "What's wrong?"

"That was Sela Rivera. Hadley is in the hospital."

He swallowed his mouthful of juice and played it cool. Since the meeting with Finn in the barn two weeks earlier, the cartel had been unnervingly quiet. The tension around the city could be felt by every underworld denizen. It had settled in their bones and made their teeth ache.

Had the cartel gone after Hadley to get Finn to agree to do their dirty work? Or was it a message to

Hector that Lorenzo could touch any person in Hector's family if he wanted?

Setting aside his glass, he asked, "What happened to her?"

"She had a heart scare last night after her niece's *quinceañera*. She had to be taken to Memorial Hermann in an ambulance. They're going to do heart surgery on her in the morning."

"That's terrible." *Thank God, it wasn't the cartel.* "But why is her mother calling you?"

"She wanted to see if I would agree to come in and handle a few of Hadley's classes."

"What did you say?" He held his breath and hoped she had declined.

She shot him a funny look. "I said yes, of course. Hadley is a good friend. She's an amazing artist. She has my paintings hanging in her house and in the arts center. The very least I can do is help her out right now."

"Of course." He didn't want to be a jackass about it so he let it go. He would have to pull Ten aside later and make sure he understood the situation more clearly.

"Galina wanted to visit the zoo. I thought that would be a nice way to spend the afternoon. I called Benny, and she's going to meet us there with Sofia and Dimitri. It will give Vladimir and Dimitri a chance to talk about Lone Star and all that." Vivian picked up his empty glass and put it in the sink. "We can come back to the house to change before we meet everyone at Samovar."

"That's fine."

"Good." She gave him a hug and kissed him quickly. "Do you want to eat something now or grab a bite at the zoo?"

His stomach soured at the thought of eating anything right now. "I'll wait."

He followed her out of the kitchen, waited while she collected Vladimir and Galina, and trailed the small group out to the backyard. They piled into an SUV and made the quick trip downtown. Vivian and Galina twittered away the entire time. He began to suspect that Galina considered Vivian family in the same way Vivian considered Sergei an older brother.

They had just entered the zoo when his cell phone started to ring. Kostya's number flashed on the screen so he stepped away to answer it. "Yes?"

"Where are you?"

"The zoo. Why?"

"I'll meet you there in half an hour."

Before Nikolai could ask why Kostya was joining them, the line went dead. He pocketed his phone and slid his arm around Vivian's waist. They slowly made their way to the bird exhibit and followed the trail toward the antelopes and zebras. They spent some time watching the giraffes before stopping at the small outdoor café. Vivian raced into the restroom while he stood in line for water.

"I figured I would find you near one of the bathrooms." Kostya addressed him in Russian.

Nikolai glanced to the left to find his right-hand man standing there. He smiled and shrugged. "The things they don't tell you when you get your wife pregnant, huh?"

Laughing, Kostya shadowed him as the line moved forward. It occurred to Nikolai that his cleaner didn't want to be seen if it could be helped. It was the same reason he was speaking Russian. The fewer people who might understand them, the better. "I'll keep that in mind."

"What's so important that you had to see me on a Sunday? At the zoo?"

"It's happening." Kostya's voice was low and quiet. "Tonight."

It?

The hit.

Nikolai nearly bolted from the line. He needed to find Vivian. He needed to stow her somewhere safe.

"Easy," Kostya urged. "It's not your wife."

His gut lurched. "The little girl?"

He shook his head. "It was someone else entirely."

The line moved forward, and Nikolai stepped up to buy the water. Bottles in hand, he stepped around the side of the café with Kostya. "Who?"

Kostya glanced left and right. "Holly Phillips."

Nikolai couldn't have been more shocked to hear that name. "Holly? Your neighbor? Vivian's stylist? What does have—?"

And then it hit him.

"Phillips." He said slowly. "Filipova." He closed his eyes and tried to remember what he had read in the dossier. "Tatiana's father had a sister. She died when they were teenagers."

"I don't think so," Kostya countered. "I think she was taken in for training."

"Training? As what?"

Kostya leveled a look that said everything.

"No." Nikolai shook his head. "That's impossible. You think Tatiana's aunt became KGB?"

"I've been digging into Holly's past."

Nikolai didn't have to ask why. Kostya might be able to hide his feelings from everyone else, but Nikolai was the world's champion when it came to pining after an unattainable woman. He could see it in Kostya's face anytime Holly's name was mentioned. "What did you find?"

"Her mother has an interesting history. Her story reminds me of my parents. I think she was an agent sent here deep under cover. I think she tried to go home during *perestroika*, but she realized she had been gone too long. It was never going to work."

"And then?"

"And then she came back to Houston and realized she was pregnant." Kostya stepped closer and lowered his voice to a hiss. "By Maksim."

The two bottles of water Nikolai held in his right hand slipped free and banged on the sidewalk. Holly Phillips was Maksim's daughter? Was that possible? Someone in the cartel clearly believed she was the daughter of someone important.

Nikolai crouched down and picked up the bottles. He stood up and stared at Kostya. "If what you say is true, Holly is—"

"In extreme danger," Kostya interrupted.

"Yes," Nikolai agreed, "but I was going to say that she's my sister."

"Half," Kostya corrected.

"Half. Full. It doesn't matter to me. She's my blood." He moved closer and dropped his voice. "No one touches my family."

Kostya's taut expression relaxed. "What are my orders?"

Nikolai embraced the brutal, violent bastard buried within him. It was high-fucking-time he remembered how he had earned his position as the biggest, strongest, most vicious boss in the city. "Give Hector and Romero the green light. I want it done. All of it. Tonight."

"I'll make sure it's quick. Clean," he added.

Thinking of Hadley Rivera and the heart surgery she faced in the morning, he said, "Take care of Finn when it's done. Make sure he's protected. Tell him that I hope his girl's surgery goes well."

"It's done."

"Make sure our boys know that they need to be seen tonight. All night," he added. "Ten needs to be at Samovar. Boychenko, too. Solid alibis for all of them." He held Kostya's gaze. "Be careful."

"Don't worry about me, boss." Kostya disappeared into the crowd like a practiced spy.

Nikolai's mind reeled as he returned to the shaded table where Vivian, Galina and Vladimir waited. *A sister! I have a sister!*

Why hadn't Maksim told him? Why hadn't Maksim asked him to keep an eye on her? Was Holly's mother the woman who had given the dossier to Eric Santos? Why? What did she expect to gain from that?

"Hey!" Vivian rubbed his arm as he sat down next to her. "Where did you go? One second I saw you in line and the next you had disappeared."

"I dropped a bottle and had to chase it down." He waved one of the dirty bottles to prove his tale. Later, he would tell her everything. Right now, he had to be careful.

"Oh. Here." She plucked some napkins from the dispenser on the table and wiped down the two bottles. He handed the two bottles he hadn't dropped to Galina and Vladimir. When finished wiping the plastic down, she titled her head to study him. "You sure you're okay?"

"It's the heat."

She smiled. "It's the vodka baking out of your pores."

"Funny." He kissed the top of her head. Relief surged through him. She and the baby were going to be safe. Hector and Romero would stage their coup. Lorenzo Guzman would fall. Kostya would keep Holly Phillips—*my sister!*—safe. Vivian and the baby would no longer have to look over their shoulders every time they went out in public.

Nikolai twisted the cap off his water and took a long, cold drink. Deep down inside, he doubted any of it would be that simple. Deep down inside, he had a sinking feeling his whole life was about to be upended.

Nikolai was keeping something from me. I focused on my conversation with Galina, but I sneaked little glances at my husband. Outwardly, he looked calm and relaxed, but I knew him too well to fall for that one. The slight tension around his mouth, and the drawn lines at the corners of his eyes told me everything I needed to know. He was keeping a big secret, probably something dangerous and terrible.

I trusted that he would spill it as soon as we were alone. I didn't think interrogating him in the Houston Zoo was the best way to get my answers anyway. Whatever it was that had him wound up so taut wasn't something I wanted to hear right now. It would ruin our afternoon and things were going so well.

"There's Benny, Dimitri and Sofia." Nikolai raised a hand and waved. "Dima!"

Our friends descended on the table with a stroller and piles of baby gear. Soon, we were walking through the zoo again. I found myself sandwiched between Galina and Benny. The conversation naturally turned to children. I glanced back at the men and smiled at the sight of Nikolai holding Sofia while Dimitri and Vladimir talked business. He cradled her against his chest, one hand gently cupping the back of her head, and whispered to her as he showed her the chimpanzees.

My heart swelled, and I looked away before he caught me staring. Benny must have seen me watching him because she bumped my hip and winked. "He's a natural."

Catching a glimpse of Nikolai in a fatherly role filled me with the strongest sense of hope for our future and for our son. We had to break the cycle. We couldn't allow our son to succumb to the same life that had taken both of his grandfathers and his father. We had to raise him to understand that the underworld wasn't good enough for him. He could do better. He *would* do better.

The rest of the afternoon and evening was spent in the company of friends. We left the zoo before five and were walking into Samovar just before eight. Nikolai left my side to do his usual tour of the restaurant. He stopped to talk to a loud table where a number of his men sat. Ten, Boychenko, Ilya, Artyom, Danny and a handful of men I recognized nodded as he addressed them. They were noticeably quieter when he left.

While Galina and Vladimir headed for the rear of the restaurant where our large party was seated, I broke away and made the rounds of the Sunday crowd. These were the regulars that kept the business thriving. They were the same faces I had served that very first Sunday I had worked at the restaurant.

And all of them wanted to get up and hug me and kiss my cheeks and rub my belly. I wasn't thrilled by all of the tummy rubbing, but I had learned to deal with it. No one meant any harm by it. They were all just so excited for us.

Unable to help myself, I pitched in when I noticed that Lidia and Jessica were getting slammed. As I picked up a tray of appetizers, I did a quick headcount of the staff and realized they were two waitresses short for the night. With our huge party in the back, they were going to be rushing and frazzled by the night's end.

"What do you think you're doing?" Nikolai swept in with a click of his teeth and took the tray. "You're pregnant. You can't carry this."

"It's some caviar, blinis, roasted potatoes and *olivje*. It's not like I was carrying a cinderblock."

"You aren't supposed to carry anything but that baby." He kissed me right there in front of everyone. A chorus of chuckles rose from the tables closest to us. "Go. Sit down."

I rolled my eyes and deliberately took the longest route back to our table. I made sure to stop and chat with as many guests as possible. Eventually Nikolai joined me on my meandering route. By the time we reached our party, they were already enjoying their appetizers and knocking back their drinks.

Sergei and Bianca looked adorable together, their brand new wedding bands so bright and shiny. Vladimir and Galina sat on either side of the happily married couple and created a perfect picture of the modern family.

Ivan had his brawny arm slung across the back of Erin's chair. He grazed his fingertips up and down her neck. She stole the caviar from his plate and earned a little pinch that made her yelp.

Dimitri and Benny relaxed and enjoyed the conversation while Yuri and Lena played with Sofia. I noticed the gentle yearning in Yuri's reflection as he amused Sofia with a noisy toy. Lena watched her billionaire boyfriend with a curious stare. She leaned her head against his shoulder and tickled Sofia's tummy. Yuri pressed his lips to the top of Lena's head, and I began to wonder how long it would be before Yuri finally asked her to marry him.

Surrounded by our large makeshift family, I had never been happier. That contented happiness followed us home. Galina and Vladimir left the restaurant with Sergei and Bianca so we had the house to ourselves. After the way Nikolai had ravished me last night, I had a feeling I was really going to be in for it tonight. My stomach did a wild, excited flip at that prospect.

Upstairs in our bedroom, I switched on the nightly news and started to undress. Naked except for a silk dressing robe, I went through my nightly routine. I had just finished brushing, flossing and rinsing when I poked my head out of the bathroom to see what the forecast looked like for my morning jog.

But the weatherman wasn't standing in his usual spot. The television showed chaotic scenes of flashing police lights and yellow crime scene tape. I spotted Eric in the background of one shot. He had a grim look on his face.

I crossed the bedroom, grabbed the remote from the dresser and dropped down onto the upholstered bench at the foot of our bed. I pressed the volume button until I could hear every word that was being said.

"...sources within the department are calling this a massacre unlike any seen in Houston history," the anchorwoman said. "There are unconfirmed reports of similar gangland-style hits taking place all over portions of Mexico controlled by the Guzman cartel. Reports indicate that this man—Lorenzo Guzman—once the richest and most powerful drug lord in Mexico, has disappeared. It appears that factions within the cartel have staged a bloody coup."

"To recap," the anchorman seated to her left interjected, "seventeen confirmed homicides have taken place in Houston tonight. All victims were tied directly to the cartel that controls the drug trade in and around the city."

Movement in the doorway of our bedroom drew my attention. Nikolai leaned against the frame and watched me. With the sleeves of his shirt rolled up to his elbows and the buttons undone almost to his navel, all those tattoos he had earned over the years were plainly visible. They were the marks Maksim, his own father, had ordered to be put onto his skin so that everyone would know what he had done for the family.

My gaze drifted back to the television screen where so much mayhem and carnage flashed before me. I was horrified that all of this had been happening while we were laughing and eating with our friends. Nikolai hadn't pulled the trigger. He hadn't used his own two hands to do this, but he had given permission to the men who had compiled this list of hits.

I cringed at the realization that I was yet again watching my father's handiwork splashed upon a television screen. He had done this. He was probably in Houston right now, kicked back in a Calaveras safe house, drinking a beer while he watched this coverage unfold. Was he pleased with his work? Would this be enough for him? Had he finally gotten what he wanted?

I glanced back at Nikolai. The mask he had been wearing since the zoo had slipped. I could see him, all of him, and he looked utterly destroyed and soul sick.

"Tell me."

Wordlessly, he crossed our bedroom and sat next to me on the bench. He exhaled a long, rough sigh—and then he told me everything. He told me about the hit that had been taken out on a daughter connected to Romero, Nikolai, Hector or Maksim. He told me about Kostya's discovery that Holly freaking Phillips was likely Maksim's daughter. Which made her Nikolai's sister and my sister-in-law!

"So then I decided to give Hector and Romero the green light to carry out their coup," he said, his voice sober and dark. "I gave them permission to do their dirty work here in Houston."

"Is that why everyone was at Samovar tonight? Ten, Arty, Danny, Ilya, Boy," I ticked off the names that matched faces I had seen at the restaurant. "You wanted them to have alibis."

He cast a sad smile my way. "I can't decide if I should be proud that you've learned to think like me or ashamed of what I've done to you."

"What have you done to me that I didn't ask for or want?"

"No, *solnyshka*. You didn't ask for this. You never wanted to be part of something so depraved." He dropped his head into his hands. "You asked me to love you. You asked me to build a life with you. You asked me to be your husband and the father of your children." He laughed, the sound raspy and sinister. "What did I do? I gave you a twisted, perverse version of the life I promised you when I married you. I've dragged you right into the middle of a bloody, violent coup." Nikolai lifted his head, but he wouldn't look at me. "I must disgust you.

I touched his face and forced him to look at me. "You don't disgust me."

"Vee, I let *that* happen tonight." He gestured angrily toward the television. "How can you even stand to be in the same house with me right now?"

"I love you." The answer was simple and imperfect. "I love you."

"You shouldn't." His voice cracked. "You should take the money and the diamonds and run. You should take the baby as far away from me as possible."

"You're probably right." Nikolai's head snapped toward me, and I was glad to see the glint of panic reflected in his pale eyes. "But I love you. I don't like what you've done. Frankly, I'm sickened by it. I can't stand the thought that all of that violence and death happened because of money and greed and your desire to protect me and the baby and Holly."

"There was no other choice," he insisted. "Hector and Romero were going to make this move whether I said yes or no. It was better to give my permission and control the situation as much as possible than to have them running wild in the city. There were rules tonight. No women, no children, no innocents."

In Nikolai's world, those distinctions meant something. To men like him, men who were more comfortable in the darkness of the underworld than in the bright light of day, tonight's events had happened in a carefully managed and wholly acceptable way. I would never fully understand that mindset. It simply wasn't possible for me because my life experiences were so different.

"I love you, Vee. I love you, and I'm sorry that I've disgraced you tonight, but I would make this decision again. I'm sure that disgusts you and angers you and confuses you, but it's the truth. I won't sit here and lie to you."

I tried to wrap my head around the fact that he could tell me that he loved me and that he would allow a night of carnage in the same sentence.

"This wasn't just about you and me and the baby. It wasn't just about Holly or your father or mine. The choice I had was to let Romero and Hector take out a handful of men or to let the entire city descend into chaos. The police would not have been able to contain this. It wouldn't have been a slow spreading cancer that crept across the border. It would have been a full-blown contagion that infected everyone."

In his view and I'm sure in the view of all the underworld bosses, he had made a decision that sacrificed a few to save countless other lives. In a different context, the decision might have been viewed as heroic, but this wasn't a war being fought for freedom or any other noble reason. This was a war being fought by my father and Hector Salas so they could gain control of the drug and gun trade.

Suddenly very tired, I reached for the remote and shut off the television. I plucked the decorative pillows off my side of the bed and tossed them onto my reading chair. When I slid under the sheet and comforter, Nikolai stood up and watched me from the foot of the bed. He seemed uncertain and bewildered by my behavior but too anxious to ask me what I was thinking.

"I don't like what you've done. I think it's cruel and vicious and brutal. I'm not happy with you right now."

Nikolai gulped. "I'll sleep across the hall."

"No." I pointed to his side of the bed. "You'll sleep here."

"But you're angry with me."

"Yes, I am." I didn't know what else I could say. I didn't trust myself to say much more anyway. I feared that I would say something I couldn't take back or that we would get into an ugly shouting match that would do nothing to solve this situation. What had happened tonight couldn't be undone. I had to find a way to live with it.

Nikolai walked into the bathroom and shut the door. I heard the shower start. Alone in our bedroom, I tried to make sense of this terrible situation. I felt like an awful human being as I searched for ways to make this ugly episode more palatable. I began to understand why so many mob wives didn't ask questions. This was complete and total hell.

Sometime later, Nikolai came out of the bathroom stark naked. He entered the closet and came back out in just a pair of boxer shorts. After turning off the lights and flipping the switch on my night light, he slid into bed but left a wide space between us. The tension in the room grew unbearable.

Nikolai's warm, strong hand found mine. His voice, thick with regret and desperate for my love, echoed in the darkness. "Vee. Please."

I closed my eyes and exhaled a slow, deep breath. I gave his hand a squeeze and then tugged on it before I rolled onto my side facing away from him. Now that I was getting so far along in my pregnancy, I couldn't sleep comfortably any other way. Nikolai scooted across the mattress and curled himself around me, tucking me into his chest and pulling his thighs up until they cradled my backside. He buried his face against my throat and breathed in my scent.

Our love was complicated and messy, but it was strong and real. Maybe I was wrong. Maybe I was weak. Maybe I was stupid. But I couldn't punish him. I just couldn't do it.

And when I felt that first hot tear splash onto my skin, I realized I didn't need to punish him. The punishment and castigation he heaped upon his own shoulders would be far more painful than anything I could ever dream up. He had made bad choices early in his life—and now he was paying for them.

28 Chapter Twenty-Eight

Five Weeks Later

"I bet Danny and Boy aren't being used as slave labor," Ten grumbled as he tapped a tiny nail into a thin piece of wood. We were seated at a worktable in the warehouse Nikolai owned and had converted to a studio space for me a few years earlier. This was a project I couldn't tackle in my home studio.

"Seriously? Are you really going to whine about helping me build canvas stretchers for the class I'm teaching?" I rolled my eyes at my hulking bodyguard. "If you wanted to babysit Bianca while Sergei is out of town with Ivan for that tournament, you should have asked."

"Sure," Ten said with a harsh laugh. "Then I'd be sitting here banging my thumb with this hammer and crying about my wired jaw. Because you and I both know Sergei would have planted his fist in my face if I had asked to spend all day and night with his hot fucking wife."

"Wow." I made a face at him. "Maybe we could not refer to my friends as fucking hot? Maybe?"

"But she is."

"Way to miss the point, Ten."

"I'm just saying—"

"I heard you the first time. We're good." I used a pair of clamps to hold a glued corner together. "Besides you couldn't have been Bianca's guard today. She and her mother are meeting Adam today at the prison. You're on parole, remember?"

"No," he stated dryly. "I forgot all about the rules and regulations I have to follow for the next four years of my life." Holding out the stretcher he had built, he scrutinized the corners. "Do you think it was a good idea for her to visit the man who killed her brother?"

"No, I think she's crazy to do it, but that's Bianca for you. If I were allowed to bet anymore, I would put money on her mother pressuring her to go to this meeting."

"It's dangerous. Especially now," he added with a shake of his head. "Until Hector tracks down Lorenzo Guzman, we're all in danger. That guy is not going to go quietly into the night. He'll want revenge, and he'll take it wherever he can get it."

The Lorenzo situation was one that continued to vex me. Instead of having more freedom after that terrible September night, I had been restricted even further. My father's crew had missed Lorenzo during their hit on the drug lord's compound. Now he was out there somewhere, lurking in the shadows and biding his time until he found the perfect time to strike at us.

"We're all fucked," Ten grumbled in Russian.

"Gee, thanks for that encouraging sentiment."

"It's the truth."

"Maybe keep that truth to yourself and get back to work."

We had another dozen or so stretchers to piece together before we started the actual hard work of tugging and stretching the canvases across them. The special needs art class I had taken over for Hadley had completed their landscapes during the last class so it was time for me to stretch and frame them so they would have gifts to hand out during the holidays.

My cell phone chirped and buzzed so I put down the stretcher I had been assembling and picked it up. "Hello?"

"Vee!" Nikolai greeted me in a voice that was aggressive and sounded almost panicked. "Are you still at the studio with Ten?"

"Yes. Why?"

"Give him your phone right now."

"Why? What's wrong?"

"Now, Vee!"

"Okay." I thrust the phone at Ten. "It's Nikolai."

"Boss?" Five heartbeats later, Ten was on his feet and striding toward the windows overlooking the street below my studio. The area was still mostly empty commercial properties and warehouses so there wasn't much traffic on the roads. Whatever Ten spotted outside made him curse so strongly in Russian that I was sure my ears would catch fire. "They're here. You better fucking hurry."

Ten ended the call and slipped my phone into the back pocket of his jeans. He raced to the door of my studio and turned the lock. He rushed to the nearest heavy worktable and hefted it up as if it weighed nothing. The muscles in his arms bulged as he carried it to the door and used it to barricade us inside.

"What's wrong? Who is here?" I finally found my voice. "Ten!"

"Get in the supply closet." He handed me a box cutter. "You don't make a noise. You don't move. You can breathe, but it better be very fucking quiet. Understand?"

"Ten, what—"

"Now! Go!"

His booming voice shocked me into a run. Thinking of the baby, I went into the closet and shut the door. I could hear Ten moving things in front of it. They wouldn't keep the attackers out, but the boxes and furniture might slow them down.

Crouched in the dark, cramped closet, I clutched the box cutter. It had to be the remnants of Lorenzo's inner circle coming for us. They must have known that my usual guard was spread thin while Nikolai made sure Bianca and Erin were protected while their men were out of town.

Ten was right. We were utterly fucked. Gun, knife, fists—he could handle his own in a fight, but he was handicapped by a pregnant woman who depended on him for her safety. If he was killed because of me, I would never forgive myself.

Please, Kolya. Hurry!

Loud bangs rattled the warehouse door. How many men had come for us? Three? Four? Five? I prayed it was a small number that Ten could handle.

The bangs continued for a long time. The lock finally gave, and the furniture pushed in front of the door scraped the floor as it was shoved out of the way. I pressed my ear to the door of the supply closet so I could hear what was happening. Men shouted in Spanish and English. I tried to count the voices, but it was so hard to keep them separate. Was that three? Four?

The sound of fighting erupted in the warehouse. Stools clattered to the ground. Fists smacked against skin. Men growled and cried out in pain. The vicious noises made my stomach churn. I gripped the box cutter more tightly and hoped Ten was every bit as good as his reputation would have me believe.

A crack of gunfire made me gasp. I clapped a hand over my mouth as Ten shouted in obvious agony. Was he badly injured? Had they hit him in the stomach or the chest or the head? Was he still alive?

Our attackers started fighting amongst each other.

"He said no fucking guns! He wants her and the baby alive!"

"I didn't shoot her. I shot this big Russian bastard!"

"He broke my arm, man! He snapped it in half!"

"Shut up, Javi. Look at Terry. He broke Terry's nose and crushed his fingers."

"The bullet could have ricocheted! It could have gone through a wall and hit her."

"Where the fuck is she anyway? She can't have gone far."

"Start tossing the place. We don't have long. That husband of hers keeps her on a short leash."

I counted five distinct voices. Straining to hear, I tried to detect any sounds from Ten. All I could hear were footsteps coming closer to the closet where I was hiding. I crouched down in the corner, going as far back as I could. The short stack of boxes between me and the door would do little to protect me.

The footsteps stopped outside the door. Breathing rapidly and on the verge of a panic attack, I held out the boxed cutter and extended the sharp razor tip. The first person to come through that door was getting slashed. No one was going to touch my baby.

The furniture Ten had moved in front of the door was loudly tossed aside. A hand twisted the knob and started to open the door—but then something heavy and hard hit the door, rattling it right on its hinges. I squeaked with surprise. Outside the door, all hell broke loose.

"Shit! He's alive!"

"He's got Marco, man. He's got Marco."

"Put the gun down and kick it over here," Ten ordered gruffly. "Now! Or else I'll snap his fucking neck like a toothpick."

A few seconds later, I heard several pinging noises. Then something metal hit the wooden floorboards. A scraping noise followed.

"There you go, man. There's the gun, but I've got the bullets. What do you think the odds are that you can take all of us? Huh?"

"I'd say they're pretty fucking good right now," Ten answered in an evilly gleeful voice.

The pop of a gunshot startled me. It was quickly followed by four more. I dropped the box cutter and clamped both hands over my mouth to stifle the scream that threatened to erupt. The lock on the door was flipped, and I squeezed my eyes shut. The door squeaked as it was jerked wide open.

Please, please, please.

"Vee!" Nikolai crouched down in front of me and hauled me into his arms. "Oh, baby. Are you okay?" He pushed me back so he could get a better look at me. His eyes were wide and panicked. His face was taut with fury. He touched my belly. "Our son?"

The baby chose that moment to kick hard against the spot where Nikolai's hand rested. Nikolai's shoulders sagged with obvious relief. He pressed his forehead to mine and embraced me tightly. "I thought I had lost you. I didn't think we would get here fast enough."

"We?" I clung to him so hard that my fingertips went numb.

"Your father is here." Nikolai helped me stand. "You're going to go with him for tonight."

I clutched at his shirt. "Where are you going? Why aren't you coming with me?"

"They attacked Bianca, her mother and Erin," he reluctantly explained. "Bianca's mother is on the way to the hospital. Artyom and his crew are already there. Danny and Boy are missing. We think they were taken with Bianca and Erin. I have to get them back. Romero will protect you."

My legs nearly buckled. "They took Bianca and Erin?"

"I'll get them back," he swore. "I'll get them home safely."

Nikolai shrugged out of his suit jacket and handed it to me. "Cover your face. I'm going to carry you out of here. I don't want you to see this."

I didn't want to see it either. I wanted to reach into my brain and take this memory out of my head and throw it away. That wasn't possible so I decided that closing my eyes and hiding under a jacket while Nikolai carried me out of the studio was the best option. It would help me avoid adding more unpleasant images into my brain bank.

"Wait." I stopped him before he could pick me up. "What about Ten?"

Nikolai cracked a smile. "Ten? They picked the wrong man to attack. He's been shot and stabbed, but he'll be fine. He's had worse."

"That's awful."

"That's Ten." Nikolai swept me up in his arms and cradled me close. "Close your eyes, *zolota*. Cover your head."

I did it, and he carried me out of the warehouse, down two flights of stairs and out into the noticeably cooler early evening. I was placed on the front passenger seat of an SUV, and the jacket was removed. Nikolai fastened my seatbelt and then draped his jacket around my body to keep me warm. He nuzzled our faces together before claiming me with a passionate, lingering kiss. "Stay close to your father. Don't even think about coming home until he says it's safe."

"I'll be careful." I touched his face. "Promise me you'll be careful."

"I'll be careful." He kissed me again. "I'll see you soon."

I blinked back tears as Nikolai shut the door and strode into the warehouse. The driver's side door opened, and my father slid behind the wheel. I hadn't seen him in months. He had changed quite a bit. He looked older and stressed out. There was more gray in his hair than I remembered and more tattoos on his hands and neck.

He said nothing as he put the SUV in drive and pulled away from the curb. We drove in silence for probably ten minutes before he lifted the center console and retrieved a couple of wrapped hard candies. He held them out to me. "Eat these. You're going to get the shakes from all that adrenaline pretty soon. The sugar will tide you over until we get to the safe house, and I can feed you."

I frowned but took the candies from him. "I'm not a puppy that needs to be fed and watered."

"I didn't mean it like that."

The crinkling plastic sounded unnaturally loud in the vehicle. I popped one of the candies into my mouth and made a face. My father chuckled next to me. "You still hate watermelon, huh?"

"I'm surprised you remember that tiny detail when you never could remember the big things, like, you know, sending me a birthday card or a letter while you were away." I didn't mean it to come out so meanly but it did. He actually flinched as if I had struck him. Guilt speared me. "I'm sorry. I didn't—"

"I deserve so much worse than that, kiddo." He kept his attention on the road in front of us. "I should have written to you. *Fuck.* I should have come back for you that night. I shouldn't have left you there in that house."

"Why did you leave me?" It was a question that had plagued me for eleven years. "Why didn't you come back for me?"

He didn't answer immediately. "I left because I was only thinking about myself. I was a selfish dick. After I got picked up and thrown into jail, I found out you had been shot and I hated myself. I wanted to die. I deserved to die for abandoning you like that."

My fingers trembled as my father finally told me the truth about something. I bit my lip and tried to control my wildly vacillating emotions as he continued his impromptu confession.

"I wanted to write you. I wanted to apologize, but I couldn't."

"Why not?"

"You were already a target. Anyone who wanted to touch me just had to go after you. I made a conscious decision to ignore you and cut you out of my life. If everyone else thought you didn't matter to me, it made you a useless target. It was the only way to keep you safe."

He reached across the space between us and gripped my hand in his callused, scarred one. "It my broke my heart, Vivian. You were the only good thing I ever did in my life—and I damn near killed you." A harsh, raspy laugh left his mouth. "I guess Wilde was right about men killing the things they love."

I blinked with surprise. "You've read Oscar Wilde?"

"There's not much else to do on the inside."

He still hadn't let go of my hand. The contact between us brought back memories, good ones, from my childhood. "I was a shit father, Vivian. I didn't know the first fucking thing about being a parent or a husband. I made every mistake in the book, some of them twice, but I'm asking you to give me a chance to be your father now."

"What does that even look like?"

"I don't know," he admitted. "I really don't, but I'd like to try. You set the ground rules. I'll follow them. I want a chance to do right by you."

I didn't know if that was possible. I didn't know if I could forgive a lifetime of hurt to forge a new relationship with my father. I didn't know if I could overlook the terrible things he did so unapologetically. Finally, after quite a bit of thought, I said, "We can try."

"Thank you." He gave my hand a squeeze and then let go. Clearing his throat, he said, "We're going to be driving for a couple of hours. You should get comfortable. Nap if you can."

I wasn't tired, but I didn't want to talk anymore. I closed my eyes and leaned my head against the window. I couldn't stop thinking about Erin and Bianca, Boy and Danny. Were they okay? Were they hurt? How quickly would Nikolai get to them? How badly had Artyom been wounded? Would he survive?

"Stop worrying about your friends and rest. That Russian of ours will get them back."

"Ours?"

"You're my daughter. He's your husband. That makes him part of my family." Signaling that he didn't to talk anymore, he turned on the radio. "Rest, Vivian. This will be over before you know it. Nikolai will find your friends and track down Lorenzo."

"And then?" Eyes closed, I asked the question that worried me most.

"And then he ends it, once and for all."

29 CHAPTER TWENTY-NINE

"What the fuck is going on?" Ivan charged Nikolai when he stepped into the barn, their arranged meeting point. "Where is my wife?"

"Erin, Bianca, Danny and Boy are being held at an old dairy plant not far from here." Nikolai clamped his hands on Ivan's shoulders and glanced at Sergei who had his fists clenched at his sides. Ilya stood nearby and patched up Ten's bloody wounds. "One of the men who took the job is on Hector's payroll. He's been feeding information to us since the women were taken."

"But not before," Sergei ground out angrily. "Why did this happen?"

"It happened because Lorenzo Guzman is desperate." Nikolai raked his fingers through his hair. "This is my fault. I should have known something this drastic and explosive would happen. I should have been better prepared." He inhaled a ragged breath. "We'll get the women and our men back—and then I'm finishing it."

Ivan's cheek twitched. "I can't be there for that. I swore to Erin that I was out. I can't go back."

Nikolai clasped Ivan's face. "I would never ask that of you. This is my problem. I'll handle it."

"Boss." Kostya stepped into the barn. "It's time."

Ten remained behind with Ilya. The rest of them piled into an SUV and headed for the dairy plant. Kostya filled them in on the layout of the building they would be entering. When they reached the plant, Kostya pointed out the men on loan from Besian and the small crew from the Calaveras MC that had pitched in to help.

Spider approached and extended his hand. Nikolai grasped it, and the biker pointed behind him to a black van. "We'll handle the assholes on the outside. That will leave the two dickheads on the inside, the two that have your women and your soldiers." Spider pulled on a pair of black leather gloves. "Ready?"

"Yes." Ivan shoved by them and headed for the building. "I'm ready to get my wife back."

Nikolai jogged after Ivan who was impossible to control when he was pissed off like this. "Vanya," he placed his hand on his friend's shoulder, "slow down."

"Fuck you, Kolya." Ivan rolled his shoulder. "My wife is in there with these pricks. They shot Artyom. How do I know they haven't shot Erin? How do I know they haven't hurt her?"

God help them all if Erin had been hurt by these men. Ivan would go insane with rage, and no one would walk away from this alive.

"We have to go in there quietly," Nikolai urged. "We have to be careful. For Erin and Bianca, Vanya. We have to think about what's best for them."

Ivan slowed the speed of his steps but remained in the lead until Kostya overtook them. He shoved Ivan back and put a finger to his mouth. Ivan managed to rein in his fury enough to follow Kostya's silent directions. They waited near a side door while Spider's crew and the small Albanian group descended on the cartel men outside the dairy plant. Once they had rounded up, gagged and tied all those men, Spider whistled in a warbling, bird-like way.

At the signal, Kostya led them into the plant in a single file. Nikolai's breaths came at a fast pace, but his hands remained still and sure. He followed close to Ivan and kept his eyes open for any stragglers who hadn't gone outside with the larger guard group. Memories of nights similar to this one, nights when Nikolai had followed Ivan into even more dangerous situations than this, came to mind. He had thought these nights were behind him, but that was just a dream.

As they neared a refrigerated storage container, the voices of two men could be heard. They pressed their bodies against the wall to listen and wait. What Nikolai heard made his blood boil. He couldn't even imagine what it was like for Sergei and Ivan to hear those two worthless fucks talking about their wives.

"Fuck that! They've seen our faces. We slit their throats and go."

"Man, I got no problem killing the two soldiers, but the girls? One of them is pregnant. I don't kill babies."

"Do you know who Ivan Markovic is? Do you know what he'll do to you if he finds out you punched his wife? He'll rip your balls off and shove them down your throat. And the other one? I saw her husband fight once. He cracked a man's sternum with one punch. One. Punch." The man chortled loudly. "No, I'm not sticking around for that show. We kill them, and we go."

"Look, Chris, maybe we should think about this. They're worth more alive than dead. The girls at least."

"What? You want to ransom them back, Juan? You think they would pay?"

"Ivan Markovic is rich, right? And the other one? Sergei? He's in tight with Kalasnikov. That's lots of deep pockets we can rob."

"What if they won't pay?"

"Then we sell them. The skinny one is really pretty. I bet Tran would pay good money for some young pussy like that. She's...what? Twenty-three? Twenty-four? Not as good as the teenagers he likes to pick up on Spring Break, but she's fresh and clean."

"And that one? I doubt the market for pregnant whores is very high."

"No, but I bet we could make nice money off those babies. I heard people pay tens of thousands of dollars for newborns. She's got two of them inside her. You could have one and I could take the other."

Sergei and Ivan were panting now. Nikolai decided he would grab Bianca or Erin, whichever woman was closest to him, and shield them while their husbands beat the shit out of those two assholes. The thought of Erin or Bianca being sold into a brothel or those sweet, innocent babies being taken from Sergei and Bianca made him sick.

"Keeping her alive is the easy part. What happens when the babies are ready to come?"

"We could have them taken out. It can't be that hard to find a doctor to do it for us. When it's done, we let her bleed out."

"Seems like a waste. She might be able to make more money on her back. Get the skinny one. Let's go."

"What about those two?"

Nikolai assumed they were talking about Danny and Boy.

"We'll send the others back here to watch them. We tell the guys we're taking these two to a new drop-off spot. Let them be the ones to greet the Russians. Because you and I both know that cleaner they keep on their payroll will find this place sooner or later."

Sooner, much sooner.

"Go!" The thud of a foot connecting with someone's body echoed in the cold storage container. "I'm not carrying your fat ass."

Hands bound and wobbly on her feet, Bianca stumbled through the thick plastic strips that guarded the open doorway of the container. Sergei leapt forward and grabbed her, dragging her into his muscular arms and lifting her out of harm's way. Nikolai stepped forward and quickly accepted her from Sergei. He pushed her against a wall and shielded her pregnant body with his.

Sergei gripped the front of the shirt of the first man through the door. He picked him up like a sack of potatoes and slammed him against a wall across from them. Sergei pounded that poor bastard to a bloody pulp with his meaty fists.

Ivan followed Sergei's lead. He grabbed Erin and handed her to Kostya. Her face was illuminated by the overhead light, and Ivan gasped at the sight of her bruised lip and black eye. He roared like a lion and attacked the man who had been pushing her forward. It was brutal and bloody and one of the worst beatdowns Nikolai had ever witnessed.

Eventually, Kostya shifted Erin toward him and jumped on Ivan's back to get him to stop. Bianca had better luck stopping Sergei who now had the other man on the ground. Bianca wrapped her arms around Sergei's neck and hauled him into a kneeling position. She pressed her face against his. "Enough, Sergei. It's over. He's had enough."

Sergei spun around and hugged his wife. He pushed her back against the wall and nuzzled her pregnant belly and face. Bianca clung to him, and they kissed tenderly and lovingly.

Ivan shook off Kostya's hands and stormed toward Erin. He lifted her right up off the ground and buried his face in the curve of her throat. She wrapped her legs around his waist and sobbed into him. "I want to go home."

"Sh, *angel moy.* I'm here. I've got you."

"Don't let go, Ivan. Don't let go."

"Never." He softly kissed her unbruised cheek. "Never, baby."

Kostya finished securing their two new prisoners with zip-ties and ambled over to the wall where Nikolai leaned. They watched the two couples for a few moments before Kostya reached into his pocket and withdrew a burner phone and a slip of paper. "There is a car waiting for you. It's fully gassed and stocked with weapons and cash. Dump it on that side of the border. Go to the second address. You'll find a getaway car there. It's clean with good tags and insurance for the trip back across the border."

Nikolai took the phone and paper. "Thank you."

"Don't worry about this, boss. I'll handle everything."

Nikolai cast one final glance at his friends before quietly pivoting on his heel and disappearing before any of them noticed he was missing. With purposeful strides, he left the dairy plant and prepared himself for the perilous journey ahead.

There was still an hour until sunrise when Nikolai carefully approached the small house on the outskirts of Piedras Negras. He had left his car farther up the road so he could sneak onto the property with stealth. He had already mentally mapped out his exfiltration route. The second vehicle waited for him a little over a mile away.

As he crept through the shadows, he screwed the silencer onto the end of the pistol Kostya had stowed in the glove compartment. The leather gloves he had found next to the handgun were supple and well-used. He supposed that said something about his relationship with Kostya if the cleaner was willing to lend him a favorite pair of gloves.

Nikolai kept his mind clear. He couldn't risk a misstep or a hesitation. He had to finish this and get home to Vivian. He wanted to put this whole fucking mess behind them and start fresh in a new underworld where everyone who was in control wanted the best for Vivian and the baby. *That* was the only way he could ensure the safety of his family.

The house was eerily quiet and dark. It was a small place, two bedrooms and one bathroom, with lots of peeling stucco and a roof that needed repairs. This early in the morning, Lorenzo was probably still in bed. Kostya had written a quick note about Lorenzo's drinking. Apparently it had spiraled out of control since Hector's successful coup.

As Nikolai drew closer to the house, he noticed the back door stood ajar. Maybe Lorenzo's drinking was worse than Kostya knew. What man on the run would leave his back door wide open like that?

The fine hairs on the back of his neck and along his arms rose as apprehension settled in the pit of his stomach. The idea that he had been set up wormed its way into his brain. Kostya wouldn't send him out here to be killed, but what if someone had fed Kostya bad information?

Floorboards squealed. Nikolai stopped moving and scanned for better cover. He ducked behind a tree and held his breath. The back door opened, and a tall figure appeared there. *Shit.*

"Are you going to hide out there all night or are you going to come inside and have a drink with your father?"

Nikolai's stomach dropped to his knees. He almost didn't believe his ears when he heard that familiar voice speaking Russian. *What the fuck is Maksim doing here?*

Lowering his weapon, Nikolai stepped away from the tree. The door was wide open now, but Maksim had gone back inside the house. Trying to figure out what the hell was happening here, Nikolai crossed the backyard of Lorenzo's bolt-hole and cautiously entered the house. He found the boss—*my father*—sitting at the kitchen table with a bottle of tequila.

Hovering in the doorway of the dimly lit kitchen, he glanced around nervously. "Where is Lorenzo?"

"In the bathroom," Maksim answered while splashing tequila into two coffee cups. "In a few hours, he'll be discovered on the toilet where he suffered a heart attack."

Nikolai narrowed his eyes. That was awfully convenient. "Did he suffer a heart attack?"

Maksim pushed a coffee cup toward the empty chair. "Yes."

Nikolai suspected there was more to that answer, but he wasn't going to ask the question. He didn't much care. He was exhausted and wanted to go home. At least now he could return to Vivian without the stain of another man's blood on his hands.

He slumped into the chair across from Maksim and sipped the tequila. He typically stayed away from it, but on a morning like this one, he wasn't very picky. Leaning back in the rickety chair, he asked, "Why are you here?"

Maksim's eyebrows arched. "You still have to ask that question?"

Nikolai swirled his cup. "I don't know what this is." He gestured between them. "You've been my boss longer than I've known you were my father. I don't know what to expect from you."

"I've known you were my son longer than you've known me as your boss." Maksim sipped his tequila and hissed. "Frankly, most days, I don't know what to expect from me either. But this?" He slashed his hand through the air. "This was too much. That man tried to kill my daughter in September and then he turns around and tries to kill my daughter-in-law and my grandson? No. I couldn't allow that to stand. He could have taken the easy way out. He was offered relocation and money, but he dug in his heels to fight. It was the wrong choice. He had to go."

Nikolai took another drink. "So Holly...?"

"It's a long story, and it's not one I'm ready to tell you. When it's time, you'll learn all you need to know. Until then? Keep an eye on her. Lorenzo isn't the only one who would try to hurt her to get to me."

"I'll watch her." He didn't mention that Kostya would probably have more than his eyes on Holly.

"Have you chosen a name? For my grandson?"

The question surprised Nikolai. He set aside his cup and nodded. "We have a shortlist. Vivian is fond of Lev."

"Lev?" Maksim tried out the name. "Lion? I like that one very much. It's a strong name for a boy. He's going to need a strong name when he inherits all of this."

Over my dead fucking body, Nikolai crossly thought. "We'll see."

Maksim laughed. "There's no escaping our destiny, Kolya."

Nikolai didn't comment on that. He knocked back the last of the tequila and enjoyed the burn that rushed down his throat and into his chest. "I have a long drive ahead of me."

"My plane is waiting." Maksim finished his drink and gathered their two cups. He carried them to the sink where he washed and dried them before returning them to the right cabinet. No one would ever know that two men had enjoyed a drink together while Lorenzo sat dead in a bathroom down the hall.

"You won't see me again until after the baby is born," Maksim said as they walked outside. "I won't miss the chance to see my grandson."

Nikolai could already see future conflicts arising with Maksim about his son. "We'll make sure a guest room is ready."

"Guest room? No. I think I'll stay at the Four Seasons, like your other Houston visitors."

Nikolai met Maksim's glare with an unwavering stare. "I won't apologize for saving Tatiana."

"Why did you save her?"

"Because she deserved a second chance," he answered matter-of-factly. "She's a good woman. She's brilliant. She's useful."

"She's a loose end, and I don't like loose ends."

"She's my loose end, and I'll tie her up if it comes to that."

Maksim grunted but didn't push the issue. He gestured to the left. "I'm headed this way."

"I'm going that way." Nikolai pointed in front of them.

"Good luck, Kolya." Maksim lumbered away but stopped and turned back toward him. "Congratulations on the baby."

"Thank you."

Bewildered by the strange meeting with his father, Nikolai walked through the Mexican countryside alone in the dark. He found his car waiting exactly where Kostya had promised it would be and slid behind the wheel. Rubbing his face between tired hands, he blew out a noisy breath.

Nikolai started the car and fastened his seatbelt. He pulled onto the road and began to retrace his route. It was a long drive home, but the thought of seeing Vivian energized him.

Everything had changed tonight, and nothing would ever be the same again in Houston. For some reason, that idea made him smile. A little change suited him just fine.

E Epilogue

April

Nikolai weaved through the raucous throng of revelers at Yuri and Lena's outrageously ostentatious wedding reception. This was the first time in his life where he had attended a party where truly no expense had been spared. He shuddered to think what Yuri had spent to give Lena the perfect wedding day.

Gorgeous and elegant in her second couture gown of the day, Lena held court at a table surrounded by her friends. He spotted Vivian seated next to her. His wife looked so beautiful in her bridesmaid's dress. She had paired the dress with the sunburst jewelry he had given her to celebrate the London art show. Later tonight, he intended to have her naked on their bed. He wanted her wearing only his gold and diamonds.

Of course, those plans all depended on the whims of their son. Nearly four months old now, Lev bounced on Vivian's lap. With his dark hair and sky blue eyes, Lev favored Vivian in his looks, but Nikolai fear his son had inherited his temperament. Only time would tell.

He wore a tiny little tuxedo but had lost his socks sometime after the cake had been cut. A curious baby, he tugged on Vivian's hair and gazed out at the dancing, partying crowd. He liked to study the world surrounding him. Nikolai had a feeling his son would be frighteningly smart and ambitious. With two grandfathers and a father who ruled the underworld, it was in his blood to be a leader, to be a king. Nikolai could only hope that Vivian's good influence would teach their boy to be kind and patient.

On the other side of Vivian, Benny held Sofia who was nearly a year old. She stared at Lev with intense interest and reached out to touch him. Nikolai smiled when his son grabbed Sofia's chubby hand and dragged it straight to his mouth. Sofia squealed with laughter as Lev gummed her fingers. His son's toothless grin lit up his cherubic face.

Yuri swooped in and plucked Lev right out of Vivian's arms. He held his godson high in the air and attacked his belly. Lev giggled and kicked his short, stocky legs. Tucking Lev into the crook of his arm, Yuri took Sofia from Benny and ordered the women to go enjoy themselves. With two babies in hand, Yuri headed for the table where the men had congregated. Nikolai trailed him and took his seat.

"Are you practicing for the future?" Dimitri laughed and took Sofia from Yuri. She had her arms out and practically jumped into her daddy's lap. "Because they don't usually come two at once."

"Tell that to Sergei," Yuri replied as he settled into his chair with Lev.

Across the table, Sergei fed Bella a bottle while Ivan made silly faces at Sasha. Sergei cradled Bella's small body in his massive hands and gazed down at her with such love. "After bringing home twins from the hospital and surviving that first week? Bianca and I are pros. If I have my way, we'll do this four or five more times."

Nikolai snorted. "Two more times, and she'll have you sleeping on the couch permanently."

Sergei just smiled at that and lifted Bella up to his shoulder where he had a strategically placed burp cloth.

Out of the corner of his eye, Nikolai noticed Lev grabbing for the Patek Phillipe watch encircling Yuri's wrist. He started to chew on the band and slobber on the watch face. Nikolai leaned forward to stop his son from ruining the watch that had probably set his friend back an obscene amount of money, but Yuri waved him away with a laugh. "When he inherits this on his twenty-first birthday, we'll tell him why it doesn't work."

Nikolai had to laugh at that. When Lev didn't get what he wanted from the watch, he started to cry.

"I think someone wants his papa," Yuri said while handing over a fussing Lev.

Holding his son close, Nikolai breathed in his sweet scent and patted his bottom in the rhythmic way that he liked. Lev latched onto Nikolai's thumb and gnawed on it. Eventually, he made a mewling, kittenish sound and then started to relax and drift off to sleep.

When Sasha started to fuss, Ivan put the baby against his shoulder and patted his little back. The baby quieted down quickly. It was clear that he had been picking up pointers from all the fathers at the table.

"Look at us," Dimitri remarked with a jovial laugh as he let Sofia squish cake and frosting between her fingers. "Did you ever think we would be sitting at Yuri's wedding with all of these babies?"

"And wives," Ivan interjected with a wry grin. "We can't forget those."

"To wives and babies," Yuri said, lifting his shot glass.

"To wives and babies," Nikolai echoed and picked up his beer. The rest of their friends lifted their drinks and saluted their families too.

As he rocked Lev, Nikolai noticed Vivian approaching with Lena and Erin. She walked around the table and stopped behind his chair. Bending down, she embraced them both and kissed his cheek and then the top of Lev's head. Smiling at their son, she whispered, "I think we may have to take him home early."

Nikolai glanced up at her with a feverish, hungry gaze. "I like that plan."

She giggled and traced his ear. "I'm sure you do."

With the promise of a long, sensual night of love-making ahead of him, Nikolai leaned into Vivian's embrace. Surrounded by their friends, holding his son and nuzzling his wife's neck, Nikolai grinned. Life was pretty damned good.

Vivian stared at him, her eyes glittering inquisitively. "What's made you so happy?"

"My son." He kissed Lev's cheek and then captured her mouth in a searing kiss that promised a night of wicked pleasure. "And my sun."

THE END.

NIKOLAI II

ROXIE RIVERA

AN AUTHOR'S NOTE

Thank you so much for reading the continuation of Vivian and Nikolai's story! This book took quite a meandering journey on the way to its release date. I was so incredibly touched by every single reader who contacted me with messages of support while I dealt with a series of back-to-back family emergencies.

Y'all are just amazing and wonderful, and I can't say thank you enough for giving my Russians (or the Connolly brothers or those dangerously sexy Albanians) a try.

The *Her Russian Protector* series will continue new books for KOSTYA, ALEXEI, DANILA, and TEN.

The series began with the FREE novella IVAN (Her Russian Protector #1) and continues with full-length novels—Dimitri (Her Russian Protector #2), Yuri (Her Russian Protector #3), Nikolai (Her Russian Protector #4), Sergei (Her Russian Protector #5), Sergei II (Her Russian Protector #5.5), and Nikolai II (Her Russian Protector #6.)

You can get updates on new releases by visiting my website, signing up for my newsletter or liking my author page on Facebook.

ABOUT THE AUTHOR

A *New York Times* and *USA Today* bestselling author, I like to write super sexy romances and scorching hot erotica. I live in Texas with a red-bearded Viking husband and a sweet but rowdy preschooler.

I also have another dirty-book writing alter ego, Lolita Lopez, who writes deliciously steamy tales for Ellora's Cave, Forever Yours/Grand Central, Mischief/Harper Collins UK, Siren Publishing and Cleis Press.

You can find me online at www.roxierivera.com.

Roxie's Backlist

Her Russian Protector

Ivan (Her Russian Protector #1)

Dimitri (Her Russian Protector #2)

Yuri (Her Russian Protector #3)

A Very Russian Christmas (Her Russian Protector #3.5)

Nikolai (Her Russian Protector #4)

Sergei (Her Russian Protector #5)

Sergei II

Nikolai, Volume 2

Kostya (Her Russian Protector #7)—Coming Soon

Alexei (Her Russian Protector #8)—Coming Soon

Danila (Her Russian Protector #9)—Coming Soon

NIKOLAI II

Ten (Her Russian Protector #10)—Coming Soon

The Fighting Connollys

In Kelly's Corner (Fighting Connollys #1)
In Jack's Arms (Fighting Connollys #2)
In Finn's Heart (Fighting Connollys #3

Debt Collection

Collateral (Debt Collection #1)
Collateral II (Debt Collection #2)—Coming Soon
Past Due (Debt Collection #3)—Coming Soon

Seduced By...

Seduced by the Loan Shark
Seduced by the Loan Shark 2—Coming Soon!
Seduced by the Congressman
Seduced by the Congressman 2

Erotica

Chance's Bad, Bad Girl
Halftime With Craig
Tease

ROXIE RIVERA

Eddie's Cuffs 1
Eddie's Cuffs 2
Eddie's Cuffs 3
Disturbing the Peace
Quid Pro Quo
Search and Seizure

NIKOLAI II

www.ingramcontent.com/pod-product-compliance
Lightning Source LLC
Chambersburg PA
CBHW020624020726
47494CB00001B/36